The Saints
of the
Lost and Found

T. M. Causey

THE ROADRUNNER PRESS

Published by The RoadRunner Press
Oklahoma City, Oklahoma
www.TheRoadRunnerPress.com

Printed in the USA

First edition published March 8, 2016

ISBN: 978-1-937054-23-6 (HC)
ISBN: 978-1-937054-24-3 (TP)
ISBN: 978-1-937054-26-7 (eBook)

Library of Congress Control Number: 2015958513

Publisher's Cataloging-In-Publication Data
(Prepared by The Donohue Group, Inc.)

Names: Causey, T. M.
Title: The saints of the lost and found / T. M. Causey.
Description: First edition. | Oklahoma City, Oklahoma : RoadRunner Press, 2016.
Identifiers: LCCN 2015958513 | ISBN 978-1-937054-23-6 (HC) |
    ISBN 978-1-937054-24-3 (TP) | ISBN 978-1-937054-26-7 (eBook)
Subjects: LCSH: Women psychics--Fiction. | Extrasensory perception--Fiction. | Brothers--Fiction. | Missing
persons--Fiction. | Lost articles--Fiction. | Suspense fiction.
Classification: LCC PS3603.A8988 S25 2016 (print) | LCC PS3603.A8988 (ebook) | DDC 813/.6--dc23

10 9 8 7 6 5 4 3 2 1

For my brother
Mike McGee
Sabonim, 5th Degree Tang Soo Do Master
02/17/64 - 12/18/12

This one's for you.
I miss your voice, your funny stories,
your crazy ideas, your singing,
your drumming on everything within reach,
your love for all your karate students,
your wonderful encouragement,
and your indomitable spirit.
You were the best brother
I could have ever hoped for
in this life or the next.

CHAPTER ONE

I see lost things.

The first loss I can remember seeing was a woman's red shoe. More particularly, a Chinese red stiletto that turned out to be a missing murder weapon. The victim was a man I had never met and would never know. I was six years old when I saw it, and what made it so unusual was the shoe was more than two thousand miles away, squirreled beneath a rotting house in the southernmost tip of snowy Nova Scotia. I had never been to Nova Scotia. In all of the years since, while I was on the run, Nova Scotia never even made my list of places to go.

Come to think of it, I've never bought a pair of red stilettos either.

The Stiletto murderer had made the innocent mistake of brushing past me while I was on a family vacation at a third-rate beach near Biloxi. This was long before the casinos elbowed their way onto the beach and displaced the ragged mom-and-pop hotels and run-down burger joints squatting there, before I knew we were a family of grifters feeding off easy marks.

Six-year-old me was a scrawny little blonde with a crisscrossing of scars on my arms, legs, and torso, still reddish from a car accident that I blessedly did not remember. The only other sign of the recent crash was a cast on my right arm from the broken wrist I'd suffered when I landed—after being thrown through the windshield. We had traveled to Biloxi to escape winter, only to find it was still winter even there, though warmer, I believe, than wherever we'd been before. We had another new last name. This time, we were the Broussards. Cajuns, my dad explained, butchering the accent, but selling it with so much charm, people bought it. People always bought Dad's shtick.

The beach was perfect—deserted, stone quiet, undemanding. Wind blew in salty gusts off the Gulf of Mexico, chilling me to the bone. Still, I had begged to be allowed to go outside, where there was space and sky. A plastic bag wrapped and taped over my cast kept it from getting wet or dirty as I piled sand into a pail to make a castle, building a fantasy world in which people were happy, one half-packed bucket at a time. Mom—or maybe it was my big brother, Latham, I can't remember—sunned a few yards away.

I was just about to top off a turret on my castle when a woman in red swept by me, and the image of a shoe—brilliant in Technicolor glare and hyper-saturated colors—curled toward me, wafting behind her like smoke drafting in the wake of a fast-moving train. The scent of piney woods and snow followed the draft, overpowering the salt air and the coconut tang of the Hawaiian Tropic sunblock Latham had insisted I wear to protect my pale skin and new scars. I remember feeling surprised when the image came in so clearly, accompanied by a sense of urgency that the woman needed to know what I knew. Of course, that was before I understood things like *murder*, or why the image bore down on me like a warhead intent on a target. I only recall the wracking pain as the loss flung its image-shrapnel into my brain. Thankfully, the pain dissipated almost as fast as it hit me, and being a helpful child, I rushed over to impart what I knew to the woman obliviously walking away. She seemed shocked by my news. Then embarrassed. She thanked me, gave me a quarter, and smiled as she walked away.

Later that evening, she tried to drown me in the hotel swimming pool.

To this day, I do not remember drowning. They say you often don't remember the details accompanying a horrific trauma, but I've been told—maybe by my parents, maybe the doctors—that I was playing near the edge of the pool when I was supposed to have been in our hotel room. Latham was flirting with some girl with dimples, distracted from watching me as my parents had instructed when he suddenly realized he had lost track of wherever I'd scooted off.

He found me floating face down in the pool. Witnesses later placed the woman in red poolside just minutes before Latham found me.

It was the first time my brother saved my life.

It would not be the last. And I swear to you that I did not know then what I had already cost him.

Standing in the Greyhound bus station in Colorado Springs, I was grateful for the cool breeze that made the long-sleeved hoodie hiding my scars not look out of place in the dead of summer. I was also uneasy. My thirtieth birthday had been the day before, and it had come and gone without Latham calling. He'd never missed a holiday or weekly check-in. Ever. He had not wanted me in Chicago to start with, much less working for the FBI, and I knew he remained upset with me. *For* me. It wasn't like my brother to be petty or vindictive, but I knew that my attachment to the Feds and the Little Princess Killer case had tried his patience. He knew I'd walked off the job three weeks ago, but instead of slapping me with a plain old "I told you so" or "It's about damned time," he'd gone radio silent. Maybe I'd missed his call while crossing the high plains of Kansas with its notorious lousy cell reception.

I had not had anywhere in particular in mind to run to when I left Chicago. Call it self-preservation, the way the press had as they began eviscerating my reputation. It never occurred to them that I was running so I could not do any more harm.

Three weeks later, and my photo was still making the evening news, along with reports of bogus sightings of me in various North American cities. I guess I shouldn't have been surprised. When you're a freak who can find lost things—except when a little girl needs you to find her—people aren't going to let you go easily.

The tang of the orange juice I was sipping helped me focus on the taste and ignore the images rolling off my fellow travelers. I stared at the wallboard scrolling destination cities, trying to remain as inconspicuous as I could as I eyeballed my departure time. People milled about, waiting for the next bus to New Orleans. I tried to ignore the pull the city had for me: Latham wasn't all that far from there in Saint Michael's, a town so small it barely rated a dot on the map.

The problem was that my parents had a house there, too, one they used between cons. Latham had mentioned they'd been around for the summer, which is exactly why I had decided on San Francisco and sweet Louise's house; I could count on Louise to hide me out for a week or two, with far fewer questions, while I figured out where to run to next.

The ring of my cell phone startled me as if I'd been shot, and several people gave me odd looks as I turned my back to the room and pulled out the phone. Exactly three people had this number: Latham, my best friend Nate, and Hank, the FBI agent I had abandoned mid-case. After the first few days of my disappearing act, Hank had given up on me answering and stopped calling. This incoming number read Blocked—so not Latham or Nate. I almost didn't bother answering, but curiosity won out.

"Hello?"

"Your brother will die, Girl, if you don't get back home now," my dad said without preamble.

I knew better than to ask Dad how he had gotten this number. A grifter never tells the truth. Ten years of frustration, anger, and hurt speared me. Ten years since we last spoke, and this was the first thing he said to me?

"Nice try, but if he's dying, you know I can't change it. You taught us that the hard way, remember?" I answered calmly, in spite of the panic I felt. I hadn't heard from Latham in two weeks. If Dad isn't lying, what if I never see Latham again?

"You've gotten better at hiding your emotions," my dad said, a reluctant admiration in his voice.

I found that suspect as well. Dad never admired anyone. I'd learned early on that to give him a single solitary inch, much less an emotion, was to give him the edge in a game that would end with you jettisoning your best judgment, and, ultimately, giving him whatever it was he had been trying to con you out of in the first place. I'd seen him do it to the best of the best. Hell, for years I had helped him, until one day I realized what our playacting really was.

"It's pretty easy to have no emotions, Dad. You're lying."

"Am I?" He chuckled. "Well, then, you have nothing to worry about, do you?"

And the bastard hung up. Just like that. I double-checked the face of my phone, but no, he had disconnected, and I knew he had done so without feeling the slightest remorse for how that would hurt me, knowing his prediction of Latham's soon-to-be demise would haunt me.

You see my dad was born with the unique ability to know when and how any person he met was going to die. To the millisecond. He and my mom had used this ability to pull off grifts all over the country. Sometimes they used the knowledge to simply go in and steal whatever they could while the family was at the hospital, or the morgue, or the cemetery. Far more often, they ran complicated grifts that I rarely understood but which had netted my parents hundreds of thousands of tax-free dollars over the years. No grift was too big or too small for my father. My dad conned like others breathe. He might have just lifted a million off a high-stakes target, but if he were to meet you in a McDonald's the next day, he'd be fumbling around, patting his clothes, and giving an Oscar-worthy performance of having forgotten his wallet, just so you'd offer to pay for his choice off the dollar menu. Any score made him happy, eyes bright, dimples displayed. He was like a winsome child coaxing just one more chocolate from exhausted grandparents. Irresistible. A master.

A master who was never wrong.

Years ago, he'd told me how I was going to die: at the hands of Jack, the only man I have ever loved.

Still, he had to be lying this time. Latham could not be dying. Nate would have called if Latham were sick. Hell, Latham would have called, not wanting things to end on a sour note with us. We cared too much for each other to hurt each other on purpose. Didn't we?

I stepped up to the ticket counter, looking at the schedule for San Francisco and freedom.

"One ticket to New Orleans," I said as I handed over the cash.

"I *know* you from somewhere," the prim seventy-ish woman said, unhappy about it. She appeared the kind who would disapprove of kittens, so it could've just been her nature. She sat a couple of seats up and across from where I had camped out on the Greyhound bus, and she'd angled herself a bit so she could look me in the eye. It was almost two days since I'd bought the ticket, and we were nineteen miles west of Baton Rouge, Louisiana. I'd forgotten how the humidity and the wilting heat of the South in mid-July could make you as irritable as an addict a few days into detox. To make matters worse, somewhere outside the swamp bath of East Houston, the A/C had died. The riders traveling on would get a new bus in New Orleans; the rest of us would escape. My new friend had been eyeing me for the last hundred miles or so, her eyes slanted beneath soggy, peppered bangs, her sagging jowls flushed as she patted at the sweat dripping down her neck with a ragged handkerchief.

I dreaded the moment she put it all together. I sank deeper into my seat, curled against my side of the bus, my ratty suitcase—the one with the faded stickers all over it—tucked safely under my feet. Diesel fumes blew in through the open window, making my eyes water as the stink settled into my frizzy blonde hair. If the crabby old lady could've seen the scars on my arms and legs, she might've guessed a little faster. I kept them covered to avoid just that: recognition. She kept knifing suspicious gazes in my direction, eyeballing my gauzy, long-sleeved shirt so out of place in the heat, frowning at the big, dark shades that hid my eyes. Just a couple of miles west of Baton Rouge, recognition flashed across her face a split second before disgust.

"You *that* girl," she accused, her Alabama drawl spitting contempt. Only in the South can you still be a *girl* at thirty. "That psychic girl that done up an' left those poor mamas and daddies and ain't helpin' them FBI find them babies."

I didn't bother to correct her. I wasn't psychic, *per se*, and I hadn't been able to help, but it didn't matter. The FBI had been trying to catch the Little Princess Killer for at least three years, and I'd only been involved as a resource in the latest LPK case.

"Yeah?" the twenty-something gangly guy in the seat across from me said, suddenly interested as he leaned forward and tried to casually angle his phone my direction. "Saw that seizure video on YouTube. Man, you were bouncin' like popcorn!" And there he went, doing a decent imitation of a headbanger, hair flopping in his face as he nearly whacked his forehead on the metal frame of the seat in front of him. "You were trippin', dude!"

"Young man," the old lady scolded, "that's a glorification of Satan. Do not mock the Lord. He was trying to exorcise demons from her, praise Him, by shaking out all her sin." She sniffed in my direction. "Didn't take, though. You got to *repent* for God to enter," she explained to exactly no one who cared.

I closed my eyes and rested my head against the window, hoping that ignoring them would end the one-sided conversation.

"Man, that video got like four million hits on the first day! She's famous." I felt him turn in his seat, the approval in his voice was coated with a thick sheen of greed. "Do something freaky," he commanded, fingering the camera on his phone in the off chance that his words spurred me to do something miraculous . . . or horrific.

Word about who I was, what I could do, had leaked out about four months ago. Five-year-old Bianca Silver went missing not long after that, and in spite of the media fascination with me—the feeding frenzy over whether or not my ability was real, the bogus tips and time-wasting calls my ability generated—we got close to finding her before the LPK had finished and buried her. Hank, the perpetually grouchy ASAC—FBI-speak for Assistant Special Agent in Charge—suspected the killer had escalated because the media had become more interested in me than him; the LPK had booby-trapped Bianca's grave, and it had taken the FBI bomb techs a lot longer than we had hoped to disengage the IED he'd put there. The medical examiner said she'd only died the hour before we found her.

We hadn't even begun to process that loss when Aurelia March was grabbed. Once again, I saw images of her in captivity like I had with the girls before her—but the images came to me sooner, clearer even, than Bianca's — and we thought the LPK was finally making mistakes.

The truth is I can often see a lost item or person, but not necessarily *where* . . . or even *when*. If you lose something, I might see that it's in a wheat field, but not necessarily *which* wheat field. Or it may be a loss from long ago. It could be something about to be lost, though I have to be deeply connected to the person who's losing the item for that to happen, and even then, it's not always accurate.

But I had seen Aurelia, alive, three days after she was snatched. Breathing. She already had the lily tattoo, like the others, but we had a chance. The FBI rushed to the scene.

To the wrong scene.

Ultimately, when Hank figured it out and went to the right place, Aurelia was dead. The site was booby-trapped as before, but unfinished, as if the LPK had been interrupted, and the FBI had just missed him. And I knew then that if I'd gotten the location right, Aurelia would still be alive. The two hours that the FBI spent in the wrong place I'd *seen* . . . well, that was the difference between the LPK being caught or slipping away to kill again, the difference between Aurelia being alive or dead. And when that realization hit me, I had the seizure. A whopper of a seizure. One the entire world saw on the news, in the tabloids, on YouTube . . . on millions of Facebook shares and tweets. So I told a lie. I told the world that the seizure had broken my ability, and I could no longer see lost things. Then I ran. And I was on this bus because I was still running.

We pulled into the Baton Rouge station to refuel. We weren't supposed to take on any more passengers with the a/c broken, but a young mom and her two little girls climbed aboard, and I felt light-headed with heartache. The girls were laughing, on a big adventure. The mom was just shy of desperate, and I could see the lost job and apartment and dreams that had led to her heading home to family without much hope. The oldest girl reminded me so much of Aurelia that I clenched my fists, digging my nails into my palms to keep myself anchored in the here and now, to keep from remembering what I had tried so hard to forget. They piled into the seat three rows in front of me, far enough away that the old woman didn't see fit—yet—to warn them not to speak to the fallen, lest their souls be in jeopardy.

"They say you saw murderers and shit, even when you were little," the young guy said, picking up his one-sided conversation as if we'd all been happily chatting, scooting so close to the edge of his seat as he talked, he was practically hovering over the aisle. "You must've been a messed-up kid."

I ignored him, but the oldest of the two girls looked shocked at the profanity and turned to whisper to her mom what the bad man had said.

"You must like that," the guy said. He propped his elbows on his knees, balancing his phone so the lens kept me in focus. "Being in the middle of a big case, being on the news. People's lives fall apart and you get famous. Must be nice."

"Hey," the driver called out as he reboarded and took the wheel. A balding heavyweight, he wore a uniform with the name Lenny over the left pocket, and he glared at the kid via the mirror mounted above his head. "Leave the lady alone, Bud, or I'll put you out. We don't got no harassing on this here bus, you *capiche*?"

"I ain't harassin' nobody," the kid whined. "I just wanna know some dope, like maybe the first lost thing she ever found. That'd set me up—I could sell that story. And it wouldn't cost her squat."

"You heard me," Lenny said. "Leave her alone."

The kid sat back, muttering about how unfair it was that *some* people got all the breaks while *some* people were just tryin' to get by, and was that his fault? No, no, it was not. I could see his losses spiraling off him in poisoned waves: the jewelry he'd stolen from his girlfriend and then lost in a poker game, the twenty grand he owed to some thugs, the lost guitar he'd hocked to buy this bus ticket, the lost girlfriend (which, frankly, after the lost jewelry didn't come as a great shock). I somehow didn't have a lot of sympathy for his lost Twitter coup. Lenny might have silenced the kid, but we could all still hear the old lady muttering about how I needed to repent. The mom of the little girls finally realized just who and what the old woman was talking about and went so pale I thought she'd disappear. She gathered both girls on her lap, as if the vile crimes I'd been trying to solve might somehow have followed me all the way to Louisiana.

My skin prickled from the young guy's stare—I could feel it angry, resentful. And though I had no intention of indulging him with an answer to his question, as I closed my eyes, the image of that red stiletto battled through the other bus riders' losses I was trying so hard to ignore: clear, sharp, as if it had happened yesterday and not more than two decades ago.

I have almost no memories before the red stiletto, but that one snapshot in time is remarkably focused and enduring. Despite my best efforts to forget it, the image swam up from time to time, and the terror of the hospital stay afterward could strangle me if I let it, anxiety swamping my limbs, my hands.

I swallowed hard, trying to shift my attention elsewhere, to anything but that memory. I made myself feel the bus as it rocked along, ambling toward New Orleans on Highway 30, parallel to the meandering Mississippi a mile or so to our right. The bleached asphalt road ran through acres and acres of soybeans and corn, interrupted occasionally by chemical plants, metal kudzu of pipe, grown tall and spreading into the countryside. To the left of the highway, a few horses grazed near dairies with herds of cattle, and the occasional silo and water tower broke the tree line. Every now and then we'd hit a spell of McMansions crammed into some former cornfield as if there were a shortage of space, with miles of nothing around them, floating islands of avarice. There were more suburbs than I remembered. More clusters of industrial warehouses along the way as well. It was an odd betrayal— knowing that memory didn't hold true. It made me antsy, filled with dread. Nothing was sacred.

Nothing.

The late July sun baked the bus as we rattled along. The old lady groused about *disgrace* and *abomination*, while her knitting needles clacked in time. She was knitting a baby blanket; she'd lost one granddaughter—a miscarriage. I hoped for her sake, as palpably as the loss was streaming from her, that she didn't lose another. She and the kid beside me probably assumed I couldn't hear them, since I had earphones in and hadn't responded to their taunts. In fact, I was listening to low, steady white noise instead of music, and I could hear them just fine. The white noise helped me focus and deal with the losses coming off everyone on that bus.

The elderly black man in front of the old lady had turned once, looked me up and down, shrugged, and then bent his graying head back over his book. He'd lost his wife a long time ago, and the image of her emanating from him was cotton soft and worn down to sepia tones, like he'd taken it out and held it daily through the years since, just because it comforted him.

In front of him, Lenny-the-driver was a mess of frayed losses: lost dreams, business losses (a hot dog stand with six lawsuits against it for salmonella), two wives (divorces), and all told, lost custody of seven children. He seemed a little relieved about the children.

For the record, I don't know how or why some members of our family have odd abilities, or if there's some trigger. My parents refuse to discuss it, and Latham has developed a convenient amnesia about it all. All I know is that after the woman with the lost stiletto, I woke up in the Biloxi hospital hurting like a birth gone horribly wrong: The scratch of the cotton sheets on my skin was as rough as sandpaper on exposed nerves; the smell of rubbing alcohol pervaded my senses, choking me; sounds from the far end of the hall bellowed as if a megaphone had been placed at my ear. Every one of my senses was working on high—and the endless blinding, iridescent images of loss streaming in from my fellow patients (not to mention the doctors and nurses) threatened to bury me in my hospital bed.

Anyone and everyone who passed by my room had lost something: keys, watches, cell phones, puppies, tax returns, marriages, divorce decrees, heirloom rings. Doctors and nurses had lost patients . . . and marriages. Patients were losing money, homes, hope, and, most excruciating, life. Visitors were losing husbands and wives, daughters and sons, grandparents and newborns. It was a swirling vortex of pain.

"You've broken her," my mother, Leila, had said at the time, standing on one side of the hospital bed as I came out of a small seizure.

My eyes had cut to her: She was thin, always thin, in a blonde wig, perfect makeup, and expensive clothes she'd bought with someone else's credit card. She looked rich and brittle. Dad, on the other side of the bed, in a slick suit, movie-star handsome, waved away her complaint.

"Nonsense. It's the losses here in the hospital giving her problems." He patted me on the head as he might a puppy. "She's fixable. We just need to get her out of here."

"The police will be all over us if we yank her out."

"Not if we have cause."

On the doctor's next rounds, he walked in to find Leila had thrown herself on me, weeping all the while, as Dad thundered about the doctor's inability to make a diagnosis. It didn't hurt that all those losses in one room triggered another small seizure. My parents ratcheted up their act—crying and braying for a whole afternoon—to justify pulling me out of the hospital without anyone getting the authorities involved. Dad's repeated threats to sue for malpractice made the hospital staff weary and only too glad to see us go.

We'd no more gotten in the car in the hospital parking lot than Leila said, "You'd better be sure you can fix her."

She refused to speak to my dad the rest of the trip home. I remember being grateful for the quiet.

It took months for me to learn control, for my dad to teach me the secrets he claimed were passed down from his Cajun mom, and hers, and on and on—family I'd never known, family as mythical as unicorns in my childhood. I committed his lessons to memory. I learned to function. And I *almost* passed for normal . . . to most people. I was able to fake that normal for years, because I had learned one very hard lesson: *never tell.*

You might have wondered about that, if you'd seen the tabloids after I was outed. Googling "Avery Marie Broussard" produces a ton of depressing, obnoxious headlines, so much so that if I'd been a media hound, I would have been overjoyed. Instead, it'd been absolute hell being in the news for something I wanted to hide. How I wanted to shed the identity of "the girl who sees lost things," like a dried-out, unwanted skin.

I wanted to be *invisible.*

The two little girls, still on their mother's lap, peeked at me over her shoulders. I swallowed hard and pretended to watch as the South, smothered in kudzu, fly by the window.

I didn't want lives depending on me. Lives like Bianca Silver. Or Aurelia March. Little girls, dead, because I couldn't find them in time.

So I ran. That's how vile I am, and you should know that, up front.

I *ran.*

I'd made a habit of running for years by then. I'd become quite the expert at it, frankly, so no one was more surprised than me when I let myself get pulled into the LPK case. No one.

The bus rattled into Saint Michael's, and I felt a weight of dread press against me as the driver slowed and pulled over at the town's only gas station, just past its one stoplight. I grabbed my little faded and dented suitcase, checked that it was still carefully locked, heaved my backpack onto my shoulder, and made my way to the exit, making sure to keep my back to the young guy with the cell phone.

"God's gonna punish you, gal," the old lady said, pointing one of her needles my way as I passed her. "A thing like you's an unholy curse."

"Shut up, Alma," the elderly black passenger said, giving me a little nod. "Don't pay her no never-mind. She's had her mean on since Houston."

I smiled a *thank-you* and kept going, stepping off the bus and onto the platform. Truth be told, I wasn't exactly sure I disagreed with Alma. I could feel my curse hovering just on the edge of my awareness. It felt like death was following me.

The driver had not been scheduled to stop in Saint Michael's. Nothing much ever did. He'd done me a favor, though he'd kept looking at me, worried, the entire trip. I think he was relieved I was no longer his concern. The bus belched black diesel smoke, kicking up dust as it pulled away.

I'm not sure how long I stood there, wishing for another alternative. Anything besides coming home to Saint Michael's. Nothing came to me, though, and honestly, I hadn't expected it to. Funny, how in the end you face your own death. I had always thought I'd go kicking and screaming.

Guess I was wrong.

I am standing in Saint Michael's. Fear scrambled my thoughts, and my hands went clammy. I closed my eyes, focused on the white noise in my earphones, and tried to remember how to breathe.

Jack was here.

If I turned left at the little crossroads, I'd be in town—a tiny little square with a post office and a town hall (one room for the city clerk, two rooms for the police, and an evidence room that did double duty as storage for the town's Christmas and Fourth of July decorations).

It was Tuesday, which meant Meryl was serving the best damned lasagna you'd ever eaten in her little diner. Zannah's travel agency was still next door, according to Nate, though in this self-serve Internet age of travel, it only survived because the chemical companies—especially the one her husband ran—still used her services. She'd gotten me my ticket out of town the first time I'd run. Not sure I'd ever thanked her for that. I'd been flat broke at the time.

Other old haunts remained: Sally's Flower Emporium, where Sally liked to foist mums on everyone no matter the occasion, insisting it wasn't because they were cheap but because they were the workhorse of the flower world and everyone should give them a chance. (We all knew it was because they were cheap.) Bebe's House of Fishing Tackle, housed in the old Texaco station, and Walter's Odds and Ends, a vintage shop in which every single item carried an astronomical price tag, mainly because Walter was both independently wealthy from oil being found on his land and also a hoarder who could give hoarders lessons. I'm not sure he ever actually sold anything. The store was more an excuse to buy what he liked than a business.

My favorite places would have to wait. I turned right, instead, heading toward a little Acadian cottage I'd seen online, having used a realtor who, blissfully, was based in Baton Rouge and willing to sign a nondisclosure agreement. She'd promised to leave me a key.

The gravel road rippled with heat, and every step kicked up dust clouds, thick and suffocating. I hadn't told Latham I was coming home.

He wouldn't like it, not one bit.

CHAPTER TWO

It took me a full day, but I finally found the courage to face Latham and let him know I was back in town.

It did not go well.

I cringed as the beer bottle shattered against the cottage's dingy brick fireplace; Latham seethed, disgusted with himself as much as with me. He turned away, ashamed; his arms braced on the kitchen counter as he tried to calm down. It was one of the many, many times I was grateful I couldn't see Latham's losses. If only my father couldn't see things pertaining to us, how different would my life have been?

I knelt to pick a few large brown glass shards off the floor, then moved on to my old rickety easel, already set up in a small nook of the dining room, next to a big bay of windows and plenty of natural light. My beloved brushes were dutifully lined up like neat soldiers, ready for work. I fished a few more shards out from the old toolbox where I kept my tubes of paint and listened for a sign that Latham's anger was ebbing.

He had arrived a couple of hours after my call with a pickup truck full of my boxes and an attitude full of vinegar. I'd shipped everything to him when I'd run away from Chicago. Didn't even write him a note; he was used to getting my stuff, holding it, and then shipping it elsewhere once I'd landed in some new anonymous place. Chicago, though—I'd stayed there the longest. The missing girls wouldn't let me leave.

For the briefest moment, I flashed back to my image of Aurelia March—five years old, with unbelievably beautiful hair the color of spun gold and the natural highlights befitting a child who loved to play outside. I had just approached the room where the FBI agents were interviewing her mother when the image had slammed into me, and we knew the Little Princess Killer definitely had her. And knowing what I knew . . . I shuddered.

"Avery?" Latham asked, and I snapped back to the present, a broken piece of glass in my hand. He carefully took it from me. "I asked you if you'd seen a broom?"

I shook off the overwhelming feeling of failure and nodded toward the little storage closet in the kitchen to answer to his question.

"You shouldn't even be here." He stared at the glass shards still covering the floor, and when I didn't answer, he sighed. "You needed to stay away. You *need*," he said, each word hammered to a fine edge, "to stay *alive*."

"I'll be fine."

"Fine!" He threw up his hands, talking to himself as he turned away from me. "Fine, she says. She'll be fine." He turned back and glared at me. "There aren't enough mapmakers in the world to map out how stupid that is. It was bad enough when you were in Chicago, for crying out loud, where there are so many people; I know the images wore you down, every flipping day. And as if that wasn't bad enough, you go get yourself involved in a freaking serial killer case, for the love of God. I thought you'd completely lost your mind over that one, but it pales to your being *here. Jack's here!*"

His voice boomed, ricocheting off the empty walls of the cottage.

"Good job on the whole calming down thing." I balanced my next words on dancer's toes, delicate and ready to leap away. "Besides, it doesn't matter."

"Like hell it doesn't. So you just decided, all of a sudden, to ignore what Dad saw? After all these years?"

Instead of answering, I dug into the box that held my paints, sorting through the tubes, wondering how on earth vermilion had ended up in the same tub as the ochers. Fascinating stuff, really.

Latham acknowledged my stalling tactic with a roll of his eyes as he moved toward the closet with the easy grace I remembered so well. He'd always seemed tall and larger than life to me as a kid—muscular and strong—superhero like. Now, ten years of being away from him had brought him into focus. In reality, he stood not quite six-foot, and he was haggard and too lean for his own good. Ragged blond hair in bad need of a cut fell into his green eyes—eyes set in dark circles with creases that hadn't been there the last time we were together. Anyone would know we were siblings from the strange shade of our green eyes alone, but we both also shared a patina of exhaustion from too many months of too little sleep. He was thirty-seven to my thirty, but it chilled me that he looked ten years older than his age.

He gave me an aggravated grimace as he pulled out the broom and dustpan. "I meant what I said. You shouldn't be here. You're just lucky Leila (we never called her *Mom*; years of being reminded how she loathed the term had ingrained the alternative in our vocabulary) and Dad are off on one of their exploits." He shot me another glare. "For *now*."

I swallowed the fear and the grief and kept my voice neutral. "Well, I *am* here, Latham. I needed to come home."

"No you didn't." He walked over to the mess he'd made and began to sweep up what remained. "You could've come home when Jack was in Afghanistan. He was gone for years, and it would've been safe." The glass rattled in the dustpan as if it agreed. Enthusiastic traitor, that glass.

"I have no intention of seeing Jack at all, so it won't matter."

"Right. Because in a town of less than eighty, avoiding Jack will be a piece of cake."

He exaggerated. Saint Michael's boasted a whopping population of thirty-eight hundred, but I saw his point. I shrugged, and he narrowed his eyes. "You know about the divorce."

"Well, the sign that said, 'Welcome to Saint Michael's, Home of Silver Star Patriot Jack Thibodaux, Single Dad and Hero To All' was a clue."

Latham laughed. "You've been to the post office."

I nodded. "This morning. In the time it took me to file a change-of-address card, I had no fewer than seven people tell me about Jack's divorce, the custody battle that followed, and, I quote, 'the woman who was almost as horrible as you were to him'—oh yeah, all seven also made a point to mention how cute his kid is."

"I'm surprised they didn't demand to know why you left. It's eaten the gossips to pieces not knowing."

"Oh, one of them did. Two different people tried to pull me aside, wanting me to tell them where something they'd lost could be found, and then JoJo Bean walked in and burst into tears at the sight of me, which distracted everyone, and so I slipped out before they could get their bearings again. No way can I go to the grocery, by the way, since Jack's family still owns it, so maybe you could run me to Baton Rouge this afternoon?"

Latham nodded. He headed back to the kitchen for the next box, and winced at the peeling horror of mismatched cabinet doors (most hung crookedly), all painted a slapdash combination of pea green and muddy brown. The previous owner was possessed (not by talent).

"What's really going on, Squirt?" His fear was palpable, piled up in thunderclouds, threatening. "You didn't just suddenly develop a love for living in half-remodeled, piece-of-crap houses. And there are a lot better places where you could blend into the crowds or hide away in the country and avoid all the damned press—so why *here*? Why *now*?"

I'd grown up working for Latham; he'd started a small construction company when he was eighteen, and it was what had fed us. I'd learned to swing a hammer by the time I was fourteen. Not from any deep desire, but for survival; we needed every penny the two of us could earn. It had become such a way of life, such a necessity, that even in the summers between my semesters at RISD—Rhode Island School of Design—I had gone home and worked. RISD was tough, prestigious, and if I hadn't had a scholarship, I'd have never managed the tens of thousands in tuition, in spite of Latham nearly killing himself taking on extra work to make sure I had that shot.

At this stage, there were some things I was far better at than my brother: painting, for one, was a given. Plaster repair, especially the detailed reconstruction work that old houses around here needed. Latham, however, was better at the big things, like walls and staircases.

But of all the things I could do far, far better than Latham, the con topped the list. And there was no way I was telling him Dad had used him to lure me home, not until I knew why. As bad as Latham looked, Dad may not have been lying.

"Avery, I know every one of your stalling tactics. Spit it out."

"That's the thing." I laced exhaustion into every word, a flurry of sighs as neat as little calculated stitches. "Dad never said when I'd die. And you know how he splits hairs when it serves one of his agendas."

"What other purpose could he have had? Self-serving he may be, but I don't think even he would lie about Jack killing you. Not when he thinks of you as the golden goose."

"He'd manipulate if it suited him." I looked at Latham then, made sure he heard me. "Believe me, I tried to pin him down. It could be now; it could be when I'm eighty. I'm tired of running. I can't . . ." My voice quivered. Failed. Tears welled up. The emotional arsenal of a little sister should never be underestimated.

"Oh, man, I'm sorry, Av," he said. "I know you've been going through hell between this serial killer case and the bastard tabloids hounding you."

"Then you'll understand why I need to be in a familiar place. Home. Or, at least, a reasonable facsimile of home. If only for a while, 'til I'm better able to handle the pressure."

"You think that's wise? You think you won't cross Jack's path? That he won't kill you, just like Dad said? This isn't just about you, Av. You dying at his hands would destroy him." Latham and Jack had once been the best of friends. I'd obliterated that, too.

Latham leaned on the counter, caught my eye, and made sure he had my attention. "And don't forget his kid. Jack has custody. If you don't care about what it would do to Jack to see you die, at least think about what it'll do to me or his kid, who'd have to live with Jack in the aftermath."

Leave it to Latham to counter my con with the one thing that could haul me back to the truth. I fought back the tears. Fought back the heartbreak and regret, and forced myself to give Latham the tone and attitude he needed to buy what I needed him to believe.

"First, Jack's not made of cotton. Never has been. As you said, he was in Afghanistan. He'll deal." If he didn't outright celebrate, I thought. Ten years ago, I had left Jack without a note, without an explanation, without a backwards glance, and I had never, ever, given in to the overwhelming desire to call him and beg him to come get me. I had run, and he had never known why. I couldn't tell him then, and I couldn't tell him now—he never would have believed me, and he would have followed me, found me, for all the wrong reasons, if I had shown one tiny sign of weakness.

"Dad said Jack would *murder* you, Squirt. Not just kill you. *Mur . . . der,*" Latham said, drawing out the last word as if I was having a slow moment. "You need to quit whitewashing that just because you still love Jack."

"I don't still love Jack."

"Please," Latham said, disgust rolling off him.

"Honest to God, I'm exhausted. I missed you. I missed being near someone who actually knows me and cares. I don't want to be alone right now. Can't that just be enough? Can't I come home, have a place—and at least one person who wants me here?"

Latham watched me, looking deep for signs I was lying. He had underestimated just how good I'd gotten at it; so good, I almost believed the lies I told him. I hated lying to Latham, but I would. For now.

"I plan to stay away from Jack, Latham, if that helps any. I intend to paint a lot—I have a show in October, and I need to get some new canvases done for it."

Latham wasn't about to be sidetracked so easily. "Jack's hell on wheels right now and . . . erratic, ever since he came back."

"I heard."

He grunted. He knew Nate kept me informed, especially when it came to any rumors involving Jack. There'd been mention of post-traumatic stress disorder. PTSD wasn't something to mess around with.

Latham opened the lone box of cookware. Sad, scuffed, and little used that it was, he began finding a place for each pot and pan in the creaky cupboards. He noticed the garage sale stickers—old, faded—still attached to a set of bowls and raised an eyebrow, waggled one of the bowls in front of me. "Do you even know what these are for?"

"Sure. I mix paint in them."

"Of course you do," he sighed, setting the bowls aside for my studio. "I am beginning to recall the futility of trying to teach you how to cook. It has failed more than once, if memory serves."

"The kitchen is where the coffee lives. Everything else needs to be takeout."

"Takeout? In Saint Michael's. Good luck with that." He stared at the stove missing two of its four knobs, and shook his head. "Never mind, we'll figure out something, if only because you've been known to set off fire alarms just trying to boil water."

He paused, his hand midway to the shelf as he stared off into space. I didn't ask him what was wrong; growing up, I had learned the dead occasionally showed up and tried to talk to him, often at the most inopportune times. Mostly, they didn't seem to realize they were dead, or that no one could see them. I knew not to interrupt when he checked out like this. Seeing the dead was something he'd kept carefully hidden from absolutely everyone, especially our parents. Leila had no ability at all, and the fact that Dad and I did, well, you'd have thought that was Dad being spiteful and selfish to hear her talk—as if there were all these sets of abilities out there to be had and we'd snagged them without inviting her to the party. If she had

23

known Latham could see the dead, she'd have had a conniption, and there'd have been hell to pay. God knows what grift she'd have cooked up for that.

Latham had realized I had a gift, he once told me many years ago, when I was about three and kept finding things he'd misplaced. He did everything he could to make me understand why our parents shouldn't know about my ability: *you don't trust grifters with your gift*, he'd warned. But I was too young to keep a secret for long.

Latham set the bowls down and drew a deep, ragged breath.

"Everything okay?"

"Yeah." Then he looked at me and said, his voice as quiet as the moon, "Please don't stay, Av. It's not safe for you here."

Unfortunately, it might not be safe for him if I left, but I couldn't tell him that. "While you're here," I said in an attempt to sidestep his next salvo, "I could use some help with the hot water heater." I needed more time with him, and he tended to talk about personal stuff when his hands were busy doing something useful.

He gave me a squirrelly look of doubt, and I pasted on my innocent expression. Oscar-worthy, I swear.

"You know how to fix a hot water heater." He had donned the big brother look; the one designed to convince you he knew what you were up to so you'd slip up and tell. "I taught you, myself. In fact, you've installed hot water heaters for me."

"Like I could forget. However, this one's ancient and full of rust. I tried to fix it, but the valve is stuck shut, and I don't think I can wrench it open without breaking the line. And as you know," I said, aiming for *hey look, I'm responsible*, "because of the seizures, I can't drive. I just figured you'd have the right tools or a spare valve."

The trick, when lying, is to never look away. Don't give in to the urge, don't embellish, and don't fidget. Just shut up. According to my parents, you let the mark jump to conclusions; let him do the work for you, and you say as little as possible. Guile—it's what's for breakfast.

In this case, though, the valve was truly stuck. I had just failed to mention that I had purposefully wrenched it the wrong direction several times to strip the threads to get it that way. He was going to have a bear of a time loosening it.

Latham stood there, quiet as a shadow, contemplating me. His way with stillness was an art form. His lips crooked in a bit of a smile, the first one

I'd seen on him since my arrival, and he came over and kissed me on the forehead as he slung an arm around my shoulder.

"Squirt, you shouldn't lie to a man who knows ghosts who'll tattle on you," he said.

Dammit. "So someone's here now?" I looked over his shoulder like I might catch a glimpse.

"No one who's staying, so don't worry about it."

I followed him into the mudroom where the water heater in question sat in all its rusty splendor.

"You look like hell, Latham. What aren't you telling me?"

He took eons to answer as he made quick work of inspecting the valve.

"I'm fine," he grunted.

"Is it the ghosts, then? Is it getting harder to deal with them?"

"It's nothing you can fix, so let it go."

"How do you know I can't help? And even if I can't, maybe it would help to talk about it." I tried to bank the anger, the frustration. "You know you can trust me with it. I'm not a kid." Couldn't he see that? Couldn't he tell it was hurting me to not be able to help him, not to know what was going on with him?

He flinched, and stopped fiddling with the pipe. I had none of his losses to guide me here. He looked up at me this time —him down on his knees in front of the tank, me leaning against the doorjamb. Déjà vu washed over me. We'd done dozens of jobs together, me trailing after him like a puppy all those years. Back then I was eye-to-eye with him, though, when he was down on his knees.

Strange, how he got smaller.

"Would you move, if I asked you to? Go away to somewhere safe? The far end of the country?"

My breath caught in my chest, and all I could do was shake my head no. And for that moment, just for that moment, anger flared and hurt. Why couldn't he just tell me? I shoved it aside and told myself he needed me here. Something must've gleamed in my eyes, because he nodded as if he grasped something I hadn't said, would never say.

"Aren't we just the Gift of the Magi?" he muttered.

I didn't answer him.

We passed the rest of his visit in our separate vaults of silence as he finished fixing the valve. When he was done, he put away his tools, stood, and turned to leave. Before he went, he tugged a curl of my wild hair.

"You'll stay away from Jack?"

"Not a problem," I answered, glad I could at least give him that.

CHAPTER THREE

The next morning I stared at the white canvas, waiting for the image to come to me—the one that would drive me, obsessively, but in a good way, the one that would take me out of myself for a little while, out of the loathing and into another place. Soaking in the colors, saturating my thoughts.

Time passed, and nothing. Instead, as I looked down at the paints, at the brush in my hand, memory flooded me, and I remembered the turn-of-the-century church, the one abandoned by the Catholic diocese, huddled, worn, and beaten, on the back of Thibodaux property, near River Road. Time had long since encroached, crumbling the once-paved drive and leaving weeds to overwhelm the church lawn. The smell of that tall grass, blades sometimes as high as my waist, filled me, tugging me back to days gone by.

The church was an old, narrow, whitewashed building, its roof as crooked as an old lady's finger; the steeple had slid a little to the side, in bad need of repair. Birds roosted, rain and humidity were slowly ruining the interior eaves, and the windows were jagged, gaping wounds from kids throwing rocks.

Oh, how I loved it.

As a child, I'd hide inside on particularly bad days, skipping school when the taunts about the scars got to be too much or when the losses of my classmates overwhelmed me. Never mind that the church was a couple of miles from school, and even farther from our home. I'd never minded running.

One especially awful day, I'd left school before lunch. It'd cost me another detention, another parent-teacher conference for which Leila would find ways to make me suffer for having inconvenienced her, but I did it anyway. Happy to pay the price. Leila made the effort to appear motherly for the teachers and clergy of Saint Michael's, and for reasons I was never told, my parents decided to make the town their home base. Before that we'd moved from town to town every few months, sometimes every other week, so to settle in one place was something new. Still, it felt odd, and I kept expecting to go home any day and hear we were on the move again.

That winter was an especially wet one, as I remember it, which made Saint Michael's feel colder than some of the places we'd traveled up north, and the day I played hooky I had huddled in the back pew of the old church, my fingers pink with cold, my breath frosting in front of me as I sketched in a lined notebook I'd scavenged from my dad's desk.

I had felt Jack's losses as he approached the church and then felt him wait in the front vestibule—where the priests used to keep a small armoire for robes and supplies, but which now only housed a broken holy water font.

I didn't call out to him or say anything that would have let him know I was there; we'd lived in Saint Michael's at that point for more than a year, and Jack and I had known each other instantly and deeply. He was four years older than me, now twelve to my eight, and he and Latham were good friends. As good as Latham would let anyone be, I suppose. But on this day, Jack had come here for me.

He eased into the chapel and slid onto the pew next to me, setting a paper bag to his right. He was already tall and rangy at twelve. Already starting to look more like the man he'd become than boy. Wild, shaggy hair the color of rich chocolate set off silver eyes. I'd have known him anywhere, even if I'd been blind. I'd have known him in a crowd of thousands, just with a glance. I didn't question it; it just was.

"That's pretty good." He'd turned my sketchbook so he could better see what I was drawing: a girl making angel wings in the snow. "You should paint that."

I cocked my head and considered the image. It wasn't right, not yet, and I didn't know why, much less how to fix it. One day, I'd know. Besides, I didn't have any paints.

I didn't answer. I rarely did. That didn't stop Jack.

"So here. You should have this." He handed me a bag, and I dug out a nice set of acrylics, complete with brushes and a pad of pure, white paper. I held it all with the reverence I've seen people use with jewels or consecrated chalices. I couldn't remember having gotten a gift before from anyone else other than Latham. I didn't know how to tell Jack that I loved them.

"Somebody gave them to Chris for his birthday, but he and his mom moved out this week. He'll never miss them. He's too little for them, anyway."

Chris was two, a full ten years younger than Jack. His mother had just finished a very public divorce from Jack's father, the philandering, corrupt senator from the great state of Louisiana, a man who'd sold his soul long before he'd held his first public office.

His stepmother had asked Jack to go with them when she and Chris left. Jack's mom had died when he was a baby, and the stepmom was the only mother he'd ever known, but Jack had said no. It was odd—I didn't see that as a loss; he'd told Latham about it. Latham thought he was nuts to stay, but Jack had just shrugged. He said he had other family here: cousins, friends. He wouldn't have anyone where they were moving, and his stepmother wasn't exactly Parent of the Year. I'm pretty sure he thought she might be able to pull off taking care of Chris if she didn't have Jack to deal with, too.

I did see the loss of the escape. He knew remaining meant he'd suffer at the Senator's hands. The beatings would return, when the Senator was drinking. We had no idea how bad it would get.

He didn't know yet that I knew about the abuse. About the bruises on the parts of his body always covered with clothes. About the Senator's proclivity for having him undress before a beating. How the Senator could place the bruises with precision, so no one else would ever know. I suspect Jack thought that now that he was getting bigger, he'd be able to stop his dad. I wasn't so sure.

Jack had never told anyone about what the Senator did to him. Wouldn't. Couldn't. But I could see losses, and he didn't know that. He just knew I somehow understood.

We needed each other. I know he stayed for me.

I put my head on his shoulder that day in the little church and drew him something beautiful as a thank-you.

I would leave him, years later, when he needed me the most. He would hate me for that. Not that I could blame him. Not one bit.

All the years after, painting was my salvation. I saved up for art classes when I started working for Latham. I'd grown up by the time Jack went to college and then the military, and I was gone to art school typically when he was home on leave. The summer I was twenty, though, I came back as I always did between semesters to help Latham, and Jack was home on leave. It took exactly the first sight of each other again to know that yes, this was still our other half, and we acted on what we were meant to be.

Until my dad's prediction.

I stared now at the blank canvas, begging it to take me somewhere other than where my mind had wandered. Some other thought, place, or time without Jack.

I made a stab at painting a different scene, something, somewhere on the beach. The phone rang twice; Hank calling to leave querulous messages that I refused to answer. The media were already reporting that I was now living in Saint Michael's. He was worried, he said, bothered by the tenor of a couple of call-ins the FBI had received on its tip line since I ran out on them. I could be in trouble.

Maybe I should have taken his message more seriously, but truth be told, he'd been saying some version of it since the week after I was outed by a junior agent who thought having a psychic helping the FBI was laughable. The agent had mouthed off after the Feds had come under pressure to find the missing girls. The press caught wind of it, and that, as they say, was that.

The first two LPK girls had been found by accident: One was dug up on a construction site. The other, found in an abandoned gas station by some kids. Police across several jurisdictions had been stumped by the identical abductions of several more girls that, at that point in time, the FBI had not been able to find.

For me, though, the involvement with the FBI had started with Jancey Taylor, who'd been missing for more than a year. By happenstance, I'd stood next to her parents in line at the grocery, and her image had slapped me, hard, brutal. I had shaken with outrage. Beyond control. That had never happened to me before, in spite of having stood by other victims and victims' families all my life.

Think about it: how many people have been the victim of something, some crime—robbery, lies, deceit, abuse? Thousands. Millions. Every day, thousands and millions more. I'd never allowed myself to get involved. Never. Had never even been tempted.

"Everybody's lost something," my dad would say. "Everybody. You can't find everything for everyone. You'll burn out, and then where would we be?"

He had said that way back when I was a kid and still helping them. He had made me promise to keep it in the family, and what Dad said was golden. I thought it proved he cared about me.

But when I saw Jancey, I could not stay away. I could not have lived with myself if I didn't try.

Jancey was five, and had once been beautiful. We found her in a tiny, locked box in an abandoned building out by the wharf on Lake Michigan, her body decomposing but perfectly posed in her princess dress, tiara, and angel wings. It was something about the angel wings—I'd seen them in my vision—that had gripped me, terrifying me in a way that the mere image of her shouldn't have, and when I found out later about the sexual abuse Jancey had suffered, I wanted to poke the eyes out of the bastard who'd done it and castrate him.

That day in the grocery, however, I had not wanted to scare her parents; they were moving robotically, glancing at every girl roughly her age in hopes that it might be Jancey and they might get lucky and find she was just around the next corner, the next aisle. I didn't have the stomach to rip that hope away all on my own. It's a cruel and brutal thing, hope. In the end, I had done the one thing I'd promised myself I'd never, ever freaking do: I got involved. I went in to the local FBI office, met Hank, with all his derision, and the rest of the team, and explained what I could do.

Maybe I made it worse. Maybe I goaded him on, the LPK. Maybe . . .

The Feds ran me through rigorous evaluations, from lie detectors to psych exams and a hundred little tests of their own devising to see if I could see things they'd lost. When I did, consistently, they listened to me about Jancey, and they found her. After that, I worked with parents and siblings of other missing girls and found each one. Several were unrelated murders, but after the girls were found, the FBI declared that several were definitely connected to one unsub, and the press nicknamed him "The Little Princess Killer," which Hank and his agents loathed.

But the LPK would do more. I'd known from the start that I didn't have much of a chance of saving the twelfth girl, Bianca Silver, and sure enough, we got there a day late. But it was my screwup that made us miss finding the last girl, Aurelia, alive by minutes. She was number thirteen. Thirteen girls, and I hadn't slept in months, hadn't eaten much, hadn't in the end helped at all. So now I sat in front of this blighted blank canvas and slathered on the images that had haunted me, images I didn't always know the origin of, images that promised absolution and lied. I painted, ignoring the phone, checking only to make sure it wasn't Latham calling. I painted all day, through the waning evening, painted as if my life depended on it. Because maybe it did.

It's funny—we worry about the big things, about the big decisions we make in our lives, and how they'll affect us. Take this job or that job? Go to school? Marry; don't marry. Move? But it's the little decisions we make that irrevocably destroy us. Dine in or take out? Turn left here or wait a block? Each one of those little decisions drives us toward our end, and we don't even know it.

I didn't know it, that day, choosing to go to Meryl's.

The bleak feeling kept growing, until it had the texture of an oil slick in my mind, with darkened images fluttering and battering against something that felt opaque, like moths trapped in a filthy jar. I chalked it up to extreme exhaustion and gave up painting for the day.

A few minutes later, I climbed on an old Schwinn I'd borrowed from Latham and pedaled to Meryl's, a squat, flat-roofed diner that faced what could be called the town square, if one were feeling generous or maybe drunk. Meryl's was the best restaurant for miles around, beating out competition in a string of tiny towns from Baton Rouge to New Orleans. There were a couple of mom-and-pop cafés that did okay, but if you wanted anything better than Meryl's, you had to drive more than an hour into the heart of one of the cities to find it.

As I stood out back, my mouth watered at the aroma of Meryl's grilled shrimp fettuccine. Meryl had offered to deliver the meal, but I'd refused. Hadn't wanted to put her out—negotiating the rutted, dirt driveway to the cottage would have demolished her little car. I regretted turning down her offer the moment I reached for the back door and realized Jack Thibodaux was inside, his losses like a thousand hornets swarming. I fought for control, turning up the white noise on my ever-present iPod, trying to deflect the images stinging me: carnage, war, losses. So many losses.

He shouldn't have been at Meryl's this evening. It was Thursday, payday, and besides the ranch, he oversaw his family's little grocery store that doubled as the town bank. The store cashed paychecks for all and sundry, and with all of the chemical plants in a five-mile radius letting out at the same time, dozens of people would be lined up to cash their weekly checks, saving them the forty-five-minute drive to the nearest actual bank in Baton Rouge. Most usually paid some on their account, charged whatever they needed for the week, and Jack made a bit of interest the way his family had for nearly a hundred years since the store first opened.

Instead of being safely where he was supposed to be, however, Jack was here, and I felt his heart breaking over his fractured relationship with his son. Right behind Jack's losses came a seven-year-old boy's: images of a home left behind, toys forfeited, security gone—the challenge of moving to a strange place, living with someone he was supposed to call Dad, a man he didn't know; he felt that loss, the loss of not having a father all his earlier years.

Oh dear God, Jack's *son* was in there with him. I wasn't sure I could stand, much less pedal. I had to get out of there, now. I turned to leave, fumbling with the bike's ornery kickstand, fighting to keep from doubling over in pain, when Meryl opened the door and tapped me on my shoulder.

"There you are, hon," she said, grinning her gap-toothed grin, nodding her graying curls toward the kitchen. "Got your favorite just about packed. Why don't you come on in while I get it ready?"

Meryl was one of those solid women, as wide as she was tall, and beautiful in that Earth Mother way, all grace and an athleticism that held you in awe, if she didn't catch you watching and shoo you away. When she made up her mind to do something, a bulldozer would have better luck stopping her, and even as I shook my head no, mumbling that I had to leave, she hauled me inside, ignorant of my pain.

It was my own damn fault. Every tabloid out there had heralded the loss of my abilities and debated what it would mean to the LPK case. Unfortunately, the lie also eliminated my good excuse to avoid people. At least half of Saint Michael's usually viewed me with downright suspicion, which, frankly, up until now had worked for me. Meryl, however, had apparently doubled up on the gene that made her determined to help when she saw a need. I was her current project. I couldn't tell her the truth without hurting her feelings for having lied to begin with. The pain from Jack's losses amplified the moment she shoved me over the threshold and into the diner's antiquated kitchen. I trembled by the back door as she bustled forward, jabbering about local goings-on. All I had eyes for was the scene playing out past the big U-shaped dining bar that surrounded the big grill.

33

Time stopped, just stopped, like some movie reel stuck and clicking, broken sprockets clacking somewhere in the background. Jack sat at the cracked red leather booth on the far left, at the end of the row. Our old booth. His once dark, wavy hair was salt-and-pepper now, cut military-short, vainly trying to make him look like any other military officer. Bland, impersonal. It failed miserably. So much about him was the same yet older: square jaw, full lips, now with a starburst of a scar lacing his right cheek. He seemed bigger, somehow, broader, as if he knew he had to hold the world on his shoulders, and that was fine. His right hand and arm had old, silver-looking scars fanning out of the short-sleeved shirt he wore, wrapping down around his wrist. A cane was propped against the back wall, just behind him.

He'd been an Air Force pararescue jumper in Afghanistan; one of those insane guys who train as hard as the SEALs, but then add trauma care to their load and go in behind enemy lines to save anyone downed and in need of medical help. He'd jumped out of planes and helicopters into enemy fire.

I felt every single one of those stinging loss. Friends killed by enemy snipers; Jack, frantically working on them, under fire himself. Images of his comrades, arms severed, legs lost, hope ripped away. Jack trying to carry one fellow soldier out and having his own leg shot out from under him, more shrapnel scissoring across his face. He'd crawled, then, dragging the man with his one good hand . . .

His son sat across from him, a shorter carbon copy, looking as polite as a scared kid could manage. Time snapped back into place, and I realized Jack was trying to patiently teach Brody how to operate a reel for a fishing rod; he had a small mock-up there in the booth. He was so focused on the rod he missed how his son had steeled himself and flinched every time Jack cast the reel into the opposite booth.

God, that voice.

Jack tried to tease a smile out of Brody, and his deep baritone magic swirled around me, lighting up the room like colorful musical notes, mesmerizing me.

I had to leave. I could not be there.

A redhead sauntered in at that moment and headed straight for Jack's booth, and I froze, recognizing his ex, Marguerite Monroe. She'd worked for the Senator before he died and had comforted Jack, I'd heard, after I left. Comforted him and nudged him all the way to the altar, not two years after I'd gone, Nate had told me at the time, disgusted. I'd never been able to hate her. Jack had needed someone to love him after I left. He deserved happiness. I just wished, for his sake, she'd been better at it.

She had always been regal, elegant, one of those ladies-who-lunch types, though I knew she had a sharp legal mind; she was now a hotshot lobbyist for some of the petrochemical companies that dotted Louisiana's backwoods, most specifically, Polyformosia.

If you looked at her—the dress, the perfect pearls, the makeup—you might write her off as soft, vulnerable. She was the type of woman my dad had once pointed out as the kind that an inexperienced grifter might think would be easy pickings. She seemed fairly fascinated with her own image and failed to care much for anyone else in her vicinity. But that was the type, he warned, who always knew exactly who was watching her, as well as who was shifting in and out of her orbit, and a grifter would as soon fleece a vicious hyena than try to scavenge off a women like that.

I knew if I moved at all, she'd see me. My one hope was that she and Jack would distract one another enough so that I could leave, unnoticed. I was afraid to breathe. They were arguing before Marguerite even took a seat next to Brody, and Brody's eyes had gone wide and frightened as he looked back and forth at his parents.

"You're not going to do this, Jack," Marguerite was saying when I tuned in. "I will destroy you before I let you take our son away from me."

"This isn't the time or the place," Jack answered.

"Oh, I think it is." Marguerite studied him, cat-like, playing with her prey. "Let's by all means let this podunk town in on your dirty little secrets. Maybe they wouldn't be such hero-worshippers if they knew some of the things I know about you."

She sounded vile, heartless, and yet, the losses spun off her, too: how much she'd loved Jack, how she'd realized he didn't love her, how much that hurt.

Jack leaned over, anger lacing every word. "You are determined to make this hard for everyone. You cannot provide a stable home life—you're never home. You kept my son away from me when I was on leave. You fought me when I got back even though you were traveling constantly. You know this is the best thing for Brody, and I'm not going to drop it. Ever. So. Back. Off. Marguerite. Or. Else."

Marguerite laughed, pleased. The artist in me couldn't help but notice the beautiful lines of her throat as she leaned her head back, the perfect ivory tone of her skin, the absolute malevolence in her stunning copper-brown eyes. The artist in me wondered if I could capture that. The rest of me shuddered, repulsed.

"Or else?" she smiled, vicious, narrowing her eyes as Jack eased out of the booth and stood, still a powerfully built man, one who dwarfed Marguerite. "You're forgetting I worked for your father, Jack. I know exactly what kind of father he was before he committed suicide. I have the file. It won't be hard to prove you're a chip off the old block, especially with your PTSD."

"I am *nothing* like my father, and I do not have PTSD," he seethed, his knuckles white as he grabbed his cane. "I love my son." He looked over at Brody, and I could feel the despair rolling off him as he watched his son begin to cry. He tamped down his voice and looked back at Marguerite. "You will not destroy my reputation, Mags, or my relationship with my son."

I couldn't bear to look any longer. It broke me, seeing the way he'd been hurt. How much he'd lost. In my head he was still—would always be—that gorgeous, invincible man. The man I loved. Seeing him scarred, aching for his son . . . I couldn't take it without reaching for him, and I knew I couldn't do that. Wouldn't do that. There was just no damned answer for us, was there? I turned to leave, and Meryl, oblivious (or manipulative, you pick), dragged me onto a stool with a loud, "Not so fast, Avery-girl, gotta get a container—wait here." Subtle, she was not. She toddled off to her pantry while hell burned fifteen feet away.

Marguerite looked up at me, and all those losses—all the times she couldn't get him to love her—raked across my soul, and then she turned her brown eyes, wet with tears, back to Jack.

Jack spun and saw me, his eyes going wide, stunned, his jaw dropping open. He finally managed a whisper, "Avery?"

"You told me it wasn't about *her*," Marguerite said through gritted teeth. "You said she was never coming back, that she wasn't why we broke up." Marguerite stood, dragging Brody with her. "What a pathetic liar you turned out to be, Jack."

Jack was still staring at me like I was a ghost. "Avery?" he said again, hurt and hope mixing together, toxic, as Marguerite made it to the door. He turned to look back at his son, to say something to his ex to stop her, but she only shook her head and held up her hand. "Save it. I'll see you in court."

Jack looked back at me, confusion, hurt, and surprise playing across his silver wolf eyes. I slid off the stool, shaking my head. His loss images changed in that moment; now they were of me. They bombarded me, an avalanche of pain and anger and fury, and I turned and ran from Meryl's while I could still move, still breathe.

I didn't slow down to get the bike. I just ran. Like I always did. All the way home. I'd barely managed to avoid Jack for three days.

We hadn't spoken in ten years.

It was still too soon.

CHAPTER FOUR

The trouble with trying to insert myself into Latham's life enough to find out what was causing his deterioration was that he had had a life for ten years without me in it. He didn't need me helping on his jobsites anymore—anything I did would only take a payday away from one of his workers who needed the money. He didn't want me in the office either, and frankly, he was wise on that front. He had a nice woman named Betty who seemed to be efficient, boringly normal, and blandly middle-aged. No drama there, though she was a trifle naive and easily distractible; I tricked her into running an errand so I could sneak into his computer to look at his books. Everything appeared to be above board; he was even making a decent profit. It was a little scary.

His doctor had e-mailed him test results—from his latest annual physical so he could renew his OSHA card—and it was all quite ordinary. There were no neon signs saying *bad juju, this way*, or *look, idiot, here's the problem*.

On the one hand, everything appeared perfectly fine, and I was relieved to see it. On the other hand, my brother looked terrible; something in his life was obviously going south, and I couldn't overlook the fact that Dad—our family's own sick version of a gleeful grim reaper—had sworn Latham would die unless I returned.

If I could have found my father, I'd have shaken him 'til his teeth rattled, but I probably wouldn't have gotten a better answer. I've never known anyone like Dad who could talk so much and say so little, so colorfully. He had a black belt in vague.

Since my brother didn't need me daily, the only way I had of checking up on him was by resorting to artifice, which had so far manifested itself in me forcing him to meet me for breakfast.

We were into the sixth day of this charade—me yawning and trying not to look like I hadn't lost all track of time and painted until nearly four a.m. It was now five-thirty, and the sky hadn't even had the decency to pink up and look pretty. On this particular morning, we sat outside at a wrought-iron café table in the little courtyard of Meryl's Diner with the rest of the early morning insane people gabbing inside and throwing us furtive scowls out the windows. I hovered over my big mug of coffee, inhaling the scent as if my life depended on it.

My phone buzzed; I didn't even have to look at the caller ID—I'd set Hank's number to his own personal ringtone a long time ago so I could ignore him with forethought. I quickly turned the phone off. Latham's eyebrows went up, but he knew, from my glare, not to ask.

The courtyard was full of ivy and ferns, potted herbs and flowering bushes, with a beautiful iron gate and a half-dozen tables tucked among the plants. Latham had built it for Meryl a few years ago. I'd suggested a small water fountain for ambiance and to cut down on the noise from the street, and I was happy to see it gurgling in the corner, water spouting from a cartoon fish with a silly face. Meryl generally didn't serve breakfast outside, but she always made an exception for me, knowing I made the other townsfolk nervous, in spite of my recent widespread declarations that I could no longer see their lost images.

"Are you going to drink it, or marry it?" Latham asked me, nodding at the mug I clutched with both hands.

"I'm still debating." I yawned.

"By the way, Squirt, I'm sending you over a horse. Her name's Pandora. She's an apple slut, a little grumpy, but she's dependable and maybe you won't so easily run off and leave her behind."

"A . . . horse? Look, dumping the bike was a one-time thing." I knew he was upset because he thought I was more vulnerable on foot, easy prey for anyone who might pop out of the bushes. It had given him nightmares to see the paparazzi footage from Chicago when people had accosted me coming out of a gallery, or a Starbucks.

"Sure, it was. Look you love horses. You have a barn in the back of your place. It's a lot less likely that you'll get trapped without transport, and she's good at jumping, if you need to go over a fence to get away from anyone. All in all, much better than a bike."

"I . . . uh . . ." I did not want a horse. The last time I'd ridden one was with Jack, though I wasn't about to tell Latham that. Best to avoid the topic of Jack. My throat closed and tears threatened.

"Look, Latham, I can take care of myself. I have been doing so for years now."

"Good. Fine. Far be it from me to try and improve your quality of life." He leaned forward and looked at me with those oh-so-familiar bottle-green eyes from under a mop of shaggy blond hair. "Move somewhere else, and I will quit interfering."

I did the adult thing. I stuck my tongue out at him and changed the subject. "I could come hang out this afternoon. Watch you work. Give you pointers."

His abrupt "No," doused my playful tone. He snapped open the menu, studying it as if he'd never seen it before though I knew it was the same one from when we were kids and used to sneak into Meryl's and filch things off patrons' plates, 'til Meryl caught us and made us peel potatoes for a week. It wasn't until the third day of the punishment that I realized the KP duty was actually so she could make us eat something in the evenings, certain we weren't getting enough food at home.

"Well, gee. I'm not talking about helping, though I'm better than you at painting, and I saw the paint buckets in the back of your truck. I just thought it'd give us a chance to visit."

"Absolutely not." When he looked up and saw my surprise, he explained, "I'll be at Jack's store. They had a water leak yesterday, and my plumbers fixed it, but not before discovering rot has destroyed the entire subfloor in the back bathroom. Unfortunately, they discovered it by Jason falling through the floor. I promised we'd be back this morning to take care of it."

My scalp tightened, especially since he wouldn't look me in the eye; he was back focused on the menu like it was about to reveal the Secret of Life.

"You're helping Jack?"

"I'm helping Lottie. She's the one who called me, and she's the one who's got to deal with the customers and employees whining about not having a bathroom. Jack can go to hell, but Lottie's Lottie."

40

Latham's first girlfriend in junior high, now a happily married mom of five, Jack's store manager was a fiery little bottle blonde whom even Jack feared, I think. Maybe that was it . . . Maybe I was supposed to prevent something between Jack and Latham from going toes up.

"Well, if you're going to be there, I could come by. It won't matter if Jack—"

"No." He had his palms flat on the table as he leaned forward to make sure I had heard him. "You stay the hell away from anywhere Jack might be."

"Aw," Meryl interrupted as she carted over a tray filled with orange juice, hot buttered biscuits, baked ham with steam wafting from it, and a heaping order of hash browns and eggs and bacon to our table and began doling it out. "Jack's on the rampage, but not because of either of you, Latham. It's just that crazy ex of his, bless her heart." (*Bless her heart*'s Southern for "that bitch," which Meryl was too polite to say out loud.) "She's up and disappeared right before the big custody hearing, and that's got him on edge."

I glanced past Meryl. What was she talking about? Marguerite was standing just inside the diner, her back to us . . . typical power suit on. I flinched as Jack's ex turned, and almost choked on my bite of biscuit. It was Suzannah, not Marguerite.

Zannah had died her hair red at some point apparently, and was now a dead ringer for Marguerite. She'd had gorgeous blonde hair that had sent hearts aflutter all through high school, so it struck me as a little odd. When she saw me staring, she did a funny little wave as she answered her phone and hurried out the front door, and I had to stifle a laugh as she plowed over sweet, patient, befuddled Father Tomas, all of twenty-five and fresh out of seminary. If you could bore the world into repentance, then Father Tomas was your priest, and I couldn't help noticing that everyone inside the diner looked suddenly busy or deep in conversation.

Meryl continued prattling on about Jack, and without thinking, I blurted, "Marguerite disappeared?" And regretted it instantly when Latham glared at me.

"Real piece of work, that ex of his," she said as she set down the hash browns in front of me and the eggs and bacon for Latham.

"We didn't order yet," Latham mentioned.

Meryl rolled her eyes. "Like you ever order anything else." She turned to me. "Jack's not upset with you, hon, either. Just that crazy woman. Walking out on their son like that."

"We don't give a damn who Jack's upset with," Latham said, but he couldn't keep a look of gooey satisfaction from settling on his face as he bit into a buttered biscuit, undermining somewhat the authoritative tone he seemed to have been going for.

"That's what Jack said about her, too." Meryl winked at me like I somehow cared. "But any woman who would raise that much of a ruckus about a custody case, who threatened Jack with every sort of thing she could come up with to avoid a court date, to then up and leave town without even bothering to tell her attorney? She's six eggs short of a dozen, God bless her. I just hope she stays away."

"She just . . . left?"

Dammit. I shoved my biscuit into my mouth before I could ask anything else, managing to both keep my gaze on Meryl and ignore Latham's angry kick to my shin beneath the table. I had forgotten once you got Meryl on a subject, you were going to hear every single detail come hell or high water.

"Oh, honey, that's just the way she is, you know, always taking business trips, leaving Brody with strangers even. That's one of the reasons why Jack's fighting her so hard. Not that I believe in gossiping, mind you."

She wiped off the table next to us, and just when I thought she was done, she leaned over and whispered, "But you know, it just isn't right. Not right at all. Poor Jack. The rumor was she was planning to go to New York, but the gossip was that she went to Atlanta instead, forgot to even tell Brody. Poor kid was left waiting at summer camp because it was her day to pick him up, and the camp had to call Jack. She wasn't answering her cell phone, which pissed Jack off, though it should also work in his favor for the custody case."

I glanced inside, at the customers waiting patiently for Meryl to come tend to them. It looked like half the town was there to hear her morning updates—better than any news channel—while the other half felt it mandatory to show up to refute them.

"Meryl," Latham interrupted when she finally took a breath, "I sure could use a side order of grits this morning."

Meryl paused, scowling in confusion. "But you never get grits on the weekdays. Said they make you sleepy."

"Good point. You got any of that crawfish pie left over?"

She grinned and patted him on the shoulder as she turned to leave.

"Sure, hon, I'll fetch you some. Good to see you eating better. I was beginning to think I was going to have to hogtie you and shove food down your throat, you're getting so skinny."

My eyebrows went up at that—so, I wasn't the only one who'd noticed.

Latham pointed a fork at me and said, "Zip it, Peanut Gallery. And I thought you were going to stay away from Jack?"

"Do you see Jack over here?"

"Keep it that way, little sister."

"You ever think maybe you're too damned bossy, and I can run my own life?"

Latham snorted as he scooped up a forkful of eggs. "How's that working out for ya?"

"Oh, shut up. I never liked you, anyway."

And I stole some of his bacon. Served him right.

A few hours later, I stood in my barn—a designation that clearly marked me as a raving optimist, since the place was more like a glorified shed, with its single stall and a tack room barely big enough to hold a saddle. It smelled of old hay, new oats, and sweaty horse. True to his word, Latham had had a horse delivered from a local ranch that competed with Jack's.

I had stabled Pandora and brushed her down, seen to all the chores in the barn, and cursed Latham all over again. I'd never owned anything bigger than a goldfish. It would have been far wiser for me to start off with a hamster than a horse. Pandora had already nipped me twice on the shoulder with a gleam in her eye that told me she knew exactly what she was doing and was enjoying herself. This, after head-butting me three times into the stall wall and smacking me with her tail. If this was Latham's definition of "a little grumpy," then he was certifiable.

Having been up all night working on a painting, I was in desperate need of sleep, something made only too obvious by my slow reflexes. I'd already almost failed to dodge a hoof when Pandora stamped impatiently at my delay in filling her trough with oats.

When I finally turned her out into the small corral behind the barn, she began to whinny but not at me—she was looking toward the long, muddy driveway, where it meandered its way through a tunnel of hickories before reaching the highway.

43

From where I stood, I could just make out an idling truck and a man fiddling with the gate latch, which I'd locked at Latham's insistence. Without even thinking, I hulloed him, waving as I circumvented the mud and met him at the gate. The truck was from the ArtShoppe in Baton Rouge. The rumpled, beer-bellied driver, in his late forties, if not early fifties, waited patiently, riffling through the bills of lading on his clipboard.

"You're a day early," I told him as I approached, and he startled back like a rabbit; his shoulders sloped with permanent insecurity. A bad haircut and heavy beard emphasized his overbite. Overly large lenses magnified his brown eyes to the point that I half expected cartoon balloons with words to appear above his head.

"Oh, sorry!" he said, lisping a little while his eyes sifted to the clipboard. "This shipped early, and it was in the way in the warehouse. They were supposed to call ahead"—he looked up at me, confused—"for a Mr. Avery Broussard?"

"It's Ms. and that's me."

He scratched his nose, reading his delivery ticket, obviously conflicted.

"You can call 'em if you want to make sure."

He shrugged. I guess the resale value of blank canvases and one easel was low enough that he didn't figure me to be some sort of master thief.

I had turned up the white noise on my iPod on my way back from the barn, but nothing overt pinged off him. I had half expected reporters to start converging on the house since I'd been seen in town for a few days now; in Chicago, they'd used deliveryman disguises a couple of times before, but I didn't pick up from Mr. Beer Belly any missed deadlines, career spiraling mistakes, or any of the other losses typical with reporters. Thank goodness.

His losses were more like those of some of the military vets I'd been around, or the FBI agents—murky and confusing and centered mostly on objects. In his case: money, a couple of necklaces, some diamond earrings. Weird. Whenever I'd had to read similar folks—especially when Hank was challenging me to read his losses in those early days in the Chicago office—I'd have to reach out and touch the person to get a clear image. I shuddered now, remembering some of the things I'd seen that Hank had lost in the course of dealing with victims of violent crime.

"Oh, okay," the delivery guy said, mostly to the clipboard, snapping me back to the present as he gazed past the fence and the gate to eyeball the deep muddy ruts in my driveway. As he sized up the situation, I noticed the cars slowing down, nosy neighbors. You could tell the locals from those passing through by who honked, impatient, and who slowed down and joined the snail pace.

He walked to the back of the truck, opened it, and pulled out the first box. It was much bigger than me. "You wanna, I can help you carry this stuff to your house?"

"Nah, just stack it by the gate. I'll get it."

He looked reluctant. "That's a long way, an' they're heavy, ma'am." He referred back to his clipboard. "Got'cher big honking canvasses, and the primo easel you ordered. You ain't no bigger'n spit. I bet that easel weighs more'n you do."

His voice was layers of accents—from Boston to Jersey to California; probably how I sounded, now that I thought of it, having worn off the Southern like an old shoe that didn't fit anymore.

"No worries. I'm used to handling big canvases."

He shrugged, pulled the box out, and stacked it as instructed, and then went to get another just as Nate pulled into my driveway in his four-wheel-drive cop Jeep and over onto the grassy shoulder to avoid the delivery truck.

The sun hit the pale blond of his hair as he exited and lit it up like a halo. Nate Barksdale—childhood friend, comrade-in-arms, partner in crime (we once filched chewing gum from Jack's family's store). Of course he would grow up to be the chief of the Saint Michael's police force. Nate had been the only one of us with a guilty enough conscience that day to return to the store, take the blame for the theft, apologize, and work to pay off the loot.

I have given him gum for every Christmas since.

Nate went away to a fancy college and earned a master's in criminal justice. He had received job offers from all over the freaking place. He returned home, instead, and worked his way up quickly through the Saint Michael's PD, which frankly wasn't that much of a challenge after the two cops who'd been in charge were arrested for running an illegal Friday night poker game out of the back of the local courthouse. Nate had cleaned things up in the department and racked up some impressive arrests, in spite of being understaffed and underfunded.

He was only two years older than me, and I could see he still worked out regularly. He was about four inches shy of Jack's six-four, so it was odd that I thought of him as "short" when he towered over me. He'd always looked slick and urbane to Jack's wild cowboy, and even without having been around these past ten years, I just knew his uniform was always pressed and perfect. Today, though, he looked like he'd rolled around in a chicken coop. I snorted with laughter as he turned to help the delivery guy and I saw actual feathers stuck to his butt.

"Shut up," he said over his shoulder as he took the next big box from the deliveryman and muscled it to the fence. "Old Alvin Hotchkins turned over his tractor trailer just on the other side of the intersection. It was full of chickens, and they were still chasing 'em when I left."

The mental image of chickens getting away (him *losing* them) made me burst out laughing, stopping the poor deliveryman in his tracks as he approached the fence to hand me the clipboard with the delivery slip to sign. Nate grabbed the board and handed it to me in a huff. I signed it and handed it back to Nate, who knew I didn't like touching, or getting any closer than necessary to, strangers—so much so, that in all the years we'd grown up, Nate had always run interference for me. He'd figured out what I could do long before Jack, and to his credit, he'd always been absolutely certain Jack would understand and wouldn't love me any less for it.

He could not have been more wrong on that score.

"You sure you don't need help carrying it up to the house?" the delivery guy asked, though it was obvious he was eager to get out of there. He already had one foot on the running board of his truck.

"I'm sure. Thanks. I've got help now." Nate mock-glared at me, and I laughed again. "Hey, at least it's not chickens."

My phone beeped a text as the delivery truck pulled away, and I rolled my eyes when I read the message.

"What?"

"It's Meryl, determined to keep me up on all news Jack-related. She hasn't given up on us getting back together."

"She's not the only one," Nate said, grinning at my scowl.

"Well, you both should know better. I'm not here for Jack."

Loss images of me and Jack, once happy together, spun off Nate, and I had to back up and raise my hands so he'd tamp it down. He'd been best friend to both of us; we'd all been inseparable, along with Latham and Sam, the latter of whom had become a firefighter. We were a party of five, and nicknamed ourselves "The Saints." I always thought it was because we were some ragtag gang like the local football team, determined to win against all odds, but the boys said it was because it made us sound like we were secret agents or spies. We blistered the town with our shenanigans. When we broke up, Jack got Sam. I got Latham (of course), and Nate was determined to straddle the fence and keep us both. I was fine with that, but his relationship with Jack had never been quite the same, though they remained pretty close friends. Another text beeped, and I griped, "for the love of God," as I read it.

"I don't care," I practically yelled at the phone, and Nate's blond eyebrows arched high over piercing blue eyes, forcing me to fill him in. "Apparently, Jack's at Meryl's for lunch, and so are some reporters, probably at Marguerite's invitation—or, at least, that's what Meryl thinks. The so-called reporters are pumping everyone there for 'outrageous Jack stories.' Of course, no one's cooperating, and the reporters are getting pushy and pissing Jack off, though Meryl claims he's just sitting there, quietly eating."

"That is exactly the kind of stunt Marguerite would pull."

Another text pinged, and I skimmed it.

"Meryl's saying the latest gossip is Marguerite flew to Atlanta, got off the plane, but was a no-show at her meeting—supposedly the people she was to meet with didn't even know about it. Everybody's wondering if she realized she couldn't win custody, that Jack was going to cream her in court, so she's up to something nefarious."

Nate went ashen with concern, muttering "son of a bitch," under his breath. "I'd better get over there."

"You're worried about Marguerite?" My question seemed to surprise him, and then he gave me a get-real grin.

"You got to be kidding. She always does this—takes off on trips, acts like her schedule is sacrosanct while Jack's is unimportant and so what if she forgets to pick up Brody."

"But she wants custody, right?"

"She wants the money that goes with custody. That woman is as tenacious as a tick in summer—she's probably just trying to goad Jack into overreacting and not displaying 'proper concern' for his son's missing mother. If she can get him to lose his temper publicly, she might be able to make those PTSD allegations stick. I'd better get over there and help."

"Really?" I asked, stopping him. "Have you ever known a single solitary minute when Jack would welcome being helped? In public?"

"He's not that bad," Nate said, and it was my turn for the raised eyebrows. He glanced away, and then nodded. "Yeah, okay, he's that bad. He'll handle it himself. Here, let me help you get these up to the house."

Nate grabbed the big easel box, and I grabbed a long, awkward, but much lighter box that had a large canvas in it.

"I thought you stretched your own canvases?"

"I do, but I shipped my tools from Chicago with the rest of my things, and they didn't make it. I think they're circling the Antarctic. I've used up all the small canvases I had shipped down." Before I could explain any more another text pinged.

Nate stopped, so I could look at it. Those little streaming news feeds on the cable news shows had nothing on Meryl for up-to-the-minute reporting. I showed Nate the text:

> Marguerite's attorney has filed a missing person's report; made some noises about having Jack's place searched.

"Dammit," Nate swore. Nate rarely swore, so two curses in less than five minutes was some sort of record. "The only way Meryl knows all that is she's been talking to JoJo Bean again."

We picked up our respective boxes and headed for my porch. "If you don't want the gossip to spread, why'd you put JoJo in dispatch?"

"She's a volunteer, and she's an organizational whiz. Still works at Polyformosia and manages to put in about twenty hours a week volunteering."

"Methinks someone's volunteering so she can get close to a few single guys." JoJo Bean had always wanted to be married to Nate, from the moment we were in second grade and she first crushed on Nate—like a lot of the girls, in fact, including Zannah before she met Peter. While pretty, JoJo was nowhere near Zannah's sphere, and that made her a little more determined. It was, Nate had once said, like being fixated upon by an overeager, OCD puppy with boundary issues.

"Well, hell will freeze over first. That said, we needed her; the files were a mess from Uncle Ned's days as chief."

"That was Ned? I thought it was Teddy." Both men were great-uncles of Nate; Nate's related to half the town.

"No, Uncle Teddy was the medical examiner. Still is. Same problem, though. I don't think either man has ever filed a single piece of paper."

"Kinda hard to say no, then."

He sighed, and I ignored the losses spilling off him: not enough manpower, too little help, too little money, and too much crime. He glanced at me, and I ignored those losses, too. We'd gone too far past those old times. Too many secrets past.

"So why are you here?" I asked him.

"Here's your hat; what's your hurry?"

I laughed. He knew I loved him. "You're here in the middle of a shift. Dressed in your spiffy, polyester shirt." That thing had to be killing him in this heat; he was drenched in sweat.

"Got a phone call today. One Hank McIver, famous FBI agent, telling me I'd better get my fat ass over here and double-check your security, and why in the hell hadn't I done that already."

I groaned as I set down my box on the porch and hung my head.

"I am so sorry. What'd you tell Hank?"

"I asked him had he actually *met* you." I glanced up at him as he grinned. "The man's real inventive with cuss words. How did the two of you manage to work together for all those months?"

"According to SAC Kowalski—Hank's boss—like two porcupines having a prick-off."

Nate laughed at that as we walked back toward the gate for the rest of the canvases. In spite of his grin, I could still feel a deep sadness at his core, something buried; images of me and Jack, apart, spun off him, and Jack—alone, miserable—bombarded me, and I held up my hand.

"Stop it, Nate. Dammit."

Nate glanced at me, confused, realized he'd been thinking of Jack again, and looked away, sheepish and apologetic. I pick up on loss images from anyone I'm near, whether the person means for me to, or not, but if someone is focused on the loss, it's much, much worse.

"Sorry, Av. I just wish you two would talk."

"Not going to happen, if I have my druthers."

"That's a bad habit you're gonna need to kick. At least call Hank back before the man drives me batshit crazy."

"Hank is a control freak who can't stand that I might not do exactly what he tells me to do, a trait common in the Y chromosome, apparently. He's just busting my chops for leaving in the middle of the case."

"He did say there'd been some attempts to hack into your sealed files."

I stopped, my boots rooted in the muddy clay. "Hacking?"

Nate nodded. "Yes, into your sealed files. He said there'd always been attempts, but this time someone got past the firewall and into the files and your personal information before the IT folks managed to shut the electronic door on 'em. They couldn't trace the hack back to anyone."

Nate turned his blue eyes on me with that cop stare he'd always had, even as a kid. "He thinks someone's after you. Thinks you're in danger."

"That's silly. I'm not helping the FBI anymore. No one knows I can still see losses. I'm not a threat. I mean nothing to anyone, now."

Well, almost nobody knew. Latham knew I could still see losses, of course, but Nate had been the only person I'd ever actually told. He'd proven over and over again through the years that I could trust him with secrets. He'd kept my whereabouts secret all those years I was away, and I knew it hurt him to do it, to keep it from Jack.

"You've *never* meant *nothing*," Nate said, and he reached for me as I flinched. He froze, appalled.

"Geez, Av, I'm sorry." He took a deep breath and dropped his hands. "But it's true. You've never been *nothing* to any of us. Especially to Jack."

He put a hand up to stop me before I could object. "We're not talking about Jack right now, I know, but obviously to someone else out there, you mean a helluva lot, or they wouldn't have hacked into your files. Does Hank know you can still see losses?"

I shook my head. "I think he suspects, and he tried to call bullshit on it, but I never admitted it, and then I left, so he could not know for sure. And I need it to stay that way."

What I didn't have to say, because as a cop, Nate intuitively understood, was that the press, and the public, had accepted—somewhat—that I couldn't see losses anymore, and that was why my retreat had worked. If SAC Kowalski found out that wasn't true, as cutthroat as he was, he'd have someone leak that I still had my abilities and didn't want to help. Kowalski was all about the solve, especially on big, public cases. Right now, his office was getting creamed for not catching the LPK. Outing me? Kowalski would think that was fair play; the press would eat me alive, especially if the Little Princess Killer struck again. I wouldn't survive it without the FBI's help; I'd have to go back in. And the FBI liked using me because it diverted attention away from the other things their agents were doing to track down the killer. Whether I helped a lot or only a little, I was good for a lot of distraction from the agency's more covert pursuits.

"If everyone there is convinced you can't see lost things anymore, then it probably wasn't a leak again from personnel, or another agent with a beef tipping someone off," Nate concluded, more to himself than to me. "If that's true, then the LPK would assume you weren't a threat any longer and wouldn't have a need to dig. The fact that whoever they were, they went deep into your file means this is probably more of a grudge thing or an overly eager reporter, rather than someone trying to grab you for personal gain."

"Way to reassure a girl," I said, with a wry grin.

Nate glanced up, about to apologize; I stopped him.

"Look, it's probably just some kid, trying to get some scoop for the tabloids. You wouldn't believe the things they did before to try to get a response from me for their headlines."

"I saw." He was grim. "We all saw. You should've let us help."

Losses started to spin off him again, but he caught himself this time and stepped away, grabbing the last of the big, boxed canvases while I reached for the smaller bag of paints and supplies.

"While I'm here," he said, "I'm going to double-check that alarm system your brother put in."

"You already did that once."

Latham had insisted on it, the minute he learned I was back in town.

"Yeah, well, I'm gonna do it again and then call him back and tell him everything's okay."

"Or else he said he'd come down here and make our lives a living hell?"

"Pretty much."

"Well, he works to his strength, gotta give him that."

Nate smiled, and we trudged back to the house.

CHAPTER FIVE

Dawn inched out, gritty and gray, overcast with a threat of rain, echoing the out-of-sorts feeling I'd had upon waking that morning from twitchy, vague nightmares I could not remember. Hank's worries, conveyed through Nate, were eating at me.

No breakfast with Latham this morning. He'd left early for Jack's store—the bathroom repair had grown into a full remodel, once Lottie realized the entire floor had to be replaced anyway. The old building had stood more than a hundred years with nary a Thibodaux willing to change a thing. Jack's grandfather had been adamantly against change in principle, and his father, the late and largely unlamented Senator, had been too preoccupied with politics to give a damn. While I hadn't been surprised to learn Jack had taken over the family businesses upon his return from Afghanistan, it had surprised me to hear that Jack had also ignored such problems. That wasn't his way, and it screamed at me to investigate—an instinct I shoved back into that dark hole in my heart that held all things Jack-related.

Sitting in front of my blank canvas again—knowing my agent expected no fewer than ten new paintings before the show in October and that I'd completed a whopping two—begged the question: What was wrong with me? When things are going well, when the images filled me and the rush to get them onto canvas overwhelmed, I was in heaven. I could lose myself for hours, submerged in color and movement and brushstrokes, lights, darks, swirls. The act of creating consumed me, and the world—and its losses—fell away into nothingness. But this morning, the canvas stared back at me bleak and empty, echoing the worry that had filled my dreams. Two days in the same week wasn't a trend, I told myself. I had *not* sabotaged my muse simply by moving home. What I needed, I decided, was a walk to clear my head—best to get out of the house and calm the sideways angles of angst twisting my gut.

My phone rang just as I was putting up my brushes; I didn't recognize the number. Had to be my dad. It was about damned time.

"Hello," I said, making sure my intonation indicated that the words *you asshole* were implied.

No response. I checked my phone. The call was still connected.

"Hello?"

Still no answer, and I hung up.

It was probably time for a new number. Back when I was first outed, the press had somehow found my old one. I'd changed it five times in the last three months, and it would seem it had leaked out again. I had a sneaking suspicion that someone at the phone company was making a small fortune off me, selling my number to the highest bidder. Tabloid reporters were a tenacious lot, made worse by deep pockets; I'd already heard about a few reporters trolling Saint Michael's, talking to locals, and getting "background" on me (given that so many of their over-exaggerated stories of my childhood in Saint Michael's had already been published by now; it was more about someone rehashing my life for the glory of a byline than getting a scoop). Some of the cockroaches had been industrious enough to come out to the house and stand at the front gate, trying to get my attention. A phone call to Nate cured that, but I knew it was only the beginning, and I hated adding to his workload. Meryl said Nate had already made it clear to the locals that anyone found bothering me with questions would face both him and harassment charges. Meryl had been enforcing the same policy in her restaurant, the few times I'd gone in—the threat of being cut off from her homemade lasagna the best deterrent going.

But still that phone call . . . a reporter would have said something, right? Maybe it was just Dad, screwing with my head. Or maybe a bad connection.

One thing was clear: any painting for the day was shot.

After putting everything away, I headed out across the back pasture, through low-lying fog clinging to bushes like dread, kicking up tendrils here, stirring eddies there, trying to remember the exact lay of the land, wary of breaking an ankle in a rut hidden beneath the fog. Crossing open pasture always made me feel vulnerable. Accessible. Exposed. It was a feeling I'd never quite outgrown. I preferred the woods, or the small hidden alleyways and private anonymity of Chicago. Or Los Angeles. Or any of the other big cities I'd lived in and run from over the past ten years. But this was Saint Michael's—tiny, claustrophobic as a phone booth, and just as old-fashioned. Someone weird, like me, would always stand out.

I took a deep breath and counted my blessings. At least there'd be no hordes of picketers or knots of stalkers waiting for me to slip my FBI handlers so they could corral me and ask for help finding *just one thing, just this one time*. I stopped, stretched, reached for a sense of peace. Embraced the quiet. Then started, only to stop. Someone's losses had brushed against me. The images were dark and jagged, and I couldn't quite make them out. I glanced around, but there was not a soul in the fog-filled pasture. Nonetheless, I paused behind a lone tree in the center of the field, watching . . . breath held . . . making sure nothing else was moving, waiting until the birds sang shrill morning sonatas the way they do when no one and nothing is stirring in their territory. I stood there 'til my heart quit racing.

The images floated away. It might have simply been someone in the woods a couple of acres over, since the images never fully reached me. Open spaces were an odd thing: sometimes, images traveled across acres, if they were strong enough. But right now, nothing. I was blissfully, thankfully alone.

Still, I jogged the back pastures at a clip, hating having to traverse Jack's land, worried he'd somehow know and resent it. I'd almost not leased the house when I realized it backed up to his ranch. But the realtor had pointed out that Jack owned more than eight thousand acres in the area, making it damned near impossible to find something in the parish that his holdings didn't touch.

When I finally eased into the woods, into the quiet of soft underbrush, loamy earth fresh from rain, I could finally, truly breathe. *Be.* Being here had always refilled the creative well, centered me in ways I could never explain; life in Chicago without woods nearby had been hell. I wasn't sure why I'd ever run there. I'd been to so many places since Boston, and I certainly hadn't meant to stay in any city for long as I lived in Chicago.

After nearly a half mile, the woods thinned; a few dozen yards ahead, the early morning gray eased into a dull, dirty haze that reflected off a white clapboard church just beyond the edge of the trees. Our church—Jack's and mine. I'd visited it the day after I'd settled in and was surprised to learn that some time while I was gone, Jack had cleaned and patched it up. The steeple was still crooked, but some extra bracing now held it in place; it made me think of a giant hatpin holding an old lady's threadbare pillbox hat at a jaunty angle. He'd managed to save the old chapel, to turn it into a welcoming place—worn, loved, fragile. The diocese had abandoned it when the Thibodauxes had bought the property, and a Mass hadn't been said there in years, but since being home I had learned that young Father Tomas still came by twice a week to open it for the few elderly parishioners nearby who wanted to light a candle or say a prayer.

In its plain, clear-glass windows, I saw the flicker of a shadow, someone moving toward the back door, and I expected any moment to see Father Tomas's smiling baby face appear as he came outside to greet me. I couldn't explain why I liked visiting this church. It had nothing to do with God or anyone's version of organized religion. All I could say was that the place felt like a balm. Quiet refuge.

I'd begun to visit daily since my return because I discovered that when I went inside, images of loss were muted, though Father Tomas's wouldn't have bothered me; his were the soft losses of youth: paths not taken, quiet dreams not pursued. There was no trauma or tragedy in Father Tomas yet. During our encounters so far, his images had shifted around him like feather down whenever he sat next to me—admirably bearing up under my mocking scrutiny of the latest abject horror of a crocheted stole from one of his parishioners. He had a lot of elderly parishioners with poor eyesight, poorer taste, and nearly nonexistent talent, but he would finger each one of the handmade stoles lovingly while we talked, smiling at the gift like a proud parent might a child's finger painting. I think he truly adored each and every one, if only for the effort his flock had put into topping each other in bad taste. The world needed more people like him. I'd only seen him a few times, but when our paths did cross, we'd talk about the weather or the latest local news. I think he meant to woo me to church with banality.

Instead of soft losses this day, however, painful images radiated from the old church, like needles piercing my skin: War. Torn bodies. Shrapnel.

Jack was inside.

Father Tomas was with him, but it was Jack's losses that blistered. His images assaulted me, and I pulled back, eyes closed, turning up the white noise on my ever-present headset and breathing deep to try to fight his losses off. His images piled, sandbag heavy, onto other layers of his losses, doubling me over: His horrific childhood. Me.

And . . . Marguerite.

The image blindsided me: A woman's eyes, open, unseeing, blood dripping across her forehead, rolling into her lashes. Her red hair caked with blood and dust. Marguerite's eyes staring up, glazed over in death.

Pain sliced into me. I backed deeper into the woods, circling around until I could see the front parking lot, see Jack's truck. I stood there, shivering with pain, knowing I should leave, unable to tear myself away.

A few minutes later, Jack came out, a commanding presence that shattered the stillness of the morning and launched a flock of birds off their perches. Even from a distance, I could see scars wreathing his right hand—the one holding the cane—and climbing his arm. Dressed as he was now—faded jeans, an old T-shirt the color of moss, work boots that had seen a better day—the scars were more clearly visible. He put his old cowboy hat on as he moved into the open and limped toward his truck. The other scars he had . . . well, those remained well hidden.

Since I cannot distinguish between past and present when I see a lost item, emotion, or person, I focus on what I *can* see: location and condition, with the latter usually being a clue as to how long the item has been lost. *Usually* being the keyword, because I occasionally see something only to learn that it was lost years before, or days before, and already found. In such cases, the initial loss was just so startling, or important, that the image burned into the person, so it hits me as if it's fresh. The unpredictability of what I do is what also made it so hard to work with the FBI. Reporting what I've gleaned after I *see* a missing girl is anything but an exact science.

The fact that Marguerite was a *loss* to Jack could mean anything, and that projection of her as a loss could account for the condition I was seeing her in. She could be a loss for his son. She could be a loss for Jack—after all, he had married her; he must've loved her. Right? I was old enough to know that no one knows what goes on in anyone else's marriage. No one knows whether or not the person quietly hits the other person . . . not that Jack would. Would he? After all that he'd been through . . . Could he? I had thought I knew him, once. I reminded myself I'd been wrong, then.

It was as if Jack had heard my thoughts. I hadn't moved. Not a hair. I hadn't even breathed for fear the motion would alert him and still, dammit, he stopped suddenly and turned my direction, his silver wolf eyes seeing far more than he should have. I suppose when you've been trained for war, you see enemies everywhere. He could feel someone watching him, even when we were kids.

His eyes locked on mine, and he took a step toward me.

I took a step back, slipping deeper into the woods. I could outrun him. With his busted leg, and his cane, I'd have a head start, but he could track me, if he wanted, and he knew where I lived; hell, everyone knew.

He took a second step, and I took another back, as well. He stopped. Stood there, staring hard at me, disgust plain on his face. Then he was granite again, and he turned away, climbed in his truck and left.

CHAPTER SIX

I could not bear the thought of going into the chapel after Jack drove away. It had been a stupid idea to come, and I cursed myself for having given in to impulse. When I emerged from the woods back at the house, I heard Pandora whinnying in the barn. I found the mare flighty and annoyed, the whites of her eyes showing her agitation; I settled her down, fed her an apple from a supply I'd learned to keep handy, and headed to the house. That's when I saw the footprints at the edge of my new flower bed. Barely discernible, but still—a man's prints stood out, since no men besides Latham and Nate had been around since my arrival.

I knelt, without touching them; the prints appeared to be from a standard issue round-toed, work boot—could've been Nate, I suppose, or Latham, come here to look for me. Jack had worn boots like that this morning. I checked my cell. No missed calls. If Latham were looking for me, he'd have called me when I didn't answer the door. So would Nate, come to think of it. I doubted it was Jack. He could have driven here faster than I could walk, and the Jack I knew would've waited if he wanted to confront me about my reaction at the chapel.

The house alarm was still on, no alert messages. I pulled out my phone, fired up the security app, and did a fast rewind through the exterior footage. Aside from a possible shadow at one point, there was nothing and nobody. No one obviously walking around the house. No one running away.

Nothing else looked amiss either; even Pandora had quieted down in the barn. I also didn't feel anyone's losses flitting about me. For all the drawbacks that sensing losses could pose, it was also a freakishly accurate early warning system that no one could tamper with: I could sense the losses of people, no matter how stealthy they were.

I knew no one was there right now. I should have felt safe. Satisfied that I was alone. But there were those bloody eyes—not just anyone's, but Marguerite's, which made no sense. And now footprints in my flowerbed, in a fenced yard with a locked gate.

Two hours later, I was no longer alone. After making the mistake of calling the police, Nate, along with two of his officers on duty, had converged on my backyard to look for signs of the intruder, and since there were ten acres that went with the house, the extra help was handy. My brother and then Nate had reviewed the footage from the security cameras, and Latham was now pacing on my porch, his fists balled, ready to punch something, muttering about blind spots and how many more cameras we needed to install.

Even Sam, the last of our gang of Saints and the only one I hadn't seen since returning to Saint Michael's, had responded with a half-a-dozen other volunteer firefighters, looking for excitement—or, more likely, for insider gossip for the next Friday night poker game. Sam, a paramedic now, leaned back against his red truck, shaking his big, ole head as he watched the proceedings. He was a ginormous, brutish-looking guy, as if God had thought gargoyles weren't scary enough and he could improve upon them with Sam—yet his fearsome exterior disguised one of the softest hearts I'd ever known, a heart he had hidden from me ever since I became Enemy Number One for having hurt Jack. Sam was nothing if not a loyal gargoyle.

"I'm not gonna lie to you," Nate said, sweating in the mid-day July sauna as we stood on my porch. "There's not a lot I can do with the casting."

He'd taken a mold of the footprints by the house, along with two more his men had found by the gate.

"State crime lab is backed up months, maybe longer," Nate explained. "I don't know when we'll hear anything back. Could be weeks."

"I know, but thanks for trying." I had already begun to feel incredibly silly that I'd called Nate out for a stupid boot print.

"Oh, look," Sam drawled, nodding toward the pasture on the left of my property. "There's a cow over there. Might be a spy cow. Could have a camera aimed at you right now, Avery. We'd better send out SWAT."

"Go home," Nate told him as Latham muttered nearby.

"Sure thing," Sam said as he opened his truck door. "And should any suspicious squirrels or birds surface tomorrow, we'll be back to construct a security bubble around Her Highness."

He slammed his door shut and pulled out before Nate could answer.

"I can't believe he's still mad at me," I said.

"He's upset you never let him know where you were, Av," Nate said, gentle, but not sugarcoating. "And then you return, and don't call him. Jack wasn't the only one who loved you, you know."

I hung my head. I hadn't a clue as to what to say to that. I could not change the past, and he had no idea how much I'd have given to be able to do so. "I'm sorry I dragged you all out here."

"Don't be stupid," Latham snapped. "Someone got past your locked gate and walked around your house and under your windows. Not to mention, that whoever it was, he was smart enough to stay hidden in the cameras' blind spots. You damned well better have called it in."

"I can compare the boot print to sample prints if we find a suspect."

"You need to look at Jack's," Latham snarled at Nate.

Nate's head whipped around to Latham, his face reddening as if he'd been slapped. "Now it's your turn to not be stupid. You and I both know Jack would never hurt her."

Latham looked at me, surprised and a little shocked to realize, I think, that I hadn't caved during the heartbreak of leaving all those years ago and told Nate about Dad's prediction. "I don't know that at all." Latham said. "What I do know is she needs to get the hell out of here."

"Her odds are better if she stays put," Nate said, turning to me. "Here, you're not alone. You move somewhere else, and it's you alone, against whoever this might be. Now that'd scare the hell out of me." He wasn't bluffing. Fear spiraled off him with images of projected losses—what he imagined was gut-wrenching—and I put my hand up to warn him, so he'd shut it down.

"Hank could keep you safe," Latham argued. As much as Latham had hated me working for the FBI, he'd been impressed that Hank had never let anyone dangerous get anywhere close to me. I think Latham finally was able to sleep through the night once he realized Hank was exemplary at his job.

"First off, I'm not working with the FBI anymore, so Hank would have no justification to put me into protective custody. That's not something the FBI does willy-nilly. Second, I'm not going to be working with the agency—I can't go back to that, Latham. Besides, it's just a boot print or two. Maybe one of the paparazzi got extra brave."

I could tell Nate was more worried than he looked, the images peeling off him told me that. The calm, professional façade was mostly for Latham's sake.

"I'll ask around." Nate tried to sound like that solved everything. "See if anyone's seen any reporters in the area."

"I'm gonna go get more cameras," Latham announced. "And lights. You don't have enough exterior lights."

"I'm not going to live in a prison." I stopped his pacing with a hand to his chest. "Remember, I do know self-defense, and if all else fails, I have pepper spray."

My brother's frown deepened as he gazed out over the acreage and the woods that sprawled past the barn and corral.

"It's not enough. Move in with me."

I started to knee-jerk answer *no way*. We were both in desperate need of our space. But what if . . . what if *this* was what I was supposed to do? To save Latham. Two birds, one stone. And it was his idea.

"I could spend nights at your place."

He flinched a little, surprised I'd accepted so easily, and he looked down, not entirely happy with the idea either. I wanted to laugh. He hadn't thought it through, and I had him now. "You're not home during the day, anyway, and all my painting supplies are here. I have the alarm; it has a panic button—*in every room*, I might add. I can easily call for help, and really, I'm kinda kick-ass now."

Nate laughed at the *kick-ass*, and Latham would have, too, if he hadn't been so determined to remain pissed off at me. I'd always been the girl who'd run and hide. I don't think he knew quite what to make of the new me. Latham grabbed my shoulders and gave me a single good shake then bent down and got nose-to-nose. His eyes were bloodshot, he had three-day-old stubble, and none of it was because he was trying to be fashionable. I could also tell he'd already had whiskey that morning. Since when did my brother drink before noon?

"Don't do this to me, Squirt," he said, low. Fear crawled all over him, completely out of proportion to a mere boot print or two.

61

"Do you know something I don't?" Meaning, had the ghosts told him something I needed to know? I couldn't exactly ask in front of Nate—Latham's ability was one of those rare things I'd never told my best friend.

I saw the lie slide into my brother's eyes, quiet as a knife. I should've known better than to ask a grifter's child for the truth.

"No," he lied, looking away. "You're just damned hardheaded."

"Now there's a shocker," Nate muttered behind us.

"I'm going to go get the cameras and wiring," Latham said. "I'll meet you back here. We'll get that set up, and you can pack an overnight bag."

He kissed me on the forehead then made his escape before I could trip him up again.

Once everyone else had left, I turned to Nate and asked, "Has anyone heard from Marguerite?" I had resisted mentioning her in front of Latham for fear of having to listen to his lecture about getting involved in Jack's life again, and yet . . . those bloody eyes were haunting me.

"Not yet. Jack has a PI trying to track her down. Her attorney did file the missing person report, but right now, we've got nothing to go on." He gave me a look that said he knew mine was not an idle question.

I told him then about the bloody eyes, and he blanched and looked off in the distance, visibly worried.

"I'll keep asking questions," he said, finally, images of losses spilling off him: Jack in trouble, Jack in jail . . . Nate's projection of Jack's potential losses. "God knows that woman's made enemies as a lobbyist, and before, as the Senator's aide—no telling who she might've crossed who'd want her dead."

"Is there anything we can do? That I can do?"

"You don't see anything else—no location?"

I shook my head, and he grimaced. "I'm not sure, then. She travels all over the country and the UK, even Australia. Hell, I'm not sure where to even start. If you see anything else?"

"I'll let you know."

Maybe I was completely wrong. I'd been wrong before. Not *this* wrong, but still, it was possible.

CHAPTER SEVEN

That evening, Latham returned home, grunted in my general direction, and then hit the shower. He ate his dinner standing up at the very nice counter (all hand-tooled cabinetry, a labor of love) in his kitchen, and barely said three words to me, still a little ticked off that I wouldn't take his advice and leave Saint Michael's.

I'd given up after the fifth monosyllabic answer and had gone to read in the guest room I'd be staying in at night. A couple of hours later, violin music wafted in from the back porch. I listened for a little while, the music a balm, curling around me, low and bittersweet. My brother had always been a gifted player, and he'd gone through phases as to what he played—classical, Zydeco, electronic. On this night, he played something heartbreakingly slow and sweet, some bluesy concoction I couldn't name. He'd probably written it. After a while, the music tapered off, and I put my book down and wandered downstairs to join him under the starry night.

He nodded to me—a little less pissed off now—and swigged what smelled like more whiskey. That was definitely a topic for future conversation but not for now. Right then, all I wanted was my brother back. All my years growing up, he'd played for me and been there for me, and it had made life bearable. Partly because of the music. Partly because it was so completely Latham, sitting with me on some back porch somewhere instead of running off with friends and leaving me to fend for myself. We listened in silence to the crickets' neighborly disputes, and when I finally heard him sigh, I knew the rigid frustration he felt was breaking into soft pieces.

"Remember how Leila used to go completely mad our first couple of years here, when the crickets would get inside and refuse to shut up?" I asked him, and he smiled into the moonlight, chuckling.

"God, she hated it here."

"For two whole years, she couldn't figure out how crickets kept getting into the house."

He laughed loudly at that one. "I'd forgotten that. She'd had me caulk every nook and cranny and was threatening to burn the place down if Dad didn't buy her an air-tight house."

"Where'd you get all the crickets? I never saw you catching them."

"Bait shop."

I cracked up. "Seriously?"

And he nodded, grinning.

"I am so impressed with you right now."

"Well, she deserved it," he said, and then just like that, the good humor was gone. "Has either of them tried to reach you since you've been home?"

"Nope." There'd been nothing from either of my parents. "Where are they this time?"

Our folks had a much nicer house in Saint Michael's than what we'd started out with, but they spent most of their time elsewhere, running grifts.

"I have no idea. Our deal stands."

He meant the deal he'd struck with them long ago: You leave Avery alone. We don't turn you in.

I hated that damned deal. I'd have broken it, but I was pretty sure Dad had something on Latham, possibly from when Latham was eighteen and trying to make ends meet to keep us fed. I never knew for sure, but as much as he disliked them, Latham was as adamant about not turning them in, as he was not having anything to do with them. The last part suited me just fine.

We sat together like that a while—Latham drinking whiskey in the dark, growing more melancholy without either of us having said a word. He looked worse today than when I'd arrived if that was possible. I was failing him, and I didn't know what else to do but to keep watch, keep nudging.

I left him there on the porch, but before I went inside, I brushed his forehead with a kiss. "G'night, my brother."

"G'night, my sister," he said. His eyes closed, and then his brow creased as if in pain.

An hour or so later, I heard the violin again, and I swear it sounded like tears flowing.

It was a few minutes after three in the morning when something woke me—a light thumping noise, something with an irregular rhythm that didn't seem mechanical or natural. I remained still for a moment, trying to place where I was and what was going on. A dim light shone from the hall, and as my eyes adjusted, I realized why the contours of the house didn't seem to be right: I was in Latham's grand old Victorian instead of my little cottage.

The rooms in the place were huge, and Latham had paid a lot of attention to detail during the restoration, despite the fact that almost no one would ever see it, situated as it was all the way out on River Road. The original house had been someone's idea of what a fancy country plantation ought to look like, built with a hope of drawing tourists; that business plan was ill conceived, because who needs to go to a fake plantation, when plenty of real ones exist nearby? The business soon went bust, and Latham bought the place and turned it into the beauty its previous owners had only dreamed it might one day be, though most of that was hidden now in the dark.

I grabbed the flashlight Latham had insisted I take "just in case"—a strong metal thing that could probably have taken down an elephant, if swung like a bat—and I tiptoed into the hallway and listened. I'd never been able to use a gun since putting my hands on one, new or not, meant that losses, terrifying losses, rippled off, completely overwhelming my ability to focus or actually defend myself. So flashlight, it had to be.

The *thump thump thump* was coming from Latham's room, and as I stood, poised, at his door, listening, I closed my eyes, waiting to see if any images would float my way indicating he was in there with someone.

Nothing.

I knocked. There was no answer.

"Latham?"

Still, no answer.

I eased open the door and peeked in, and then paused, confused and a little shocked. Latham stood in the corner of his room, his back to me, banging his head against the wall. It sounded like he might be crying, and he was pleading with someone I couldn't see.

"Go away, I can't help you. Go away, I can't help you," he begged, so anguished, it broke my heart.

"Latham?"

He spun and looked at me, his eyes peeled back wide like something wild and broken. I held my hand up the way you would to gentle a horse.

"Easy, Latham. It's just me. Avery."

He shook his head, confused at that, and then, slowly, as if he recognized me through a foggy window, he nodded.

"You're alive, right?"

So it was the ghosts bothering him. "Yes. Very much so. Are you okay?"

That's when I smelled the bourbon. The room reeked of it, but I'd been so focused on what I might see and trying to understand what I did see that I hadn't noticed the smell. "Holy cow, have you been drinking all night?"

"Pretty much," he said, weaving his way to the bed. "Too many girls. Too many. Tell 'em I can't help 'em."

"Girls?" *What . . . girls?* My chest ached, just looking at him and the red welts rising on his forehead.

"Dead girls. Some came . . . with you. Lots and lots of them, little sister." He swatted at something in front of him as if brushing away a fly and grimaced. "They're asking me questions."

My hands shook, and my throat tightened, and I tried to think which one of the million questions I had to ask first.

"Does this happen often?"

He flopped backward onto the mattress. "More and more."

"Why? Has something triggered this?"

"Little sister," he said again and then brushed at the tears on his cheeks. "You're so sweet. Go to bed. Gotta go to bed now."

And he passed out.

My back ached from having slept slumped in the old wingback chair beside Latham's bed. I'd covered him with a knobby white quilt and kept the bedside lamp on a low amber glow so I'd be able to see if he worsened. I knew he wouldn't call out to me if I were in the other room, and I'd worried that he'd get up in the middle of the night for some reason, pass out again, and hit his head, or worse go wandering and fall down the stairs. Maybe this was what Dad had seen: Latham sick, maybe falling. Maybe I could help him after all, and once he was safe and sound again, I could move on.

I shrugged up from too little sleep, jittery with the memory of nightmares that had perched just beyond my vision with sharp teeth and rabid claws. In the dim morning light, I fully expected to see Latham snoring, still passed out. I rubbed my eyes open. Latham's bed was empty. Not only was my brother not in his bed, but his bed was made.

He wasn't in his room or the hall bathroom when I knocked, and I could not help noticing that the house felt hushed, poised, as if waiting for me to discover something awful had happened to my brother while I'd slept.

The back screen door screeched open downstairs, and I yelled his name, taking the steps too fast in hopes of catching him. I found Latham sagging against the back door, dressed for work in jeans and a sour attitude, coffee in one hand, his hard hat and keys in the other. He glared at me like I was the one who had shoehorned two whole fifths of whiskey down his gullet when he wasn't looking last night.

"Where're you going?"

He waved his hard hat at me, and an unvoiced *duh* hung in the air. Okay, not my finest moment, but it was 6 a.m., and he'd only passed out a few hours ago. How he was upright, dressed, and more coherent than I was, when I hadn't had a single drink, was beyond comprehension.

"I fed Pan already," he said.

I'd ridden Pandora over yesterday—she'd overnighted in his barn.

"Are you going to your house?" Latham asked.

"Um, yes. What happened last night?"

"Nothing. I drank too much. You need to be sure to lock your doors when you get inside your house. I know how you forget. I have already double-checked the security footage from last night and this morning—no activity. Still, check it on your phone *before* you go and walk in on something. And don't leave here without letting me know."

He started to pull the door closed, but I grabbed the knob and yanked it back open.

"What the hell, Latham? You don't just drink like a fish every work night, sleep for two hours, and go to work as if everything's okay."

"Everything's fine, Squirt. I don't need you to take care of me."

"Really? So you *normally* stand in your room at three-freaking-a.m., beating your head on the wall, talking to dead girls?"

"I had too much to drink and bad dreams. It was nothing. I'm late." He gave me a kiss on the forehead, like he used to do when I was twelve and asked too many questions. "Go back to sleep, Avery. Lock the doors. Turn on the alarm."

With that, he pulled the door shut, as if that was going to work. I was not twelve anymore. I flung the door open and barreled out after him, shouldering through the blanket of summer heat determined to smother us before seven. My hair had matted to the back of my neck by the time I caught him—right as he reached his old truck. There were oil spots on the limestone drive where the old truck had leaked, and that was just one more for the worry column. My brother would never let his tools and truck go like that. He never drank to excess either. I couldn't shake the feeling that something awful lingered between us.

"Look, Latham, you're not going to go off to work and pretend like everything's fine."

"Everything *is* fine." He reached for the handle of his truck.

I stepped into his path.

He tried to hip-nudge me aside, and not terribly patient, said, "Dammit, Av, I've got a meeting with Manny this morning, and I'm already late. We'll talk tonight."

"Tell me what you meant about the dead girls."

He didn't even flinch. "Let it go, Av."

"I'm not going to let it go! You scared the crap out of me last night. You look terrible; you're losing weight; you're drinking like a fish. What the hell is going on with you?"

"It's nothing, Av." He tried to climb in the truck, but I still blocked his way. "Dammit, get out of my way. I'm late."

"Well, you can either tell me now, Latham, or I can follow you to the store and badger you all day in front of your crew. Pick one."

I crossed my arms and glared at him. And that's when I saw the tears. He was fighting them, in that way men do when they pretend they have something in their eye and turn away from you, but I'd seen them, and I did the good, dutiful, sisterly thing. I pushed harder.

"I'm going to bug you every minute of every day, Latham, until you tell me. Might as well get it over with now."

"God," he sighed, "you're annoying."

"Yep."

"I love you, Squirt. And I appreciate what you're trying to do. But there's nothing to tell, and trying to insist on it is just going to force me to make something up. Then you'll be wondering all day if I conned you or if I told you the truth." He leaned closer. "Go inside. Go back to sleep. And if you go to your house to paint, text me so I know."

With that, he nudged me aside, climbed in his truck, and drove away. At least he hadn't lied. He hadn't done what Dad used to do when he didn't want to answer a question: simply made something up, and then made sure you knew what he was doing, because he wanted you to feel foolish. Dad and Leila could invent lies out of any little snippet, and any line overheard could be spun into a story so convincing you'd lay money on it being true.

For a moment, I closed my eyes, and when I opened them, I could feel and see *frost* as I exhaled. I caught a crystal clear image of myself as a child, dressed in rain boots (red) and a too-thin coat, standing in the boulevard of some fancy-housed street white with winter, bony-fingered trees scratching the sky, and hearing my dad say, *"Now, you remember what I told you to say, right?"*

"I'm s'posed to cry, 'cause I lost my dog."

"Right."

"Daddy, I don't have a dog."

"It's pretend, remember? Just long enough for me to talk to the man."

And long enough for me to read his losses, which I would recite to my dad later.

I shivered, pushing the memory away, wishing to hell it had stayed buried with the rest of my childhood.

CHAPTER EIGHT

I should have known better than to try to paint, not in the mood I was in from worrying and lack of sleep. Hours later, the *work in progress*—a euphemism for *unholy mess* if ever there was one—stood angrily on my easel, as different from the image I'd wanted to convey as burlap is from silk.

Would my life have changed if I'd taken the hint right then and there and gotten the hell out of the house? Out of Saint Michael's? Maybe. I didn't, though. I kept trying to fix where the image fought itself, a tug of war of lights and darks, rough textures where smooth should be, despair instead of joy. I'd been feeling this same level of despair all week, building up like barometric pressure before a killer hurricane. I stepped back to look at my work and did a double take: there on my canvas, a dark forest had erupted in the middle of my placid lake. The sight rattled me.

I can usually control this sort of mental wandering that I'm occasionally prone to while painting, this pulling of mood and lines, drawing from some dark place, some image maybe of someone in the vicinity that my ability has latched onto and let fester. I reached for the cerulean blue and a few seconds later, realized I must've dipped back into the burnt umber without thinking, as I had unwittingly scratched more hulking tree trunks into the scene. Instead of the soothing peaceful comfort that a scene of the woods normally gives me, menace emanated from the canvas as palpable as hooves thundering.

I could feel the hoof beats rumbling up through the wood floor, vibrating the house on its pier foundation, the rhythm growing louder, discordant, fighting with the music streaming through my iPod, and I realized this quake, this threat, was made by an actual horse, not my feral imagination run amok. One glance out the front windows and my inner dread began to thrum in time with those hooves: Jack was coming, riding his big black gelding instead of driving his truck, galloping up my barely navigable dirt road. I cringed, dreading what was surely to come: Would I see Marguerite's image? Nate hadn't found her yet. Was this about her? No . . . Marguerite didn't appear in the images that raced ahead of Jack.

Jack closed in on my house and his images shot into me fast, going for the gut, curling their fists, aiming to strike again. I'd lost a great deal of my childhood ability to control the pain and backlash of the images on that dark day in Boston after I'd left him, but Jack couldn't know that, couldn't know that it had taken me years to recover what little control I now had. I'd never told him, or anyone. I didn't want his pity.

Not that pity would have stopped him on this day. I could see his determination as he rode hell-bent for my house. Everything in me said *run*.

The picture window showcased me for Jack, and he fixed me with a glare and came off his horse like fury unfurled, grabbing his cane from the saddle. He limped hurriedly up the steps and onto my porch, his losses swirling away from him, inky, staining. He banged on the door and—typical of Jack—stormed in without waiting for me to answer. I had been so caught up in my work I'd forgotten to lock the door and set the alarm. I silently cursed my stupidity. Latham would be apoplectic.

Even when things between Jack and me had been wonderful, it was hard for me to look at him all at once for any length of time; it was like staring at the sun—interesting in theory when you're young and not smart enough to know better, but sure to leave you blind if you did it long enough. My gaze slid from the terror in his eyes, taking in the worn, soft faded blue of the work shirt, the ripped jeans coated with dust, the fresh scratches on his suntanned forearms, the work gloves and pliers he'd shoved into a loop on his work belt. He must've been repairing barbed wire somewhere on the ranch, which explained the horse outside . . . just not why he was *here* in my house in such a mad fury.

He was speaking—I think he was speaking—but waves of images drowned out his words, and I realized with a startling clarity that I was not prepared to handle losses as visceral as Jack's up close like this, not after my last seizure in Chicago. I realized I had been plain stupid for coming back home, because this had always been inevitable.

I closed my eyes for a moment, thoughts of Latham standing in the corner of his room, lost, drunk, banging his head against the wall, tormented by something he wouldn't or couldn't tell me. And as much as I desperately wanted to, I couldn't run away. I took a deep breath and faced the devil. Jack was already standing way too close. He leaned on his cane, his left hand flexing with tension as if he were trying to hold himself back from grabbing me and shaking me.

I knew he was waiting for me to respond, but I hadn't completely fought through the images yet to hear much less clearly answer him. I tried to ignore how he filled up the space. There was too much of him, and he couldn't know what his nearness did to me. I'd never told him.

"For God's sake, Av, pay attention. We need to hurry!"

I shook my head, struggling to push my words out past my panic.

"Jack, you need to leave."

"Jesus, I need your help. Quit backing away from me."

I had absconded with six more inches of space, and he closed it back up with one step. Every square inch of him screamed that he was about to snap. Was Marguerite right about the PTSD? I don't know how he had ever managed to live with the losses pummeling me.

I shuddered, fighting to get the words out. "I can't talk to you, Jack."

"Like you running from me wasn't a clue?" Anguish poured off him. "Give me a break, Avery, I know you hate me. Got it, loud and clear. And yet, I am here, which should tell you it's damned important."

He bit hard on the words, fighting not to shout. Jack never shouted. It was something of a code of honor with him. He meant to never be like his vicious father. He must have sworn that a thousand times when we were kids.

My hands shook as I fumbled with the iPod trying to switch over to white noise to help me block the images rushing in. Jack took a step closer and tugged my earphones out. His losses hit me sledgehammer hard, crushing, no chronological order, shimmering in saturated hues that hurt, they were so brilliant. The air around us smelled singed, like a grass fire racing across a pasture.

"It's Brody," he said, his voice tinny and distant around the images as they fought to take me over. *Heartbreak heartbreak heartbreak* as images of his son poured over me. "My son," he clarified, as if I didn't know. "He's missing."

No—no! Not this. Not here. *Jack's son.* Sweet God, no. Everything inside me went weak as water.

"We think he's run away. CJ over at the bed-and-breakfast said he saw him crawling into the back of Latham's truck when he left the store, and JoJo Bean saw him climb out when Latham stopped at Meryl's. Brody's upset. I need you to do your thing." He waved his hands my direction as if that explained everything. "Your crazy voodoo or whatever the hell it is."

He meant the single thing I'd hidden from him all our years growing up, the one thing that, when he finally found out, had destroyed us. He paused and looked at me expectantly, as if I were a gumball machine and he'd just put in his penny.

"Av, he's just seven years old. Alone. Lost. Where is he?"

Jack's fury and impatience made it harder for me to see the images one at a time—he stood too near, his other losses bombarded me, flaying at my senses. I closed my eyes and shook my head, trying to clear it.

"Bullshit." He'd misunderstood the shake of my head, but there was no mistaking the rage and disgust in his voice. He'd become so absolutely motionless, it took me a minute to realize that he was shaking-the-rafters furious. Not that I could blame him. "You're lying. I don't care if you've told every damn TV network, every tabloid reporter, that you can't find things anymore. I don't care that you turned tail and ran when that girl died. I know you. You can still see things. Marguerite is missing. I don't know where the hell she is, or why—but if she snuck back and took Brody? Or if he is hurt or in trouble. Believe me, I wouldn't be here if I didn't have to be. We've been looking for Brody for hours—and nothing!"

Jack ran his free hand through his hair. "You have to help me find him." His voice broke and unshed tears gleamed in his eyes. "My God, Avery, my son's out there"—he waved toward the forest—"somewhere. If you have any compassion at all, help me, help me find him."

His words stabbed me, cut me. He had always been an expert with his weapons. Images, thick, coiled, roiling smoke-filled images. I tried to pluck through them, through his pulsing anger, to find . . .

"Get out."

I choked the words out, barely able to speak. I couldn't spare the energy for an explanation; I needed him gone, if I was to help.

73

Instead, he moved closer, clueless, crowding me into the easel. Frantic. His voice softened, pleading. "I've got a hundred people combing the woods and the fields south of the ranch. But you—you could see him. You can help. Something like your ability doesn't just go away. Avery, for God's sake, Brody's *missing*."

The word *missing* chopped the air between us, hatchet bright.

"He's new here, Av. I've only had custody of him for the last six months. He's scared of this place still—and he doesn't really know anyone yet. I can't believe he'd just go out on his own. It's getting dark. He's out there. Somewhere. *My son*." He pounded his heart on those last two words, and the blow shook me as if he'd hit me, instead. He had no idea how much he was hurting me with his words, those blows.

I tried to swim to the surface long enough to tell him.

"If," I said, putting the edge of a blade in my voice, harsh jagged serrations to make him hear me, "you'd back off, Jack, I could tell you that *I can't see where he is*."

Shock paled the scars of his face. He narrowed his eyes, choosing to believe I was lying again. How could I tell him that the reason I couldn't form words or string together a sentence was because his images were so horrific? Instead, I held up my hand to stop him as I searched through his images, trying to see the kid. Trying to see if the image I was getting was a current one—not an old loss of Jack's spinning up for me to grab by mistake. All I could see was that Brody was alone. He seemed okay in the image; the trouble was I wasn't sure when the image was from, and because of that, there was no point in giving Jack a false reassurance.

"Avery, please."

I closed my eyes, trying once more. Shook my head. Held a palm up to shut him up, fighting off the pain just to see. Sometimes, I misunderstood the images, and people died. Kids *died*. Do you know what that's like, holding a life as precious as a child's in your hands, in balance, and not knowing which direction to go, knowing people believed in you, in spite of the insanity of the idea that a woman could see lost things? And knowing they would go wherever you told them to go—even if it was wrong? And that child could die because of you?

Parents always want you to guess, always assume that you're just being modest, or worse, selfish. They think that if they push a little harder, explain with a little more anguish, hold up their bloody heart in front of you, that you'll give them that last piece of information they're sure you were holding back. They want to believe. Parents will do almost anything to try to find their kids. They will even hold you at gunpoint, if they think it'll help. Once they latch onto that hope, they are incapable of understanding that I might not be able to see their missing child.

Jack grabbed my shoulder. Shock waves from his many losses pounded into me: Mutilated soldiers and wounded civilians under Jack's care. In a transport helicopter, by the side of a destroyed jeep. Marguerite's eyes, blood running down her forehead, dripping over the bridge of her nose. Eyes dead and glassy, unseeing. Then me. Images of me at twenty, from Jack's point of view as he waited for me at his cabin; his point of view as I walk toward him, all smiles and joy at seeing him and then all that ripped away, destroyed.

That was the image that caused him the most pain.

I flinched, doubled over, breathing hard. *Breathe in, out, in,* I coaxed my body.

I didn't want to know any of this. I should not know such intimate thoughts. His images were bright and fiery—he'd seen too much, lost too much. Too much blood and too many of the tragedies so common in war. I stumbled backward.

"You have to help," he begged, moving near me again.

"I'm trying," I answered.

Eyes closed, every nerve ending firing. I edged sideways away from him, nearly overturning the stool I'd been sitting on earlier, knocking into a table that Jack caught and righted before most of the tubes of paint rolled off onto the floor.

"I'll come help look for him. That's all I can do."

He had no idea what saying that cost me.

He fished a few of the escapees out from under the easel. "Avery," he said, trying hard to rein back his terror as he methodically put each tube back in its proper place, remembering how I liked them arranged, "you can't possibly hate me so much that you'd let my kid suffer just to punish me."

Memories, or something like them, shouldered up against me, reeking of desperation, foul odorous quicksand, pulling me under. There are giant swaths of darkness where some of my childhood memories ought to be, but this time I sensed something bubbling up, something specific I hadn't remembered before: myself as a child, hunched down below a house, a house very much like the one I lived in now, built up on short piers, where airflow beneath the house kept the interior temperatures a notch or two below intolerable through the broiling summer. I appeared to be about five in the image. Pre-beach and stiletto, I think. I had a backpack with me, one stuffed with the things a kid knows she'll need for survival: a Barbie, two books, my favorite shorts, swim goggles, three candy bars, some pretzels (mostly broken), and a box of Band-Aids. In my pocket, I had my dad's poker winnings, filched while he napped. I would later learn I had carried around a thousand dollars that day. I could've made it out, if I'd only understood.

Instead, I squatted there under the porch for hours, fending off mosquitoes and chiggers, mites and spiders, legs cramping, stomach growling, the dirt packed hard beneath my feet, smelling of mold and decaying leaves. There's a blank of time prior to that memory—and another afterwards. The only thing still tangible was the terror—I was terrified my parents would find me and almost equally worried they would not, and the taste of that in my mouth was the ashes and copper of desperately wanting . . . something. Something else.

I don't know how I suddenly knew or saw all of this, when it had been lost to the ether before, but I knew it, bone deep. I didn't want Brody to have that sort of memory. There had to be some other way for Jack to find him. Some other way. I told myself I couldn't help anyway. I didn't know where the boy was. For one rare moment in my life, I wasn't lying. I didn't know for sure if someone had taken Brody and hidden him, or if he'd run away. My one image of him safe could have been from last year or last month. What I did wasn't a science, but it never mattered how much I tried to explain that, especially to a frightened parent.

The FBI case swam up in front of me, the thirteen dead girls, all of them looking serene in their graves. My seizure when I failed Aurelia.

Jack stepped closer, and I backed away. He stood there, all lights and shadows and fragmented images, shards of loss, at a moment when I could barely handle my own images and remain sane. I tried to block the heartbreak rippling off him; I forced myself around the table and willed myself upright for the three steps to the door. I held it open for him, summoning every reserve of strength I had to speak, to hold my voice steady and not betray the pain I was in. It was none of his business. He did not need to know.

"I can't track him, Av. He could be miles away."

Images reeled off him. He hadn't known why I had left. Hadn't understood the terror that had driven me to run and hide. Hadn't had a way of asking me. Blood pounded in my ears. We stared at each other, neither moving. We had tightroped out over canyons, miles to fall, and each held the other in perfect balance. I would not fall first. I'd had ten years to practice.

I closed my eyes, gritting my teeth against the bile rising in my throat, and motioned him to leave.

He started to go, stood in front of the door, then spun. "I can't believe you'd do this. I'd keep your damned secret. You don't have to lie to me."

"I can't tell you what I don't know!"

"You'd lie, though."

His voice had gone quiet. Deadly. He'd been more patient than most of the families I dealt with on the LPK case; it wasn't unusual for them to quickly escalate from begging to bribes to threats—anything, anything at all to get you motivated to hand them the clue to find their child.

"You've been lying to everyone," he continued in a low voice, and I hated the calm more than the terror. "You still have your abilities. You're lying just to save your own hide some inconvenience."

He white knuckled his cane, his gray eyes riveting me with that sniper stare; his shoulders hunched forward, aggressive, as if he barely held himself back. He stepped so close his images hurled themselves against me, stinging, bloody, and mean.

My pulse thumped; my vision blurred. It was everything I could do, just to stand there in front of him without showing the strain, bracing my weight on the door. Dear God, please don't let me have a seizure right now. He's never seen me have a seizure. Please give me that. I'll give You three seizures next time if You'll just hold off on this one.

"No, Jack. The freak show is *over*."

My voice sounded ragged even to my own ears, like an old-fashioned party phone line with poor service. I planted my palm in the middle of his chest and pushed.

Caught by surprise, Jack stumbled backward out onto my porch.

Everything he'd lost hit me with that touch. Everything. I'd only ever had the appetizer, and hadn't even realized. I managed to slam the door behind him, my arms heavy, moving underwater slow, and then I slid to the floor. There was pain—my own, his, Brody's—I was grateful for the darkness as it closed in and dragged me under.

CHAPTER NINE

There are odd hollows that surround me when I wake from an image-induced overload: Light refracts strangely, as if bent through water, and sounds feel tinny and dim, carried over great distances. I am there, but I'm not, stuck in some half-world, some plane one step or two out of sync with reality. Colors seem muted, dull compared to the kaleidoscope of brightly lit fractured images that burst against my mind's eye just before I pass out.

This time it took more than a few minutes to settle back into myself, into the present, to feel the cool wood floor beneath me and recognize it for what it was. My head lounged at an awkward angle against the door, blood coating my face from a nosebleed, my T-shirt soaked red.

This was not the pretty aftermath most people expected from this sort of talent. Most imagined some type of mystical music, sweet-smelling incense, and a smiling bangle-wearing gypsy glomming onto their hands, gleaming with a knowing wink, willing to spill the information the person secretly wants but was loathe to admit to craving.

People, well, most people brave enough to accost you and demand your help, wanted to strike a simple contract—this one piece of information for their gratitude. They want to believe that their gratitude is all I'd need to make the exchange worthwhile, because who wouldn't want that? A nice, pleasant trade, the information for their smile and a thank-you. What they didn't want was a woman who could see not just that one loss but all of their losses, their vulnerable bellies, their whimpers in the dark, their curled-in-fetal-position bad moments, their indiscretions. No one wants those exposed.

I had thought about wearing bangles, once, just to humor people. Made me itch at the thought. So instead of some whimsical, ethereal, big-skirted-ballet-shoed-tie-dyed-beaded-junkie woman, people get me. I'm skinny, muscular, and you could put a gun to my head before I'd be seen wearing one of those floaty skirts. Too hard to run in. I favored worn work jeans and sneakers and am generally covered in paint splatters and linseed oil. I never looked particularly ugly to my knowledge—I've never seen anyone actively flinch when I entered a room—but I'm not exactly pretty either. Forgettable, mostly, which is exactly what I aspired to be, so maybe that's one for the résumé: accomplishes goals.

By the time I regained consciousness, the buttery evening light had faded to the early smoky blue of dusk, and every muscle I had ached flu-like. I thought for a moment that I'd oblige and just remain on the floor for a few hours but the ruined painting stared down at me, pulsing with gnarled trees, and I finally realized what I was seeing.

Dammit. With so much of the town looking for him, Brody being missing was like a shocking loss to everyone, and that communal loss had saturated the air around me and had been doing so all the time I'd been painting earlier. The answer was right there on the canvas.

It took me five minutes to wash the blood off and change into dark clothes. I grabbed the first shirt I could find, and it must've been a dirty one I had cleaned my brushes on, the way it smelled. But it was already almost night, and I didn't have time to be picky. I shoved my hair under a black cap and grabbed a backpack of supplies—first aid, flashlights, a candy bar, cell phone—just in case I needed them.

I thought about calling Jack, but if I was wrong, I might derail the rescue he could have made if he had kept searching wherever he was currently looking. My gut clutched at the memory of Aurelia March, dead only minutes when the FBI got there. They'd have been there sooner if not for . . .

I shuddered, and held the doorframe to stabilize.

Calling Nate created the same dilemma. He'd be helping Jack, and I didn't want to risk the call routing through to dispatch. Once JoJo Bean knew, word would spread—especially at the next poker game at Meryl's. It wouldn't take five minutes before the entire town—all 3,803 of them—would know I'd *seen* where Brody was. From there, it would be a heartbeat before the first tweet went out, and the maggot tabloid reporters returned to crawl all over my life, at least the scraps of it that were left.

Besides, I could get there faster on my own. Stealthier, if I left Pan behind. I suspected if he heard me coming, he'd try to run again; if he'd just stay put, Brody might live.

The woods whispered around me, quiet. Welcoming. When we first moved here from . . . well, I don't actually remember where from. I keep thinking one day I'll be able to finish that sentence. When we first moved to Saint Michael's, I'd travel through the forest over unseen trails, burrowing into bushes or skipping across limbs, wild, determined to stretch out every moment in my own personal paradise 'til the green hues of the canopy leeched into grays and blacks and the stars kissed the inky sky.

From the time I was maybe six, or seven, I was also convinced that if I searched long enough, I'd find my real family—the fae, or elves, or any assortment of magical creatures I was sure existed and that I came from. I was certain they'd left me by mistake when I was born, rushed out of the woods from fear of humans discovering them, dropping me in their hurried escape, and then unable to retrieve me, once humans had me in hand. I could think of no other way to explain how I'd been born to a mother who had not a lick of magic and resented mine, as profitable to her as it might be, much less to a father whose main focus was the grift to the exclusion of anyone and everything else, even his children.

When I was eight or so, I thought I'd solve all our problems by leaving the fae notes with extensive crayon-drawn maps as to where I lived. I marked the spot with a star and marked my window, as well, so there would be no confusion, lest they take Latham by mistake. I'm thirty now, and I sometimes still find myself wanting to leave a note, breadcrumbs to my heart.

In the woods, quiet brushes of branches caressed my aching shoulders. Misty fog billowed over the creek; bullfrogs sang arias with the crickets; musty smells of moss and earth wound through the canopy to the moon. I could breathe here, at peace. I never got ugly images from the trees, never saw losses for other trees long gone; the trees felt no remorse, felt no longing for times gone by—tree swings rotted and were forgotten, little girls skipped beneath their branches never to return.

Brody was about two miles southeast of my house, somewhere near the gnarled oak I'd apparently seen and had started painting. If he went any further south, he'd be in dangerous swamp territory, where idiots had been feeding alligators, showing off to the tourists, forgetting (or not caring) that alligators don't make the distinction between a chicken dropped in the water and a child.

Thick summer foliage overhead smelled of honeysuckle and wisteria, pungent sweet from a late afternoon rain, and the loamy carpet of deadfall was springy and soft underfoot. I moved the beam of the flashlight around, looking for signs of the boy, listening for his breathing, his heartbeat.

Losses drifted from above me, behind me—I had the wrong tree, or else he'd moved from the time I'd left my house. I turned, shining the beam in the crook of another oak, a white oak this time. The beam lit up the gray-white bark of tree, but not the boy—he must have been clinging to the other side of the branch, hiding.

I switched off the flashlight; let my eyesight adjust. Waiting. The forest waited with me, tense.

"Brody?"

The dark night air did not answer me. "Brody, I'm Avery Broussard. I'm a friend"—I tried not to pause on the word—"of your dad's. Get your butt down here. I'm tired. My head hurts, and if you don't come on out right this minute, I'm calling your father."

A breeze swished through the limbs, bending them in unison, and his silhouette stood out for its lack of movement. Brody hadn't learned yet how to be a part of the tree; he was a city boy, raised by his mom in DC until a few months ago. I'd give him less than a year before he tried this again. By then, he'd have discovered how to be one with the trees. He'd be harder to track next time. The one thing I learned from a lifetime of running away is that a smart adult will make you think going back home is your own idea. Kids sometimes have nothing of their own save for the little scrap of pride they carry around, close to their heart, as fragile as spun glass.

"Fine," I announced, sounding resigned for Brody's benefit. "I'm calling him." I pretended to dial and then put my cell to my ear. "And while I'm at it, I'm going to tell him it was you who lost his Silver Star, not him. What were you using it for, anyway? Stupid place to throw a medal, if you ask me."

"Don't!" a boy's voice squeaked, pleading. "He'll kill me."

I clicked on the flashlight, nailing him with the bright circle of white.

"I'm gonna help him, if you make me stand here much longer getting bit by mosquitoes. Get down here."

He disappeared from view long enough to slide and scrape, boy versus bark, around and down, landing a few feet from me. He sauntered over, all seven-year-old bravado squaring his shoulders. Spitting freaking image of his father. He had Jack's angled face, black hair, and build, but the brown eyes must've come from his mom. I throttled the sick feeling in my gut, the drowning feeling of what might have been.

"So, you're the pain in the ass everyone's looking for."

"Yeah? Well, you're the town weirdo."

Make that *belligerent little ass* . . . definitely Jack's DNA.

"You ready to go home?"

"I'm not going back."

He crossed his arms and glared at me, setting his jaw in strict determination. I kinda admired his pluck. I'd have been more impressed if there had been a backpack or some sort of luggage and supplies to back it up, but as it was, he was all daring and air. He wore his best tennis shoes and one of those graphic T-shirts that said something smart-ass most grown-ups think doesn't mean what it really means. Both were covered in mud and twigs, and if my eyes weren't mistaken, his arms had the faint beginnings of a poison ivy rash.

"Got plans, then?"

"I'm gonna go to Cleveland."

"Cleveland, really? Huh."

Cleveland was good a place as any, I suppose, if you're running away, but Jack's son could use some pointers when it came to his disappearing technique. I'm pretty sure his father would frown on my helping out with that. Still, I have to say I was tempted.

Brody put his hands on his hips, and I had to shake off the déjà vu— Jack did that whenever he thought he was about to be challenged.

"Sounds fine to me, then. Good luck with that. See ya."

I clicked off the flashlight and turned to slip out of the woods.

"Hey!" Brody yelped as soon as the light snapped off. "Wait."

I kept going, quietly, quickly. He might be a monkey boy who could climb above all the rescuers—I'd spotted fresh adult footprints in the soil, along with hoof prints, signs that Jack or someone had passed this way at least once—but I'd slipped past more people than Brody'd ever met in his life.

"Slow down," he begged.

"Why? You're headed to Cleveland. I'll let everyone know so they can quit searching and wasting their time. I'm going home. I figure you have this all worked out."

He caught up to me, smelling of boy and sweat and fear; his losses fluffed around him, a little puff cloud of confusion as he continued to follow me.

"You've probably figured out what you need to do about money and transportation and food and all. The basic rules, like don't take rides with a stranger. And no matter how hungry you get, don't give in to eating dumpster food—it goes bad pretty fast. You don't wanna get food poisoning and end up in the hospital—they'd call your dad for sure, and if you think he's not happy about a lost medal, you don't want to see the look on his face when he gets that medical bill. So"—I paused, eyeing him over my shoulder where a patch of moonlight illuminated us both—"you're good to go, right?"

"You're gonna just let me go?" He didn't sound entirely happy about that.

"Sure. What's it to me?"

"But you're supposed to be looking for me."

"Yeah? Well, I found you. You're okay, so see ya." I turned and took a couple of steps and then added, "Oh, and the black bears out here can climb. So if you're spending the night, you need to find a better place to sleep than that tree."

"Bears? There's no bears in Louisiana."

I snorted my derision. "Seriously, kid, how you're going to make it out of these woods alive if you don't know Louisiana has black bears is beyond me. But hey, you're a smart kid; you'll figure out something."

I kept walking, and he kept trailing right behind. We'd made it about a half-mile before I asked, "I thought you were going to Cleveland?"

He didn't answer. He just tagged along in silence, wrestling with the question for another quarter mile.

"I hate my dad."

The forest confessional muffled the heat of his declaration, but not the hurt of it.

"Yeah, well, I'm not terribly fond of him, either, but even you've gotta admit this is a pretty crappy way to treat him." I ignored the little voice inside my heart that said *spoken like one who should know*. "The least you could've done is say good-bye like a man."

83

The kid went stone still, and I felt the blow of his losses. His mom, gone, with no explanation (or at least not one that the police were sharing). He had images of hundreds of times she'd forgotten to pick him up on time piled against images of her crying and furious, slamming a door on Jack, packing her bags. "My dad doesn't tell me stuff," he confided.

I found I had a sudden interest in shining the flashlight on the trees around us, checking out the pattern of the bark, the mottled grays and browns, as he surreptitiously wiped his eyes. This was Jack's kid. I wasn't falling for Jack's kid. I reminded myself then that there was nothing on the planet that could make me like him or make me care. He was too soft and whiny and runty. He sniveled for God's sake.

"Tough noogies, kid. Grown-ups don't always tell kids stuff. It's part of the job description. Deal with it."

He gave me the look, the kicked-puppy look. I hated that look.

"Ha! Don't even try that one on me, kid. I don't care what your dad does or does not tell you. That's your dad's damned business, not mine."

"He thinks my mom is dead," Brody whispered.

Leaves rustled above us, but the world was carpeted in heartache just then, and I barely noticed as I doubled over, pain shooting through me. I gritted my teeth and braced my palms on my knees, pretending that I'd just meant to get eye-level with the kid. I could see bloody eyes, again. Marguerite's bloody eyes. Still, no idea where she was or if she was dead or alive, much less when the image had happened.

"What makes you believe your dad thinks she's dead?"

"I think maybe he killed her," the boy whispered again, the words dropped like pennies in a well, wishes tossed, hoping what he voiced wasn't true. "Or maybe hurt her, and made her go away. They fought a lot."

My heart screamed. I did not want to know this. I started walking again, him trailing beside me, closer than before, like I'd passed some litmus test.

"Mom didn't let him come over much. I didn't know he was my dad 'til last year because Mom told him he didn't got no rights. She was always yelling at him; said he made promises and broke them."

"I don't think your mom would be happy that you're telling me this."

"You won't tell her I told, will you?"

"Not a chance, but you should probably not say anything else."

He was quiet for all of forty-five seconds, as we moved through the trees. "Dad wouldn't yell back, but I could tell he wanted to. He'd go outside and hit things. When he'd come back in, they'd fight some more." (He had yet to take a breath.) "And then, one time, she threw a big vase at his head. He was real mad then."

"Look, kid, grown-ups fight. It happens, and it's not going to always be like that."

"He hates her. She told him she was gonna see him in hell, and he said 'you, first.' Then just a little while after Christmas, she went on a trip and forgot to pick me up, and they called my dad, and he said I had to come live here."

Things could change so swiftly when you're a kid. One minute you're leaving notes for the fae, hope still living and breathing and sustaining you and the next, Garry Adaonais, two years older and practically a giant, already as tall as a lot of high-schoolers, is holding your note in class, reading it out loud in a high-pitched voice, emphasizing all the awkward feelings and longing and making cloying faces and you know, suddenly, that the woods have betrayed you.

I'd never liked kids. They broke too easily. I should know; I'd been one of the broken ones.

"Do you think he kilt her?" he asked, so softly I almost wasn't sure I'd heard him right.

I stopped, turned, and sucked in a long breath, a vain attempt to make my body quit rattling as I thought about what to say. "Look, Brody, do you know how your dad got that Silver Star?"

"Something he did in Afgannis . . . in the war somewhere, he said one time, but he said it wasn't important. 'Til it was gone, and then he was pretty mad."

"Yeah, well, he did a lot of stuff in the war, mostly saving other men's lives. He risked his own life to save other people while taking fire. There's a long list of reasons why I don't like your dad, but does that sound like the kind of guy who would hurt someone?" *Someone besides me.* "Ever?" Dear God, please let me be right about this.

Brody thought for a minute and shrugged, half nodding, still uncommitted. It was probably the best he could manage, as palpable as his fear was.

"Well, as much as I dislike him, that's one thing I know about your dad—he would never lift a hand against anyone. It's not in him." How could I expect Brody to believe something I didn't fully believe myself?

Brody studied me while I studied him. Finally he said, "You sure?"

"Have I ever lied to you?"

He thought for a moment.

"I dunno about the bear part," he said, and I laughed.

"Google that one when you get home. Now here's the deal—we're about a quarter mile from the road where your dad and Nate have everyone searching." I could feel their losses, urgent, tangible, even from this distance. "I'll take you as far as the road and point you in the right direction, but I'm not going out there with you. You gotta walk to your dad on your own."

"Why?"

"Town weirdo," I said, pointing at myself, "so I get to make whatever rules I want. That's my rule. And here's my other rule: you don't get to tell anyone—not a soul—that I helped you tonight. You just tell them you found your way out of the woods. And then I don't tell your dad that his Silver Star got flushed down the toilet at fishing camp. Deal?"

I put my hand out for him to shake, which was my second big mistake of the night, because he took it and immediately the image of two bloody eyes drilled through me with the force of a diamond bit grinding through rock. I nearly passed out right there; it was everything I could do to hold it together for the kid. I must've yelped and jumped back from the contact, because suddenly I was standing—when I was aware again of my surroundings—a good three feet away from him.

"You okay?" His eyes were big as his face.

Even in the moonlight, I could tell he'd gone all pale.

"Fine. Something stung me. Let's go." I got him to the road and nodded toward the search party a little farther down from us. I kept my flashlight off, as I stayed hidden behind a large tree. No way was I going to head home and find out the next day that the squirt had had a change of heart and was now dead on the side of Interstate 10 because he'd tried to hitch a ride to Cleveland. He paused as if he still had a choice, and I let him think so for a while, and then he turned and hugged me. Hard.

"Go, runt. Quit stalling."

I turned him back toward the road, and gave him a little shove he wasn't exactly thrilled over. He glared at me over his shoulder, and I smiled, giving him a thumbs-up. He flipped me the bird. Kid might stand a chance in this world after all.

I stayed out of sight, easing from tree to tree for a few feet so I could keep watch over him while he slogged reluctantly forward, as if I'd sent him to a firing squad instead of the many car lights gathered at the fence line. Finally, Jack shouted, "Brody!" and ran, first with the cane, and then after throwing it to the ground, at a fast limp for his son, scooping his kid up in his arms and hugging Brody like he'd never let him go.

Somewhere far past the little clearing, Sam shouted, alerting some of the others that Brody was found.

Jack finally set Brody back on his feet, kneeling beside him as he ran his hands over the boy, inhaling him as if to scent any injuries.

"Are you okay? Are you hurt?"

Brody's voice came muffled from his dad's shoulder as Jack hugged him again. "Dad, I'm okay. Lemme go."

I could hear Jack's sigh of relief, even from where I stood. It was the sound a soul makes after a plane survives a near-crash landing or when a boat rights itself after nearly swamping from waves. Jack set his son away from him, his hands still on Brody's shoulders, and he leveled one of those famous *you're toast* stares.

"Where the hell have you been?"

"Lost," Brody answered, having clearly thought ahead as to what he'd tell his dad.

"Fine. Who helped you?"

"Nobody." A nervous warble pitched Brody's voice off-key and sour. "I can do stuff by myself. You never think I can."

Jack scanned the forest a little too casually, and images spun off him: watching me paint, helping me set up my easel, cleaning up the *linseed oil*. Damn. I glanced down at my shirt, feeling the imprint still of Brody's arms around me. Not terribly likely that Brody would encounter linseed oil in the forest now, was it? My chances of escaping Jack's wrath appeared to be fading, but maybe I was wrong. Maybe I still had a chance to avoid him outing me in front of everyone. I went still as a prayer. I'd spent years blending in, hiding in plain sight, but right at that moment, I wished I could disappear. Of all the superpowers in the world I coveted, that now topped my list. I was well enough hidden, but even so, I had to stifle the reflex to bolt. Jack would spot movement, no matter how slight.

"You never think I know when you're lying." Jack's voice dropped another few degrees. "But I do."

Jack's eyes scanned the woods again, before fixing on a spot right in front of me. I didn't breathe.

"There are consequences to lying, Brody. You hurt people. Everything you do has consequences. That's something you're going to have to learn."

"I hate you!" Brody shouted, standing his ground, all seven years of Jack's DNA screaming back at his father, fists balled, ready to fight. "You don't care about *nobody*. Just being *right*."

Jack's gaze broke away from the forest, and then fell on his son. I could feel the tsunami of grief at Brody's words. Jack's images of how he was losing any hope of fostering a good relationship with his boy swallowed me whole, but the damned man didn't utter a word. Didn't comfort his kid or tell him he cared. Nothing. That wasn't the Jack I'd known growing up; it was the man I'd feared since my return, though. Silent as an abandoned battlefield, then a sharp nod as he stood.

"I can't ride with you in the car. I've got Gambler"—he nodded at his big black gelding—"over there to ride home." He bent to get in Brody's face. "I'm not angry with you, but you scared a lot of people, son. I was worried. So were they. Nate will drive you home. He and Uncle Sam will stay 'til I get there. I won't be long."

Jack was mentally packing up images of his own losses at his father's hands: the loud, gregarious Senator, good-ol'-boy to the world, easy-going, quick with a smile even when in the midst of a heated public battle, the same one who didn't tolerate disagreement at home. I could feel Jack shove the images back down into the dark hole deep inside where such memories are kept, and I knew what it cost him. He was determined to remain calm, to give his son what he had never been given. Maybe too much calm. Calm like that, ratcheted too tight, is destined to eventually explode anyway. Especially if pushed too far.

I'd seen that firsthand and in his images, too. It would anger Jack to know I could see into him so easily, read him so well, despite the walls he had built just to keep such intrusions out.

I ventured a half-inch lean to peer around a limb; I could see Latham at the fence line near the gate where the cars were parked, and next to him, Sam in his firefighter blues. Then there was Nate, standing a couple of feet behind Jack, awkward, when Nate was never ill at ease. Heartbroken. He loved Jack as much as I did, and losses spun off him: not being able to reach through Jack's hard shell anymore, not being able to help his friend.

This was the first time we'd all five been in the same place since I had run away all those years ago. Once it had been us against the world—the five Saints. We'd been a team, looting dragon lairs, fighting aliens, claiming victories at sea in a tree house fabricated from old tires and wishes. It broke the last pieces of me to see what we'd become.

"Jack," Nate urged, his voice pitched as if he were dealing with someone who was stretched to his limit, patience-wise, "it's late. Everyone's relieved and exhausted, including you. Why don't you come—"

"I'll be there in a bit," Jack interrupted, and I could tell from Nate's images of me just then that he'd guessed I'd helped Brody and was trying to protect me, yet again, from Jack's wrath. I had no doubt he'd pieced it together—I'd found Brody and walked him back here *without calling Jack and letting him know.* Nate knew there'd be hell to pay for that.

"I have something to check first."

"Of course." Nate forced a smile in his voice, one of those fake smiles that cops use when everything is a little south of hunky-dory. "C'mon, Brody, let's you and me and Uncle Sam"—in the South most everyone our parents' ages, if they were close friends with the family, were honorary aunts and uncles—"take a ride to your house. I'll let you run the lights, if you want."

Jack's back grew rigid as Brody walked away with Nate and Sam; the boy only turned once to look over his shoulder—not at his dad, but back toward the forest where I stood. If Jack had had any doubts of an accomplice, the poor kid had confirmed his worst suspicions. I thought about moving silently backwards in hopes of maybe still being able to avoid what was fast becoming inevitable.

I had barely shifted my weight when Jack said, low, "Don't even think about it."

"Wouldn't dream of it," I muttered, as we watched everyone climb in their cars and reverse away from the field. The caravan filed down the old highway, a gentle ribbon of red taillights sliding away from us until Jack and I were left alone in the gulf of dark beneath a fickle moon playing hide-and-go-seek behind the clouds.

Something crept up on me as we waited. Something black and evil, and I realized I was again feeling losses that had no images, losses I couldn't define but that sucked at me, as if trying to pull me under. I wasn't alone in the woods—someone was behind me. My skin crawled, and I turned in a full circle but could see nothing. The cloying scent of roses stole around me, which made no sense—the woods had too much heavy foliage for a rose bush to survive. I shuddered wanting desperately to run.

Time skipped, disjointed, and hopscotched over my perceptions of reality, and before I could make sense of it, Jack was there, inches away, though I could barely see his silhouette in the moonlight. He must've moved before the last car disappeared; I hadn't had time to brace myself for his proximity, and his writhing, furious losses carved into me, hacking away at my soul.

"Why did you lie to me earlier today? We could have found him *hours ago*," he snapped as I doubled over, gripping onto consciousness by my fingertips. "Then you teach my kid to lie to me? I don't deserve that, especially not from you. All his mother ever does is lie. I am trying my level best to build a relationship with that kid, and I will not have you teaching him to lie to me, too."

I couldn't stand; the pain had doubled me over and now crippled me.

"What is wrong with you?"

"Feeling winded is all. Got your point. Stay away and don't lie. *Check.* You can go now."

"You think what you did was okay?" he asked.

He was talking about more than just Brody, though I'm not sure he realized it. He was too wound up from the adrenaline to let it go.

"You knew where he was hours ago, and you waited. What if something horrible had happened, Avery? Did you think of that while you were making me suffer? You let me agonize, terrified for two extra hours just for kicks and giggles when you could have made one phone call and said, 'Hey, Jack, I know where he is.' You made a bad situation ten times worse. Hate me all you want, but if you ever let him stay in danger again to serve your own purposes, you can bet I'll make sure you're on the front page of every newspaper and tabloid and on every TV show out there. You got me?"

It's hard to know that you're about to pass out when you're already standing in near pitch-black darkness. It's not like your vision gets fuzzy, because you can't see anything to start with. Plunging forward, however, onto your enemy's boots is a sure sign that things aren't going according to plan.

"Bite me," I said, as I hit the dirt. Or, that's what I tried to say, but the consonants refused to line up properly.

CHAPTER TEN

The next thing I knew I was propped up against a tree, with the beam of Jack's flashlight blinding me.

"Dammit, why didn't you tell me?"

"Oh, the nosebleed?" I closed my eyes and tried to pinch the bridge of my nose, but my hands felt as heavy and awkward as an anvil. "I hope I bled all over your good boots."

"Shut up, Av." Jack pinched the bridge of my nose, a viselike grip that both stemmed the blood and held me in place at the same time. He checked my pulse, which decided to do the rumba as soon as he laid hands on me. Terror tried to push my limbs to move, urged me to lever upright and get away, but all I could manage was a feeble swat at his hands. I could feel the light behind my lids, but I kept my eyes clamped shut and focused on keeping his images from drowning me.

He whistled for Gambler.

"Oh no, I'm not getting on that horse with you." I tried to push his hands away, and his grip clamped tighter.

"Do you really think you have the strength to fight me right now?" he asked, seething. "Be still. Lean your head back. There. Hold the bridge of your nose." He guided my hand into place. "Good."

I heard him stand and rummage in something—probably a saddlebag. I could smell the gelding, the sweat of him, all horse and pride and idle curiosity, his oat-filled breath snorting my direction a time or two. I drifted then, thinning out like watercolors after a rain, barely enough pigment to hold a place on the canvas. It was easy to forget for a moment where we were. I felt lax and quiet, or maybe that was blood loss doing the thinking for me, but for just a single minute, we were in a bright pasture by a lake, where the future was breezy with hope, dandelions floating on the wind.

"Did you do this in front of Brody?"

Jack's voice yanked me back to the hard ground, the scratch of the tree trunk at my back, the night air a hot sticky blanket, suffocating me.

"Yes, Jack, that was the plan. Come out here in the middle of the night, bleed like a monster, and scare the bejesus out of the kid. I'm sure he'll think twice about running away now."

"I simply want to know if my kid's been traumatized, Av."

"Right." I sighed, too tired to keep fighting him, and damned myself for that. "No, I did not have a nosebleed in front of your kid. He's fine."

He wasn't fine, but Jack knew that already.

A kid doesn't run away because he's fine.

Jack knelt back down in front of me, broke one of those chemical ice packs, and then put it on the bridge of my nose, the better to stop the bleeding. As a former medic, it didn't surprise me that he had supplies, especially since he'd been looking for his son. It just felt so . . . official. It felt like a formal demarcation between the Jack of the *before* and the Jack of the *here and now.* I wondered if this was how a cartographer felt, going over old terrain after an earthquake. I no longer knew this man. Not really. Maybe, I never had.

"I'm going to wash your face while you hold that pack in place."

His voice tethered me to him in the dark like beautiful, gossamer silk; he could have been that young man of ten years ago, with that voice soft between us on a moonlit night in the back of his truck, before he'd known what I was. What I could do.

I pushed his hands away. "I can do it myself when I get home."

"Sure," he said, still all soft and reasonable, a steel hammer inside a velvet glove, "but I'm going to do it now, so I'll know if the bleeding's stopped. I'm not asking your permission, Av. Be still."

The world was a study of opposites just then, and I was adrift between them: the cold of the ice pack on the bridge of my nose, the warmth of Jack's hand steadying my head while he used a damp cloth to clean away the blood, the impatient huffing and stamping of the gelding versus the methodical, unhurried way Jack cleaned my face, replacing the cloth and cleaning again. His images circled like crows, ready to have at me, and I shuddered, blocking them as best I could.

Marguerite's bloody eyes, though, refused dismissal. The image glowed, phosphorus behind my eyelids, and I tried to think of pleasant things—waterfalls, rocking gently in a hammock, birds singing, a sky so brilliant blue that I had to squint to see the sunlight dancing with the clouds.

"You've been checked?" Jack asked, breaking apart my carefully woven net of defense. As I mentally ran through all of the possible retorts I could make to that, he amended, "For the bleeding. Does it happen often?"

"I'm not getting into it with you, Jack. Are we done here?"

His hands paused as his momentary lapse into kind inquiry folded back in on itself like relationship origami. He pulled off the ice pack, and I finally opened my eyes to find him watching me with the detached assessment of a trauma tech checking to see if the patient needed anything else, and then he nodded, satisfied I was out of danger.

"You're done. C'mon."

"I'm fine. I know my way home." I stood without taking his offered hand, then braced myself a bit on the tree until the woods quit spinning. I'd made a habit of not looking at Jack since I had returned. I saw no point in breaking that habit now. "Go away."

"You're not walking home." He said this as simply as if saying it made it so. As if he were in charge. I kept forgetting this tendency of his. "It's a good two miles."

His concern would be touching if his earlier threat to expose me hadn't been tattooed on the air around us. It hung there, pulsing a garish red, like one of those permanent mistakes you try to blame on too much drink or too little sleep.

"I'm not getting on that horse with you, Jack."

I forced my voice down to normal. I remembered too well the last time we were on a horse together. I could still feel the engagement ring, phantom-like, on my left hand. I wouldn't recover from another ride.

"You're not going to walk two miles with that leg while I ride. So I'll go to my house, and you go home. And before you say anything, no. No, I won't teach your son to lie to you again. I'm sorry about that. In fact, I'll make it easy on you. Leave me alone. I didn't ask for you to barge in my door today, and I didn't ask for the kid to be lost. Thank you for your help just now. I'm going home."

"Dammit, Avery, you suddenly appear, but you won't talk to me, you won't say you'll help, then you do, and I, well . . ." He looked away and shook his head, grief replacing the anger. "I should have thanked you."

"Don't. This wasn't for or about you or me."

"We need to talk."

"No, we do not. You have a kid on his way home who's terrified about his missing mom, who needs you. I, on the other hand, do not need you, much less your help getting home."

I left him then. It took nearly an hour to make it to my house; I had to stop and rest three times. It didn't help that Jack had ignored me completely and followed me home anyway, keeping me in sight every single step of the way. I'd heard him call Nate to let him know why he was running late but he had refused to let Nate come help. I pretended he didn't exist.

We said not a word, but then words were never what I heard loudest. He shed a stream of images of too many men down, bullets whizzing over his head as he fought to save them, dismantling a series of IEDs to reach a hurt fellow soldier, someone who couldn't possibly be saved, though Jack hadn't let that stop him. He wasn't in the stop-when-it's-not-convenient business. It was in his DNA to keep going—no matter what the cost to him. I remembered loving that, once, long ago. I had never known anyone like that before Jack. Now, though, it just carved me up from the inside, all those images. It made it harder for me to put one foot in front of the other. He couldn't know that; and God knows I wouldn't tell him. I would not concede defeat. Not to Jack. Not when I knew what was at risk.

Not ever.

I don't know why the visions were affecting me so much more since my seizure, but they were, and I seemed to be getting worse. I wasn't sure if it was fear for Brody, or the anxiety of seeing Jack, or our own history that had pushed me to the edge, but the answer was simple enough—keep away from him—and since Jack wasn't likely to repeat the experience of this night, it was an easy solution as well. As difficult as the day had been, I might be safe from him from now on. At least, that's what I'd tell Latham, when he figured out why Jack had stayed behind. I'd be safe.

Marguerite was not safe. I knew it in my bones. Nate had not told anyone about my vision of Marguerite—I knew him well enough to know that was true. Which meant that Jack had figured out that I still had my abilities all on his own. And if he'd figured it out . . . or told . . . Hank would come. If anyone looking for Brody tonight realized I'd helped, that I could still find lost things, especially lost children, everyone who had ever wanted help finding anything would be on my doorstep tomorrow, and Hank would be first in line.

No one thought the LPK killer was done. I just did not dare try to help. To steer the police or FBI wrong again, to lose one more child? I couldn't take that kind of loss.

Even when it came to Marguerite, I was useless. I didn't know anything for sure about her bloody eyes except that the image of them was a fragment in time. It could have been from a fight last year. Could be from ten years from now. It could have been from her teenage days for all I knew. All I could see were those eyes, and their age wasn't obvious.

I shoved it aside. Marguerite wasn't my business. Nate was on the case. I would be stupid to make it my business. People got hurt, all the time. People died, all the damned time. People went missing, all the damned time. Getting involved just got me into trouble. It had nearly killed me before. I would not go down that path again. *Not my freaking business.* I was back here for Latham. Only that. Period.

When I finally saw my house, an oasis of amber light against a curtain of heavy, dark trees, I thought I'd feel relief, but it still felt miles away. Miles and miles and way too many memories away, that warmth. I wondered if I'd ever feel warm again.

CHAPTER ELEVEN

Hours later, I stepped barefoot across prickly grass, carefully avoiding the burrs of small sticker weeds by skimming each foot along the tips of the blades until I felt a safe patch of Saint Augustine to hop onto. I was almost certain I was dreaming, except my toes protested whenever they struck the next burr. The sunlight refracted glorious rainbows as if it were shining through the facets of fine crystal sheets. Rivers of scent eddied past: honeysuckle, sweet olive, bitterroot, and lemon verbena.

I needed to leave this dream. I hated this dream. I'd had it off and on over the years, but far more frequently since I had started helping with the Little Princess Killer case.

Everything about the woods I stood in was excruciatingly beautiful, and the weight of that beauty pressed against me, pinning me in place. The bark of the tree I touched was knife-edged, and when I lifted my finger it bled crimson, blood flowing so fast it puddled and became roses that rotted in the forever moments it takes for dreamtime to pass.

"Would you care for a cup of tea?" an old woman asked.

I took a deep breath and steadied myself before facing her. Each time was a shock: Parts of her were always missing. Bloody stumps where an arm and a leg should be. Old Woman was older than the mountains I sensed beyond the forest of this dream, older than memory. Her eyes were mere creases of heavy lids. Her hair glinted silver in the sun, each strand razor sharp, whipping about her head, lacerating the plush chair she sat upon. A chair so out of place in this wood that I kept staring at it, knowing I'd seen it before, somewhere.

"Darling Avery, your tea." She pushed a cup across a table I had not noticed before, and the lemony smell gagged me. I tried to retreat but had grown roots where my legs used to be.

"No," I told her, though not unkindly. She could not help being in my dream, and I sensed she was not pleased to be there, either. "Not today."

Her shoulders sagged, and her wan smile trembled. "Soon, my dear. Soon."

"Never." I'd answered the same for as long as I could remember. It was necessary, that *never*. As important as breathing. It was my last defense, though I could not tell you why.

Old Woman closed her eyes and nodded, waving her hand against the brilliant light that glinted off her spoon, reminding me that the stump of her other arm just kept bleeding and bleeding and . . .

A whiff of strong coffee snapped my eyes open, and I woke to find Latham standing in my bedroom doorway, holding a cup of freshly ground, freshly brewed, dark, dark coffee. His haggard eyes had a hundred-yard stare. He looked away quickly, not able to hold my gaze, as if something he saw hurt him.

For as long as I could remember having the dream about the Old Woman, Latham was there when I woke from it. Once I moved away, he'd call, although the clanging phone was a poor substitute for the cup of coffee he'd always brought me before, no matter what time of day or night. I was just grateful he was here now. In all my years on the run, Latham had been my lifeline back from that dream. It was an odd job for an older brother to perform: waking a now-grown sister from a nightmare. Yet he'd always done it without fanfare, without comment, all my life.

He never let me ask him why or how he knew.

He said one day I wouldn't have to ask.

"Jack called to let me know you were here, exhausted. He told me about you helping him find the kid."

In all the Brody hoopla, I'd forgotten I was supposed to spend the night at his house again, though I'm not sure how wise that would have been given our last overnight. I held my hand out for the coffee, refusing to produce words until I had had a sip. My eyes were pits of grit and sand.

"This is getting out of control. You need to get out of here. Find somewhere else, somewhere safer."

I wiggled my fingers in the universal *gimme* sign for the coffee and grunted something unintelligible, and he gave up, handing it over.

"If you're not too worn out, I could use some help today with the McGinnis plaster job."

It was only the sheer unwillingness to waste a drop of coffee that kept me from handing it back and pulling the covers over my head. Of course he knew this, the jerk.

I inhaled a few ounces before I reminded him of my status in town. "You know they're not going to be happy if they learn I'm the one who did the work." The McGinnises were very Catholic. "Mrs. McGinnis told me I was an aberration last week when I saw her."

"She did not."

"Did so. Sprinkled holy water on the money after I handed it over to her."

He rolled his eyes, knowing it was in the realm of possibility for Mary McGinnis, the local postmistress. "You can't actually be Satan's minion if she took the money."

"Duh. Why turn down money when you have holy water on standby? And seriously—think about that—she had *holy water* on standby."

"I'll have Father Tomas come over to bless the repairs, then, just in case."

"Oh, goody." I winked at him above the rim of the cup.

"No pretending to speak in tongues."

"I think that's a violation of my civil liberties."

"And no pretending to hex Mary, either."

"She beaned me in the head with her rosary when I asked for extra stamps."

"She did not."

"Did. And I think she consigned me to hell when I asked for that new one with Gloria Steinem on it."

"I don't know why you provoke her. You know her mother ran off with—"

"The plumber," I interrupted, knowing the story all too well, "after Leila made her hocus-pocus prediction."

When we were kids, our mother liked to pretend she had "the sight," as she called it, and she constantly roped in poor, naive people who just wanted to hear something good was going to happen to them. She kept it low-key, here in Saint Michael's, since it was where we lived most of the time. What the town didn't know was that my mom, ace grifter, had a keen ability to read body language, and she had me, back when I was small and could be forced to help, as a secret weapon.

"Mary put peanut butter in my hair at lunch time, every day, for almost a year. I think she deserves to be hexed."

Latham tried to summon a glare, but the corners of his mouth were already twitching.

"C'mon, you lazy rugrat. I need to get the crew organized, and you're dawdling."

I slurped down the last of the coffee—slurped it loudly, just because I knew it annoyed Latham—and as I set the cup on my night table, I saw the paint on my hands. Hands that had been completely clean of paint when I'd fallen into bed, exhausted after finding Brody.

"Damn."

⚜ ⚜ ⚜

I ran into the living room, the gray light of dawn shifting into purples and blues and tinges of early morning honey pink. My easel held a new captive—one of my bigger canvasses yet. Latham followed as I padded across the cold wood floor, tensing more with every step.

He didn't have to warn me that I wouldn't like what I was about to see, though I'd known immediately from his expression that he'd already seen it on his way in. I rounded the easel and flinched. There were Marguerite's dead, cloudy eyes. Her forehead covered with rivulets of blood running like paint spatter. She was nearly decapitated. One red stiletto lay nearby. It was difficult to identify what I'd painted of the scene around her—it looked sort of like a worn wood floor, but there was nothing more to go on as the majority of her body was out of the frame. I gritted my teeth to keep from throwing up. It was almost photorealistic, more so than I usually aim for in a painting. The colors pulsed off the canvas, so super rich they reached out and enfolded me. I had no clue how I had accomplished that in one night.

Mere seconds after coming face to face with the canvas, pain struck me on my left side, a body blow, and I felt the runaway train of a seizure coming on. The image seemed to fill me. Drown me. My head throbbed with a sharp

99

blinding hurt; I had to get rid of the painting. Couldn't think. Breathe. Had. To. *Get rid of it now.* Couldn't think. Now—*now now now.* It was all a blur; I grabbed the open jar of mineral spirits, ignoring Latham's rising panic behind me. Splashed it on the painting. Lighter, lighter—*there*, the fireplace lighter in my hand as Latham shouted, "What the hell? Avery?"

The whoosh of the flame singed everything around it—ceiling, wall, me—as the pain from the image slammed me to my knees.

"Jesus, Avery, are you out of your mind?"

I could taste the metallic of the seizure, felt the tremors start somewhere, fault lines moving, warning quakes rumbling.

"Avery?" Jack shouted from the door, and my head split with thundering images. "*Son of a bitch*—are you crazy? Brody, *get back*. Latham, get a fire extinguisher. Brody, over there—porch. Now!"

"What's wrong with her?" Brody shouted, scared.

"Get out," I garbled back, brain not working, the tremors bowing my back as I folded into myself. "Get out, get out—*get out get out*," tore through me, ripping me limb from limb.

"Get him out of here—Jack," Latham boomed beside me, firing up the extinguisher he must've somehow found beneath the kitchen sink.

"You said she was okay! Last night, you said you didn't hurt her. You said she was okay!" Brody's shriek was sharp enough to slice through steel.

"She is. Will be. Dammit, Brody, wait on the porch."

The roar of the extinguisher stopped just as abruptly as it had started, the last of the powder falling, like snow, quietly to the floor. I could feel that the image remained mostly intact, in spite of the tremors closing my eyes. I needed that canvas to be gone, needed it obliterated, but with the seizure having hold of me now, there was no way to communicate that to Latham.

I didn't know if I'd live through this one, what with the image being right there, those eyes staring down at me. The lacerations on the woman's face, the dripping blood. It was killing me. Burned, but not gone. I didn't remember hitting the floor. When I came to, I was still bouncing against the floor, my head slamming the wood over and over until I felt someone catch it and hold it tight.

"She's none of your business," Latham seethed, as he released my head and rolled me onto my side. "Leave her be."

"She is my business," Jack said, closer now as another spasm hit, my mind floating in some middle space, disconnected from my muscles as they tensed and released, tensed and released, rapid fire. I felt Jack's hands as he eased me away from Latham. "That's Marguerite up there. That makes this my business, Latham. Now move that damned painting somewhere Brody can't see it."

"Get the hell out, Thibodaux," Latham threatened, and I could feel his hands on me, as well. "She needs you to stay away from her."

They were two old Samurai, warring over a conflict so old I could barely remember the time when they'd been best friends. Latham's disgust with Jack ran so deep now, so wide, it dug chasms into the earth.

"That's between me and Av. Go. Get that painting out of here, Latham. I can tell it's still upsetting her."

Latham kissed me on the forehead—Latham, my beautiful big brother Latham, who never gave me images, who only gave me blessed rest—murmured, "I'll be right back," and then stood and grabbed the painting, swinging it over me as he pulled it off the easel.

It was airborne at twelve o'clock, when the second wave of the seizure struck, full force, *on off on off on off* contractions clicking through my muscles, bouncing my body for its pure vindictive enjoyment.

Jack's hands ran over me, soothing, feeling my pulse, brushing the hair from my face. I wanted to hate him for it, but his voice crooned in that deep singsong he knew I loved. He was my Pied Piper, the one I wanted to always follow, and he led me step by step, convulsion by convulsion, compelled by the folds and russets in his tones to believe in the promise of sunrise after a long, dreary night. I melted into Jack's song, the bass of it running through me to some hidden place, calming the seizure, calming me. I needed him to survive, though I wished I would not. I'm not sure what he said. I know only that he did his best to make it easier on me, and I knew the entire time that he'd have never done so if he'd known the whole truth, the lies I'd told, the things I'd held back, or omitted.

Whose sin was greater? His, for something he'd yet to commit? Or mine, for what I had?

I heard them, some time later, arguing, words crashing in the other room like thunder and lightning. The soft, worn folds of my favorite childhood quilt, one Latham had saved, wrapped around me, as if it could protect me from the monsters. But there was no protection, and the dark in my bedroom was heavy with want: wanting to run, wanting to hide, wanting to scream.

At some point, I became aware that Latham stood outside my door, blocking Jack's entrance, while Jack paced before him.

"You think I'd hurt her?" Jack kept repeating, incredulous.

"I *know* you would," Latham answered, low, bitter.

He couldn't tell Jack the prophecy. We'd sworn not to tell. I'm not saying we weren't tempted through the years, but Dad had always said the one thing he'd learned the hard way was that messing with the predictions only made them worse. We never understood how, except maybe they sped up, or hurt random others. We couldn't know if Dad told the truth, but what if he did? How do you tempt something like that? It was why I knew I had to come home when he said I needed to, to save Latham. I couldn't risk questioning that.

I must've dozed, because when I opened my eyes again, Jack and Latham had moved away from my door and were shouting at each other in the kitchen—from the sound of it, they had been at the argument long enough for it to boil over and seep through the walls. I couldn't parse much of it, so deep was I in the trough of darkness. I did catch snatches of words, though, mice scurrying by my consciousness, rustling, making me shiver.

". . . and now you care? Ten long years, Jack, and you have no clue what she's been through . . ."

". . . Because you hid her! She needs tests! There are medical advances."

". . . you think I wouldn't take care of her? Get her the best help possible? We've done that. Everything there is, experts, every test, every . . ."

Dark rippled over me, covering, welcomed.

I sank into it and was gone.

CHAPTER TWELVE

Somewhere in that dark, Jack's voice surrounded me, tugging me back to when I was eight years old, about a month after Jack had given me the paints. I was burrowed in my closet behind a pile of clothes Leila had never once noticed. I felt Jack pass by the house and linger a moment, quite close, and then fade away from the door, deciding not to knock. His images spread out before me, a nasty briar patch of losses and grief.

It was winter, and it turned out that winter was always especially bad for Jack. Winter meant more clothes, which meant the Senator had more options for places to leave bruises. Jack's stepmother and brother had been gone about two months, and the Senator, who was drinking more frequently now that the ex-wife had vacated the premises, embraced his alone time with his oldest son with irrepressible glee. I'm not sure if Jack would have stayed had he'd understood how the abuse would accelerate before he could finally grow big enough to put a stop to it. Jack's losses that afternoon told me it had already been a particularly bad day for him.

It took an hour to escape the house—not that Leila was being especially watchful, but because I needed to swipe the bandages, and Leila was in the bathroom, coloring her hair the brassy orange she preferred when in Saint Michael's. I think she thought it was evocative, sexy. It reminded me of a lit matchstick. To get her out, I lied and said one of her customers was at the back door, someone wanting to buy some high-priced makeup, one of those pyramid money-making schemes Leila didn't care a whit about. No, the makeup was simply her lure. She would have me slip into the cabinet behind where she sat at such sessions, and then she would go into a spiel about the latest lipstick or moisturizing cream; meanwhile, I'd see the client's losses, pick one, jot it down on a slip of paper, and put it in a slot cut into a drawer above my head. She'd start pawing around for some sample as an excuse to open the cabinet drawers, read the note while she was at it, and then in a sort of oblique way, imply that she'd had this awful vision, that the client had lost said item, and had the woman thought to look in such and such a place.

Leila could be quite theatrical when she wanted to be, and generally, the tips she pocketed from these little one-on-ones were huge, far larger than any makeup commission might have been. No one wanted to admit they'd ever consulted a psychic, but under the guise of buying makeup? Genius. Leila did a booming business in a place where she said they prided themselves on being uptight in public and eccentric in the shadows.

I hated the con, but at least it meant we were home, and I could run with Jack and the rest of the Saints so long as Leila didn't have any appointments. It was a vast improvement over the summers we'd go on family vacations in the cramped RV, like a circus caravan of one, camping in hole-in-the-wall towns, places that weren't as likely to be surprised by an itinerant family roaming from state to state. We all had new names each trip, part of a game advertised as *fun* and *pretend* but heaven help you if you forgot them. I'd be stashed in a cramped cupboard, doling out losses while Leila, dressed in some outlandish getup, would commence to contacting lost relatives and finding beloved items for the locals. As a child, I never understood why some of the locations of the customers' lost items were never shared with them—where they could find their missing diamond earrings or gold bracelet or a particularly valuable work of art. I just knew Dad was always especially happy those days, and we'd sometimes come home early as a result.

On that particular day, when Jack didn't knock, Lelia had been griping at Dad that they needed to just take me out of school for a year and travel, so I knew I needed to warn Jack that we might disappear soon without warning. It would have hurt him for me to leave without some kind of good-bye, and it killed me to think he would have to face the Senator alone if we left.

Leila had assumed I was in the cabinet by that point, and I watched from the tiny opening of my bedroom door as she sashayed down the hall. She'd put her hair up in a turban, and when she headed to the front door, I snuck in the bathroom, stole the bandages needed for Jack, and then shimmied out my small bedroom window. I'd catch hell for it later.

Winters in Saint Michael's have a way of biting into you that surprises every time—probably because mild is the norm here, and we're used to being spoiled. But winters are also high in humidity—a cold so wet it cuts clean through you like you were nothing but air. I was shivering before I got to Jack. I could have tracked him from his losses—they'd have grown more hostile and menacing as I drew near—but I already knew where he'd go.

I pushed open one of the side doors to the old church and saw a path created by dead leaves that had drifted in. Jack was curled nearly fetal on the scarred wooden floor behind what used to be the altar.

I hated the Senator, right then. I wished him dead. Able to see Jack's losses, even with Jack fully clothed, I could have marked each place where his dad had ever struck. Jack was twelve and still skinny, and he wore big bulky sweaters and joined the junior high football squad, mostly so he had an excuse for the bruises. There were flashes of other losses: Jack, shivering, standing naked while the Senator berated him for some infraction, a bottle of whiskey in one hand, his belt in another. I bit the inside of my mouth to keep from flinching at each swing of the belt, the buckle landing hard on flesh. Images flashed of other things, and I fought to ignore them. The big, hulking Senator grabbing Jack. Turning him around. I didn't understand the other things, then.

"I told you last time not to come," Jack said, biting back the fury he longed to scream. I could see him fighting that scream, holding onto it with the thinnest of restraints.

"I'm always going to come," I told him, "and so would you, if it was me."

We belonged to each other. As if we always had. Always would. This is what we did for each other.

He thought about that and then finally nodded. We patched up the worst of the cuts as best we could, and then curled up like puppies, keeping each other warm, watching the rain that had finally made good on its threat.

I'd since broken that promise. I'd made Jack think I was never coming back, and then even in coming home had abandoned him.

As I started waking up from the seizure, back in my thirty-year-old body, in my room at my own home, I felt him there, felt him standing by the window. My leaving had been a blow far worse than anything his father

105

had ever inflicted on him. How do you ask forgiveness for that? Especially when you have so much worse to confess?

Jack leaned against the window frame, facing me; his body cast half in shadow, half in moonlight. It seemed the sharpest, truest image of him I'd ever seen—dark shadows in the caves of his eyes, their steel-gray color piercing the moonlight. His jaw was set in anger; his hands, thrust in his pockets. He was violence, restrained. My hands itched to paint him. Hold him. Traitors, my hands.

Memories of how I'd left him ten years ago rushed in.

"I told you to let it go!" he'd shouted.

He was twenty-four to my twenty, and in all the years I'd known him, he'd never shouted, not at me, not once, and I had stood in shock, vibrating with fear and adrenaline and the need to run.

"I swear to God, what the hell were you even thinking, Av? It didn't matter if he didn't want us to get married. He had no say in our lives! I'm never going to be a politician, even if he wanted it. You were my choice—my choice! I told you to ignore him. Told you I'd take care of it, that I would protect you. He's dead now, Avery. What the hell? Do you know what you've set in motion?"

"He threatened me, Jack; he threatened . . . us." I shook until I was on my knees; my hand still on the handle to the big front door of the Senator's stately mansion. I hadn't even made it across the threshold before Jack's anger had hit me. "I'm so sorry."

"Sorry?" He turned then. "Sorry? My father told me what was in that file. I can't believe you'd do that. I can't believe you think so little of me, that you'd use something like that, tell a fucking reporter!"

"I . . . I just wanted him to back off." I couldn't explain why, not seeing the disgust now in his eyes. There was no excuse, and I knew it. It didn't matter that his father had practically kidnapped me the day before, dragged me into his office past all his aides, and tried his dead-level best to humiliate me. Threaten me.

I had blindly latched onto one telling image—and truth be told, it had felt so damned good to see the mighty windbag Senator fall back into his chair, ashen at the mention of the file. It didn't matter that I had no idea what was in the file, why it was important, or who'd left it in the campaign office. All that mattered was the Senator was being hunted for corruption charges, and his enemies were circling. I knew where the file was, and where to tell a reporter to go look. I implied I already had, and that the reporter would use it—whatever was in it—if the Senator didn't back off and let Jack and me live our lives.

I'd been twenty and in love and finally in a position to defeat the man who'd made Jack's life a living hell. I walked out of that mansion feeling like the Queen of the Universe, telling myself no one could touch this power I had, telling myself it made me special, better somehow.

What an utter idiot I was.

The next day I realized I had to tell Jack what I'd done, because no way would the Senator not aim his rage on his son, his favorite target. Never mind that Jack was now a grown man and far more capable of handling himself than the Senator could ever have known; the Senator's sudden vengeance would still surprise Jack, and I didn't know how he'd react. He was home on leave, already on edge from losing friends in Afghanistan on his first tour, and I knew he was not himself. I'd gone over to apologize but instead walked straight into Jack's fury.

"He said you told him you have the ability to find lost things. Said you knew stuff that no one else could know, and that you'd exposed him to the world. Is that true?"

I had nodded, bent by his fury.

"I can find lost things. There was a file. I wanted him to back off."

"Damn, Avery, you do something like that, like there aren't consequences, without talking to me first? Something so big, something so . . ."—he pulled at his hair, in denial. "It's unreal. Something like that could infect our kids?"

He waited for me to answer, and by the time I nodded, tears rolled down my face.

He looked at me in disgust: "You're nothing but a liar."

"You . . . you don't mean that," I said in a voice gone small and tight from hurt. "You're still grieving."

"That's what you think this is, grief? That I'm upset the bastard's dead? Hell, no. I'm happy he's dead."

And I couldn't see anything of the Senator's death being a loss to him. Not a single thing.

Jack had been there when they fought. The Senator's face twisted in anger, a loss . . . a loss of opportunity. Jack wanting to stop him, shut him up, take away the threats to humiliate him, even now. Did he? Did he pull that trigger? Dad said I'd be murdered at his hands . . . did he mean now? Could I know what Jack would do when pushed this hard?

"This is about trust, Avery."

I flinched on the word trust. Every lie begins with an implicit "trust me."

"Screw trust. I trusted you. I thought you trusted me." Jack stepped forward, rage and disgust building in his voice. "You know every dark thing, every horrible thing about me, but you're capable of doing something so huge, and you don't tell me. Not a word. No heads-up that you're going to confront him. If what he said is true, and you say it is, you've lied to me our whole life. I don't even know you. You're some sort of freak show."

He shouted those last two words, his expression hard enough to cut stone, and then he stomped toward me, his hand up, a knife there, yelling, "Get the hell out of my life," and all I could think was: Run. Run, and don't stop. Don't stop.

So I ran.

And I've been running ever since.

Jack, the older, broken Jack, stepped forward now, and I flinched. He froze. "Dammit," he muttered, and turned back to the window.

Even in profile, I could see his pain. There was a part of me that wanted to reach out to him, to hold him, to tell him how sorry I was. That part of me had the self-preservation instincts of a moth. I shoved away the pressure inside my heart and pulled myself up, leaning against the headboard. My door was open, and Latham was in the living room, talking to someone on the phone. He stood, though, where he could keep an eye on us. Jack would resent that, I knew. I could feel nothing of Jack's losses. That was both the beauty and the curse of a seizure—everything goes numb for a while. Even if it did not last long, I loved that for a few rare moments in time, there was no direct conduit to other people's pain, but it was also like having a part of me amputated. I felt ill at ease in my own skin. Vulnerable, because I didn't have any way of knowing what Jack was thinking.

I flipped on the lamp beside my bed, and my gaze moved to the mounds of paperwork spread across the room. Everywhere I looked were piles of medical assessments, notes, tests, results, research. It was one of the things the FBI had insisted on; Hank hadn't exactly given me a choice. And still, it had not helped. There were no answers in the realm of logic or medicine or science to explain what I could do or how it affected me. How do you run medical tests to measure how seeing images of lost things might affect a person? How do you diagnose where the ability to see such images comes from? In the end, no one had any answers, in spite of the ferocious resolve with which they began.

"I'm not going through all of that again," I said. "Don't even think it."

"Latham already made that clear. And these," he waved behind him, "are exceptionally thorough." He didn't sound happy. "Though it wouldn't hurt to keep tabs on those two little lesions in the back of your brain."

"You will not ambush me with more tests, Jack. I'd never survive them."

As for those lesions, I'd always had them; Latham had explained that to me after the particularly scary tests had come in. The doctors had found them long ago in Biloxi, although no one knew what had caused them.

"Your brother emphasized the no-more-tests rule already. Told me what hospitals and stuff do to you—all those losses so nearby." He looked away, some middle distance, like he was calculating another chess move. "I'll keep researching. Must be something out there—"

"No." I hammered the air with the word. I could not do this pretense of caring. "Leave it alone. Leave *me* alone." *Hate me*, I wanted to say. "I don't want your help. I don't want anyone to know about this. Ever. I helped you find Brody. All I'm asking is for you to keep this to yourself."

Jack didn't look back at me. Didn't nod. Guilt emanated from the tightness of his shoulders, the way he held his breath. Guilt and fear.

"What did you do?" It came out harsh, more bitter than I meant it to.

"I'm not your enemy, Av. I never was."

He was wrong. He had been, and I'd known it and ignored it. He would be, again, when he learned the truth. He had yet to look at me.

"That's something else we have to talk about," he continued, and I stiffened, afraid once more. "Before I explain, Latham tells me—reluctantly, I might add—that after a seizure, you have a brief window of time in which you don't see images, or feel that pain. Is that true?"

Damn Latham. I didn't want him discussing my ability with Jack. We had a deal—neither of us told on the other. Ever. "Why?"

"Is it true?" There was ache in his voice now. Craggy, harsh, an open wound I hadn't seen before. I looked away from him.

"Yes."

"How long does it last?"

"I don't know. It's always different."

He turned back to me; his expression shuttered. "Talk to me. Please."

I closed my eyes and leaned back into the headboard, my will right then as thin as rice paper and about as useful in the face of his determination. "Sometimes hours. The bigger the seizure, the longer I'm sort of burned out, like a short circuit. It can sometimes be days. Images will start filtering back in slowly—not all at once, so I at least have some warning. Why?"

"Why didn't you ever tell me about this?"

"You never asked."

It hit him like a hammer to his heart, and I could see that in the way the dark etched deeper around his eyes, the grim set of his mouth. Sometimes I wanted to shake him, tell him everything I had done, watch him recoil and just know. Know everything, including why I had run away from him so long ago. And then common sense kicked in, and I ground my teeth and crossed my arms, barring him from my world. I'm not entirely sure I'd survive Jack knowing everything.

"How was I to know to ask about something you hid from me?"

I shrugged. Begged my heart to keep beating in spite of how close to home he was getting. "You knew, Jack. You saw, over and over, that I found things, knew where things were. Knew things I shouldn't have known. You might not have understood, as we were growing up, how I did it, but you noticed and you could have asked. Instead, you ignored it. You didn't want to know what a freak show your friend—and later, your girlfriend—was. You wanted to live on the surface of perfection."

My words enraged him, though he hadn't moved a single fraction of an inch. I didn't have to look at him to know the muscle in his jaw flicked a little as he watched me.

"What beautiful bullshit you've been selling yourself. You don't believe those lies any more than I do."

They aren't lies, I wanted to yell at him. You hated what I was. "Now look who's believing the beautiful bullshit," I said instead.

"You never had a seizure when we were kids," he continued, still focused on the medical side of the issue. I should have expected that as a PJ—he was all about triage—a *solve the medical problem first* kind of person. "There was never a nosebleed or even any kind of dizzy spell. I'd have known, Av; I'd remember."

We were going to dance right past that last horrible night, and deal with the now, and I couldn't tell if I felt relief . . . or grief. I focused on my hands, scrabbling in the dirt pile of my emotions to unearth words, actual syllables and consonants that would make sense. He wouldn't go away with half of an explanation; I knew that about him. I knew Jack would never just take half.

"I used to be able to control it more. Keep everything at bay."

"Block the pain?"

I nodded.

"So what happened? Something must've happened in the intervening years. What made it worse?"

My gut churned, and I refused to say *my losses*. He'd want to know what those losses were. I clenched my hands across my stomach, fighting for control. "My own business, Jack," I said, my voice shaking. "Why do you ask?"

"Brody wants to come in here to make sure you're okay."

I ignored the sudden relief swamping my heart, such a stupid, stupid organ.

"He's convinced I hurt you," Jack said, watching me, "and when I tried to take him home, he got hysterical, so I've kept him busy out on your porch with a video game. But I know that was Marguerite in the painting, and I need to know why. I have a PI looking for her—so far she's covered her tracks, and my gut tells me she's up to something, trying to do some damage to me. Maybe to you. But that image, that's her."

"It's possible it's her, I grant you. It's also possible it's a projection of someone's potential loss. Losses are weird. They can be real. They can be projected—what someone thinks they've lost—they can be old losses that festered, changed as people's memories added on, or subtracted. It's not exact, and they don't always make sense, even to me."

"So she might not be dead?"

I was pretty certain she was—the hairstyle and color were current, and Marguerite changed her styles frequently, but I'd learned never to be certain. I was more puzzled by Jack. He seemed worried and aggravated at the same time.

"She might not be dead, Jack, at least not yet. If you can find her, you may be able to protect her."

"And if she *is* dead, that's a loss of Brody's. He'd be devastated to find out like this, and I'd rather we know for certain, and find some way . . . I don't have a clue how . . . but find some way to help him when I have to tell him. But in the meantime, if he comes in here—into the house—I don't want it to set you off on another seizure. I need to know the symptoms, how often it happens, and what to do to prevent it."

"And?" There was an *and* coming. I could feel it.

"I *saw* the painting, Av," as if naming Marguerite hadn't made that obvious. "That's Brody's mom. I can't just let that go." Then the bombshell. "I had to call Nate and Marguerite's attorney."

Nate would have kept it from Jack that I'd already told him about the images I'd seen of Marguerite before the painting, but now he'd have to open up an official investigation, which meant informing people.

Which meant the FBI would know.

It was over. This refuge. It was gone, just like that.

Fury warred with panic. I had to leave. Pick up and go again. Fast. Surely there was someplace I could run without Internet or tabloids, someplace in need of an awkward woman who could fix a hot water heater and paint. I wondered what Africa was like. And then I heard Latham's voice in the living room, and I knew I would stay. Despite all that might come, I had to stay.

Jack had used my distraction to his advantage; he now sat next to me on the bed. I had his full attention. Up close, like this with him, I could barely breathe. I had hoped what I'd felt for him was long dead and gone. Silly me.

"Please don't run, Av," he said, and I stiffened—he was too close to the mark, and his tone was pleading this time, not an order. His voice had gone soft, wrapping itself around me. "I'll help. Just don't run."

"You can't help."

"I can. It's my fault people will know—at least let me try."

"You were overseas when I was in the tabloids; you don't know what you've unleashed, Jack. You have no clue."

"I have more bloody clues than you realize."

My gaze snapped to his gray eyes. He turned, a faraway expression on his face. "Marguerite was a friend when nothing else made sense. I barely saw her when I was home on leave. She was simply supportive, seemed genuine, and, like me, was alone in the world. You were gone—and for two years I didn't care if I lived or died. She became a friend. I never fell in love with her, though I cared. She knew that. Accepted it, I thought." He looked at me then. "I need you to know that."

"It doesn't matter—"

"Yes, it does. I wanted to forget you, and she seemed to care when I needed someone to care. I thought it was all we'd both have, all we deserved, and then she got pregnant with Brody. We were arguing one day, and she blurted out that she'd thought I'd be able to love her, now that she was having our baby."

I flinched. "Jack—"

"Stop. I need to say this."

He waited, and I nodded. He'd thought about it too long; if I didn't hear him out, he'd always tell himself that if he had just said this one thing, it'd have made the difference. He'd always have hope. I had to stop that.

"Marrying her was a mistake, and I think I knew it five minutes after we exchanged vows, but I thought we could try. She wanted more than I could give her, more than I could be with her, and once she had Brody, she had a weapon that could hurt me. She made it a living hell for me to see him.

"In a way, I don't blame her. I'd given up actively searching for you, but I hadn't given up hoping you'd come home. I thought about you every single day, sometimes all damned day long, and I didn't hide that from Marguerite. Our divorce, when it came, was a relief. Then a few months ago, I went back to the rehab hospital for a final surgery so I could be officially discharged, and you were on my mind more than usual. I kept thinking I heard your voice. I wanted you to be home, in the worst way possible—I wanted to talk to you about that night, about how sorry I was, and how much I missed you. I was so angry for so long, but more than anything I wanted to talk to you, and that day was particularly bad, thinking I heard your voice.

"At first I thought *I'm losing it*, and then I realized, no, I really was hearing you. You were angry. I'd never heard you that angry before. I made my way into the waiting room, and there you were—on TV in Chicago being hounded by a dozen reporters as you tried to get on the 'L' train. They shoved cameras in your face. One reporter guy tried to grab you."

I remembered that encounter and nodded. It had been a couple of weeks after I'd been outed, and just before someone tried to kill me and the FBI stepped in and put me in protective custody.

Layers of rage smoldered behind Jack's eyes, and the power of his words was all the more devastating for how softly he spoke next. "It took four doctors and three orderlies to keep me from leaving the hospital—and that's after I'd already been sedated. I tried to call you."

"I know."

Shock creased his brow, and then pain. Letting him know I had purposefully avoided him so recently was like pulling duct tape off skin; fast hurts, but slow is torture, and it was the only course of action given that there was no hope for this, for us. None. Embarrassment seeped into my chest and up into my face.

"I tried to find you, that first year you left. I looked everywhere."

"I didn't want to be found, Jack. Not then. Not later, especially after I'd been outed. That wasn't my choice. This, right here, this isn't my choice. Please don't do this. Please—just leave."

He leaned forward, practically nose-to-nose. "No."

I wasn't surprised. Jack had never known how to stop. It's not who he is. I had no more hope that he'd quit than an elephant does to fly. I started to argue the point, and he interrupted.

"I didn't kill my dad, Av. I think you ran that night thinking I had. I know I scared you, how angry I was, how out of control. I was furious with you—but I was wrong to blame you. I hadn't had time to process any of it. I'd just seen him, and it was a shock. Everything that had gone wrong—that could go wrong still—was circling in my head, and I was out of my mind about what I thought you had cost us.

"Thirty minutes after you left, I realized that. I wanted so badly to call and tell you how stupid I'd been, how wrong I'd been to lash out at you, but the cops were holding my phone. When I got it back, you didn't answer. I went after you after the police let me leave the scene, but I couldn't find you. You'd already left."

He touched my cheek, a longing in his eyes that ground my heart into dust. "I did not kill him, Av. I promise you, I couldn't do something like that—even to him."

I had told myself the same thing: that he wasn't capable of killing anyone, but he had—in Afghanistan, and the war at home was so much worse. What if I'd been deluding myself? What if he was lying—to himself, to me—even now?

Some losses are obvious, and others are subtle. Someone can lose something and then realize she's relieved—it still shows up as a loss, but muted. Here's the problem—if someone murders someone else and feels no guilt? Feels the death as a relief or justified? As something that needed to be done? *I wouldn't register it as a loss.*

I knew Jack didn't see the Senator's death as a loss, because even at that moment when I first found out, when I approached him at the door, Jack had had no loss images of his own dead father. I could not blame him for that, but it also meant he could have killed the Senator that night, and it wouldn't have registered as a loss. I can't tell when someone's lying—only the losses they feel.

What mattered when Jack confronted me on the porch was that I had grasped that he'd been capable of killing the Senator. He was capable of *killing*. My father's prediction that Jack would someday kill me had slipped between us in that moment, cutting my last thread of hope loose.

I hadn't wanted to believe that. In the end, Jack's father's death was ruled a suicide, but I was long gone by then, and even now, I didn't know for certain if the ME had gotten it right.

Was Brody safe with Jack? Was I horrible for not quite knowing? Was I wrong for wanting Jack to be able to defy what was predicted for him, knowing my dad's predictions had never once not come true?

Jack leaned back, but our gazes held. How could I say, *but you will one day kill me, and I'm trying to spare you that as long as I can*? He wouldn't believe it. But he would know that I did. And that would destroy him. I'd rather he hated me. When it happened—not if, but when—Jack wouldn't mean for me to die. That is what my heart told me. In spite of everything, in spite of how much I tried to hate him, I'd always known he was a victim, too.

Stupid hearts.

"Why didn't you tell me about what you could do? The truth, this time."

Because I loved you, I wanted to say. Because I wanted to be loved by you, because I wanted to be normal, to be thought of as normal, to have that chance, and I worked so hard, so hard, to hide it. And it was okay, because you made it go away, sometimes. I remembered whole days he'd transformed into spun gold, beautiful and shimmering in the sun.

I wanted to tell him I ran because he'd been right, I *was* a freak show, and I knew in that moment, in the violence I could see barely held in check in him, that one day I would be dead at his hands. I wanted to say, because you told me to get out of your life, to get the hell out, that you regretted even thinking about getting married to something like me. That I had grasped we could not have a life, could not have children together, because a death sentence hung over us both.

"Maybe we never knew each other," I said instead.

Brody's voice washed up in my memory, an incoming tide, that quiet confessional in the woods: *I think maybe he killed her.* Could that violence erupt again? Could he have snapped when Marguerite pushed back? I don't know if we can outrun fate. She'd threatened him, threatened to expose his past. What had she learned? What if she knew more about that night? I shook, and Jack assumed I was cold. He pulled the quilt up around me.

"You're wrong," he said, gently, letting his hands rest on my arms as his heat seeped into me. "I knew you. I knew the part that matters." He tapped my heart. "I know you, now. I won't let you take that away."

He was killing me.

"I want you to go, Jack. I want you out of my life. Tell Brody he can come see that I'm fine for a couple of minutes, then take him home."

I had meant to sound angry. Emphatic. I'd barely managed weary. He reached up and wiped away the tears I hadn't realized I'd been crying, betraying myself. I closed my eyes, wanting nothing more than to sink into the warmth of his hands.

"I'll be back tomorrow," he murmured.

"No, Jack."

"Yes, Av. Nate will be here. And I'm not letting you face that alone."

His voice cradled me, gently, gently.

"Nate's the least of the problem, but I'll be fine either way. I've handled this alone before. I do not need you to take care of me."

He gave me a wry grin. "I know. I'll be here for moral support, and in case dredging up that image starts to do"—he waved at me on the bed—"this again."

"*Don't. Even. Think. About it.* This is not your fault, nor your problem. You can't help that I saw Marguerite and painted her, so it's not your responsibility. You have to do what's best for Brody. I get that. Take that good Catholic guilt elsewhere. I don't need it. I don't want it. And I don't want you here."

He traced the contours of my face with his hand, and I felt my traitorous body ignoring my resolve and relaxing beneath his touch.

"I'm going to be here, Avery. Unless you're well enough to physically kick me out of the door, you'll just have to suck it up and deal."

I looked at him then. I was not the girl he remembered. She had died in a cold Boston apartment, the first place I ever ran to. I was someone else now, not some sentimental memory full of sunshine and tinted with nostalgia, and it was stupid to let myself think any differently, just because his hands were warm and his words soft.

I pushed his hand away and steeled my voice.

116

"We are not doing this, Jack. I don't want this. I don't want you. I left once; I will leave again, if I have to, to make that point. Now get the hell out."

He pulled away and stood; his face had turned once again to granite, all concern erased from his eyes. He stared at me then, his hands on his hips, his shoulders rigid.

His voice was dangerously soft when he spoke again.

"You forget that I do know you, Av. I know your heart, your body . . . all your little tells. I know you want me, still, the same way I want you. I know you, Av. You have always been right here," he said, tapping his heart.

I swallowed hard and bit the inside of my cheek to keep from nodding, from sobbing, from reaching for him.

"I know you're not telling me something," he said. "Something important. For the very first time since that night you left ten years ago, I understand there's something else going on with you. Something that scares the hell out of you."

He waited, and I forced myself to hold his gaze, to not look away.

"We've been doing this a long, long time," he said, gesturing at the two of us, when he realized I would not fill in the blanks. "I don't think either one of us can stop it. Even if we should."

He paused then. A glint flashed in his eye—and it terrified me, because I recognized it for what it was: sheer determination, the same determination that had seen him through the hell his father had dealt him, the torture his training to be a PJ had demanded, and the danger of being shot down behind enemy lines, doctoring wounded men, and dragging them back to safety.

And when I looked again, I realized that no, this was worse than all of that. He had the gleam of the newly converted. A man with an epiphany is the most dangerous man of all. He will believe, no matter what you tell him. I could see that in Jack.

Whatever it was he thought he'd learned from this latest seizure of mine, it had reframed for him what had happened between us, and it had given him hope.

"I'm going to find out what you're hiding, Avery. Trust me. You're going to tell me. I know what I lost once. I know how stupid I was. I'm not letting you go again."

He left then, closing the door gently behind him.

117

For a moment, I calculated the weight of the possible against a lifetime, however long I might have, of having to lie to him to keep him.

Not even hope weighs enough against that much hurt.

Not even hope.

CHAPTER THIRTEEN

Less than a minute later my bedroom door creaked open a crack. I looked up where Jack should have been and saw air. Then down: Brody, face red, hair sweaty, cheeks stained with tear tracks. Dammit. Jack appeared behind him and mouthed an apology as Brody tried to push into the room.

"Not today, Brody," Jack said, holding the door in place, his gaze meeting mine.

"You promised we'd make sure she stayed okay," Brody said to his dad.

"We have and we are. She's had a rough day. She's a little cranky," Jack said, more as a plea to me to play along than as an actual complaint. "We'll come back tomorrow."

"No," I said. "No, you're not coming back, because I have said no, Jack. Brody, you come in. Jack, wait outside. Let's get this over with right now."

I didn't believe tomorrow or the day after that or the year after that would change anything. It couldn't reach into the past and make us different people. It couldn't erase a single thing from the past decade, good or bad. I pointedly ignored Jack and focused on getting rid of Thibodaux number two.

For what it's worth, I knew what I was going to say to the runt. It wasn't exactly my first rodeo, having a seizure in front of a kid who mistakes it as having been somehow his fault, or worse, something he could catch. When it happens, it requires a quick and firm response. Kids never believed you when you told them it was no big deal, that it was something unique to you that they couldn't catch like the flu, that there was no chance of them suddenly having seizures themselves. Kids are a lot smarter than us; they know the world is filled with scary things they can't control.

I had a plan on how to not only absolve Brody of any worry or guilt, but also convince him he didn't even like the idea of being friends with me. He was going to think it was all his idea when I was done, and be pleased with himself about it to boot.

Everything I had planned, however, evaporated the moment Brody scrambled up onto the foot of my bed, settled cross-legged, and started unloading his backpack. This was another reason why I hated kids: they were wholly undependable.

"You look kinda bad," he said as he arranged his things on my quilt: some firecrackers, a watch, a few comic books, and something that looked suspiciously like the baseball cards Jack used to collect as a kid. "Kinda zombie bad."

"Thanks, kid. Just what every girl wants to hear. What are you doing?"

"Trading," he said, so matter of fact, I could practically hear the *duh* hanging in the air over his head. "Mom says you have to trade if you want something. If you want it bad enough, you trade something of real value. You don't offer junk for something important."

"So this is a business meeting?" I said, holding a hand up to stop Jack from stepping in. I pulled myself into a cross-legged mirror of Brody, scrutinizing his expression.

Something in his brown eyes—an earnestness, an urgency—arrested me mid-motion. One second I was sitting on my bed—worrying the old-fashioned quilt between my fingers—and then I was somewhere else. It was as if I had been jerked back in time, back to a smaller body, back to when I was four or five. Snow covered my favorite red boots. Actual snow, on the cold, concrete floor of a garage or a workshop. Yet I knew I'd never been in the snow as a child. Never once, not even on a vacation, and I wondered whose images these were.

The small past-me peered up at tables higher than my nose, tables overflowing with locks and safes and odd tools and drawings—what I would later learn were schematics. They seemed so familiar, and yet they weren't. I'd never seen them before. So how could I know them?

My father was bent over something on the workbench, his hair not yet gray. I remember him like that; I'm constantly surprised when I see him that he doesn't match the way he lives in my memory. He was working a few feet away, and I remember I craved his attention. He was busy with a small drill, and I'd been warned not to interrupt. Warned repeatedly.

Sweat beaded on my forehead, my hands shook, and only then did I realize I was holding someone's hand. Someone off to my right. I tried to say the words, to clamor above the noise to get his attention, but the words would not form.

I wanted to be older that day. A grown-up. He'd listen, then.

I knew he'd listen then.

Then I blinked, and there I was, sitting back on my bed, across from Brody, Jack still hovering by the door, frowning at me. Confusion played across his brow, as if he'd seen me leave and reappear. That other place, the snowy place, seemed so tangible that I bunched the quilt in my hands to make sure this place was real. Shaking and clammy, I shoved my hands in the crook of my knees to hide them. I'm not sure if I was hiding them from Jack, or Brody, or myself.

"Yeah, it's business," Brody answered, not aware I'd traveled somewhere else and back again since asking him the question. Should I be worried that I could still feel the crunch of snow beneath those red snow boots?

"Mom says you don't ask people to do stuff for free. Nothing's a free ride. You haggle. Negotiate. Make a deal."

"I see," and I took a split second to spare admiration for Jack's restraint. We all knew where this was going. It was a slide downhill to hell, and I had a snowball's chance of surviving it. "Well, your mom's pretty smart. So what do you want?"

"Can you find her?"

He didn't tremble or hesitate or show one fraction of how much he wanted his request. He was exceptionally professional. I suspected his mom would have been proud of that. I couldn't look at Jack; it would give it away, and I didn't want the kid to learn before we knew for certain. That sort of limbo wasn't fair. I'd seen that before.

"I don't know, Brody. I'm kinda broken right now."

He nodded, assessing me. "You looked like a fish flopping around."

"Brody!" Jack admonished, but I snorted, laughing.

"It felt like that, too," I told him. "I'd like to help you, but I don't know when I'll be able to find anything again—if ever. I'm not always successful."

"Like with those girls?"

The air whooshed out of the room, and what remained was thin and greasy with regret. Jack stepped into the doorway then—headed for me.

I shook my head. "You Googled that?"

Only then did the kid blush, and I saw freckles that had to come from his mom.

"Just your name. And I saw a bunch of pictures, like from the news. I can read a lot of stuff." Then he looked at his dad, saw his dad's face, and tried to amend, "but I didn't read a lot 'cuz I'm not s'posed to 'less Dad's there with me."

That was bad, that he'd had free rein to find those stories. Jack cursed under his breath, and I wasn't entirely sure he wasn't going to smash a fist through the door. I leaned forward and whispered, "I think you just lost your unlimited Internet privileges."

Brody glanced over to where Jack now paced and curtly nodded, confirming to his son that he'd screwed up. Brody sighed and faced me again.

"I saw them FBI guys on some video on there about the girls. They said you tried," he said, adding as if to make me feel better. "Nobody else knew nothin', neither."

Trying doesn't matter I wanted to tell him. It's about as useful as wishing, especially when a little girl is dead and if you hadn't interfered, she might still be alive.

We were sitting almost nose-to-nose at this point, this seven-year-old-going-on-a-hundred kid and me, and I couldn't explain to him how wrong he was. He wanted his mom. He'd have believed I could pull a freight train out of my ear, if that's what he needed to believe to live with the constant ticking of the clock as the number of days she'd been gone grew.

He'd believe anything.

Anything I said.

"The TV people said that you don't take money for finding stuff, but Mom says that sometimes you have to show people good faith. And I know Dad has money, but you don't like Dad, so I figured you wouldn't want him to buy you stuff."

"Got it nailed exactly right," I told him. Jack went still as deep water by the door. "So what do you aim to trade?"

"I got these," he said, pointing to his loot on the bed between us.

There were treasures: A dog-eared comic book. An autographed baseball. A couple of interesting coins, a pocketknife, a flashlight, and other assorted items added to the first ones he'd pulled out. "And this," he said, digging into the pocket of his blue jeans and pulling out a ring.

I heard Jack inhale, and I thanked God I wasn't standing. The ring was a two- or three-carat, square-cut diamond, with other smaller diamonds piled around it.

"Would this be enough?"

I took the ring and examined it, holding it up to the light. It was a beautiful ring, and I could tell from the way Jack had stiffened and gone ashen that it was the one he'd given to Marguerite. It made me nauseated to hold it, but I was proud I managed to stay expressionless.

"Not my style, kid," I said casually, "though it's a beauty. I'd just get paint on it. Besides"—I held the ring out to him—"never negotiate away your heart, Brody. You can't get it back when it's broken. And this is your mom's. Keep it."

"But—" he stammered, worry flooding his expression as he shoved the ring back in his pocket.

"I'll take the rest."

He jerked ramrod straight; I think he wasn't sure whether to be surprised, or relieved, or somewhat disappointed. But life costs. I didn't want him thinking later on that he hadn't offered enough for me to do my best. I was almost certain I didn't know where Marguerite was—usually, the location of the lost item is either obvious in the first moment I see it, or it's forever obscured in the image. Marguerite's was obscured.

"I'll take it and try. If I don't find her, you get everything back. If I do find her, I keep it. Deal?"

He nodded and started to ease off the bed.

"Hang on," I said, "we're not done. For the duration of this contract, there'll be no running away. I am not going to go tramping through the woods to track you down to give you my report. Got it?"

He nodded.

"Good. Now go away. Take your dad. Don't come back here. I'll find you when I have something to tell you."

Brody tugged his dad out of the room and out of my house with a tenacity I knew Jack would learn to dread in the years to come. I stayed put, cross-legged, staring down at the treasures the kid had left behind. I don't know how long I sat like that. When I looked up again, Latham was sitting in a chair, watching me.

The light had changed in the room, shifting the shadows into a new landscape.

"You've been gone a while," he said. "I was beginning to worry you wouldn't come back."

"You owe me ten bucks for poker—you're not getting out of it that easily," I said, with a shrug.

Yes, I see lost things—something which has always been a boon to my poker game, because every losing hand at the table stands out like neon Day-Glo for me. Not that I had ever mentioned this to anyone I ever played. Latham thinks his gift of talking with the dead gives him the edge, and even after all these years, he still thinks he can enlist them to tell him what the others are holding. Only, the dead don't care anymore what cards someone holds, and they're not terribly reliable about telling the truth. It depends, I suppose, on whether they valued truth when they were alive. My feeble attempt at humor failed to amuse or distract him. And if I knew my brother, he was fair to bursting with frustration and anger about now.

"You might as well yell and get it over with," I told him.

He put his coffee down and pointedly leaned forward, both elbows on his knees, like he wanted to jump up and stomp around but had thought better of it. "Are you *crazy?*" he asked. "I heard Brody tell Jack on the way out the door that you were going to help him find his mom."

"I am." I held up my hand before he pounced. "I've got to try."

He jumped up anyway and started pacing and muttering. Latham had a thing for muttering; I was never quite sure if it was to himself or if some ghost nearby was getting an earful. Somewhere in there, I made out, *Dammit I told him not to ask you* . . .

"Who?" I asked, and he stopped, brows knitted, confused. "Who'd you tell not to ask?"

"Jack, of course. He comes in here all blazes and glory and acts like he gives a damn and then—"

"He didn't ask me, Latham. Brody did." My brother paused mid-pace, shock in his eyes. Then grief.

No good can come of this his eyes said.

"You know I couldn't tell that kid *no*."

He stared out the window a bit then nodded. He wouldn't have been able to either, and we both knew it.

"Do you know where she is?"

I shook my head. "No clue. I didn't recognize the area in the painting."

"And now it's burned to a crisp." He cocked his head, worry warring with curiosity in his eyes. "I've never seen you do that—burn a painting. Not even the violent ones."

I'd had a few other moments of savagery burst out of me on canvas. I'd never enjoyed painting them, but they gave me no choice. They just took over, command performance, and I had learned to get rid of them as fast as I could. This time, though, Latham was right. This time was much, much worse.

"I've never seen me do that, either. Not sure where it came from."

We both knew he'd be confiscating the lighter later on tonight. I also knew he'd sleep at my house, so I didn't have to be moved. He'd probably spend the next hour or two hiding anything particularly combustible or dangerous. He'd pretend right now he wasn't going to worry, but we both knew it was a lie.

"So how are you going to find her?" he asked. "Usually, you either know, or you don't."

It was my turn to give him the evil eye; he held up both hands and began backing away.

"No, Avery."

"If we go to her house, we might learn something."

"No!"

"One of us might be able to sense something there. Either something that she lost or . . ." I left it at that.

"Absolutely not!" Latham threw up his hands, and began pacing again. "You're supposed to stay away from Jack. Don't you remember? This will just involve him more. Look what's happened to you with just one interaction! You had a nosebleed last night—oh, yeah, Jack told me all about that while you were *unconscious* from your seizure."

"So I'm grounded?" I stared at the ceiling to stifle a grin.

"Yes!" he shouted, as if this were the absolutely perfect solution he'd been looking for, and then he had to face the wall so he wouldn't laugh, in spite of how furious he was. He'd had exactly zero success in grounding me all those years ago when I was a teenager and lived with him. "Forever," he added, muffled, to the wall.

It was tearing him up, not being able to help me. I knew that. But it had been tearing him up no matter where I lived, so that part wasn't new.

Something else was, though, and I waited, hoping he'd tell me. When he didn't say anything after a long moment, I said, "Latham. Jack's kid asked me. I have to help; you know that."

We avoided each other's gaze, like magnets pushed apart. He stared out the window where storm clouds gathered like they had an agenda.

"Ah, dammit, Av. He's going to break your heart again."

I knew that. I just nodded. There was nothing more to say. Latham didn't even try; he just left.

After he was gone, I didn't have the energy to repack Brody's things into his bag. Instead, I slid them over and pulled the covers up as I wriggled back down and drifted off to sleep. It was only after I was warm and completely comfortable that I remembered I had forgotten to ask Latham about the snow and the red boots. He'd know if we'd gone on vacation somewhere in a snowstorm. He was seven years older than me; he'd remember snow.

Suddenly, my feet were freezing, and in spite of it being nearly eighty degrees at night in this little sauna of a town, I never quite warmed up again.

CHAPTER FOURTEEN

At 8 a.m. the next day, the heat was already so sweltering, it felt suicidal to choose to go outside. Dread crawled up my spine as I waited on the porch for Latham to arrive. He'd left early to make sure everything was going well on the job before he took the day off to help me.

I did not want to do this today. I closed my eyes as I leaned back in the rocker, and Brody's face loomed up from memory. Damned kid. Whatever anyone else thought of her, Marguerite was his mom, and I was going to be the one to deliver her, dead. I hated that. Hated it. But short of wandering around like a human Geiger counter, hoping to ping on someone's loss, I wasn't sure what else to do. Jack had hired a PI. Or had he? Would he lie about that? Nate had said there was nothing else the police could do, though he did plan to stop by and talk with me about what I'd seen, in the small hope that I'd remember something else about the image. All in all, the odds were not in my favor.

I shuddered, despite the heat. The dread I'd been feeling for the last hour scratched at the base of my skull, swamping me with adrenaline; my arms iced over with cold. I wanted to run, and had no clue why. Something dark brushed against my mind, something evil, reminding me of that night in the woods when Jack had come storming toward me, furious over Brody. I wanted to cry—though I never cry—and run. Dear God, I wanted to run and run and run and . . .

Latham pulled up just then, and I bounced up from the rocker as the dark blackness slowly receded from where it had touched my mind. I turned to set the alarm, and the sharp scent of piney woods mugged me, though the air was still as death. And when I spun back, I gasped.

Small snow flurries fell, creating small mounds of white on Latham's truck, coating the green grass and the daisies. Snow on the porch, beneath the roof where it couldn't have blown in, and on my palm, freezing pin-points of nothing. I looked up at the ceiling, almost expecting to see a hole through to the sky, but the porch roof was perfectly fine; the snow seemed to fall from it somehow, *soft soft soft*.

The ripe smell of roses filled the air, and I glanced down. At my feet, dead roses, broken apart. Bloody red petals, black with rot, spread out in the snow drifts and from far, far away, I heard Latham open the door to his truck, heard the creak of metal on metal as the old hinges protested, and heard his foot hit the gravel.

"Squirt?" he called, worry threading his voice, and when I looked up at him, the snow was gone. Triple-digit heat shimmered from the hood of his truck, and at my feet, there was only the decking of the porch. "You okay?"

Honestly, I didn't know. All my life, I'd seen images, but they were always distinctly separate from the world, like watching a pack of cards thrown in the air. Sometimes they rained down on me, biting into my mind, and other times, they brushed against me, but caused no real pain. Generally, after a seizure, my ability to see images would come slowly back online, and the pain stayed dull until I was back to normal. My version of normal, at least.

Never before had I seen things out in the world, overlapping reality so fully that if I hadn't known it was the dead middle of a Louisiana summer, I'd have believed it was winter and the middle of a snowstorm. I could still feel the crisp frigid air, still feel the light touch of the flakes on my skin. Latham's boots hit the steps, fast, and he grabbed my hands.

"Squirt?" he asked again, bending down to peer into my eyes and then, "Jesus, your hands are freezing. What happened?"

"I don't know," was all I could say, as he rubbed my arms to warm me. I worried that if I told him about the snow, he would refuse to take me to Marguerite's, and Brody would have to wait longer. I shuddered.

"We shouldn't do this today," he said.

I shook my head. "I have to." I knew bone-deep, I had to. I couldn't have any more turned away than chosen not to breathe.

A scowl creased Latham's face as he looked over my shoulder.

"No!" he said on an explosion of air, and I had the distinct feeling he wasn't talking to me. The sickly smell of rotting roses drifted up again for the briefest of moments, and then was gone. Were the roses, the snow, connected to him somehow?

"Is someone there?"

His gaze swiveled back to mine, and for the longest time, he simply watched me. He seemed paler—sicker, and thinner—than he had only the night before, as if pain were leeching the life out of him. I knew if I asked, he'd deny it, deny that whatever it was he saw, hurt him.

He shook his head. "No, Squirt. It's just us. Are you sure you're up to this? We can wait a day if you want."

"There's a little boy waiting for his mom to come home, Latham. I can't do that to him."

Valerie Romano, Marguerite's divorce attorney, stood outside the lakeside mansion as we drove up; she reminded me of a linebacker primed and set to sack the quarterback at any given moment. Broad shouldered with spiky, short blonde hair standing up every which way, like she didn't give a hoot what she looked like and wanted you to know it, she wore a basic navy suit with flat heels and kept the jewelry to almost nonexistent.

The house was grand, easily triple the size of the McMansions around it; built in a Greek revival style, both opulent and cold. Giant columns lined a porch the size of a promenade at a coliseum. Someone had gone to great expense to make the columns and the stucco look ancient, as if they hadn't been built a couple of years ago on this peninsula that jutted into one of the lakes near Louisiana State University. As I looked around at the wealth obvious in the neighborhood, it was a pretty good bet not a single professor at the state's top university could afford a driveway here, much less this house, which begged the question: How did Marguerite afford it?

Latham had driven, and he paused in the driveway, his pallor graying so suddenly that I flinched.

"What's wrong?"

"Nothing," he said, but his voice sounded muffled, like something you'd hear underwater. "Bad place. The lawyer's no picnic either."

"How so?" He was distracted enough that he answered.

"There are eight suicides hovering around her right now. Three murder victims. Probably what gave her those worry lines."

I gaped at him a second—it was the most he'd ever said about what he could see—but he didn't notice me. He was focused on Ms. Romano, and when I looked back, I realized he was right about the lines—they were as deeply grooved as a ditch.

"Is Marguerite one of them?"

He seemed to come back to himself then, and shook off whatever it was that had had him in its grip. "No. Let's get this over with, Squirt."

Nate had pulled up behind us, and Zannah climbed out of the passenger side of his official squad Jeep, an incongruous sight what with her spike heels and perfectly white dress.

"What's she doing here?" I whispered to Latham as Zannah daintily balanced on the balls of her feet and gingerly made her way up the irregular surface of the slate walkway. Halfway to us, she wobbled (purposefully, it seemed), so that Nate had to pause and put his hand on her elbow so she didn't fall.

"Polyformosia—aka, Peter—owns the house," Latham explained. He'd been on the phone with Nate in the insane predawn hours of the morning making arrangements, in spite of protesting the effort. "The company is willing to let us into the premises for a wellness check—and to see if you get any hits on something lost that will tell us where Marguerite is. We're not supposed to touch or open anything. Zannah's here to protect Poly's interest. Romano's here to protect Marguerite's."

Losses spilled off Romano, who stood at Marguerite's front door. My senses had apparently come back online sometime in the middle of the night, and the losses clawed at me: Lost cases, files, dreams. A charm, a lover named Judy, a missing tiara, which nearly undid my poker face—especially her loving image of herself wearing said tiara while wearing a spangly green boa and, well, nothing else.

"Ms. Broussard. Mr. Broussard," the attorney said as we reached the house, "You will now be considered in my employ. Sign this nondisclosure agreement."

So much for *hello* and *how are you*. Clearly, Romano had no intention of wasting oxygen on niceties. Latham had made all the arrangements with her the day before and briefed her as to what I could do, keeping it purposefully vague and relying on Romano's curiosity to get us in the door. Word had already leaked out of Nate's office about my intended visit to Marguerite's house, and so he had issued an official "no comment" statement to the press, which were already flocking to the area, parking their beaters along the exclusive street, and hauling cameras and tripods out, lining the sidewalks. We ignored the catcalls and whistles for our attention. There were only four of five bearing logos from Baton Rouge or New Orleans. Maybe it was the press that worried her, but Romano warned us that we would not be allowed to disclose anything we saw that might impact her client negatively—which, of course, begged the question as to what she had to be so protective about. I couldn't sense specific losses from her that were Marguerite-related, so maybe she was just being cautious.

We both read over the brief statement she handed us, signed the agreement, and had the papers whisked away by an assistant I hadn't noticed hovering behind the giant urns with the prickly firs as tall as the roofline. Zannah and Nate reached us, and Zannah's losses of time, clients, and Nate cartwheeled out of her; I gritted my teeth. Nate's losses of Jack, me, cases, and victims sliced into me, and I stepped a little away from them all, shoving in the earphones and dialing up the white noise on the iPod while Latham briefed Romano.

"She's still recovering from a bad day yesterday," he warned, "so we'd ask you all to try to think about positive things in your life right now. Things you love, things you cherish, good days, happy thoughts. It'll block some of the pain she feels and allow her to clear through any images she gets and pinpoint them to Marguerite's whereabouts."

"Pete's real worried," Zannah offered, her voice breathy and catching. She shot out images of her lost happiness with Peter, and mixed with it was an image of Peter and Marguerite together. Zannah sounded very concerned for Marguerite's well-being. Her acting skills went up in my estimation.

"This way," Romano said, and she marched us to the door. "Remember we have agreed you will disclose to me, and me alone, anything you discover. I will decide if it's anything the police need to know about. In your capacity as my consultants you will each be paid a dollar"—the assistant whipped out two checks for one dollar each—"and you will honor your employment contract. Should the state ever call you as a witness, I will act as your attorney. If you disclose anything here to anyone else without my express, written permission, you will be sued. Do we have an understanding?"

We both nodded. Just what, I wondered, had Marguerite been up to that her attorney felt the need to go to such lengths in the name of protecting her?

"Chief Barksdale," Romano continued, "will remain outside, but he'll be here if, for some reason, we need him."

The attorney's losses, most of them associated with Marguerite in distress—screaming fits, throwing things in Romano's office, crying jags—lashed out and sucker punched me. I held onto the door, hoping neither Latham nor Nate noticed. Latham's eyes narrowed on me, anger washing across his expression, then gone again. He knew I wouldn't leave. Not yet.

We followed Romano and Zannah inside.

If the exterior was grand, it paled in comparison to the interior. Exceedingly formal, the entrance was all about the bling—chandeliers that cost upwards of a hundred thousand dollars apiece, Venetian plaster, a marble staircase that wound thirty feet upward to a second floor, creating such an immense entryway I was afraid to speak, certain every syllable would echo.

The startled cry of a newcomer greeted us, and we spun to see a young woman, no more than eighteen or twenty, standing tentatively in an inner doorway, her body poised for flight.

"Ms. Romano?" she asked, wide blue eyes scanning the rest of us. "Have you heard anything? About Ms. Monroe?"

Images of Marguerite slid off her in small piles—a difficult boss, impossible requests, losses all. Then she glanced at Zannah, and her gaze skipped away, as she studied Latham's face, mesmerized. Or so she pretended; in actuality she was thinking of when she had stumbled across Zannah's husband, Peter, in Marguerite's arms, loss of her innocence that day, a loss for Zannah.

Romano shook her head. "Not yet, Natalie. Please meet Avery Broussard and her brother, Latham, as well as Zannah—"

"We've met," Zannah and Natalie finished together—Zannah with steel in her voice, Natalie with a blush on her baby face.

Romano turned to me. "Natalie is Marguerite's housekeeper and the babysitter for Brody." She turned to the young woman, marshaling every bit of courtroom authority, the kind of imposing tone that sent lame prosecutorial witnesses quivering from the stand. "Exactly what she's doing here, I have no idea."

"Oh, um. I was worried. Ms. Marguerite never has missed paying me, even when she's out of town, and she missed this week. I knew it wasn't her turn to have little Brody, but I thought she might have written the check and left it here on the counter. She does that sometimes. But she didn't, and she's not here." She shifted from foot to foot, like a first-grader scared to ask to go to the bathroom, and I knew before we left that Latham would make sure she was paid. Her gaze angled my direction and shifted away as soon as I caught her looking. Losses—her grandmother's wedding ring, her sister's favorite sweater, her dad's best coffee cup, and a flurry of other odds and ends shuffled by, including her virginity, and I flinched.

"Underneath a red dresser," I told her, and she furrowed her blonde brows. "Your grandmother's ring. There's a red dresser. The ring is underneath, against the wall. Kinda wedged beneath a green rug."

Recognition struck her face, lightning fast, as her eyes went wide enough to float her up to the ceiling. "Oh, wow. You're—you're—"

"Yes," I said. "Did Ms. Monroe mention where she was going?"

"Oh, no, ma'am." She almost genuflected, and I cringed at the *ma'am* and Latham's low chuckle. "She didn't say. I saw she was packing, and I asked—on account I didn't know if she was gonna need me or not. When she's out of town, she doesn't need me to clean. An' she said she was going on a quick trip, and she'd call. She also told me she'd have me paid regular, like, on Friday, but she didn't. I've been callin' her, and she doesn't answer."

"Was she going away with someone? Meeting someone?" It hurt Zannah that I asked, I think, but I couldn't rule her out as a killer, if Peter had intended to leave with Marguerite.

Romano gave me a sharp look. "Why on earth would you need to know that?" Romano knew anyone Marguerite had planned to meet would be suspect in her disappearance. Was Romano protecting Marguerite? Or someone else? "Just trying to get a feel for her," I answered, waggling my fingers, implying a bit of the *woo-woo* for effect and avoiding Latham's glance at my own dissembling. He knew more than he was telling, too, if his paled complexion was any indication. "I typically do this with the parents of a lost child, but it's not a good thing to do with the child of a lost parent, so that rules Brody out. Which means you'll have to do."

I held out a hand, faked a foggy expression, as if I was tuning in and seeing into the past or some such bullshit. Leila and Dad would be so proud. For the record, I *never* did this with parents, but Romano didn't know that. I either saw their children, or I didn't, and either way, it was going to be hell on them. They didn't need the theatrics. Romano did, though.

133

"I need to know if the reason I'm picking up a male's losses is because of someone who is usually here visiting, or if it's an intruder's."

Total BS, but Romano bought it. She clearly didn't like it, but she bought it. Natalie, meanwhile, was trying to make herself invisible, so she wouldn't have to answer anymore intimate questions about Marguerite's paramours in front of Zannah. Latham, however, had walked away from us, and he seemed grayer somehow. He kept his back to me as Romano answered.

"There was someone." Romano kept it vague, which suggested she knew who the someone was, and she was clearly torn. If Marguerite were in trouble, she wanted to help; if she wasn't, Romano didn't want me prying where I didn't belong. "I understand, however, that he's been out of town. If there has been foul play, I'm sure the police will look into it."

"Hmmm." Out of town was not exactly an alibi, since Marguerite was supposedly out of town also. If Romano was referring to Peter, Nate would have a lot of questions for Zannah in the near future. I turned in a circle, stretching my hands out; my eyes closed. "I'm sensing a serious problem. I need to see some of her personal things." I stopped and gave Romano my most honest, earnest expression. "If that would be okay?"

Luckily, Romano didn't notice Latham rolling his eyes behind her.

We wound through the house, and the deeper we went into Marguerite's personal space, the more disheveled it became: Designer outfits strewn recklessly across chairs; shoes that cost upwards of a thousand dollars tossed haphazardly wherever she'd last taken them off; and enough jewelry lying around to make a thief's mouth water. I half expected to see one of my parents hiding in the closet waiting for the coast to clear.

"Ms. Marguerite made me leave while she was packing," Natalie, who tagged along, told Romano. "Maybe I should clean up?"

"No—if there's been any sort of"—and she glanced at Natalie to see if she was steady enough to hear the supposition—"foul play, the police will need to go through her things. Do not touch anything."

Latham tensed, his eyes darting to the side once too often to be ignored; I could practically feel him paling as we walked. I elbowed him behind Romano's back, and mouthed *What's wrong?* but he didn't answer. Just shook his head and frowned at Romano's back, indicating he couldn't explain now.

The kitchen was bigger than my house—literally—all gleaming porcelain and stainless Italian ovens, with plenty of other high-end appliances hidden behind custom cabinet doors. I knew it was the current trend, but really, how confusing that must be. There were miles of granite, along with refrigerator drawers, warmer drawers, and dishwasher drawers. You could have gotten lost in the walk-in pantry.

Latham paused and leaned in the doorway. Romano didn't notice that he needed the wall for support, but I did. He gave me a grim, sick expression but shook his head at me; he was seeing a ghost, but not Marguerite.

"Did she actually cook much in here?" I asked the attorney to keep her attention on me. Marguerite struck me as a room-service kinda gal.

"It was my dream kitchen," Zannah said, and then startled like a fawn, obviously surprised that she had spoken out loud. She reached out to touch the granite, then thought better of it. "I helped Pete design this place when we were first married. It was right after you left, Avery, so you wouldn't have seen it. But Latham did a fabulous job."

I blinked, looked at my brother, who shrugged. The handiwork was amazing. Why wasn't he doing more of it?

"When did you move out?"

"Oh, a couple of years ago. Pete had always had his heart set on buying the old LaRoux plantation and had been after them to sell it for years. They finally did, and now we're stuck out there. I wanted Latham to come out and give me a price to remodel it, but he said he won't do a plantation."

She sounded brokenhearted, and had slid a sideways gaze at Latham, but if she was hoping to guilt him into her job, she was wasting her time. The LaRoux plantation didn't look like one—it wasn't like Tara in *Gone With the Wind*, all majestic and gleaming in the sun. It was pretty simple, as I recalled: a two-story house with a jumble of add-ons and hodgepodge redesigns over the years so it was now the Frankenstein's monster of plantation homes. It had also been the site of multiple slave murders, if the rumors held true, and Latham would have seen every one of the ghosts from that time, if he worked there. He looked sick just hearing her talk about it.

"If you could show us around," I told the attorney, "I sometimes get hits off personal objects. It helps if it's something she's used a lot, like a computer, or iPad, or the like." I smiled beatifically, and Romano frowned at me, her lawyerly skepticism increasing.

"If it comes to light that you had anything to do with my client having gone missing, Ms. Broussard, I will make sure you are prosecuted to the fullest extent of the law." She leaned over, her nose in my face. "I will bury you."

135

"I think you'll have to take a number. But no, I had nothing to do with Marguerite going missing. I promised her son I'd look for her, and I'm going to keep that promise."

She watched me a moment as if trying to decide if I actually had some ability to help, or if I was secretly there for some nefarious purpose. She did her best, but I'd worked with Hank McIver, a man so thoroughly distrusting, he probably had his own mother background checked before allowing her over for meals. Thanks to Hank, I'd learned how to conjure up an innocent expression my own grifter parents would have been proud to borrow, so much so that even Hank couldn't read me. Someone like Romano was a picnic to convince.

"Fine, Mr. McIver vouched for you. I'll show you around."

Crap. I hadn't expected her to call Hank. That meant he would either now suspect—or know—that I could see things again. He was going to want me back on the LPK case. *Dammit.* I may have managed to shoot myself in the foot with this attempt at helping Brody. I'd turned off my phone to walk the house, and now I dreaded turning it back on.

We toured the house long enough for me to learn a couple of things: For one, Marguerite Monroe was a woman who loved bling and felt entitled to it. She had a Titanic-sized closet—one of the adjacent bedrooms had been commandeered and converted—strewn with shoes and handbags and clothes, like a whirlwind had whipped through it. I saw her luggage in one corner, an expensive set; only the smallest carry-on seemed to be missing. It was difficult to tell what else was gone.

Her office made clear what her priorities were: She had a stellar filing system, everything color-coded, annotated, very OCD. I was impressed. Her desktop was the latest Mac with a gargantuan monitor. The only thing amiss in the room was the closet door, and a quick glance from across the room indicated it was filled with neat, blue, silk-covered storage boxes, all with labels printed in a calligraphy font.

I strolled closer and nudged the door open a little more with the toe of my shoe and froze: the boxes were labeled things like *Senator Thibodaux—Corporate Papers, Senator Thibodaux—Supporter Files, Senator Thibodaux—Laws Introduced and Failed, Senator Thibodaux—Laws Passed, Senator Thibodaux—Contacts, Briefs, & Miscellany.*

I don't know how long I stared at that wall of blue, the screaming in my head splitting me in half—half of me here in the now, half of me back in the Senator's office, twenty years old, never as young as Natalie, not even as a child, understanding just how the Senator meant to destroy me and everyone I loved, simply because he wanted a young woman with a fancy pedigree to marry his son, to carry on the political Thibodaux legacy. He had lived in denial so long he believed he could make Jack bow to his will. Either that, or he planned to blackmail his son—the same way he had tried that night to blackmail me.

Was the infamous file I had seen back then, the one with the Senator's corruptions mentioned . . . here? In one of these boxes? I reached out, forgetting everyone around me, until Romano stepped in my path and nudged the door of the closet closed with one toe of her very practical pump.

I had the sense to shrug, turn away from Romano, and caught Latham as he slumped and braced himself against the wall. His eyes closed, and I could see his hands were shaking. Mine were, too, but for entirely different reasons, I suspected.

"Do you see anything that gives you a read?" Zannah asked, snapping me back to the matter at hand.

"Not yet. Nothing specific. Weird vibes, though."

On Marguerite's desk, there was a dock for the laptop, but the computer itself was gone. There was a slightly crumpled boarding pass in the trash from a commercial flight—the kind where, when you print it, the stupid advertisements for car rentals and hotels print out with it. She must have printed it, realized she'd printed the ads, then reprinted it again without the ads. I wanted to pull it out and open it to see the destination, but I knew Romano would stop me.

"Zannah, didn't Marguerite book a flight through your agency?"

Zannah, who stood in the center of the room, arms crossed, very much the princess awaiting her entourage, sighed.

"Yes, for the umpteenth time, yes. I already told that to Ms. Romano, and the Baton Rouge police, as well as Nate, of course. We have a charter service—Polyformosia shares a small jet with a couple of other enterprises. Pete didn't know about the flight—Marguerite said it was company business, but she was going to pay for it herself because she had some personal stuff to tend to as well. She said she was going to New York, but she had the pilot stop over in Atlanta. She told him to come back in two days to pick her up, but she didn't show. Nobody knows why she went to Atlanta, though. According to Pete, Polyformosia has no interests there. He seemed pretty steamed, actually, that she took off with a big bill pending in the legislature that we didn't want passed; it's Marguerite's job to stop it. She's not here to do that, though, and I think the vote is tomorrow."

The cascade of losses from Zannah all tuned to the same channel: everything she'd given up by marrying Peter—a man who hadn't been faithful, who clearly hadn't made her happy, even though she'd been the beautiful trophy wife that all of the nerdiest of nerds prayed for, and goodness knows Peter was king of the nerds. Truth was, all she'd ever wanted was Nate, kids, and a little house in the country. It was odd, seeing her standing there, glittering with diamonds and wrapped in Chanel, knowing what she actually longed for and knew she'd lost forever was the chance to have a little house in a middle-class neighborhood, where neighbors shared recipes and gathered for barbecues. I forced myself away from her losses, and wondered instead why Marguerite had printed out a ticket from an online booking site if Zannah had booked her on a chartered plane that could have taken her wherever she wanted to go. *What were you up to, Marguerite?*

"Anything?" Romano asked, and for the first time, I realized she was afraid. Images seeped off her.

I nodded, and then tilted my head toward Marguerite's desktop. "Do you know her passwords?"

"No. What do you see?"

I told her the truth. "I think she's dead, Ms. Romano. I see her looking up, blood running into her eyes. I just can't see where she is."

Natalie started sobbing in the corner, Zannah gasped, and Romano sagged against Marguerite's desk, jostling the computer, which popped on. Across the screen spread a collage of photos.

They were of me, Jack, Jack's father, Nate, Chris, Sam, Latham, and headlines of the Senator's suicide. She'd created a visual storyboard of the Senator's death, everyone involved, and had drawn lines and circled things I couldn't see, because Romano had seen them, too, and had stepped in front of the screen.

"I think we're done here," Romano said, suspicion crusting each syllable in flash-frozen regret that she'd allowed me inside the house at all.

Outside as we split off to our respective vehicles, Zannah paused, blocking Latham and me from our car. Behind her, I could see Nate on his police radio; Zannah leaned forward, reaching out as if to grab my arm, but Latham gently counter blocked her.

"You don't even want him," Zannah said, heartache rippling off her, and it took me a moment to realize she meant Nate. "Avery, please just tell him that, okay? Let him go. Let him heal and move on? He's never going to give up on you until you do." Tears gleamed in her eyes. "That's just cruel, Avery, and you've never been cruel." She spun, then, and walked toward Nate.

As Latham and I climbed in the truck to leave, my brother asked, "Why'd you let her get away with that? It's none of her business what Nate feels for you."

"And that's why I did. Nate and I know where we stand. We're okay. That's never going to satisfy Zannah, because she thinks if I wasn't in the picture, Nate would have saved her from her bad marriage."

"In other words, she's delusional, and you're protecting Nate."

I shrugged and looked away. What Nate and I had was something beyond friendship, nearly as close as what I had with Latham.

"Get anything on Marguerite in there?" Latham asked, changing the subject.

I shook my head and fought the nausea, clamping my teeth tight and staring out the window. I had never liked Marguerite—not since the day I met her. When she started working for the Senator, she'd been all charm school and polish, sheathing a razor-sharp mind and a cruel streak. Early on, I noticed how she lit up whenever she saw Jack. I would have felt awkward if I hadn't been able to see all of her losses, even then: parents (car crash), family home (no insurance), lost dates, lost opportunities (scholarship money didn't get you into the clubs you needed to join for the best networking). She wasn't a good person. She could be cutthroat in her job, and she made a better lobbyist than a mom, but I do think she loved Brody. She didn't deserve this. And Brody surely didn't deserve to lose his mom.

Someone was responsible. And I had to find out who, if only for Brody. He didn't know it now, but he was going to need whatever closure that could bring him.

"You?" I asked him. "You saw someone. Was it Marguerite?"

"No. And I don't want to talk about it."

Usually I'd have argued with Latham, except he actually looked worse than when we were inside, and I hadn't thought then he could look worse.

We rode in silence for a few minutes, and I drifted back to Marguerite's whereabouts and what she might've been up to.

"I wonder what Jack's PI has found out?"

"Dammit, Avery!" he snarled, and I jumped as he slammed the palm of his hand on the steering wheel. I hadn't meant to say that out loud.

"Get real! The man's a walking time bomb, and you're his next target. You can't hide the truth from him forever. And you'll die because you're too damned stubborn to leave. You need to be as far away from here as possible."

Absolutely true, but I couldn't leave. I was pretty sure, just by looking at him in that moment, that my dad had been telling the truth—Latham was going to die, if I didn't do something. I was beginning to suspect that it was the ghosts creating the problem, which meant there wasn't anyone else on the planet he could turn to for help. If only I had a clue as to what to do for him, or at least how to get him to talk to me about it.

"I can't take it, knowing you're putting yourself in danger, Squirt. Marguerite's dead. You saw the computer screen. She was after Jack. It's a pretty easy guess as to what he would do if he found out she was going to drag him and his dad back into the limelight."

We stopped at a red light, and a chill ran through me, a horrible sense of oiliness and dread, of cold evil; I sat up and looked around us. There were several cars in both lanes, and I felt a trickle of images flowing from each car, but nothing like the horrible, icy bleakness that had slicked its way into my gut. I thought I might throw up.

"I'm sorry if it bothers you, but you know I'm right. You know this. You need to leave town."

I shook my head. I couldn't have spoken then to save my life anyway. There had been one other time I had felt this way. It was while I was helping Hank and we thought we'd cornered the Little Princess Killer.

I shivered, grateful I'd be staying at Latham's that evening.

CHAPTER FIFTEEN

We drove in silence for the next forty-five minutes; a wreck between two eighteen-wheelers exiting one of the chemical plants had clogged Highway 30. I closed my eyes, my head against the window. Mentally, I walked back through Marguerite's house, pulling up the images of the Senator's files, wondering: Had she used something in those files to blackmail someone? Had she exposed some buried secret that could have triggered a violent reaction from Jack or maybe someone else? I tried again to get a lock on where Marguerite's body in my image might be found from the fleeting impressions I'd felt in the house, but I got nothing.

Flitting dagger-like between those thoughts was the image of Brody and what this knowledge about his mother might do to him. I fought back a rising tide of dread. I couldn't go there. Not now. I wasn't entirely sure I'd survive it. No good could come of dwelling on negative possibilities, and I tried to shift my focus to a safer subject.

"Did we ever live somewhere where there was snow?" I asked Latham.

"Maybe," he said, a tad too carefully.

What did he have to be careful about? "We either did, or we didn't. Snow would be hard to forget, especially after living here, in this heat."

"Then you don't need to ask me."

"I mean from before," I said. He knew so many of those early years were a blank for me.

"I don't remember much either, Av. We moved around a lot. The folks weren't as good at the cons back then, and we lived in shacks, camps, whatever they could find. There wasn't a lot of food."

He spared me a glance. "I was focused on us—you and me—surviving. Everything else is a blur."

He was lying. *Why?* Who was this Latham who'd ramped up the drinking, saw dead girls in the middle of the night and suicides by day, looked a little sicker every time I saw him, and was now lying to me. That it was all connected, I had no doubt but connected to what? And why *now?* He'd been going downhill before I moved back, if Dad was to be believed, so it wasn't my proximity. But eliminating that left me with no better clues.

"So basically, you're not going to tell me."

He shrugged. "Nothing to tell."

I wanted to smack him, but knew it would get me exactly nowhere. So we rode in silence. A calm settled between us like it used to—each locked in our own private hell, but a hell that only the two of us would ever understand. We stayed that way, prison mates, until we bumped across the entry to my driveway, and Latham suddenly slammed on his brakes and swore.

Some days are dainty and graceful, and they whisper into your life with soft-footed pirouettes and eager smiles, hoping to please you. Those are the days you save in your scrapbook with bits and pieces of your heart—a train ticket home, the ribbon that held your first flowers from a boy. Some days, on the other hand, are like a pipe to the skull, a thief bent on rendering you helpless while they rifle your pockets and steal your soul.

Leila, with her bright orange hair like a perpetual gas flame, was standing on my front porch. I could practically feel the lead pipe whizzing through the air. Beside me, Latham cursed and slammed the truck in reverse.

"We're going to my house. They won't bother you there, and I'll come back for your painting supplies and clothes."

I whirled and faced him. "No! I need to talk to Dad."

Wherever Leila was, Dad was never far behind. He hadn't been taking my phone calls—my efforts to figure out how I was supposed to save my brother and from what—yet now he'd taken time to show up here?

"No, you don't," Latham growled as he put the truck in gear.

I hopped out my side of the pickup before he could take off. I heard him cursing as I approached Leila. I had sometimes wondered why she chose that particular name, but then there had been a lot of first names through the years. At least she'd finally settled on one I could remember. "Where's Dad?" I asked.

"Where have you been?" Leila demanded, her shoulders drawn up, trying to make herself look taller, all five-foot-even of her. Her hands lay fisted on razor-thin hips, making it all the more obvious she was barely more than a wisp of skin and bones loosely held together by a low-cut, yellow mini-dress that would have made a hooker feel overexposed. "We could be making a fortune, Avery Marie. I expected more of you. Why would you help the FBI but not your own family?"

And bam, it began. She'd been calling me for months, always with the same complaint. I'd gotten to the point of forcing her calls to voice mail. And since I'd met Leila before, well, let's just say I knew, without going to look and without using my ability, that the five bucks I'd found in my jeans before washing them a few days ago—the five-dollar bill I'd shoved in a kitchen drawer underneath the old flashlight with no bulb and the pair of rusted gardening shears—was now comfortably residing in her purse. Or bra. Or whatever pocket she'd had hand at the time.

"Maybe because what you want to use it for is illegal?"

"Bunk," she snorted, her sharp green eyes glaring at me over the rims of her bright pink tortoiseshell spectacles.

She adopted this *I'm an eccentric, take no never mind, move along* persona whenever she was in Saint Michael's. In such a quiet little town, my mother had the soul and finesse of a carnival barker, playing to the crowd in the line for confession at church or while not so quietly buying my first box of tampons at the grocery. In other cities, she wined and dined with the elite, rubbed elbows with diplomats (picking their pockets without them ever having a clue), or faded into the background, a poor, suffering doormat of a housewife—whatever suited her objective best. The entire world was Leila's stage, and I remember being drop-jawed shocked the first time I saw her in action as a sophisticate, complete with auburn hair, killer heels, and diamond bracelets. She never once broke character. I had giggled as she darling'ed me in public. She covered by telling everyone I was a little slow, forcing me to pretend to have disabilities every time she and Dad pulled that shtick in that particular community.

Leila stomped her foot. "Don't you lie to your mamma, Avery Marie. I'll keep quiet about your YouTube seizure not being real. All those acting lessons we gave you finally paid off. I'm glad to see you coming to your senses," she said, edging toward me like a bright yellow beetle, "but it's time you remembered you owe this family. I'm gettin' too old to keep havin' to go on the road."

"That seizure was real, and I did lose my abilities."

Even as I said it, I knew I was wasting my breath; Leila knew too much about my seizures and their repercussions to believe the lie I'd told the world. She knew I'd be offline (her description) for a few days afterward, and then back to work within a week, just like when I was a kid.

I was also not surprised she hadn't tattled on me to the press—it was potentially much more profitable for her if I could be blackmailed into helping her and Dad in their cons. She knew I didn't want the limelight—something she'd never understood. I still remember her trying to pitch Dad on the idea of submitting footage of me for a reality TV show when I was a teenager—under a different set of names, of course, and with stage makeup to hide my scars. Dad, at least, had had a keen sense of self-preservation and had shut that ridiculous idea down immediately, something for which I'm pretty sure Leila still hadn't quite forgiven me. It never crossed her mind that someone from another city might recognize us, or her, in particular, from one of our old cons, much less the price we would pay if someone did.

At some point, I'd tried to step back and be objective about my parents, about what made them tick, looking beneath the obvious for their humanity. Despite years of looking, I had yet to find even a flicker of a soul.

"I have this client," Leila said with all of the sly discretion of a flasher in the park, "in Omaha, who's lost a small fortune in—"

"Stop right there. The FBI knows I'm back *on* again. It's common knowledge in town. I imagine I'm about to be outed to the world. That means, reporters."

My parents had never been overly worried about their aliases passing legal perusal; whoever did their paperwork and inserted it into whatever national databases it needed to be inserted in to make it look like those personas had always existed was damned good, because my parents had never thought twice about sailing into waters requiring the kind of background checks that would have made a diplomat nervous. No telling who my dad had coerced into that little bit of legerdemain. But up close and personal with the FBI? Answering questions? Leila drew away from me the way fourth-graders scurry away from a classmate with cooties.

"I could introduce you to them if you like, *Mom*," I said, smiling sweetly.

"There's no need to go gettin' nasty, Avery Marie."

"Where's Dad?" I asked again, moving past her. Latham wasn't going to wait much longer in that truck. I had things to ask Dad that I needed to ask quickly before Dad used Latham's presence to clam up.

"Leave him be, Avery Marie. He's tired, and he's just in there taking a little nap."

I gawked at her. "You're kidding, right?"

"Don't use that uppity tone with me, young lady. I'm still your mother."

"You expect me to believe that y'all drove all the way over here and broke into my house just so Dad could take a nap?" Then I realized there was no car in the drive.

"You left your gate unlocked, which frankly, Avery Marie, was disappointing. Have you learned nothing? Locks won't do you much good with reporters if you don't use them."

We all knew locks didn't keep determined criminals out—especially not the ones with my parents' skill set. If Dad had picked the lock, Leila would have been quick to insult me for having bought something so inferior; since I knew Latham had put a top-of-the-line lock on the front door and she wasn't insulting it, it must've actually been opened when they arrived. I knew we'd locked it before we left. *Hadn't we?*

Dad ambled out my front door as if he'd been doing it for the past twenty years and saw nothing out of the ordinary about it. When he dressed the part, Dad has the look of an elder statesman actor, someone who'd have starred in fabulous old black-and-white movies and have all the girls swooning. His hair had gone silver long ago (well, silver in the cities where he didn't dye it), and when he dressed in a suit, he reminded me of Gregory Peck in *To Kill a Mockingbird*. I think he'd even used the name Gregory Peck for a con or two. Dad loved irony.

Now, though, he looked hunch-shouldered, his sweater buttoned askew, his glasses magnifying his eyes four times larger than normal, giving him the confused, bumbling professor air that he tended to use in Saint Michael's— quite a foil to Leila's over-the-top hussy persona. He patted his pockets as if he'd forgotten something and scratched his head, deep in thought. Damn, my parents had missed their calling. Oh, wait. No, they didn't.

"You can cut the act, Dad. No one's here but me and Latham."

Dad peered over his glasses, mostly to confirm I was telling the truth, and then he straightened up, shoulders back, gaining another six inches in

145

height in the process. For a moment, I saw what Latham would look like when he got older. If he were to get older. I barreled up onto the porch, brushing past Leila before either of them had a chance to launch into whatever con they were there to pitch, grabbing his arm, and pulling him close.

"You're going to tell me what's up with Latham, Dad. Or I'm going to out you to the world."

He pulled off his glasses, pretending to clean them as he stalled. My dad has 20/20 vision, if not better.

I clamped down on his arm, harder. "I'm not kidding. Spill."

"It's not that simple, Daughter."

He had a tendency to never call me by name. Sometimes I wasn't entirely sure he remembered what it was, since he and Leila changed theirs and mine so often.

"Anything I tell you could backfire," he said.

"You know, I used to believe that, but that's just a little too convenient an excuse, isn't it?"

If I hadn't been watching for it, I'd have missed the spark of, well, pride, in his eyes, for me pinging to the con, but it was gone in a half a heartbeat, so fast I couldn't swear it had been there at all.

"Well," he said, putting the handkerchief away, "the only way to prove I'm wrong is to tempt fate. I did that once, and it had such a horrific outcome, I've never allowed myself to do it again." Then he looked at me, giving me his full attention for once, and said, "I've shared with you as much as I can, without outright risking everything. Your choice, though. You want to risk it with your brother's life in the balance? Go ahead."

The man was good. I'll give him that.

While I floundered with how to respond, Sam drove up and parked. Latham climbed out of his truck and the two of them met in the middle of the drive, conferring.

Sam headed for the barn, and Latham, for the porch, obviously tired of waiting for our powwow to end. To me, he said, "They disabled the cameras and somehow bypassed the alerts when they entered the grounds. I've changed the passwords, and scrolled through all of this morning's footage."

Ah, so that's why he'd stayed in the truck.

"They missed the outer cameras."

He turned to our parents. "It's not like you to be sloppy, so either you were proving a point, or you're messing with us for some reason." Latham held out his hand and waited until Dad reluctantly pulled some sort of computer gizmo from his pocket and handed it to Latham, who turned it over and frowned. "Pretty sophisticated jammer, Dad." Then he looked up at them. "If you put her in danger again, I will end you. We clear?"

Dad smiled his big movie-star grin, and patted Latham on the shoulder, resting his hand there proudly, like Latham had done exactly what he'd hoped he would do. "See, Darling," he said, addressing Leila without glancing her direction, "I told you she was safe here."

"Humph," Leila muttered. "We got past it, and you're gettin' rusty." She looked at Latham. "You need to upgrade to the—"

"I'll handle it," Latham said, stopping Leila cold.

Latham had stiffened and paled at the brief contact with our dad. Dad dropped his hand.

"You'd better see that you do," Leila snapped, almost as if she cared, which raised the hair on the back of my neck.

All three of them just stood there staring at each other, the silence screaming all around me.

"What?" I asked.

"Nothing," Latham said, finally, and then turned to me. "I have a security-expert friend on his way here from Baton Rouge to see what we can do so that this doesn't happen again from the likes of them, or anyone else. Meanwhile, Sam is going to check the barn, the house, and the entire perimeter, so wait here 'til he gives you the all clear. He'll stay until Nate arrives for your meeting."

I wasn't about to protest. The alarm had been off that long? God only knows who had been prowling around. I've had reporters show up in disguises, paparazzi jump out of trash cans, and people who were desperate to find things climb out from under cars to waylay me. If I had to pick someone to scare everyone off though, it'd be Sam.

"Time for you to leave," Latham told our parents, who shrugged and smiled as if he'd just thanked them for dropping by.

"I want you to think about Omaha," Leila said airily, as if that was still a remote possibility.

Some days, I truly felt like I needed to reintroduce myself to these two. "How did y'all get here, by the way?"

"A friend dropped us off," Leila answered, not looking at any one of us in particular. "We wanted to check on you."

"You wanted me to help the client in Omaha, Leila." I said with a sigh, knowing I would never get the truth out of either of them. Somewhere inside of me, there was a seven-year-old who was still trying, though.

"Never going to happen," Latham told Leila, his voice like a hatchet in the hot summer air, slicing off the rest of her plea. He pointed to his truck. "Now."

My parents sidled his way without actually agreeing. I was never sure what power Latham had over them; whatever it was, it was strong. He could give them a look, a simple *you know what I'll do if you don't cooperate stare*, and like two recalcitrant teenagers, they'd bow their heads in mock guilt and do whatever it was he asked.

Ticked me off that I didn't have that knowledge. Anytime I'd ask him about it, he'd just say, "I'm a lot older than you, Squirt. Just leave it at that."

Some days, being the youngest sibling sucked. When I had once pointed that out to him, Latham had squinted his eyes closed and hugged me tight, resting his chin on my head. Later when he didn't think I was watching, I caught him wiping away tears. I never mentioned it again.

I would never understand my family, and I wondered, then, if anyone ever really does.

I also had to give it to Latham—he'd managed to give me private time with our parents and still blocked them from destroying my heart and my home.

The debts just kept piling up.

CHAPTER SIXTEEN

It was funny how the word *home* had begun to slide off my tongue so quickly sometimes, like a runner hurtling into a stolen base, rushing head-long to grab purchase of that small square of real estate before being declared out of the inning. I had spent so many years running away from home that it felt like cheating to have rounded third and to be back here and using such a word so casually.

I didn't belong here. I knew that. I felt that.

I kept waiting for the umpire to throw me out on that technicality.

Latham's truck had disappeared down the drive when I heard Pan snort from the small corral near the barn. As rough as yesterday had been, I had failed to give her enough attention, though I knew Latham had tended to her basic needs. Still, the Diva was a prickly pear, even when I did fawn over her. I needed to hire someone to help me with her, especially if I kept having seizures. Pan wasn't a bicycle I could lean against a wall and come back to later, rain or shine.

Sam came out of the barn and noticed me heading that way.

"All clear, Brat."

I grinned. If Sam was back to calling me names, he wasn't as pissed off as he'd been the last time I saw him. He might look like a mobster's idea of an enforcer, but in truth Sam was a big marshmallow; he couldn't get a solid grip on a grudge to save his life. He tipped his head toward the house.

"I'm going to walk around, check the perimeter, and then give the inside a look. Latham said he could not see anyone in there on the footage, but I'll double-check."

"Thank you!" I called after him as he headed off with a little wave, without looking back.

The smells of warm hay and oats, old wood and leather hugged me as soon as I entered the tiny barn. I loved the feel of the rough-hewn wood of the stall against my hand, the fresh-cut-grass fragrance when I broke open a new bale and spread clean straw on the stall floor, the way the sun melted through the upper windows like a benediction. I still remembered laughing, though, when the realtor had called it a barn. It was a glorified shed, barely laced together by mold and peeling paint. Still, if anything were to smell like I had wanted childhood to smell like, it would be this place. Safe. Warm. Inviting. The fictional world of little girl dreams.

When you're a kid, there are things you never understand about your family. You think what you have is normal. The summer I was eleven—when I'd had the temerity to outgrow the cabinet in the RV—was the first summer we didn't go on vacation anywhere. When I asked why, Dad only said we were "between plans"—which, I realized later, meant he hadn't quite figured out what con they would run now that I wasn't able to participate the same way I had before. The way Leila had complained, you'd have thought she'd never heard of the concept of kids growing up. It baffled me, the armed truce we seemed to have in our home; Leila was so unhappy with me, I took to tracking down Dad in his workshop, a mysterious place, full of tools and oddball sculptures made of found items.

Dad would never answer direct questions, like "What are you making?" or "Are you gonna sell it?" But whatever his creations weren't, they were most certainly imaginative and bizarre and swiftly shipped off to some gallery to be sold overseas. I remember being impressed with their popularity. It wasn't until years later that I realized that many of the items I had seen as *lost*—and had mentioned to my parents during one of their client sessions—had never actually been returned to their clients, but rather had mysteriously appeared as a part of an art piece that my dad then sold abroad. Especially jewels—Dad once mixed real diamonds in with cubic zirconia and plastered them all over a Picasso-esque dog sculpture he'd made. It was hideous. It also sold for more than a million dollars I found out later. Nice way to fence stolen goods. *Finders keepers.*

When it became obvious that he couldn't bore me out of his workshop, Dad had kept me out of his hair by teaching me the fine art of lock picking, and once I could break into most anything, he channeled his not-so-inner Fagin into helping me hone my pickpocketing skills. He would place a wallet in a suit hung from one of Leila's dress dummies until I could lift it without knocking the precariously balanced egg off of the dummy's shoulder. Since I had to clean up the egg, I learned fast. I liked it much better than five-fingering images.

It wasn't long before I had progressed beyond the single-egg phase. Dad added a second egg and fined me a quarter for every one I broke. I'd perfected even that, when Latham came by early from work one day. He was eighteen and had his own place, a tiny apartment he'd sublet over Meryl's Diner. Latham had taken a job with a small construction company instead of going to college, and I didn't get to see him much anymore. I had just high-fived Dad when Latham walked in. Even then, young as I was, I understood his puzzlement—seeing Dad engaged, much less animated, was a singularly unusual sight. That, alone, made it a special victory for me.

Latham did that half-smile thing, where his mouth cooperates, but his eyes are wary. "What are we celebrating?"

"Watch!" I exclaimed, and I reset the wallet in the innermost pocket of the jacket, both eggs, and then stepped a few feet away. "See, they're walking along, and they think I'm just this silly kid," I did a sort of twirling dance step—something to distract the mark, Dad had said—and *nimble nimble quick* had the wallet in my hands with no eggs disturbed as I turned to high-five Latham.

He stood frozen with the most inscrutable look on his face as he looked at Dad.

"Latham?"

Dad's face had smoothed out, plain brown wrapping covering the momentary pride he'd beamed just moments before.

I wasn't sure what I was more frantic about, Dad's reaction or Latham's.

"It's okay," I told my brother, "it's just for fun."

Latham tore his gaze off Dad, and blinked at me for a few seconds.

"And how are you going to feel, Squirt, if the people ever realize they've lost something important?"

"She would've been fine," Dad said, turning back to his workbench. "Nobody has radar like she does."

"I'm not gonna use it on somebody real," I told Latham, trying not to look at Dad or feel his disappointment in my protest. Latham knew the images of loss coming off anyone after I had stolen from them would break my heart, but I didn't want to let go of Dad's pride. "And I'm good at it!"

Latham put his big hand on my head to stop me from bouncing on my toes. "You're good at a lot of things, Squirt. You should hear that more often. Go pack. We'll come back and get your bed and stuff later."

"What?" It was sometimes hard to keep up with the non-conversations my family had. I hadn't realized I was moving.

"Clothes, books. Your paints."

"But," I glanced over at Dad, who'd turned his back on us, "you only have one bedroom. Where will I sleep?"

"I like the couch a lot better. You'll get the bedroom."

As much as I loved Latham, my heart choked. I desperately wanted Dad to turn around and say, "No, she's staying here." I would have crawled in any cabinet Leila could design. I'd have pickpocketed God, if they'd asked.

Dad didn't even protest, just put on his welding helmet and fired up his cutting torch. In seconds, he was hard at work splicing two former chair frames into some grotesque shape for his next sculpture. The roar of the torch echoed through my body.

"If you hurry," Latham said, guiding me out, "we can go pick out a color to paint your new bedroom. I think we could get it all done over the weekend."

I ended up painting a mural of the woods, the way I see them, on the walls. If it disturbed Latham to have a room that felt alive, he never said.

Pan shifted beside me, and I suddenly realized the sun now slanted into the barn from a different angle, having gone from the buttery white of mid-morning to the blinding neon sear of noon. I'd lost at least an hour, standing there. No telling how long I'd been petting Pan but she was now entirely unhappy with the stunning lack of apples accompanying those pats, and she huffed her disapproval. I led her back into her stall and began to work the curry brush over her; she seemed to sigh, and finally settle, happy at last that she was being properly groomed. Maybe Latham had been right about Pan. I wasn't ready to concede that just yet, but the ritual had become a comfort to us both in the short time I'd had her. I let my thoughts float for a while until one bumped up against violent darkness creeping in from someone nearby, something oily and slick and filled with an anger so old, so deep, I couldn't identify it. There were images, this time, something I hadn't been able to see the last time in the woods when I'd found Brody, or at the house or even in the traffic the other day; they were oddly familiar. Dim, so smoky I could barely make out the shape of a girl. Four or five years old, maybe, and she looked like . . . *Me.*

The sickly sweet smell of rotting roses curled up around me. Pan picked up on my panic and moved to put herself between me and the stall door. The images of a younger me changed, and now I was wearing a threadbare winter coat, one I didn't recall having. I gagged on the smell of the dead roses . . .

. . . and the bombardment slid *away, away, away* until new losses sifted in. I felt Jack before I saw him, felt the drumming of his losses, and wondered if the others had been his, too, just buried so deep, I hadn't known them before. He moved as quiet as a secret through the barn, like every step was navigating enemy territory. Maybe it was. He didn't bother with a hello; he just eased me aside as he took the curry brush; from the way Pan practically stretched with glee, it was clear with each pass he knew what he was doing far better than I, and I was too tired to argue that I should be doing the job. I should have told him then about those other images. I should have asked, at least.

"Where's Sam?" I wasn't feeling any of our old friend's losses, and couldn't really pinpoint when that had stopped.

"He left when I got here—said you'd been daydreaming out here, and he didn't want to interrupt." Jack glanced at me, grief written all over him. "You look tired, Av. I've got this."

"I'm fine. You don't need to stay. Nate's on his way over, I think. Or Latham is."

"Latham needed to go buy an encrypted router," Jack said, "and Nate had an emergency callout and called me. I hope you don't mind. I think we have a few things to talk about."

Latham was going to have kittens over this. Jack wasn't going to leave until he had his say, though, that much was clear from the frustration rippling off him.

"You didn't bring Brody, did you?" I'd had enough of the kid for a lifetime. The last thing I needed today was to be reminded of just how much the little rugrat looked like Jack, and how the boy was counting on me to find his mom. He was going to hate me, once he got the answer. And it was going to kill me to give it to him.

"He's with Gail, playing with his cousins." Jack's words were terse. He'd had time to think about last night, about me kicking him out. He'd almost always taken his time about getting angry in the past, like he needed to study the location on a map and case it before launching an attack. He was careful that way in a way that people hadn't been careful with him. Once fully staked out, though, he did his anger justice.

"You shouldn't be out here," he said, still talking as much to the curry brush as to me. "You're supposed to be resting—this morning can't have helped."

He knew where Latham and I had gone.

I imagine all of Saint Michael's knew by now.

"I have things to take care of here."

"Then, dammit, ask for help."

He let that sit there a while between us, festering. Pan shifted her weight as he moved to her other side and finished the job, put down the brush, and ran his big hands over her, easing her away from where I stood so that she didn't trample me. I'd seen him do this as we grew up—he'd practically lived in his family's stables. It had started off as a maneuver to escape the Senator, and turned into something he loved, marrow deep.

Jack picked up the hoof pick and pulled Pan's foreleg up smoothly, like he and Pan had been long acquainted, and she wouldn't dare think to nip him the way she tried to do me when I cleaned her hooves. She nuzzled him with affection and relaxed, the traitor. Jack, though, seemed barely tethered, at the end of his control, and he breathed in deep, hanging onto his calm by shreds of honor or, maybe, of hope. Hope beneath a long, slow, simmering anger, one brought to a nice boil after last night.

"You don't always have to do everything alone."

"I'm fine, Jack." I tried not to lean too obviously on the stall wall. The morning at Marguerite's had in fact worn me out, but I couldn't tell him that, much less why, not with the nondisclosure I'd signed. Leila showing up had nearly finished me off. I was still wrung out from the seizure, from the day before. "I don't need any help."

"Right." He stood and moved to another hoof, edging me back a little to give him room. "That explains why I found you in the throes of a seizure yesterday. But God help you, far be it for you to ask for anything from any-one, because you're fine."

Jack dropped Pan's hoof and threw the hoof pick on *fine*, startling Pan, who flinched and nearly sidestepped onto me. He shushed her again and then turned away from me, facing the stall wall, and I could see him fight-ing that anger; I could also see the losses pouring off him in a tsunami, the times we'd been together, the stolen nights when he was on leave, making love under the moonlight.

He'd enlisted the day he'd turned eighteen to get away from the Senator. Two years of Superman School—going through basic first, and then the PJ training, and then deployment, and I hadn't seen him much. I'd grown up in those years. Gone off to college and home in the summers to work with Latham. When Jack came home on an extended leave because the Senator had pulled some strings and wanted to piggyback on Jack's hero status (he'd already won the Silver Star) in hopes of improving his failing senatorial cam-paign, we saw each other for the first time in four years. We'd kept in touch of course. I was twenty to his twenty-four, and it shocked us, the attraction. The bone-deep need.

"Please don't do this, Jack. I told you to stay away."

"Yeah, about that. What in the hell do you take me for, Av? A monster?" His voice was low and coarse, like he'd sawed off pieces of his soul to wedge out the words. I couldn't see his face—his voice had cracked on *monster*.

"Do you really think so little of me, that I'm the kind of guy who'd just blithely waltz into your life, get you to help me find my kid, cause you a major seizure, and then waltz back out, like it didn't mean anything?"

I sighed, staring at my feet, at the hay on the floor. I flashed for a mo-ment onto an image of the two of us in the afternoon sun, sitting on a hay bale out on the back of Jack's family's property, him watching me with won-der, ignited with joy.

Who was that girl back then, I wondered, the one brave enough to step forward and say *I want*? She was foolish, stupid beyond repair, and my soul rent apart because I wanted her back. Dear God, *I wanted her back.*

I glanced at the stiff line of his shoulders and knew something about the hell he felt. "I know, Jack, that you're a compassionate man. You saw me hurting yesterday, and your instincts just kicked in. I know your motto, the PJ motto—*That Others May Live.* You wouldn't know how to walk away from someone hurting, even if your life depended on it. You were always good at that, but I'm not a downed soldier. It's not your job to save me. You didn't cause the seizure."

"No. I sure as hell didn't, but my ex did, or something did, and there you were"—hurt wobbled through his voice—"and I had no idea what your abilities did to you until I saw you in the throes of that seizure." He leaned his forehead against the stall wall as if it was all he could do to remain standing. "I never let myself watch the one on YouTube. I had heard about it, but I knew I couldn't watch you in that kind of pain. Told myself it was a once-in-a-lifetime thing, that seizure. I thought surely the FBI would get you medical help to keep it from happening again. It couldn't be possible that no one would be able to do anything. I should have known. I took the easy way out, when I should have stepped up and done something to help."

For a moment, I felt like one of those shopkeepers who starts pulling in merchandise, boarding up windows just before the hurricane, aware of having waited too long to batten down. Debris from our relationship flew all around us, images of what we'd lost as childhood friends, as young lovers, as a couple torn apart.

"It's not your job to take care of me, Jack."

He turned, heartbreak warring with anger in his eyes.

"It should have been, Avery. Damn you, it should have been."

I turned to walk out of the stall, and Jack blocked me.

"Wait," he pleaded, visibly struggling to rein all the pain in, battling to shove the hurt aside, fighting for every square inch of calm he could claim. "Avery, please. I remember a time when you were my best friend. I remember when you were the love of my life." He looked away from my poker face. "Damn you, Avery, I can't forget that."

I could be in San Francisco by tomorrow. Four pieces of luggage to pack; two, if I shipped the art supplies. I wondered how shocked my sweet friend Louise would be if I showed up tomorrow claiming my old room. I could run, if only Latham's life wasn't on the line.

"It doesn't matter what we remember, Jack. Those people don't exist anymore."

He drew a deep breath and seemed to dig deep for resolve. I'd seen him do the same thing in high school, when he'd played baseball and was seven innings into a bad game, pitching poorly. He'd done the same, when dealing with his dad's political business as his dad rose from local mayor to state representative to a U.S. senator of national prominence. Jack had hated that life. Hated being on display, having to be the perfect son for the cameras and the voters. He used to take deep breaths before facing his old man, even when he was a kid.

Looking back now, I'm not sure what did more damage: too much attention, or too little. We were a pair, the two of us, broken as bottles on the sidewalk, our jagged edges somehow matching. Later, I think we convinced ourselves we fit, ignoring how those edges could also draw blood. It bothered me, more than I was willing to admit, that I hated he had to draw that breath, force himself to deal with the pain I had caused him.

"I did not mean to do this," Jack said, closing his eyes and shaking his head as if he were trying to clear it of vapors. Or ghosts. And then he caught my gaze. "I thought, when you first moved back, that it didn't matter. I wasn't going to be affected. It was ten years ago, and we've both grown and changed. And I thought, when I saw you again I wouldn't feel anything. I'd breathe like normal, think of you in some nostalgic way, and all those memories would just fade away. I think we both know after last night, that's not true. I don't think it's true for you, either."

I shook my head, not trusting myself. We'd known each other too long.

"You have always been my other half. I tried to let go when I went off to the Air Force, to give you a chance to grow up, make your own choices. I stayed away, dated, tried to—well, to see if what we had was real. I had a hard time even bothering to remember their names on a date. It's always been you. Who finds their other half at twelve and eight? That's crazy, right?"

But true.

He eased in, effectively boxing me between himself and the horse as he reached up to scratch behind Pan's ears. His losses pinged around me. My senses were back online full bore, and his emotional imagery was driving them over a cliff. I hadn't thought to bring my iPod out with me.

"Why'd you stay away, Av?"

He asked it with the gentleness he showed to Pan just now, his plea soft, luring. I stepped back from him.

"I just did." It was the truth. "It was for the best."

"I don't believe that." Emotion heated his voice, and the gravelly roughness of it broke. "I'm still . . . damn, Avery, I want to say furious, but that's not it. You left me. No word, no way to know if you were alive, and I went crazy. Stayed crazy." He closed his eyes. "I knew, all this time, that something happened that was more than just that night. I want to understand why. I hope you will talk to me. We used to be good at that."

I had to stop him. Looking back was a trap, swallowing me whole, promising nothing but pain.

"Have you not been paying attention? I never told you, growing up, what I was. Not once. Not until it was inevitable, and even then, I would have avoided it, if I could have. I lied to you, back then. I lied again, when I came home and told everyone I couldn't see things anymore. I would have kept on lying to you, if there hadn't been a kid in danger. I never told you about the seizures, or the pain, and I had absolutely no intention of ever telling you. Talk? Ha. We didn't talk back then. We just lived. We were kids, infatuated—that's an entirely different thing."

"You know that's a damned lie."

Of course he was right.

"Then you're an idiot." *I destroyed your family.* My chest hurt. My throat hurt. I bit down on the emotion, shoving it back into the box where it belonged. "I'm done with this."

I moved to go, and he took my arm. Gently. Firmly. His losses swirling through me, taking me over.

Pandora shifted in her stall, laying her head on my shoulder, her chest to my back as she glared at Jack. I heard the rumbling whinny start in her chest, felt the tension as it moved through her, and understood she thought she was protecting me. This difficult, wayward, stubborn beast that not five seconds ago I was thinking of leaving behind. I cupped a hand over the bridge of her nose, shushing her, soothing, running my palm up and down as she steadied. Never before had I felt roots rise up from the ground and entwine around my ankles so clearly that if I had looked down and seen them there, I wouldn't have been surprised. I wanted none of this, but I didn't know how to stop it.

"If it was just kid stuff, Av, then why is your heart breaking? I can see it in your eyes. You're afraid to tell me something. You don't have to be, Av."

Dad said you will die at Jack's hands.

"Here you are," Nate said from the door of the barn, and then, looking back and forth between us, he coughed. "Um, am I interrupting something?"

"No," I said, emphatically. "There's nothing here to interrupt."

CHAPTER SEVENTEEN

"You won't know what to do if she starts to seize," Jack said.

Jack and Nate were arguing. Nate was there to do my interview, and Jack was insisting he be allowed to stay for it. We stood on my porch, where Nate had blocked Jack's entrance to the house because Jack was, technically, a suspect and shouldn't be there. The ex is always a suspect when someone goes missing, and as much as I knew it hurt Nate to not let Jack stay for my questioning, I also knew he intended to record the interview and do everything by the book—on the off chance that he needed the documentation for a trial later. He couldn't very well have it documented that he had let a suspect attend an official interview.

Jack glanced at me, and then at Nate, anguish sharpening the angles of his face, the grim line of his mouth. "You didn't see her yesterday. You didn't see how serious the seizures are."

"What if she's the only lead to finding Marguerite? You want Brody wondering—"

"Dammit, no!" Jack slammed his hands through his hair, fear palpable.

"Then you need to leave," Nate told him. "Look, I trust Avery to tell me if it's causing a problem."

"And if she can't? If it happens too fast?"

"It won't," I assured him. "I get symptoms, first. Blurry vision, pain." I could see him get angrier with each word. "I'm doing this, Jack. I have to."

"Didn't look like you had much warning on that last seizure. You couldn't even get words out to let Latham know what was happening."

Nate stepped closer. "Do you think I'd purposefully hurt Avery? You told me about the painting, knowing I'd have to follow up with her."

"I thought you'd simply come take a look at it," Jack said. "Not try to use her like some sort of human metal detector."

He glanced back sharply at Nate, and the silence stretched thin as Jack measured Nate's expression, the way an engineer would scrutinize the smallest hairline fractures in a girder stress test.

"You knew," Jack finally said. "You weren't surprised at all when I told you. You already knew she had the ability to find lost things."

Something was off between them. I didn't think about it, didn't plan it, just grabbed for Jack's images that were shuffling around me and closed my eyes, focusing, feathering them out like a giant deck of cards.

I pulled at one I'd seen before: me at the train station. This image had made no sense earlier, and since it hadn't been as graphic as so many of his other losses, I had missed its importance. It was the devastating moment he'd learned just how much Nate had betrayed him by helping me run away. It was a loss he'd projected. This image he'd imagined—however incorrect— was real to him, because it was the defining pivotal moment when he knew I was gone.

"I made Nate promise, Jack. That day, I made him promise not to tell you."

Both men started, as if they'd forgotten I was there.

Nate grimaced. "You've every right to keep your abilities to yourself."

So many images of loss were sliding off both of them, I felt as if I was under an avalanche. My body shook, but I stepped back with my hands raised in defense when they both stepped forward to help.

"No," I said, shaking my head, not wanting to wait and let Jack's assumptions fester and poison their friendship any longer. "I'm not talking about now. I'm talking about ten years ago. He's just realized you've always known what I can do. And he knows about that night."

I looked back at Jack. "You had the details wrong—the clothes, the time of day, but you're right—he drove me to the station ten years ago."

Jack stiffened as he realized what I meant. He knew, then, that I'd reached into him again, found a loss and exploited it. He tried to hide the shock at my intrusion; he failed. He tensed, holding himself so rigid, I thought he'd split in two. There was no mercy in avoiding that night any longer. God help me, mercy was all I had left to give him.

"I made Nate drive me to the train station that night, Jack. I made him swear not to tell you. Nate has never broken a promise. You know that. He hated it, but he promised because he was worried about what I would do if he didn't help. You can hate me, only me, for that. Don't blame him for what I wouldn't let him do."

Jack turned and gripped the porch railing, the tendons in his arms standing out against the strain. I could feel the struggle, the losses sliding around, clamoring for my attention. He turned around finally, and nodded at me. Grim. I'd just shown him how easily I could pluck his images from the air and use them to hurt him. I waited for the disgust to ripple up, in spite of his best efforts to control it.

"How long have you known?" Nate asked. His face flushed with anger. It was now his turn to grasp the fact that Jack had been aware of the betrayal. Jack's fury at him, his disgust, was not lost on Nate, and I knew what that cost Nate. I knew, and couldn't stop it.

Jack uncoiled from the railing, deadly calm.

"Eight years ago. Aimee Toussand ran into my cousin Gail, and I apparently came up in conversation. Little Aimee commented on how everyone agreed I was lucky to have dodged that bullet a few years back." He jerked his head at me, and the absolute distaste everyone had for me ten years ago came flooding back. I shuddered as he kept going. "Apparently, she thought it was a wonderful thing I had such good friends, after the *disaster*."

No one in town ever called it a suicide. Nothing so vulgar and common could have happened to the great Senator Thibodaux. It was always, *the disaster* or *that awful night* or some other euphemism, as if the Senator was somehow less dead if we were polite about it.

Jack took a step closer to Nate. "And when Gail asked her what she was talking about, she said, 'Well, when Nate got rid of her. Rode her right out of town. Plopped her on the train, and made sure she left.' And Gail e-mailed me to let me know just how damn lucky I had been that my friends had been looking out for me that night. Only, you had told me nothing about it. The night she left, when I was frantic, searching for her, *you helped me look for her*."

So he'd known. For eight years, he'd known Nate had helped me . . . and lied to him. A few weeks after discovering the betrayal, he would up and marry Marguerite. I looked down at my clenched hands, wondering why they felt wet, and realized tears were streaming down like a runaway waterfall.

Images boiled off Jack: me running out of his house, him showing up to my apartment that night and seeing the closet half-empty. My bags gone. His engagement ring on top of my cheap bedside table.

He looked at Nate. "You knew I was out of my mind with grief over what I'd said to her. I couldn't find her anywhere; I couldn't let her know it was just pain lashing out, and that I was wrong to have hurt the one person who always"—and he looked at me—"*always* meant more to me than life itself." He focused back on Nate. "You let me go nearly insane. You didn't tell me you knew where she was or that she was okay. I thought at first, when I first found out, that you'd been in love with her. Were you? Are you?"

"You really are a stupid sonofabitch," Nate swore, and not in his usual calm, I-have-this-under-control way.

I don't think I'd ever seen Nate's demeanor crack. Not once, in spite of his job, and there I was, detonating what little friendship the two of them had left. Nate did not have much he could call his own: He made little money. He came from a very poor home. Still, he had always had his integrity and his loyalty, and his love for his friends. He loved Jack most of all.

"He begged me to call you," I said, my words rusty and hard, and Jack's attention snapped back to me. Stunned. "I wouldn't."

"Avery," Nate said, desolation running through his voice.

"No, Nate, he needs to know." My gaze never broke with Jack's. "He begged, Jack. He made a case for you, every time we spoke for years. I always said *no*. It was my decision. If you want to hate someone for that, hate me. I didn't want you there. You would have come barreling back into my life, not because you loved me but because you felt guilty."

Jack started to counter and I held up my hand—of course he'd disagree. I turned to go back inside, with one last glance at Jack's ashen face, now set like stone.

"Go home, Jack. There's nothing here for you."

"Why didn't you confront me?" Nate asked. "Eight years—why in the hell didn't you just punch me out once you heard?"

Jack's pause was excruciating as he stared at Nate. "I figured you were either in love with her, and since she didn't run away *with* you but just got your help, you were hurting, too, or you were helping her as a friend, and you still had contact with her—and for some reason you didn't think it was safe to let me know."

With that, Jack broke down, turning away from us both. I felt like a mountain had fallen on my chest, the wanting to fix this hurt so much.

"Avery, you're wrong, you know," he said, his voice cracking with grief. "Everything I ever wanted is here." He looked over his shoulder at me. "I would have come barreling back into your life because I knew I was an idiot. I wanted you, the way you are. And nothing else mattered."

He looked at Nate. "I'll be over by the barn. If she shows even the smallest symptom that her vision is blurring or a seizure is starting, you damned well better yell."

We stood together, unable to turn away as he walked across the yard, grabbed the axe from the barn, and began chopping wood from my woodpile as if God's own wrath possessed him.

"I have to give him credit," Nate finally said as we watched him work. "He handled that a lot better than I would have expected. I thought he'd be a lot angrier."

"I don't think he's done being angry."

"You underestimate him."

Nate watched Jack, and images of what might have been—how Jack might have been happy, how we might all have grown old together—spun off him. That's another trouble with loss images; I can't always tell if it's something the person actually lost, or if it's some sort of loss they're projecting. Images aren't concrete. They're ephemeral, changeable.

"He was wild back then. I half thought he kept flinging himself into some of those missions overseas, hoping to die, just to ease the pain of losing you. I kept telling him that if anything had happened to you, your family would have been notified, and he'd know." Nate glanced at me. "It was the closest thing to the truth I could tell him without breaking my promise. It never seemed to help."

He watched Jack again as wood chips flew and the strike of the axe echoed off the barn like gunshot.

"He calmed down a lot, once he saw you on TV earlier this year and knew where you were. That you were alive. That, right there, isn't anger. That's hurting."

"He may be hurting," I said low, aware of the truth in Nate's words. "But he's also the angriest man I've ever known. That's a bad combination.

163

No matter how much you want him to be okay, Nate, wanting isn't going to make it so."

I didn't try to explain to Nate how well I understood his best friend. Jack had the lid on tightly—as tightly as he had before everything blew up with his dad. The only thing I could do in this life was hurt him and force that lid off again.

"Av, I don't know what all happened between you two back then, but are you sure you're doing the right thing now?" He looked at me. "He loves you, Avery. You love him. Why can't it just be that simple?"

I met his gaze.

"We have a dead woman's eyes to talk about."

CHAPTER EIGHTEEN

"You sure you're okay to go over this?" Nate asked, as we settled in the living room on the couch.

I clasped my shaking hands behind my back, swallowed the grief that threatened to choke me—grief for Jack, grief for all of us—and nodded. Nate did that cop assessment thing that I hated, and managed to remain professionally still throughout until he finally sighed, resigned. More than anyone else, he probably knew I was lying about being okay, but Brody's mom was dead somewhere, and I'd promised I'd help find her.

"What we have," he began, "is almost nothing. You already know from our meeting this morning with Romano and Zannah that Marguerite re-routed her chartered flight to Atlanta, without filing any sort of itinerary. Zannah can't give me a good reason why that was approved, since it wasn't the norm."

I thought about Zannah's losses—Pete's infidelity with Marguerite, and the way she looked at Nate as her biggest loss, and I absolutely *hated* that I knew these things. It wasn't fair, much less right, yet there wasn't a damned thing I could do about it.

"Did Pete approve the flight?" I asked him, and his eyebrows went up a bit, a knowing look in his eye.

"Surprisingly, yes," Nate said, "though I'm told that task normally fell to the accountant. Why?"

"Zannah seemed defensive about it this morning, which is odd if you care about the person who might be missing."

Nate nodded. "I have the sense that Zannah wouldn't be all that torn up if Marguerite were to turn up dead, with Pete on the hook for it."

At my gasp of surprise, he sighed. "You've forgotten what a small town Saint Michael's is, and how quickly gossip spreads. It's pretty common knowledge that about a month after Marguerite arrived she started sleeping with Pete; you'd also have to have been blind not to notice that Pete began sporting flashier threads, driving a sports car, and taking an excessive amount of trips out of town. He even got his teeth capped."

I thought about the Pete I knew, the proud geek who, in college, was the poster-child for successful nerds everywhere, his big, gapped-tooth smile one of his best features. I had problems reconciling that guy with a guy who'd cover up his most prominent attribute and let someone make him over. He hadn't even done that for Zannah, and he'd lusted after her all through high school and college. Zannah had been proof to the world that he'd become successful without compromising his true self.

"Do you think Zannah could have done this?"

He shrugged.

"I never got a sense that she loves Pete or is excessively jealous, yet this kind of murder seems very . . ." I searched for the right word. "Passionate."

"It's difficult to know what people feel," Nate said, "but I do think she likes the security Pete provides, so that could be a motive. And because of that, my gut feeling is that she hopes Pete is behind this. Zannah's family has never had a divorce—something her mother has been known to announce on a fairly regular basis at church socials, and Zannah isn't going to rock that boat. But if Pete went up for murder?" He shrugged again, unsure. "She'd feel justified and could probably walk away with at least half of Pete's money, which isn't a small amount. We need to find Marguerite's body and get an accurate time of death so I can pull those strings and see what falls out."

Getting an accurate TOD wasn't always as quick and easy as it looked on TV, as it depends largely on the condition of the body when found, and the temperatures and surrounding environment of that location, as well as how long the body has been decomposing. Nate needed that time in order to start pinpointing who had alibis and who did not.

"As it stands," he said, "there's no way to know if Marguerite actually met anyone in Atlanta, much less if it was a business trip or a personal one.

Maybe she had another boyfriend—there's been local gossip about other flings, and it's possible she had men lined up in other cities. I reached out to Atlanta PD, and its records show zero reports involving anyone of her description. No Jane Does anywhere near her age. So she either booked a different flight, which the boarding receipt you saw would indicate, or she left that there to throw us off yet again and took a cab, bus, or a boat. Or she's hurt or dead. Maybe Jack's PI will find something."

"Nate, you know I'm not a hundred percent sure what I saw in that trash can."

He measured me a moment, then nodded, as if to himself. "You've always been observant, and I trust your gut instincts. But you're right, it's not a fact, yet, and it's not specific enough to give us a clear course of action."

"Why, though?" I wondered. "Why buy a commercial flight when she could have taken that chartered plane wherever she wanted to go?"

"Exactly, which begs the question: Why did she need it? The most obvious answer was that she was trying to disguise her ultimate destination. Until proof of foul play, we can't access her credit-card accounts to see what flight she booked."

"We can't do any sort of wellness investigation?"

Nate shook his head. "It doesn't work like that. She's a grown woman. She has the right to travel and the right not to tell anyone what she's doing or where she's going. Without a clear-cut piece of evidence that she has been harmed, there's not much anyone can do. The Atlanta PD can't just canvas the entire city and surrounding area for her. Especially now that we know you've seen evidence of another possible itinerary—"

"Was she involved in anything dangerous? Work? Former clients?"

Nate shrugged. "No idea, yet. Until we find her, or proof of harm, we don't have reasonable cause to do any sort of in-depth background check on her, or impound her computers. Her attorney has made that quite clear."

I nodded; I knew he was right. Romano would probably sue me for telling Nate about what I'd seen, but my priority was finding Marguerite, not what she may or may not have been up to that her attorney felt she had to keep quiet. "So she wasn't running scared or panicked. She was too stealthy, and that takes planning."

Nate thought about it, and nodded. It was clear from the lack of *loss images* from Nate that he thought Marguerite being out of Jack's life was a good thing.

"What about company credit cards? If she was supposed to be there as a lobbyist—"

"Already checked, with Pete's permission. JoJo Bean's in accounting at Polyformosia, if you remember, and she says there are no other charges to Marguerite's company card after a glass of wine the night before. We can't check her personal ones yet, not without a sign of foul play. Are you sure she's . . ."

"Dead." I thought about the Atlanta scenario a moment, but my gut instinct screamed foul. "What's bothering me is that I think she's somewhere local."

"Why?"

"I don't know." We hadn't pulled out the painting yet, and I wasn't sure I could handle it if we did, though I wasn't about to tell Nate that. "I don't remember painting it, so I have no idea what I was painting from—what sort of image I saw originally. Everything surrounding that image feels blank, like there's no point of reference. All I can say is the location feels like it's here, and that I've seen it before."

I stared at a photo Nate had of Marguerite in the file he'd opened on my coffee table. Latham had left Brody's baseball card collection there as well, and it felt somehow obscene that these things should be side by side. I moved the cards to the kitchen counter.

"Avery?" Nate said a little loudly.

I stopped, realizing he'd been speaking. "Sorry. What?"

"You're trying to put up a good front in front of Jack, I know. But are you sure you're okay to do this?"

"Let's get this over with, Nate."

He nodded, knowing me well enough to also know when to move on. His voice was low and gravelly on the first few questions, like he had to fight to make himself do this, to hurt me. I tried to help him along.

"Their custody fight," I asked, "it was all about Marguerite being unreliable?"

"Right." I hadn't let him tell me the details before, though he'd wanted to and had tried. "While Jack was on tour, he didn't get to see Brody much. Marguerite never Skyped with him, always managed to be traveling with Brody when Jack was on leave."

"So how'd she manage to lose custody to Jack?"

"Roughly eight months ago, Jack was finally discharged on a medical."

I knew Jack had been hurt two years before, and had undergone surgeries and rehab for a long time. Nate didn't look at me as he glossed over that part, knowing how often he'd begged me to call Jack during that time, telling me over and over that Jack needed to hear from me. I hugged myself as he plugged on.

"Jack had been fighting through the court system to see his son, and Marguerite was refusing to even let him visit. The original hearing happened while he was overseas, and it turned out the judge was an old sorority sister of Marguerite's, who ruled Jack was too volatile as a recent veteran with PTSD. He'd volunteered for some near suicidal missions to get men out, and Marguerite used that against him. Whenever he got home, he fought to see Brody. Then about six months ago, a call came in from the DC police that Brody had been left home alone while she was out of town, after the nanny was called away on a family emergency. The nanny had left Brody with the doorman who should have called the police but the guy claimed he was waiting for Marguerite to return. Apparently this had happened before, and she was known to tip him big for keeping it quiet. One of the maids, though, thought it was wrong and called the police, who finally convinced Brody to give them his dad's name when they couldn't find Marguerite."

"Jesus." I wanted to smack the crap out of Marguerite, but that was long past an option. It was a stupid, stupid thing to do, but she didn't deserve to die for it. Brody loved her. At one time, she had been a good friend to Jack, been there when he needed a friend. She wasn't a horrible human being. Flawed, self-centered, maybe, but dear God, I'd done so much worse.

"So Jack's had custody for over six months. What's the big showdown now about?"

"Marguerite made the case that she'd been delayed due to canceled flights out of Europe, and that the nanny had assured her Brody was fine. In the aftermath, she immediately moved down here, went to work for Polyformosia and Pete, and set out to prove she was the best mom ever. It looked pretty good that she'd gain back at least fifty-fifty custody. Then Jack's PI found out she hadn't been in Europe at all—her tickets there had been faked, and no one had thought to double-check that. The bottom line is, she had no explanation for abandoning Brody."

The skin crawled on my scalp, and dread swamped me. My voice felt small, tight. "When did Jack find out about all of this?"

Nate started shaking his head. "No, Av, it's not like that."

My gaze sharpened on him, reading his loss images: Jack being imprisoned was one of his projected loss-fears, and I snapped, "When?"

"Five days ago."

"So he found out she'd lied about why she'd neglected and abandoned their son just a few days ago? Two days before Marguerite went missing?"

Nate sank his face in his hands, sick at giving me ammunition against Jack. "It's not what you're thinking, Av. I can promise you that. Jack would never hurt the mother of his son."

Nausea threatened, and I swallowed hard. Maybe he wouldn't mean to hurt his son's mother. But if Brody's losses were anything to judge him by, the kid had been terrified. Traumatized. I didn't have to stretch my imagination much to imagine Jack losing it over his own child being left alone in a big city, much less what could have happened to Brody had the doorman not been a somewhat decent human being.

"Does Brody ever talk about it?" Thinking maybe he had, and that's what had pushed Jack over the line.

"No. Though Jack's probably not the person he'd confide in. Brody told the officer who picked him up for us that his mom had told him that his dad killed people in the war, and Brody couldn't trust him. That Jack could snap any minute, and she was protecting him, keeping Jack away. That's why Brody never called his dad even though he had a cell phone and had Jack's number. He said he didn't want his dad to kill him. I was there when Jack finally heard the whole story from Brody, and I can tell you it devastated Jack. He wouldn't make it worse, Av."

I doubled over, filled with such intense heartache I had no words for it. What Jack must have gone through. What that poor kid had gone through. The anxiety, the confusion.

"Are you able to handle seeing this again?" Nate asked, nodding toward the back porch where the painting was. "And Avery, Jack cannot be in here while I'm questioning you on this. Do I need to call an EMT? Do we need to reschedule?"

"No, I owe it to Brody. Let's do this."

Nate pulled the scorched canvas inside, and as he did, horrible, bloody images of Marguerite spun off him, his cop sense extrapolating off what little was left of the painting. Marguerite's bloody eyes were mostly still visible, although a line of flames had eaten through the right side of her face and blackened most of the background that might have held a clue as to her actual location. Once Nate had wiped off the residue from the fire extinguisher, the rest of the canvas had a hint of an old wooden floor, or it could have been the pecan brown of mud.

"Jack and Marguerite argued a lot," Nate continued. His gaze fixated on the horrific image before him. "I don't know how to explain her. She could be soft and vulnerable, even kind. She had real moments of friendship with people, though if I hadn't seen those for myself, I wouldn't have believed her capable of it. She'd be fine with Brody sometimes. Amazing, even. Other times, it was like he'd ceased to exist, and she'd as soon leave him with complete strangers as on the street. I don't doubt she loved Brody, and I think, deep down, she's a lot more fragile than any of us thought."

I don't know what Nate said next because the world went all white noise and harsh cymbals clashing. Grief sucked me down, covering me, squeezing the air out of my lungs, burying me.

When I opened my eyes, I saw nothing.

CHAPTER NINETEEN

Blackness filled and surrounded me. I recognized this place, this despair. Grief has a way of becoming your whole world, making living so painful, that dying seems easier, welcome. Everything in me begged me to succumb, but my brother's life was at stake, and now there was Jack's son, a boy whose mom was gone, who needed my help.

I wanted to help.

Please, I said, somewhere in that vast darkness. *I want to find the truth.*

That phrase echoed, bouncing off the distant walls of my mind, as if to say, *are you sure?*

Yes.

Terror squeezed my breath away, and I suddenly knew there was more here, more than I wanted to know, even though I'd said *yes*. I began to shake so violently, I thought for a moment it was a seizure, but it was only ever fear. Plain fear, and that's when I felt someone take my hand, and a woman's fingers entwine with mine.

And then, as simple as blinking, I was gone from the room and standing in a clearing in a forest. It took a few moments to adjust to the bright midday sun; the air around me smelled crisp, fresh, as if just after a rain, and I could feel the breeze on my skin. I knew two things: I hadn't been sleeping, so I was pretty sure I wasn't dreaming, and this was no seizure.

The colors before me weren't the soft shades of watercolors, but rather rich, vibrant hues, so crisp I could nearly taste them. Dewdrops about to roll off leaves paused, like wishes not spoken, and everything—from tree limbs to blades of grass to a bird midair—was frozen in place in the brilliant sunlight streaming in from above. Somewhere just outside of my periphery, I could make out the swish of a tail of a big dog as it moved—it was the only thing moving—under the shrubs like a whisper. Maybe there, maybe not.

I wanted to step forward but was afraid to take a step, and when I glanced at my feet, found I was standing at the edge of a muddy stream. It all seemed so familiar, and yet a terrible sense of dread flooded every cell of my being. If I were smart, I would go back. I wasn't sure exactly how, but I knew that if I were smart, I'd try. But Brody needed to know about his mom. Somehow, the answer was here.

"Would you care for a cup of tea?" The Old Woman spoke from my left, and I could feel a gentle squeeze of my hand, meant, I knew, to reassure me. In all of the years that I'd had the nightmares, the Old Woman had never once touched me, and chills ran down my body as I nearly convulsed.

"Ah, it's still a no, then," she continued, regret etched deeply into the sigh that followed. We stood there like that for an eternity—me afraid to turn and see her, her sadness weeping over me for reasons I did not understand and did not want to know.

Finally, she said, "You weren't wrong to go back home. You needed home. Home needed you. Latham needs you."

Sweat poured from me. I couldn't look at her. Not yet. My heart raced, and I squirmed in this sunny, surreal place where the wind was music tilting in the trees and everything sparkled, diamond-hard, sharp-edged—teeth that would rip me apart if I moved the wrong direction.

When I glanced over my shoulder, there she was: the Old Woman from my nightmares. Whole, for the first time since I'd met her. Not a single limb sliced off, and once again she was holding my hand. *I could feel her hand in mine.* I knew that was significant, but I didn't know why. Her once-silver hair was darker and plaited, two long braids on either side of her head. The light though, oh how the light loved her. She seemed luminous, timeless, beautiful in spite of her, well, I would have said *her wrinkles*, but as the light caressed her, I could see I'd been wrong about that, too. Her skin was stunning, barely lined, as if she might be only a few years older than me.

Where had I gotten the idea that she was old, older than the world? I fished for the exact image I'd held of her before, and found it faded, blurry, though she wore the same old khakis and soft cotton shirt with tiny roses in the pattern.

"Who are you?" I asked, knowing that something had changed, and now was my chance, maybe my only chance, to ask her. "I should know you, shouldn't I?"

"You do." Her smile was sad. "But I cannot tell you until you remember."

"If I remembered, you wouldn't need to tell me," I snapped, and she smiled, the first genuine smile of hers I'd ever seen.

"Ah," she said, "maybe so."

She was about my height, though I couldn't quite tell, because there seemed to be no beginning or end of her, the way she filled my vision. The perspective was also all wrong, as if she was drawn looking up at me from a position on the floor, but instead, I was facing her, nearly eye-to-eye. I don't know why knowing that made a difference to me, but it did: I was seeing her from the wrong angle and so everything was skewed. I shuddered, and then looked around again, mostly to avoid her terribly patient eyes. A leaf dangled overhead. When I touched it, it felt cool, brittle, and dead in my hand.

"Where am I?"

"Where do you think?"

I took in the lush ripeness of everything around me—the blackest of blackberries on a bush tangled in a fence line, yellow jasmine against a stump, low palmetto shrubs green and spiky, dangerous to the touch. The sun dappled overhead through birch and white oaks and pine; the water at my feet should have been burbling, tumbling over rocks, but instead was frozen mid-cascade, a singular moment in time. Holding its breath. My eye followed the line of the stream where it widened into a bona fide creek about a hundred yards away.

"I've seen this spot," I told the Old Woman, who nodded and waited. "There are bad things here."

I felt her nod again in agreement, though I was now focused on an old tire swing. I knew that swing. I'd played on that swing at Jack's house, when we were little kids. Well, when I was a little kid.

"The guys used to fish over there," I pointed out to the Old Woman. "They would let me fish, too, but usually, I'd sit in the swing. Sometimes, Jack would give me a push, and I'd fly up and up and up until I was dizzy."

I kept moving forward, toward the massive tree, dread crawling all over me. Part of me half expected to see Jack and Latham and Nate and Sam sprawled by the stream, cane poles propped up on rocks, waiting for the bream to bite. Part of me knew something awful lay ahead, and I desperately wanted to turn and run.

"Memory is a funny thing," the Old Woman said as she put a hand to my arm. I could feel it there—warm, real, firm.

Her touch stopped me in my tracks, as did thinking of her as real, as standing there, not some ephemeral dream I was somehow creating in a bid for insanity but someone who existed that I should know.

"Memory," she said, spacing out the words with careful diligence, like they were fine crystal that would shatter if they were spoken too fast or too close together, "curls around and connects things, but you must pay attention. You have chosen to learn the truth, and so it will be. I'm so sorry."

And then where her left arm had been she was now slashed and bleeding. Slashes appeared across her face and torso, and I recoiled, struggling back and away from her, some inner chant beating a drum to *no no no no no* as I almost fell on a body at the edge of the creek.

When I looked down, for a brief moment, it was the body of a small girl, one who'd also been slashed, her arm severed, lying in a bed of snow, snow everywhere, and blood, so much blood, and I screamed and jumped backward, and in the blink between one second and the next, that body became Marguerite's. The snow was gone now, and she was lying on wooden planks and bleeding into the grass.

My world spiraled out of control, the colors mutating and knifing me, and I could hear the shrieking, knew it was coming from me and couldn't stop it.

Marguerite's eyes opened then, as blood dripped down her forehead just as it had in my painting. "Tell him," she said, hatred blazing in her eyes. "Tell him he did this to me."

And then everything went black.

CHAPTER TWENTY

I ran.

I cannot explain to you how I got out of my own living room, how I eluded Nate, or how I knew where to run when I couldn't even see.

But that's what I did. I ran.

Everything was a blur, a dark tunnel, with a dim light at the other end that I knew I absolutely must reach or die trying. I felt the mud of my driveway beneath my feet and then the soft dirt of the woods, the branches whipping past me, scraping my arms, thrashing against my face. *I ran*, the screaming in my head so loud, I could barely hear anything else, barely sense other sounds, like someone calling my name, relentlessly *calling, calling, calling*—pure instinct pushing me blindly along.

Nothing and yet everything was around me. The colors so disjointed, lights and darks melting into each other, a river of confusion flowing around me, not connected to form or function, and if I had been called to speak under oath, I could not tell you how I moved from one place to the other, except that I ran, *dashing jumping bumping falling stumbling flailing* . . . My hands had blood on them. Bright red, thick. Not my own.

My feet were leaving a path in the *snow*, with blood dripping from my hands making it so obvious, might as well have been pointing *follow me, follow me*, and I knew, I knew I would die if I didn't hide. Had to hide. *Must hide, must must must must run through the underbrush, hop rock to rock, find a tree, there, there up, up icy branches, sliding, sliding, hard to hold, have to cling. Quiet, quiet, breathe into the crook of my arm so my breath doesn't frost the air, so no one sees. Soft breaths, hunker down into the snow piled on the limb in the crook of the tree.*

Something held me, stopped me still as ice, and then shook me. Shook me hard.

He had me now. Time to die.

He shook me hard again, and said, "Avery."

The name floated there, floated as if it didn't quite belong, and then soft, soft, like a well-worn sweater, I pulled it on. My name. *Mine.* Something cracked through the dark, broke through the ice and snow, and warmth flowed back in. Warmth . . . and I reached forward, out, out, into nothing, reaching, and reaching again, and finally I felt hands. Strong. Safe. Calloused. Heat radiated from them as they enveloped my fingers, coaxing, tugging. My own hands fisted inside of roughened fingers as the rest of the world seeped back into existence, and I found myself near the same spot as where I'd started off in the image—by the stream, a dozen or so yards away from . . .

I flinched, confused. The light was odd, the sun much lower than before. Was this real? The voice shushed me, holding onto me, as if soothing a wounded animal. Terror reeked through my pores. Little gypsy thoughts of losing my mind scampered up and down my internal scaffolding. If OSHA had been there, they'd have shut me down, it was so unsafe inside my head.

"It's just me," the man's voice coaxed, and I focused on the source and finally saw the lights and the darks of the scene coalesce into discrete items: *It's Jack. There is Pandora over there. That is the bright sunshine—it's not dark. Why did I think it was dark? That is the creek. Those are the trees. There is no snow.*

The screaming in my head died away, and I could hear the burbling water as the stream laced through and around fallen logs. That water flowed to a body and then over and around it. I shuddered so hard, my teeth clattered, and I bit down, trying to control it. I had expected Latham to be there—he'd always been there, either by phone or in person, after a nightmare of the Old Woman. Then I remembered I'd silenced my phone when Nate and I were talking about the painting, and honestly, I wasn't sure where *here* was yet, so how I thought Latham might know was beyond me.

"Avery?" Jack asked, and something in my expression must have appeared more alert, as the tension in his jaw eased. "Are you here, now?"

177

I focused on his eyes at first and then registered—there were branches around me. *Branches?* I blinked and the rest of the bush came into focus: knobby bark and crooked limbs on three sides of me where I had snuggled up against the trunk; Jack knelt in front of me.

My fingers clutched at Jack's hand. I am hiding in a bush. A bush. I had been in my house having some sort of image, and then there was all that screaming and blood and . . . snow? . . . and now I am hunkered down inside . . . I glanced around . . . inside an azalea bush, with Jack kneeling in front of me. Well, that seals it. I am officially crazy.

I wonder who'll win that bet?

"Jack?" I kept the panic just barely squashed flat, out of sight, despite the fact that I was reeling inside. "Why am I sitting in a bush? And how did I get here?"

A smile twitched at his lips, though it didn't ease the concern in his eyes, and he squeezed my hand, a clean hand now with no blood that I could see.

"I was beginning to think you flew. I tried to track you after you lit out from your house, but I lost your trail. It just vanished. And I finally realized you'd gone up. That was a half mile away."

"I ran half a mile?"

"About a mile, actually." My pulse slammed up a few hundred beats, and I knew he could feel it, as he oh-so-subtly held my wrist. He notched his voice down, smoothing the words. "I lost you about a half-mile back, so I widened my grid and found your trail again—that's when I realized you were going in a zigzag pattern and were using the trees." His own hands shook. "You scared the hell out of me, Av. I kept calling, and you never answered."

A mile? My brain had lodged right there, setting up camp on those words. I'd run a mile, all but blind. I saw the scratches and scrapes on my arms, and twigs and dirt on my jeans. I remembered rough bark against the palm of my hands, and looked up and saw limbs interlocking overhead, a bridge I'd apparently crossed. I used to blank out as a child, missing hours sometimes, and would find myself perched in a tree, miles from home, Latham stalking through the forest, calling my name.

Noises filtered through my shock, and I looked past Jack and saw that a good dozen people—most of them in uniforms—were gathered over across the clearing, where the body would be. My hands were still ice cold inside of his, and Jack kept rubbing them, almost absently, as we both scanned the crime scene and the people. I couldn't tell who they all were, and I was almost grateful for that. Some of them walked the perimeter, putting little evidence tags on the ground. Someone had cordoned off the crime scene. Others seemed to be photographing various angles or bagging evidence.

Sam was over to one side with several other volunteer EMTs, a few yards away from where I sat in the bush; they were trying not to be obvious but I could tell they were curious about me. Nate stood near the crime scene, and though I could see his tension, even from here, as he occasionally glanced over to where we sat.

"How long have I been here?" I didn't ask the question I wanted to ask. The need to ask what had happened burned like acid in my chest. *Would it happen again?* Was I a danger now? To myself? To Jack? To others? I felt trapped as a moth against glass.

"Couple of hours. Give or take." Jack sat, then, and stretched out his bad leg. He nodded toward Pandora who was munching sweetgrass a few yards away. "I grabbed her when I saw how fast you were going. Once I found you, I called Nate, and then everyone else arrived. I sent Sam back with her for your saddle after I got here, so you'd have a way home."

"So I've been here awhile."

He nodded, kindly. I knew I didn't deserve his kindness, especially not after he'd just had to confront the truth of how I'd left him all those years ago. Whatever anger he felt about that, it hadn't stopped him from trying to help me. That was the Jack I knew. I scrubbed away the tears forming and tried to figure out what I'd done. "So you ran after me?"

"You ran across Mahaffey Highway—right in front of JoJo Bean."

Oh. Dear. God. "I ran across Mahaffey?"

"Yes."

"Across, like . . . across?" I couldn't wrap my mind around it, even though Jack nodded. That's when I realized he looked a little green. He couldn't look me in the eye. He was afraid for me. Mahaffey was a busy highway. I could have run in front of a car going sixty, easy. Wait. Apparently I *did* run in front of a car, one driven by none other than JoJo Bean, who would live for the next decade on this piece of gossip alone. I wasn't sure what was worse— the potential accident or the certain future exposure at JoJo's hand.

"She almost hit you."

I stared at him. He had his hands clasped around his bent knee, but I could see they were trembling. He'd been in battle, and in his loss images,

179

he'd been steady—even when disarming an IED. This? This had scared the hell out of him.

Losses spun off him: Seeing me move from tree to tree, precariously, nearly falling, him not able to get to me in time. Loss of a chance to begin again. Loss of hope. Loss of the good use of his leg. If he hadn't been injured, he'd have been able to track me faster, overtake me, keep me safe. These losses shuffled around other losses, a veritable stew of things and stuff and hurt and people gone.

Jack kept talking, unaware of what I was picking up from him.

"That's how I found your trail again—JoJo called 911, and Nate and I realized how and where I'd lost you and I tracked you here. By then . . ."

"I'd found her." I said it on exhale, resigned.

"Yeah," he agreed. He knew better than to sugarcoat the obvious. "I'm so sorry you had to be the one to find her. Especially like this."

It seemed an odd thing for him to say about me finding his dead ex-wife. Like it mattered how I'd found her? I'd seen worse, with the girls. Well, maybe not worse. Still, there was no remorse that I could tell in his expression or words—just a general deep sadness, like none of this was connected to him. It was cold, and almost heartless, and it plucked at my fears. He should at least care for Brody's sake, or for their shared past. He should be *something*.

Talk grounded to a halt. I didn't want to confront him, and he was steadily focused on how close he'd come to losing me again—not something I wanted to get into just then, because he was going to lose me, and he was going to have to face it.

As soon as I knew Latham was okay, I was gone.

I stayed silent, and we both scanned the clearing, while more and more official-looking people swarmed, gnats at a hot summer picnic. Reporters were already clamoring for quotes from Nate as a couple of his officers tried to keep them cordoned off from the crime scene.

I crawled out from under the bush and sat next to Jack; we were just a foot or so from the stream and the exact location where I'd stood and talked to the Old Woman. It had been real. Hadn't it? I had stood there. I'd known to come here. Somehow, I'd known. How? Yet I saw no tracks to the stream—my own, the Old Woman's, or the dog I thought I had seen.

180

Had all of that been a vision? A dream? I could see the tire swing, the rope mostly rotted now, and the gnarled roots the boys had once used as seats because they were near enough to the stream that they could sit and fish. I could almost hear our laughter and the shrieks as someone inevitably fell in. Finding Marguerite here was a punch in the face, a crime against those few happy times. We'd had so little childhood we could hang onto, Jack and I, and now this was gone, too.

"Where's Brody?"

Jack tugged his gaze off the crime scene and turned a puzzled expression my way. "He's still with my cousin Gail and her kids. I called her as soon as I saw this, and asked her to keep him and to make sure she kept all of the kids away from the news. They're up in Saint Francisville, so they won't be home 'til this evening. I want to know more about what's going on before I talk to him. I've left a message for Father Tomas. He's been great, helping me with Brody. I hope he can meet us back at the house. Help Brody put it in context. Give me some advice."

Context? *Context? What the hell?* It all sounded so cold.

Nate cast worried glances our direction, nodded at me, now that I wasn't sitting inside a bush.

"Father Tomas is a good choice. He even makes me calm," I said.

Jack looked appreciably surprised. "You're not a fan of religion."

"I'm not a fan of being told God hates me, and I'm going to hell, which seems to happen on a daily basis. Father Tomas came by the house the day I moved in, and I started to not answer the door, but his losses were so soft. Mellow. It made me curious."

We watched the crime scene techs get started, and I had to wonder where they'd come from and how they'd gotten here so fast; Saint Michael's didn't have a department big enough to have techs, except the little bit that Nate could do on his own.

"And?" Jack asked, and I realized I'd drifted off topic.

"He smiled, so sweetly. I could tell he was a kind guy. Good choice, for Brody."

"All that, from soft losses?"

"Well, that, and he said, in his opinion, God didn't make mistakes. So if I had an ability, then there was a reason, and eventually, I'd have a chance to see why. He thought that who I was, was a blessing. He meant it, and honestly, was probably the first person from an organized religion who did."

"I'm glad, and he was right."

I shrugged, but I didn't miss how much Jack's opinion had changed about what I could do. I wish I could have agreed with them both. Personally, I wasn't so sure God wasn't using the ability to punish me for something I had done but couldn't remember. That possibility ate at me daily.

Suddenly, I blinked—a parsed set of images was coming off of Jack and they matched something coming from Nate.

"Jack—did you recently lose a pair of work boots?"

He swung his gaze back around to me, confusion furrowing his brow.

"Well, yes, actually, a couple of days ago. That's an odd thing to focus on, Av."

I shrugged. Tapped my forehead. "We apparently do odd here daily."

Then I recognized what it was about Nate's tense stance that was bothering me: He was angry. *Worried* angry. And he was rigid with a kind of fear I understood: fear of losing someone he cared about. I could feel it emanating in waves off him, and it was aimed at us.

"From the expression on Nate's face, Jack, I think they're going to find your boot prints at the crime scene."

He stiffened, wanting to argue when enlightenment dawned.

"Son of a bitch," he swore, low, so the words didn't carry.

It was odd, sitting there, calm. Together. So much like old times when we were kids and would sneak out of our respective houses and meet up in the woods to face some new adventure Jack had planned. There were always forts and tree houses to build, rope swings and fishing holes to find, critters to capture and release, and miles and miles in which to run our own small Country of Five Saints, as Jack called it.

But this felt more like the day we'd wandered too far into the backside of the gravel mine, and nearly lost Sam in a small sinkhole that had been poorly covered up with rotting wood planks. One minute Sam was there, in front of me, and the next, he'd disappeared. I'd have plunged after him if Jack hadn't jumped forward and snatched me back to safety. It had taken EMS and firefighters hours to pull Sam out, and I think it was the memory of that moment that formed his determination to become a firefighter. The shock of that sudden almost tragedy stayed with me for months. Nothing was quite the same, after that. We grew careful. We grew aware we were mortal. It was an awful lesson to learn so young, and one we couldn't confess. Not even to each other.

Now it felt like Jack was stumbling over a sinkhole, but I had no way to reach for him, to pull him back from what lay ahead. I hadn't expected to feel the agony of that notion, but it weighed as much as all of my other fears together and knifed me in the chest. It was all I could do to fight down the bile without him seeing.

"I wonder if someone was trying to implicate me, or if it was just convenient," he mused, anger bubbling beneath that smooth surface as he looked out over the scene where the ME had arrived—Nate's Uncle Teddy, his stooped shoulders forming a perpetual question mark. Teddy Barksdale was maybe seventy, but he looked ninety, easily. Despite the family similarity, Uncle Teddy clearly had ascribed to the *why exercise, we're all just gonna die philosophy*—though his toothpick arms belied their strength. He stooped near Nate, whose blond hair and vitality shone like a beacon.

". . . near here," he was saying and I tuned back in with a raised brow. "As I was saying my back barn is the structure nearest here. It was muddy out here when she went missing; he may have just grabbed the boots as a convenience."

"Whoever did this wasn't thinking very clearly," I said, musing aloud. I watched Nate's shoulders bunched in fury as one of the news photographers tried to sneak around the crime scene tape.

"Why's that?"

"Anyone who knows you knows you aren't stupid enough to put the body on your own land and tromp around on it in your own boots."

Jack went very still. His gray eyes seemed lit from within, and the fury etched on his face made me wince. He pitched his voice low. "God forbid you simply believe I'm innocent because you know me well enough to know I wouldn't kill anyone, Avery."

I hadn't meant it like that, and that realization seized me with fear: *This was the man at whose hands I would die.* I'd known this for the last ten years. It had governed every decision I'd made since that fateful night of his dad's death, and yet here I was sitting comfortably with him, so comfortably that even his losses weren't making me ill any more. What was wrong with me? Was I truly that stupid? That desperate for him that I'd give up and give in, even knowing anything between us was doomed? God knows I wanted to. How sick was that?

Jack leaned in a little. "I don't know who turned you against me, Av, but we grew up together. You know me. You know me better than anyone else in this world. Whoever turned you against me, whoever made you think I'd ever hurt you, they have some kind of ulterior motive. They don't want us together. You need to think about that."

He stood up, and reached a hand out to help me up as well, and it took a minute, that hand calmly extended, before I gave in and put my hand in his. And then everything we might have been slammed into me, everything we'd lost when I'd left him.

"Jack," I whispered, barely able to get the words out around the pain, "please quit thinking about us . . ."

I swayed, and he did what instinct told him to do: He reached for me and held on tight, tucking me into him, his chin against my temple.

"I'm sorry," he said, "I know it's going to take some adjustment, and I know you're hurting, but you were going to be my wife, Av. As far as I am concerned from this point forward, you still are. I'm angry, and you're not telling me a helluva lot, and it's killing me not to be able to help you, but I'm not giving up. Get used to that. Get used to the fact that you can trust me."

I was shaking my head as best I could with it against his chest, when he put his palm on the back of my head, sliding his hand into my hair, still whispering, "Whatever it was. Whatever. I'd rather know, and face it with you, than not know. If it was someone else—"

I gasped and looked up at him. "No—never!"

He stared down into my eyes and the world fell away, and then he nodded, satisfied. "Then anything else, we can face together."

I shook my head again, and he thumbed away a tear, just as Nate and the rest of the cops headed toward us. Jack let me turn to face them, but he didn't drop my hand, even when I tried to tug it away.

Jack leaned in, "And very soon, we're going to talk about who turned you against me, and why. I think I deserve to know that."

No, we weren't, but I couldn't tell him that. I only realized I hadn't heard a part of what he said, as if my brain had subtracted the last three words as they had hit the air, but now that I stood and could see who was on scene, my entire body went weak with stark madness. Jack had said, *But God forbid you simply believe I'm innocent because you know me well enough to know I wouldn't kill anyone . . .*

"Especially *a child*."

CHAPTER TWENTY-ONE

"Jack—" The word ripped from me, a stone crashing against a windowpane, shattering the quiet of the morning. Without thinking, I stepped closer to him because I'd just seen who was standing on the other side of the clearing: Hank—tall, weary, wearing his FBI field vest. "Hank's here."

He only worked one case.

Dear God, no, please no.

Hank must've sensed my eyes on him because he glanced over and immediately headed my way.

"Yes, he is," Jack answered, and I could hear the confusion in his voice. "Av, he's been here an hour. He tried to talk to you earlier, but you wouldn't answer him. He told me to wait—that you'd done this a couple of times on other sites, and he'd learned to wait you out."

The images I'd seen earlier now slammed against me again, but this time in context: a child, a child brutally sliced.

I turned and threw up. When I stood again, I was shaking so hard that I'd have fallen if Jack hadn't braced me. He said something over my head to Sam, who tossed him a wet handkerchief and some rinse, and he handed each to me in turn. I could barely get either of them to my mouth my hands trembled so hard. *A little girl. Maybe three. Maybe four. Not Marguerite.*

He could see my terror, and he wrapped his arms around me, obviously confused. "You didn't know?"

I shook my head. "I saw Marguerite dead in the images, only this time her corpse talked to me." I couldn't bear to look at the site. "Jack? How long did I sit in that bush?"

He cupped my head to his chest, and I listened to his anxious heartbeat as he said, "About three and a half hours."

I had lost three and a half hours? I remembered now the little girl's image, and more bile rose. I had to breathe through it, closing my eyes, pushing the images away. I'd seen both her and Marguerite. Why? That had never happened before. I'd never had overlapping images of different victims, especially two so wholly unconnected. I couldn't even comprehend it.

"Who is it?"

Jack didn't answer. Hank had reached us now, and he glanced at Jack first to gauge how I was doing. Jack gave a small, reluctant nod.

"Kid. You look like crap."

I took in the exhaustion in his watery eyes, the map of wrinkles that seemed to have cut deeper into his lean face, and the familiar pallor he took on when he hadn't slept in several days.

"Yeah, well, you are obviously rubbing off on me." I bit my lip, dreading the answer even before I asked. "Who is it?"

His phone rang, and he stepped aside to answer, just as a little bulldog of a man stepped up. The shiny shield on his belt read Baton Rouge Police Detective, and he relentlessly tapped it just in case I was blind and had possibly missed it. I put him to be around forty; he was fit, like a fighter, a light heavyweight, with a face and hands carrying enough scars to vouch for a few bar fights over beer or women through the years. Probably both. He played up the role of redneck country boy—worn Wrangler jeans, plaid cotton work shirt, a half-chewed toothpick dangling from the corner of his mouth, but nothing could disguise the snakebite in his eyes.

"I hear you're that crazy psychic chick that gets off on seeing dead people."

Hank was still on the phone, but his eyes narrowed at the comment. Most people annoyed Hank by breathing; this guy was toast.

I could see a whirlwind of hundreds of losses spilling off the various people working over at the crime scene, and had no way to tell any single image's origin, but this detective stood so close, his images came through with a rancid smell to them. The pain was already at a crescendo when Nate belatedly introduced us—"Avery Broussard, Detective Donnelly"—then threw me an apologetic grimace as the detective reached out to shake my hand before Nate could stop him, however, it wasn't only Detective Donnelly's losses that hit me. *Sisters. Blonde. Playing in the park not far from the town square. Gone. Gone.*

"I've got her," Jack said to someone off to the side—Donnelly, I think, and that's when I realized we were sitting on the ground again. I was in Jack's lap, and he was holding a cold pack against my nose. I had blood all down my shirt, and losses spinning the air into dizzy hurricanes of hurt. I had a split second to think about Latham, about how he'd have a coronary when these images hit the news, or worse, the social media feeds, but there wasn't anything I could do about that or him right now.

At Jack's words, Nate waved the paramedics off as Donnelly squatted eye-level with me and applauded with the slow clap of the cynical.

"Nicely done, Ms. Broussard. Do you charge a fee for this act?"

"Donnelly," Hank barked, off his call now, with his voice pitched low so the reporters wouldn't overhear. Several of them were positioned on the other side of the clearing, carrying boom mics so big, they could probably pick up an ant moving. "I vouch for her. She's been through more," he said, stepping into the smaller man's space, "than you and any two cops you know. Leave her alone."

"You ask me, she's a quack. She left you high and dry in Chicago, and now she's brought your son of a bitch here to my territory." Donnelly pushed himself up and puffed out his chest, and I realized that some of the loss images were coming from him. The dead little girl by the creek was the daughter of a close family friend, something he hadn't mentioned to anyone, I'm sure, or he'd have been off the case.

"I'll cut her some slack," he continued, "when she quits screwing up this case. The fact that she was on it so long and you *still* haven't caught the son of a bitch? Should tell you something. She's a fake or worse she's the killer or the killer's girlfriend." He glanced at Jack and then back to Hank, "and you're too damned starry-eyed to see it."

I could see Hank respond but I couldn't hear what he said past the chant of *the LPK is here the LPK is here the LPK is here* running through my head.

I gritted my teeth, stood, and faced my accuser.

"I'll tell you what, Detective Donnelly, let's talk about you, shall we? You've lost your wife and your kids, probably because you're so freaking closed-minded and a bit of a lush." I put my hand up before he interrupted me. "You lost your first girlfriend in the tenth grade, you lost the final game of your high school's state championship by drawing a penalty on the final play of the game, and just last night, when you were alone, you lost seventeen tries at the scratch-off lottery cards."

His narrowed, cynical eyes widened in shock; he glanced at Hank, no help there. Then came the anger—then confusion over what kind of trick I was trying to pull. People believe what they want.

"I could go on, but we're wasting time here. We've got a killer out there, Detective, and he has your best friend's daughter." (He blanched at that.) "Let's just agree I'm the least of your problems."

Donnelly folded his arms across his chest, his biceps bulging, his right hand fisted like he'd like to take a swing at me. I could see that swing as a loss for him, the one thing he wanted right now that he couldn't have. He said, low enough so only I could hear: "You're a world-class bitch, you know that?"

"Card-carrying, Detective. Your point?"

"My point," he said, leaning closer, the mints not quite disguising the alcohol on his breath, "is you don't impress me, Ms. Broussard, and I don't buy the damsel in distress act. I'm not fooled, like the Chief here, or the Feds. Awful convenient to have you arrive first on the scene if you're not the killer—and that means I'm going to have a few questions for you."

Hank stood there, a fifty-something, pissed-off Lone Ranger, and I would have sworn in that minute he'd been reincarnated from the Old West, a gunslinger who'd shoot first and ask questions later. He looked past Donnelly, and locked onto my gaze. Behind us, I could hear Latham had arrived, already yelling something about Jack getting his damned hands off me, but all I could see was what Hank was projecting: *Another girl, another blonde. A lily left at the scene where she and her little sister were abducted like before. That little sister, dead. The other one . . .*

"He's escalating," I said, the whispered words cracking the air. An explosion of images roared in carried by a wave of pain so great, I staggered, careful not to grab Hank's outstretched hand as he'd reached to steady me. I would never have survived it.

"Taking two at once. He's changing tactics."

Hank shook his head. "No, not as much as you'd think."

CHAPTER TWENTY-TWO

Latham waded into our small group, pushing, shoving, and reeking of bourbon. His skin was ash pale, and he shouted something at Jack that I couldn't quite hear. Reporters over by the crime scene immediately ran our direction, their cameras flashing as they ate up the scuffle that ensued, with Nate not so gently restraining Latham.

I stood in the middle of the storm, only able to see Hank's newest loss—the most recent little girl taken by LPK—a tow-headed cherub with wide green eyes. She looked to be about five years old.

"You're drunk," Nate snapped, turning Latham around, "and this is a crime scene. You need to go home. Sleep it off. You have no business here, Latham."

Sam, looking a little overwhelmed and shocked, had apparently stepped closer when he saw the melee forming, and now, he moved to help get Latham under control and away from me.

"Sam?" Nate asked, "Can you drive him home?"

"Like hell, he will," Latham snarled back, stumbling a little, like the ground was trying to buck him off his feet. The bourbon wafting from him nearly choked me. He'd only left me a little while ago to get our parents away from me . . . wait, no. If what Jack said was true about how long I'd been zoning out, our joyful little reunion with our parents had been much longer ago, more than an hour before Jack had been at my house, and then Nate, and almost another four hours under that stupid bush—plenty of time to drink too much. Had something gone so south with our parents that he'd needed a few stiff drinks? Or was it that he hadn't protected me from all this?

I peered into his eyes, trying to see past the barrier that always blocked Latham's losses from me. I would have sworn that he looked infinitely worse than when I'd last seen him that morning.

"You must be the brother," Hank said. "Your sister's spoken of you often. She's very proud of you."

Like magic, the fight went out of Latham, and he looked away, muttering, "She shouldn't be."

Donnelly eyed him speculatively, like a hyena might watch a particularly weak antelope on the edge of the herd.

"Kid," Hank said to me, "we have work to do."

I nodded as Donnelly said, "She's coming in for questioning first."

"No," Hank said, "she's not. She's my CI, and under my jurisdiction. Take it up with your local special agent in charge if you have an issue."

"We'll see about that," Donnelly said, snapping open his phone and stepping off a few paces.

"She can't do this," Latham told Hank, his voice very near tears. "She's not well."

"I'm standing right here, Latham," I snapped, "and I can take care of myself."

"She had a bad seizure yesterday," Jack explained to Hank, "and another episode or break this afternoon when she suddenly knew where the body was." Jack nodded toward the crime scene. "She's not in any shape for this."

"Jack," I elbowed him. "Cut it out."

I was trying my level best not to cause a bigger scene, if only to thwart the media, gathering now by the dozens on the borders of the clearing, looking for something interesting to shoot. That meant no dramatics. "I know what I'm capable of handling most of the time, and honestly right now, none of that matters. There's a little girl missing. Alive, for now, but the clock is ticking."

Hank nodded.

"You're not facing this alone," Jack said, leaning into my ear to keep it private. "You know you're better when we have some sort of contact."

I started to argue and then stopped and realized . . . he was right. There wasn't nearly as much pain from the images circling around me, and those same images had been causing me stabbing pain a second before. I must have looked surprised because he volunteered: "Your pulse rate evens out when I'm holding you. Your eyes aren't nearly as dilated, and your color is better, even though you're not using your iPod with the white noise. So something about this"—he gestured at his embrace—"seems to help you in a crowd like this."

"You need to get your hands off her," Latham mumbled, so slurred, I could barely understand him as he tried to shove away from Sam.

"You're not taking her anywhere, son." Hank laid his hand on Latham's shoulder. "She's with me. I'll make sure she's fine."

Something in Hank's voice seemed to quiet Latham; I'd seen Hank have a similar effect on frightened parents and scared witnesses. He squinted at me and asked, "Kid, you gonna pussy out on me again?"

"Bite me, Hank."

He grinned. "That's my girl. I know you can't meet the parents at the police station. Where would you like?"

"Why not the station?" Nate asked, as if his sanctuary had somehow been found lacking.

"Too many violent losses at a police station," I answered, and saw the epiphany—why I'd yet to visit him there and never would—flash across his face. "And not my house—their losses would become associated with the place, and I couldn't live there anymore. We need somewhere neutral."

"My store?" Jack offered. "We can close for an hour, use the back offices. It's a pretty happy place, I think."

I nodded—he was right. The store had always felt positive and neutral, and since I wasn't going to set foot in there again, because I wasn't going to see Jack again, it was probably our best bet.

"Wait a minute," Donnelly argued, having hung up from his call in a huff. "This is still my case. Y'all ain't doing anything without me on it, like white on rice."

"Even so," Hank said, having already fought this battle and won, "that call just told you that I'm taking lead here."

"You asswipe—"

"Donnelly," Nate said. "Shut up. You're the kind of cop that gives cops a bad name. You know we need the Feds' help. We need everything we can throw at this guy."

My legs wobbled, and as Jack braced me, he looked at Hank and said, "She's got to rest. At a minimum, a few hours."

191

"Can't do that," Hank said, looking at me. "You know the odds—the first few hours are critical."

I nodded. He was right. "I'm fine. Lottie'll have some orange juice at the store; that'll help."

"You can barely stand," Jack pointed out, "and you've had multiple incidents in less than twenty-four hours. You're going to crash and seize out, and what good will you be to the investigation then?"

Hank pulled out his unlit cigar, fiddling with it, all the while never taking his eyes off Jack. "We have federal, state, and city cops, as well as sheriffs all flocking here to help, and even so"—he pointed at me with the cigar—"she's our best bet. You think you're gonna be able to comfort and protect Avery if she doesn't try to help this girl and the girl dies? Because if you think that, then you sure as hell don't deserve her, because she won't be able to live with herself. And one thing more"—he leaned in a little, his voice leveling a threat Jack couldn't miss—"you don't talk for Avery. She decides."

"Not when you're manipulating her, you son of a bitch," Jack said. "You'd use her 'til she dropped without giving it a thought, as long as it closed the case."

"True," Hank said, and he didn't seem bothered by that at all. "You telling me that's wrong? That the little girl out there in this monster's hands isn't worth some pain?"

Hank was right. Jack couldn't see how much losing the other girls had already cost Hank. How the thought of losing this one was killing him. How much he hated putting me back through the pain but how he also knew he had no other choice. It surprised me, somehow, how well we'd gotten to know each other. Hank hadn't been wrong when he said I wouldn't be able to live with not helping, especially not if the little girl died, especially not if the LPK had followed me here to my hometown.

He just hadn't admitted he didn't think he could survive it, either.

I elbowed my way out of Jack's embrace. "Let go."

I'd gotten only a few feet when Jack said, "Avery," and when I turned around, he was staring at the ground, his hands on his hips, like he was fighting to figure out what to say. Images—losses of me—piled out of him, and I flinched.

"I'm sorry." He looked up at me. "I know Hank's right. You decide. Just know it's who I am to try to keep you from getting hurt. It's who you are to risk everything you are to help someone else. We've always been that way.

We've always loved what and who the other *was*. Is. Please let me drive you and be on standby. I've got my med kit in the truck, so if you have another seizure or anything else happens, I can help. At least let me do that."

Latham snarled something, but I ignored him as I thought of the new little victim and how little I'd be able to help her if I seized again.

I looked at Hank. "I know it's not procedure to let him accompany me, but he might be the only thing that keeps me from seizing in front of them. You okay with that?"

Hank nodded, and as I turned to reach for Jack, he was already stepping forward, reaching for me.

Sometimes, there are just no good choices. I was going to die at Jack's hands. And I was starting to get the feeling that was going to happen a lot sooner than I had thought.

CHAPTER TWENTY-THREE

The first time I ever set foot in Thibodaux's Grocery, I was almost seven. I had a death grip on Latham's hand, and for a thirteen-year-old, he was remarkably tolerant about it. I'm not sure what I had expected when my mother allowed us to go shopping with her that day; I have a vague memory of anticipating something vast and sterile, like the big-box groceries where we'd shopped in other cities—a place of thousands of pre-packaged options and very little soul.

It was summer as I recall, and the parking lot rippled with heat as we wound our way to a dilapidated, once-white, two-story, clapboard building that looked like the gentlest of breezes would flatten it. It reminded me of old churches, and I couldn't say why—except that the white siding and skinny profile begged for a steeple. Cobwebs as big as Latham filled the corners of the porch overhang, knitting the whole place together, and a rusted ice machine hummed along without a care in the world (or even a lock) next to a front door plastered with faded garage sale notices, stapled one on top of the other, layers and layers of lives, sold cheap.

Inside, Leila beelined for the proprietor—someone they called Old Jacques—while Latham tugged me in the opposite direction, over floors so old the linoleum had exposed the warped, gray plywood beneath. Aisles jumbled with shelves where goods teetered and clung to ledges as if they had grown there, moss in the cracks of rocks. Sepia-toned lights hung from soaring ceilings dimly illuminating the place, as creaking fans lazily stroked through dust motes as if they begrudged the effort; someone had carved out space for an actual bar in the back right corner of the store, with Bud and Michelob neon signs wedged in between LSU sports memorabilia. The whole place smelled like roast beef from the deli, and my stomach growled.

Somewhere beyond where we stood, pool balls clacked together followed by boys' voices rising in triumph. Latham drew me toward the sounds, and we found a hallway beyond the little bar, and beyond even that, a back room with a pool table that to a skinny, short, not-quite-seven-year-old looked the size of a frigate set afloat amidst hideous orange paneling and lime green shag carpeting. We entered another universe when we entered that room: a gaggle of boys lounging around in shorts and T-shirts, laughing, living. Several of them tussled playfully in the corner (one would turn out to be Sam); two more were shooting pool. Nate—the slimmer of the two players, his hair a shock of white-blond—didn't look particularly dejected as he lost. He just racked up the balls again.

"Good game," Latham said to the older boy holding the pool cue.

"Lucky day."

The older boy's losses spun out and held me pinned. There were bad problems with his family, with his father at their core, and I understood him immediately. I was only seven and he a worldly eleven, but I knew him. He was as trapped as I was in my cage of silence. With his gray eyes and dark shaggy mop of hair, he already looked as grown up as Latham.

He glanced at my brother. "Hey, I'm Jack. You must be the new kid—Latham, right?"

Latham nodded, angling his head at me. "This is my sister, Avery."

The boys all stopped mid-fight, mid-game, curiosity winging through the room as I stood there, half-hidden behind Latham. I was in shorts, my scars having paled to a rosy pink against my tanned skin, and they didn't stare. Instead, they shrugged and then proceeded to completely ignore me.

It was *wonderful*.

Voices rose in argument in the outer store, and I cringed. Leila and Old Jacques were hurling insults at each other with religious fervor. This came as absolutely no surprise to either Latham or myself. Somehow, I sensed, it didn't surprise Jack, either.

"So," Jack offered to Latham, "you know how to play?"

Latham shrugged. "Little bit."

"Oh, thank God," Nate said, with completely genuine relief, thrusting his pool cue into Latham's hands. "Here. I think it's something like six hundred and forty-seven games to three. You try."

Jack glanced at me, understanding more in that one glance than most anyone had in all the years I'd been dragged from town to town. "She gonna be okay?"

"Squirt?" Latham asked, and I nodded.

From the store, we heard Leila's voice raise with hacksaw sensitivity, "You stupid bumpkins wouldn't know a real opportunity if it bit you on the ass. Tarot-card reading is the coming thing. I'm offering you the chance to make real money just for the use of a small corner of your store."

I didn't actually understand all of the words Old Jacques spat back, being that some of them were in Cajun and some of the (possibly) English words profanity I hadn't actually ever heard before, but all of the words were angry. I did know that Leila didn't actually want to set up a Tarot card corner—she just wanted to establish the persona she and Dad had chosen for this town—eccentric, Southern-fried crazy. From what I could tell, she was succeeding on all accounts.

Jack broke the balls on the table with a sudden fierceness I appreciated.

Leila appeared at the door, and her retro-seventies mini-dress and tall, white go-go boots were strangely appropriate for the decor. She had a placid expression welded in place, always a dangerous thing to see. I retreated into the corner a bit more as she said, "Come along, children. We have better places to go."

Latham looked over at me, and then without turning to face her, said, "We'll stay here."

"I said come on," Leila insisted. "Right. This. Minute."

Jack missed his shot and silence ticked in the room; a million years later, Latham bent over the table, cocked his head to the side, and stared at her with an expression of resolve that would have made God quaver.

"We'll stay here." Then he slammed that ball into its pocket. And the next. And the next.

I'm not entirely sure when Leila drifted away, as the shock and awe of Latham running the table turned that room into a chapel of worship; no one had eyes for anything but those balls going home.

Hours later, after we had been given mouth-watering sandwiches from the deli, and were sitting out behind the store on the backsteps, and all of the continuous praise for Latham's skills had ebbed, one of the boys, Sam, piped up and said, "It must be a drag to have to watch after your little sister all the time."

I studied my sandwich; it had almost gone to ashes in my mouth, when Latham answered, very quietly, "It's a privilege. I take care of her."

They never asked again after that. Not once, in my hearing. Instead, I became their unofficial mascot, the girl who didn't fit in. For years afterward, the grocery was my safe place, an altar to normalcy. It was more home than home, that store.

With vehicle lights flashing, our caravan pulled into the crowded parking lot—Nate in his police jeep, Jack with his volunteer firefighter lights on, Sam behind us in his own truck, and then a parade of officers and God knows who else. Heat shimmered off the parking lot limestone, and I fought back a well of emotion at bringing the darkness we carried to a haven such as this.

I could almost see us as kids racing around the corner, back from some adventure or other, exploring some utterly important part of the woods, making kingdoms, pirate ships, and eventually campfires as the guys got older and talk turned to more serious subjects, like girls. I glanced at Jack, and he saw my battle, the tears fighting to brim over, and he reached over and squeezed my hand.

"Home," he said, understanding my nostalgia and sad little smile had nothing to do with the pack of reporters trailing us—a couple of whom were at that very moment rushing his truck. Jack twisted around and rummaged behind the seat until he found a jacket. "Put this on."

I did, gratefully, despite the stifling heat. God knows I didn't want the girl's family freaked out anymore than they already were because of my bloody shirt, courtesy of my nosebleed.

"Wait here." He stepped out and came around to my side, blocking the paparazzi. Jack, at his most menacing, will scare the fur off a hyena, and these bottom-feeders were no hyenas—though they backed up as one, giving him room to help me out of the truck.

Hank joined him in keeping the scavengers at bay as I climbed out, the parking lot dimly lit from a single streetlight. It was nearing dusk, and the grocery was usually pretty empty this time of evening, but thanks to the crowd that had followed us, the lot was now packed. I focused on the white noise playing on my iPod, which had somehow managed to remain in my

197

pocket on my run to the crime scene; on the way over to the store, Jack had pulled his earphones from the glove box for me, since mine were lost somewhere in the woods.

We moved as a unit toward the door, the group of reporters seeming to swell, along with a host of newcomers wanting me to find stuff. The quiet in Jack's truck had given me a few minutes to regroup, but I was still wobbly as we approached the store. I tried hard not to think about that little girl out in the field, or her sister, somewhere in hell.

At the front steps to the store, I noticed a small cluster of locals, people who'd just cashed their checks, or gotten groceries. They glared at me, hatred bubbling off them. Their stares said *abomination*, *sinner*, and my personal favorite, *media-whore*. I guess the crime scene footage had already hit the news. I caught myself searching the crowd for Father Tomas and his bright purple stole—or would it be blinding yellow today? He'd shut down several critics before when I had first visited his little church, people who thought I was desecrating the pews just by being there, and I knew he'd have intercepted these busybodies, asking them to consider their own sins instead of what they perceived to be mine.

Reporters crowded in behind us as we entered the cool of the old market; inside, the store was already jammed with people. I assumed the line was long because people, as always, needed to get checks cashed to pay on their accounts and to shop for the week.

"Lottie," Jack shouted above the din. "I told you to clear the place out."

"I tried!" a harried-sounding woman yelled back from somewhere over by the deli counter. I could barely see her for the crowd. "They," she nodded toward the reporters squeezing into every spare inch of remaining space, "got wind the family was here and that Avery was on her way. I didn't have enough help to clear everyone out."

Jack nodded, disgusted, looking around the room for who he could appoint as bouncers. He and Hank flanked me; Hank was also scanning the room, I presumed, for the family we were supposed to meet. I was pretty sure he would never have agreed to this location if he had understood how crowded it would be.

The place reeked of losses, like dead fish floating to the surface. I was drowning in them. Somewhere far away, Hank asked questions, and Jack answered, but none of it seemed real. *Real* was the one overriding image of oily, evil blackness I'd encountered a few times before since returning to Saint

Michael's. It dominated and obliterated all the other images, threatening to choke me with its malevolence. Yet other than the reporters, everyone in my sight seemed ordinary: Lottie, a dead ringer for Marilyn Monroe, in spite of five kids and her hair up in a bandanna, as she made sandwiches at the deli for the people wanting a snack for the ride home; Zannah digging in her purse, looking for something, maybe a lost car receipt, no, no, a check card, buying a few last-minute groceries still sitting on the counter. She glanced our way and images of Nate, lost to her, spun into the crowd, along with her certainty that I was what had come between her and the man she'd always loved. Emanating from Nate, lost images of Jack and me again, while Jack's losses were a muddle of war zones, combat, and the crowd pressing in as a possible threat to losing me. Fear rode shotgun behind his steady façade, a resolute expression that fooled everyone but me.

Piling on were the reporters' lost images of stories, and prizes, and paychecks, and prestige, lost images of books and belts, phones and keys, every image glowing bright, almost an afterburn. My vision started fritzing again, multicolored misfires, when my gaze landed on a woman I didn't quite recognize. She looked familiar, high cheekbones, her flaxen hair limp and dirty, as if she couldn't bother to care, and a face so hollow with sorrow, I couldn't place her. As we'd entered, she'd spun away from where she'd been examining the paltry selection of chips and headed right for me, recognition in her eyes, recognition tinted by rage.

I still had Jack's earphones in, and as I reached for one to pull it a little loose to get a handle on who she might be, she stopped in front of me and said, "Well, finally. I've been looking for you."

I felt, rather than saw, Jack and Hank rush for her, but neither fast enough to intercept the hand I never saw coming as she slapped me so hard I landed on the floor before it all clicked: Aurelia March's mom. I spat blood onto the grayed plywood (that was going to stain) as she bent over me, struggling against whoever was trying to pull her away.

"How's that for publicity, you bitch," she cried, her voice ragged with grief. She must have headed south as soon as she heard I'd resurfaced here. "You could have saved her. You let my baby suffer; you dragged it out, they told me. You played it out *two extra hours*, because you love the attention. I hope you rot in hell."

All around me, the cameras whirred and clicked.

CHAPTER TWENTY-FOUR

Pandemonium reigned in the grocery, and my world shrank to a tight circle of shoes and boots, of ankles and knees and darkness as people bent over me or crowded closer, blocking the light into my cave of hell. Everyone was shouting—someone heaved Aurelia's mom off me, but the voices . . . the voices stabbed and babbled, cut and bled; it was a feeding frenzy, half of the onlookers cheering, half appalled. Flashes popped, and people moved, people shoved. I felt around for my earphones, blinded and sickened by the images windmilling through my mind.

Someone nearby spoke to me, and I reached for outrage, but I had none. I wasn't the victim here. Shapes and colors melted together and swirled and made no sense, no sense at all, like multiple colors of paint stirred into a vat of black, and panic hit me, wave upon wave.

Suddenly someone lifted me, patted me down, and helped my trembling hands put the earphones back in. I needed something louder than white noise, and I clicked on a song, a track of one of Latham's favorite violin pieces that I'd uploaded years ago. It reached into my heart and soothed, pushing the images and pain out, and the world back into focus.

I opened my eyes to find Nate standing by me—he had been the one to help with the earphones—while Jack steered the gawkers out of the store. Hank stood beside what appeared to be another family—*little girl, blonde, dimples, laughing at her birthday party, balloons, blowing bubbles with her brother in the backyard*—their terror and grief so palpable in the air, I felt as if I could scoop it up in both hands.

Many of the reporters had pinched, frustrated expressions; they were furious with Jack for ejecting them with military precision. I didn't understand how Nate had arrived so fast. I heard Hank bark orders. People listened to him. Maybe it's his voice, the deep authority of it. Maybe it's because he's Hank, and if you take one look at him, you think of Clint Eastwood's Dirty Harry. You just want to make him happy so he won't shoot.

"Stop," I told Jack when a reporter tried to slide by him, and he shoved the guy into someone else, starting a domino effect in the crowd. He meant well but was just making matters worse. He ignored me or couldn't hear me past his own rage, so I shouted again, "Stop!"

Movement ceased, like a video on pause. Whatever Jack saw in that moment stopped him cold. His hands shook. "You're hurt." The cut of his words scratched like a record of his own failure. "Lottie—get her some ice!"

And then it was as if someone had yelled: action. Two of Nate's officers—I have no idea where they'd come from—each took Aurelia's mom by an arm, and the cameras began to whir again. Time expanded and then recoiled back to the last time I'd seen her, standing in the FBI office in Chicago, having just gotten the news that they'd found Aurelia but not where I'd had them look. *I'd been wrong.*

Aurelia had only been dead a few minutes when they got there.

I wish I could say I had never seen a person fall apart so completely at the death of a child. I wish I could say that. But I had seen it before. I saw it again that day when Aurelia's mom learned all hope was gone. It shattered her, scattering pieces of her sanity so far and wide, I knew she'd never be okay again. There is no *okay* when your child dies.

There is never an *okay*.

What remained was a naked stillness, a grief so deep that so much of what she used to be was gone. I understood that, too. Retribution had carried her this far—all the way from Chicago, all on the promise that I was here, and now she had absolutely nothing left.

"Let her go," I told the officers. My words hung in the air between us. Both of the officers scowled, confused. I turned to their boss. "Nate, you and I both know it's your discretion. Let her go."

We both glanced over at the woman, and it was impossible to tell what she was thinking—her face carried a strange, vacant wax-like expression.

Nate seemed to think she might still be dangerous. "Not here. We'll process her at the station."

"No, Nate. Please. That's Nonnie March. Aurelia's mom." He recognized the name. Most anyone in the country who'd seen a paper or TV in the last month would. "She's grieving."

"I can't let every grieving person take a shot at you, Av." His voice so low, I knew I had won. "Legally, it can't be open season just because someone feels like they have a justified grievance against you."

If he'd been adamant, nothing I'd have said would have mattered.

"She deserved that shot at me. Let her go."

Before Nate could answer, Jack was there, pressing a small bag of ice to my cheek. He cupped my other cheek with the other hand. "You don't owe the world, Avery, for your existence. Your ability doesn't mean that you have to save everyone. You have to quit thinking like that. Nobody deserves to take a shot at you."

"Can you blame her, Jack?" I met his gaze, and we stood there as everything went silent around us. Maybe we'd stepped through time again. Maybe it was ten years ago, and he'd just seen his father, his brains blown out. Maybe he'd remembered how much he'd hated me then, how much he believed I shouldn't have revealed to the reporter that a file of the Senator's secrets existed, one that could put the Senator away. "Of all the people in this room, Jack, I'd think you'd be the one who'd understand what she's going through."

"I wish I didn't," he said, finally, self-disgust flaking off his voice.

Somewhere far away, Nate interrupted, his voice calm and authoritative, capturing the room. "Everybody settle down. Right now." To me, he said, "I'll get Bailey to help Mrs. March."

I nodded as he dialed his friend, a grief counselor. I didn't expect that to help—there's really nothing a grief counselor can do, you know? You go through losing a child, and you rant, and you rave at the world, and you hurt, and you ache, and you go over every single step, every second, and think, *What could I have done differently,* and there are a billion things you could have done. You torment yourself until you're worn down to a nub, and you're so exhausted, you can't remember the last time you breathed without pain or bothered to eat. And when it's all done, when it's wrung out every ounce of humanity you have and left only a husk of who you once were, you don't get your baby back. The Universe doesn't say, *Well, it's horrible what you've gone through, no one should have to go through that, you've convinced us: here's your child, alive and well.*

It's the finality of such a loss that threatens your sanity. And when that vicious swing of the sledgehammer hits you, you are destroyed all over again, because you finally realize, *this doesn't end.* You will get used to the grief, the pain, the hell, the absence of that child, and then you will feel guilty for getting used to it because it *should* hurt. It should always hurt.

I don't remember letting go of the ice pack or it falling. Instead, I felt the glacial wind whistling past my ears, chapping them, and then flakes of snow landing on my face, freezing to my lashes and crusting my cheeks. The smell of piney woods overwhelmed me, shutting out any of the sharp aromas of deli ham and cheese and pickled potato salad. There was only the strong sweet bite of sap, the cool crust of salt air, the cold of the snow.

My hands clasped at my stomach, and when I looked down at them: blood. So much blood. Blood pooling at my feet, snow falling all around.

All color leached from the room as if I had stepped into a monochromatic world. Snowdrifts piled onto the worn linoleum, and an unearthly silence blanketed the store, even though everyone appeared to still be talking, shouting. I heard nothing; something had cut off that sense as if to say *pay attention.* White lights flared in slow motion as camera strobes flashed for what felt like minutes instead of a split second, and not a single click or pop pierced the hush entombing me.

The blood from my palms stained the packed snow, *drip, drip, drip.*

The snow turned to sand . . . and back to snow again. Sand. Snow. Sand. Snow. An icy wind breathed down my neck, chilling my ears to the point of pain, creeping, creeping, into my soul. Fear washed through me. Over where Lottie stood, the deli counter dissolved into rocks, and I could see ocean waves crashing against them. The sea was strangely silent when its waves should have been thundering as they showered icy mist over me. Panic pushed up inside, choking me, yet no one noticed. Not even Jack, who also seemed frozen, moving in such infinitesimally small increments, I wondered what dimension he existed in and how I had stepped out of reality.

Then in a snap that seemed to crack time, people moved and kicked up snow flurries in their path, and everywhere I looked, flakes were coating the surfaces: hair, eyelashes, purses, the canned good displays. My breath puffed white frost, as did Jack's as he seemed to be trying to speak to me. I heard not a sound, except the low whistle of the wind through treetops. Trees, instead

203

of the ceiling fans I knew were there. I was now in a clearing, and there were trees and snow fell from a gray sky, except I could feel the hard floor of the store beneath my boots, and when I looked back down, eye level, I could see the shelves, the piles of groceries, the randomness of Lottie's system of putting canned baked beans next to bags of brown sugar, and once again I could smell the pastrami at the deli.

The drifts on the floor grew higher and higher. Sometimes they were sand, and I swear I could see a girl with a sand bucket just on my periphery, but when I turned, she was gone, and the dunes were snow again.

Was I losing my mind? And a little part of me wondered if that wouldn't be better than trying to fight the pull of wanting to be with Jack, knowing it was the worst choice I could make. Seeing him standing there, holding back the tide of reporters, trying to help, knowing what it would do to him one day to know the truth? There is a special hell for people like me, and maybe I deserved it.

Sand. Snow. Sand again. Snow. Was Latham losing his mind, too? Was this what the problem was? Was his ability careening out of whack? You can't play God with other people's lives without ramifications. We'd played God a time or ten, hadn't we?

The snow and sand fought for dominance, and I scanned the room. Someone near the door—a tall man I didn't recognize; a reporter?—made me shudder. He stood in a drift where a little girl's snow angel had started forming as if a small, invisible child lay there, raking her arms and legs *up and down, up and down.* The man stepped toward me, his foot landing on a wing. It hurt. Hard, wrenching pain cut through me just to see his shoe touch that snow wing. I looked down at my own feet, and spread before me was another snow angel, this one only a little bigger. Freshly made, and I could almost feel the snow crunch beneath my jacket, as if my own arms had fanned out to make that pair of wings.

Whose images are these?

They are yours, Old Woman said, and I glanced up fast, without thinking, and there she stood, in the middle of the crowded grocery, her arm severed, bleeding all over Nate's shoes as he talked to an unresponsive Nonnie March. I didn't know what else to call this aberration—she had been Old Woman to me all of my life, but she was even younger now than when I'd last seen her at the clearing by the creek. She seemed more familiar. And I couldn't place why. She was easily my age, and if I focused on her face and not her severed arm, I could see an inherent kindness that comforted me. *How do I know the images are mine?* I asked her, and maybe I said that out loud, since the room seemed to hush, everyone gaping.

I could feel Jack's hands warm, so warm, on my arms, clenching as if to shake me. I knew he stood there. I could *feel* him, but he'd become invisible. I could almost see him on the periphery of my vision if I turned my head just so; beyond him, the store looked hazy. Mostly, though, I saw a clearing in woods I didn't know, taller trees, big boulders—bigger than me—landmarks I'd never seen before. I could feel Jack's gaze, and knew, without hearing him, that he was calling my name, trying to bring me back.

Dread thrummed through me, as if a precipice had formed beneath my feet; I was going to fall if I kept looking, and yet, I couldn't stop myself.

I pulled away from Jack and knelt in the snow, so cold, so very cold, frostbite nipped my fingertips, and suddenly, deep red roses grew up out of the other angel; they grew like magic beanstalks, taller and taller, until the blooms were abruptly sliced off. The heads of the roses fell to the snow, sprinkling across the littlest angel's wings, breaking apart, and petals flew.

And blood stained the snow where the petals had been.

LPK's little girls had been cut beneath their beautiful dresses and perfect wings.

He had kept them alive during the torture and redressed them in white, always with a lily tattooed between their thighs.

Were these images from Hank? The parents who were around here somewhere? Aurelia March's mom?

But if the tattoos were of lilies, why was I seeing roses?

I wanted to look at Hank, to ask him, but a big dog's paw prints now appeared around me, tracking through the snow, and something growled fierce and furious; I could almost feel the ruff of its fur under my palms, feel it press against me, protecting me, its teeth bared against someone.

Run! I must run from . . .

Someone in this room.

Run! Now! Now now now—now!

Someone is here.

Run!!!

I spun, feeling the evil, feeling the dark, and *there*—there was the man who'd been standing on the little angel's wing, and I watched as he turned and slipped out the front door. Fear crawled all over me, and every scar that crossed my body burned. I wanted to run, but Jack still held me, asking questions I could not hear. I tried to talk but no words would form, no sound would come. I couldn't breathe, couldn't breach the cold, and I shook, oh, how I shook. I panicked and looked at Jack, and he read the panic in my eyes: *I can't get back to you.*

I felt glass brush my lips as he put a tumbler to my mouth and tipped it up.

"Orange juice," Jack was saying, as I drank. "Lottie's fresh-squeezed, Avery. Drink."

And he tipped it again; little by little, as sound ebbed back into the room, and then color.

I looked over at Hank, who seemed, for the first time, not stoic, not hardened, but scared and . . . expectant.

I grabbed his sleeve, struggling to form words, shivering so hard—in spite of the withering temperature. "I think he was here."

"Yes," Hank said. "I already told you," and he motioned to the devastated, expectant family behind him waiting for me to be their miracle.

"No, Hank, I mean here, LPK in the store. And *here.*" I tapped my head. "I think I have some of his images now."

Hank, Nate, and Jack went on instant alert.

"What did he look like?"

"I didn't get a good look. Tallish, a little shorter than Jack, older. Dirty blond hair. Mean."

"I got it," Nate said and grabbed one of his officers as they ran to see if they could spot anyone of that description leaving the parking lot, or someone who might have seen such a man get into a car.

Hank was running right behind them, and as he hit the door he looked over his shoulder at Jack and said, "Please tell me you have security video in this place."

Jack shook his head. "We've never needed it."

CHAPTER TWENTY-FIVE

I closed my eyes and cranked up the volume on the iPod as I focused on breathing in, breathing out, and staying conscious. Jack encircled me with his arms, his chin resting on the top of my head, and I grabbed for his losses, stacking the images around me like armor against the razored edges of the others trying to reach me. The devil you know. I'd gotten used to Jack's losses now, and somehow they didn't hurt like the rest. Maybe that's why I could never see Latham's. Or my parents? Proximity, repetition, familiarity—whatever the reason, it was an unexpected gift.

Jack's warmth settled me, and the icy cold inside of me receded until I could no longer see the snow, feel the cold. My muscles relaxed, slowly, slowly, until my breathing eased back to normal. I didn't realize he and Hank and Nate had been talking until I felt vibrations from Jack's chest under my cheek. The rhythms of his words, the beat of his consonants hypnotized me like a long, lazy drive home.

"You're back?" Jack asked, his cheek pressed to my temple. He put a hand beneath my hair and rested his fingertips on my carotid artery—checking my pulse, waiting for signs that I had calmed.

Disappointment washed over Hank's expression when I looked his direction. "You didn't find him?"

He shook his head, grief and frustration warring on his face. "Too damned many people outside. Reporters, locals, gawkers."

Hank didn't have to explain. Now that the news my ability had returned was out to the public, I would always draw a crowd.

"I have a couple of officers questioning some of the people from the parking lot and store to see if anyone saw anything or has any photos," Nate added. "Someone may have caught him while trying to get a shot of you."

"Where's the girl's family?"

"My office," Jack answered.

Hank cocked his head, worried. "Kid, you up to seeing them?"

We both knew the answer to that was a decided *no*, but I nodded anyway. My worst day as a paparazzi target paled in comparison to that of parents who have lost a child.

"They know the youngest daughter has been found," Hank explained. "Her name was Melody, and she looked very much like her sister."

I'd need to know that, to be able to know and distinguish what images I was seeing; Hank and I had developed an understanding of what I needed to know beforehand that would make this easier on the parents and require less of my time with them.

"The girls were playing in the park with a babysitter yesterday morning—the mom works from home. The sitter was knocked out cold, and when she came to, the girls were gone." Hank looked at his notes. "The sitter was an older woman—the mom's aunt, I believe, and she's in the hospital recovering from her injuries and the shock, I think. We have a national alert out so that if any girl matching our victims is taken, we get immediate notice. I was en route when you found the sister today."

I could see images of lilies spinning off Hank. The LPK always left a lily. We didn't know why, anymore than we knew why he tattooed his victims with them. Hank had never released either to the public, and so far, they hadn't been leaked, which meant it was very low odds this was a copycat.

"How can I help?" Jack asked.

It startled me to realize he already had. I felt steadier. This was the slippery slope Latham feared and my dad had warned me about ten years ago, when I'd first chosen to keep seeing Jack despite Dad's prediction. This was the slippery slope of my heart. I knew what the consequences of following it were going to be. Sooner or later, what Dad had predicted would come true. But, God help me, I couldn't stop myself. It was as if I'd been out in the cold for a million years and had finally come inside to stand by the fire. I hadn't felt so safe, so connected, in so long that I wanted to weep from the sheer comfort of it. Sometimes you see your life barreling toward an exit; the brakes have failed, you can't turn the car, and you can either choose to panic or you can make your last moments count as much as possible.

"Hold my hand," I told him, "and don't let go. I'm using your losses to help me through all this other pain—I won't get through this meeting without you."

My admission shocked him, and his expression turned grim.

"Will this hurt you?" He meant his hand as he clasped mine.

In more ways than you know.

"No," I told him and laced my fingers through his.

I wasn't prepared for what I saw when I stepped into Jack's small office. The last time I'd been there, it had been his grandfather's—Old Jacques—his Senator father having never deigned to step foot inside to my knowledge. Old Jacques's idea of office décor had been "early cardboard," with enough junk scattered about that you had to wonder if he robbed garage sales as a hobby. Since the store hadn't changed from the time I'd first set foot in it— well, with the exception of having every last LSU front-page championship headline shellacked, decoupaged, and hung on the wall—I hadn't expected Jack's office to be any different. Instead, it was clutter-free and streamlined: military shipshape, simple lines, nothing expensive, everything functional.

But it was the painting on the wall opposite his desk that drove a spike in my heart. Shock stopped me in the doorway, despite Hank snarling at me to enter. Jack, following right behind me, had to have felt the shock ripple outward. He squeezed my shoulders gently as we moved inside the room, and he bent to my ear. "That painting kept me alive, Av. Please don't be upset that I bought it."

I couldn't answer him. I couldn't parse the feelings, the fear that he'd known why it was so important to me. Why I had painted eight variations, since. Why it haunted me, still. I'd been dreaming about him for weeks when I'd painted it just a little over a year ago. The canvas almost filled the wall; I'd intended it for a large space and always wondered about the anonymous buyer who'd taken it off the market the day the show opened this past spring. The painting was of a lake at the cusp of sunrise: the blues and purples and blacks of the quiet, still water mourned the death of something innocent while the smooth surface of the lake mirrored the brilliant violets and magentas and golds of a beginning day. The colors were so saturated and hyper-real, they infused the senses. Barely visible at one edge of the image, where a pier was almost hidden in the luminous early dawn, a couple lay. It was their first time to make love. If you looked close, you could see her scars. And you knew they had never mattered to her lover. He had never known or thought of her without them, and before doing anything else he had kissed every one. No one else would know that. No one else, but Jack.

I'd titled the painting: *Broken Hallelujah*.

Usually, that is how I let go of things, by painting them out of my system. Through the years, I have let go of so many things, one by one, I sometimes wonder how I'm not invisible. But I couldn't let go of this, and maybe I never would. Maybe I'm not meant to.

I had wondered, before we made love, if it would be a disaster, a flood of losses destroying the joy, the mood, the chemistry. Instead, it had been the opposite: so much connection and thrill, excitement and trust, pure *feeling*, that there were no losses swirling around us at all—only what we gave to each other. I had everything in that moment, everything I could have ever hoped for, and my father's prediction hanging over it, making it all the more precious because I knew it wouldn't be forever . . . or even for a year.

I glanced at Jack, knowing he'd seen the other, almost hidden, image to the far right of the canvas, the one that could have been a trick of light and swirls of pigment: the same couple broken apart. She reaches back for him but you know it is futile. It was one of those once-you-see-it, you-can't-help-but-see-it things. Yet I knew most people never saw it. I had tried to exorcise Jack from my memory by committing our moment to canvas. Determined in each incarnation that the woman would not reach back for him. She'd move on. She'd stand on her own. I never managed it.

Not everyone sees my double-images, the play on lights and darks, and I sometimes don't even realize they're there until someone points them out to me. My biggest breakthrough sale had been like that: a snow angel made by a small girl with a red rain boot lying on its side in the upper left . . . I froze.

Amidst the earlier barrage of snow and images at the store, I'd almost forgotten the other painting, but that painting had also sold quickly and anonymously, and hidden in it was the image of a dying rose overlaying a snow angel. I'd painted it almost four years ago. Had the LPK focused on me as long ago as that painting? Was he the source of that image? Had I brushed up against him at some point, and grabbed this loss? The original *Snow Angel* wasn't something I could mention now, not in front of the family of another lost girl, but somehow I knew that painting might be the lead Hank needed.

"Av?" Jack asked, squeezing my hand. "Did you hear Hank?"

I looked over my shoulder at Hank and Nate, who were both giving me their version of stoic-but-worried. Cop worried is never good.

"These are the Gavins," Hank said again. "Russell and Rachael."

It startled me that I'd been so overwhelmed with the painting that I hadn't even seen them yet. Seen their losses. The parents clung to each other in a corner of the office, as far away from me as they could get without merging with the warped paneled wall, as if proximity to me made their suffering more real: one daughter brutally murdered, another held by a monster.

Russell Gavin, balding slightly, was short and stocky with a lot of muscle from wrestling whatever it was he delivered when he drove his big truck; he subtly leaned against the desk as if he might not manage to hold himself up without it, and he clearly he was the only thing holding his wife together. Rachael Gavin, bright bottle-blonde hair, matched her husband's girth but in soft, girlish curves, one of those women you instinctively know is a hugger who calls everyone *honey* in such a nice way, no one would think to object. Her eyes, watery from recent tears, and his, bloodshot and bleary, implored me to save their baby. They were cracking from the strain. I don't think either of them was even thirty, yet. Their images and losses swirled across the room, etching themselves, acid-like, into my world.

I tightened my grip in Jack's and half-stood behind him, terrified of what else I was about to see. Their faces were filled with so much fear, but it was the glimpses of hope that hurt the most. Hope is always the worst.

"How," Russell cleared his throat as his wife pressed her face to his shoulder, "how does this work? Do you need something of Calliope's?"

Before I could answer, Rachael interrupted, begging: "Please find my baby. Please find her. I'll give you anything I have. We lost her sister—we can't . . ." and unable to finish she broke down in sobs.

"We can pay," Russell offered, his words clacking together like bowling pins tumbling of their own accord. "Our car, our house—anything. You just . . . you just name it," and he bowed his head, his own tears flowing as Hank stepped forward.

"Anything at all," his wife cried.

CHAPTER TWENTY-SIX

"I'm sorry, it doesn't work like that," I told Russell, and then turned to Rachael. "Mrs. Gavin, I promise I will do my best, but I would never in a million years take or make money off someone's loss. You also have to understand: the images I get are often limited—like a zoomed-in close-up. I often don't see enough to know the exact location of what's in the image. What I might be able to do is help the FBI narrow down the possibilities or give the agents another lead. You have to understand that, going in."

They both nodded, but they would have agreed if I'd said they needed to throw themselves onto a bonfire; hope shone from them, unstoppable.

"I don't need anything of Calliope's."

I turned the volume on the iPod down a few notches as I stepped around Jack and closed the distance between the Gavins and me.

"I will need to touch your hands. Before I do, I need to emphasize something. Please focus only on Calliope. On how she looked the day before she was missing. Other than that, please focus on positive things, happy things—smiles, birthday parties, Christmases—because I see losses, and if you start focusing on all that you have lost—or think you might have lost—well, it's like sifting through a thousand grains of sand while trying to find the one that we need. So, happy moments, okay?"

I felt Jack inhale sharply behind me, and he squeezed my shoulders where he'd rested his hands. I knew he was keeping one finger on my pulse to monitor me, though he'd made it look casual to everyone else. I could also see his losses spill out—how he'd yelled at me when I was trying to see the lost images of Brody, how he'd been focusing on all that he'd lost, and how that had cost me.

I reached up and squeezed his hand. "Jack, stop. You didn't know. I need you to do what I just asked of the Gavins if you're going to stay in here."

By now, terror coated Russell and Rachael in slick, black tar; they probably would not be able to help themselves in their panic—they would see losses. I would have to deal with it.

"Ready?"

They nodded, and I slowly unstacked Jack's images—softer now, no physical pain or punch to them—and mentally shuffled them. *Huh, who knew? I can move them.* I hadn't thought of trying that before, though I had always been able to search through images as they flew toward me. The higher the volume of images, though, the harder it was for me to see one long enough to know what I was looking at, especially as they dug and cut into my mind, barreling around like a hurricane made of barbed wire.

Still, I now knew Jack's images—and Hank's—so intimately I could handle them almost as if they were my own. I'd just never tried to move them before, and the fact that I could gave me an idea: one by one I took Jack and Hank's images and stacked them until they formed a tent over and around me, igloo-like, with a small opening in the front for the Gavins' images to enter. If I could slow down their images, maybe I could see something helpful, faster.

What if it didn't work?

What if I screwed up again, and Calliope paid the price?

Jack squeezed my shoulder, sensing my terror.

Reassured, I reached out a hand and placed it over the clasped hands of Russell and Rachael; the images of Calliope and Melody streamed through the tent's opening, swirled around and around like black crows determined to rip me to shreds. It was a lot to take in, but my fortress held so much more at bay, I was able to pluck one image and then another and sort of paste it against the wall of Jack's and Hank's images. I don't know why that worked, but it did, and the images started forming a timeline of little losses of Calliope: a lost binky (under the dresser), a lost stuffed animal (behind the dryer), the five seconds she'd run out of her mom's sight at the grocery store—all the way to the present, and bam, there she was.

I grabbed that image and focused on it hard, my breathing shallow, my pulse no doubt racing, while in the background Jack asked if I needed to stop. I shushed him without losing focus on little Calliope, who was tied— hand and foot—to a chair in a dark room.

Just as I felt I was making progress, someone began screaming in my head; it took all my willpower to push the screams away, to push away my own horror and panic and heartbreak and focus, something necessary if I was going to be of any help to this family. The first girl, that very first time, I'd broken down in front of the parents and made it so much worse for them.

I focused on opening up my senses, and as the pain slammed into me, I used it to concentrate on the room where Calliope was being held.

Roses bloomed at my feet, and I ignored them as they climbed the people standing in the room with me. I ignored their strong scent, and then tried to avoid being distracted by the feeling of being crushed under the weight of something so dark, so heavy, that I struggled to breathe.

It had always been like this, every time I'd helped Hank. The killer tattooed lilies on the girls, but I always saw dead roses, and it never made sense. I pushed that away now, focusing again on what I needed to see in that room, and as I sifted out everything else, until all that remained was an image of the room where Calliope cried, tied to a chair.

It seemed familiar, and yet, once again I had no markers for the room— no specific wall color that I could see, no windows, no shapes. Just the sense that it had a tall ceiling, with something that looked like a wooden chair for Calliope, placed next to a wooden stand of some sort that I couldn't fully see, with a long purple-ish drape (or maybe that was just a shadow) over it. The latter hung so close to my viewpoint, I thought I should be able to identify it. Yet no matter how I tried to force the image to be clearer or sharper, it grew darker and fuzzier instead.

I couldn't see any exterior light entering the room, but it was dark outside—and so even if there were windows, I might not have been able to tell. I also knew this could be an image from earlier today. No way to know yet. There was no other furniture visible: just the chair with Calliope—her face swollen from crying, tears silently falling. She was in shorts and a sleeveless shirt. I gasped when I looked down and saw the lily tattooed on the inside of her left thigh. It was fresh—still red and scabby.

There were also shallow cuts on her arms and legs. She had blood dripping down her legs. I didn't know if she had been raped already or just cut.

Horror and regret swamped me, and I fell to my knees. I willed her to open her eyes and see me, as if I were somehow there and could comfort her, and as I strained to make a connection I felt Jack's arms tighten as he whispered in my ears to come back. I couldn't. I had to find a way, some way, to reach this beautiful, sweet little girl and protect her, and I just couldn't pull back from her and leave her alone.

But Jack could. I felt him pull my hands away from those of her parents', and the image faded, though it didn't disappear. I blinked a few times and, wiping the tears from my face, looked up into the absolute fear of her parents. I would not tell them everything I'd seen.

"She was alive at the time of the image," I said. "I can't promise you any more than that. I can't even promise you that she's still alive right now, but I think she is."

They were on their knees now in front of me, collapsed in a heap, sobbing, holding onto each other, terrified of touching me again but so desperate to know more. Pain, so much pain, and I shook from it.

"She was alive, and it's recent," I told them again, fighting to push the words out, fighting not to scream from the pain. "Hang onto that. She's alive. I've never seen anyone else this early. We have a chance."

I lost track after that—there were so many words and prayers and so much begging; Nate seemed to realize I was spent and stepped forward with a gentle, "Come with me, folks. I have a place where you can be alone for a few minutes."

He led the Gavins out as Jack knelt next to me.

"Av, how in the hell do you stand it?"

"How do I not?" I asked him. "She's there, Hank." I looked up at my old nemesis, the man who'd become one of the few people in this world I could count on, tears streaming down my face. "She's there. He's already started with her."

Hank's color went ashen. "The tattoo?"

"And cuts," I told him, "on her arms."

Jack lurched up, his eyes locking on Hank, who shook his head and waved him off.

"It's not something we've ever released to the public," Hank said.

The two of them seemed to be saying volumes, just short of arguing, but I was in too much pain to dissect the losses reeling off both of them.

"Kid. The cuts—just her arms?"

"Enough," Jack shouted, staring at Hank as if he couldn't believe Hank could be so clinical. But you had to be; he had to be, to get through this, to find her. It was hard for Jack to see a child scarred for life. I understood that. My scars were at least from an accident. Calliope's were from a monster. They would be a reminder the rest of her life, and that would be difficult for Calliope, growing up with scars, but if we found her... she'd be growing up.

"I didn't see any other cuts, but there was blood running down her legs."

Hank steeled himself, and I knew he would carry that revelation every minute of every day to come.

"He hasn't torn the clothes she's wearing yet, or put on the other dress." I knew he would know I meant the princess outfit every girl had been wearing when we found them. The FBI had tried to track down sales on those dresses, but they'd been sold by the tens of thousands in stores around the country and online.

"The tattoo? You think it's fresh?"

I nodded. The medical examiner had told Hank that the LPK put the lily tattoo on them just hours—maybe a day at most—before he was done with them. But he was moving faster now, and even if he stuck to his routine and old timetable, we didn't have much time.

"Any hits on the place?" Nate asked when he reentered the office.

"Not specifically." I described what I'd seen. "But it's somehow familiar. Some place around here that I've been or know."

"Recently?" Jack asked, hopeful. I hadn't been back long—the list of places to look would be short.

"I can't tell. So much hasn't changed—could be from when we were kids."

"But it's here?" Hank asked. "Not somewhere else you traveled with your parents or while we've been working the case?"

"Here, I think." I'd never be able to answer Hank's questions with anything close to confidence. Not after Aurelia. "I feel like there are things in the image I should recognize, but didn't. It's like having a word on the tip of your tongue. You know you know it, but it's not there. The room's mostly dark—there was a single light overhead, and it was dim. I can't tell if it's an issue with the light itself, or just how I'm seeing it. But the ceiling is taller than I would have expected."

"Like a warehouse or a barn?" Nate asked.

I closed my eyes and pulled up the image. "I can't tell. Walls are white, but I can't tell if they're metal or sheetrock—not with the poor lighting."

Hank paced the little he could in the tight space. "I have to get the local teams started on this. We'll start with all of the old warehouses around here."

Nate spoke up. "I have officers who're off duty who'll be happy to help. We have a pretty damned good volunteer system here—more people will help us cover more ground faster."

"Officers," Hank answered, "not volunteers. He'll be armed, and he's got nothing to lose—he won't blink at taking out a bunch of innocents who stumble across him. Your officers can go with some of my agents, act as liaisons, and help with pinning down locations. And remember that our unsub has escalated to using IEDs at the burial sites. So far, they've been sophisticated enough to create a serious obstacle for the bomb squads. This guy knows what he's doing."

"Don't forget chemical plants—we have a lot of abandoned ones around here," Jack suggested, but I shook my head.

"No, it wasn't a plant. I wouldn't have been in a plant—or a warehouse. But an old house remodeled from past years—yes. It could have been something like that. There are a lot of those old southern plantations that Latham and I worked on when I was in my teens."

"Can you get me a list?" Hank asked.

"Betty—Latham's secretary—would be able to get that for you faster." I gave him the number. "She's scarily efficient."

CHAPTER TWENTY-SEVEN

It was excruciating to wait, unable to do more. Back in Chicago, as a layperson, I couldn't go into the field and search for the girls. To this day, I didn't know if I had whether it would have helped me zero in on the location physically and helped me bring the images into better focus, or whether it might have made the difference in finding a little girl alive, or dead.

The images were always one small piece of a giant jigsaw puzzle, and I had always argued that I might see something on site that would give me a point of reference, or simply help me recognize what I was *seeing*, and thereby allow me to narrow down the actual location of the girl we were looking for on a case. Hank, understandably, couldn't let me ride with the agents, who might be going up against an armed serial killer, and couldn't legitimately put me into the field without the risk of the media chronicling my every move and exposing how close—or not—the FBI was in its search. When the LPK added IEDs to the mix, every cautious instinct Hank possessed had grown exponentially.

Once Hank was out of earshot, working with Nate to coordinate an incident command center, Jack offered to drive me around.

"Really?" I squinted at him, wondering why he was willing when he'd been so worried, before, that helping would hurt me.

"You mean, why would I drive you around instead of thinking you should stay put given there is a serial killer out there, and you're so close to another seizure, even I can taste it?" He looked at me knowingly. "After all, you're so docile, you'd just sit tight. Right?"

There was no point in denying it; in the beginning, I'd lifted car keys from an agent so I could drive around and try to get a hit off a location—something that resembled the images I'd seen. That had proved a disaster. It was nearly impossible to both see the images that burned into me as I hunted for the LPK and notice what was happening on the road in front of me. It was a miracle that I'd only hit a streetlight and not an individual—and the accident ended my attempts to hunt down the LPK by myself.

I smile as Jack grimaced.

A few minutes later, he picked me up at the back of the store, and we were headed to my house so I could change out of the bloody shirt I still had on underneath his jeans jacket.

"I texted Gail to bring Brody to my house," Jack said, "and to explain what was happening, so he wouldn't be afraid. She's going to stay with him. I'll have to tell him something about his mom soon. I just don't know what to say. As difficult as our relationship was, she loved—what the hell?"

There, parked in front of my house (having navigated a gate I thought again had been locked) was a beautiful late-model, powder blue BMW.

"That's Marguerite's car," Jack said, swallowing as he looked at me for an explanation.

I was too stunned to answer, and the fear she might be dead inside made me shudder.

"I have no clue," I finally managed when I realized Jack was still waiting for a response. I started to climb out of his truck; he put a hand on my arm to slow me down.

"Let's call Nate and let the police make sure who is in there. If it's her kill—" He stopped, gaping now at the front door, and when I turned, I felt my blood drain to my feet, all the air in my lungs whooshing out in shock.

Marguerite stood framed in my doorway, perfection from head to toe, looking at us all the world like we were the intruders. Then she turned and walked back into my house.

"Where in the hell have you been?" Jack snarled at Marguerite before he had even cleared the threshold.

"How'd you get in?" I asked, following on Jack's heels, knowing Latham had installed the new encrypted router earlier that morning, and the place should have been as secure as Fort Knox.

"The door was unlocked," Marguerite said, with a shrug, never taking her eyes off Jack. "Really, Avery, anyone could've wandered in here. It's like you want to be in danger, just to keep Jack running over here at all hours. How incredibly clever of you."

There was no point answering her, much less trying to deny the accusation—she'd never believe anyone female wasn't as manipulative as she'd always been. But the door not being locked—as far as I knew she had no breaking-and-entering skills, which meant it had been open. And that was weird. Then I remembered Latham's boozy breath at the crime scene and wondered if he'd been a little bit too drunk to close up properly. Still, it wasn't like him to be sloppy when it came to my safety.

"I want an answer," Jack said to Marguerite, glancing at me in bewilderment. I shrugged, equally confused. I'd been certain she was dead.

"I see you got my note," Marguerite said.

"What note?" Jack asked.

She sighed, aggrieved. "I left a note at your house that I was here, and for you to meet Avery and me here, but I guess I should have known you would already be with her." She glared at me. "You sure don't waste any time."

"What Avery and I do or don't do is none of your business, Mags." Jack said it calmly, not quite gently, his anger curdled just beneath the surface. "And you still haven't answered the question. Where have you been? We thought you were dead."

Jack's hands closed in fists at his sides as he moved to stand a little in front of me. "Avery? You okay?"

I felt so watery thin, as if I were barely there. She wasn't dead. The thought electrified me, burning through to my core. How could I have been that wrong? Am I wrong about Calliope, too? Am I leading Hank in the wrong direction again?

What have I done?

"I'm confused," I mumbled to Jack as I stepped into the kitchen and poured myself a glass of fresh squeezed orange juice from a big pitcher I always kept in the fridge. I took a sip as I tried to buy some time from having to answer. I couldn't help noticing that Marguerite's losses were razor sharp, centered mostly on Jack, with me as the culprit. I couldn't tell her how wrong she was without causing her even more grief.

"Oh, I assure you, I am quite alive," Marguerite said, warmly. A little too warmly, and my nerves tingled in warning.

I stared into the remnants of the juice glass, surprised to see it almost gone. The tang of it was helping me handle the pain she was throwing off. I poured another glass as she reached into a briefcase and pulled out a sheaf of papers. Whatever the documents were, they didn't signify a loss. Quite the opposite, she seemed practically euphoric, as if she'd just crossed some critical finish line and was about to run a victory lap.

Jack's patience was gone. "Then where the hell have you been? You left Brody at camp without telling me I needed to pick him up, you planned a trip without telling me or making arrangements for Brody, and you missed the custody hearing. We tracked you to your hotel and lunch, and then you disappeared, and yes, I even went so far as to hire a PI to find you, for Brody's sake. He's devastated. For someone claiming to want her son, you have one helluva way of showing it."

Then he pinged on something she'd said earlier. "And by the way, what are you doing here? At Avery's of all places?"

She smiled. The hair on the back of my neck stood on end as images of her losing Jack to me washed over me and then, like a light switch had flipped, evaporated.

"I'm a hell of a mom, Jack," she answered, and there was no anger, no fire, in her words, only calm. The calm of a victor who's about to fillet a fish she's caught. She looked at me then, tapped the sheath of paperwork in her hands with a manicured nail. "I'm not the kind of mom who'd let my son's father be duped again. I've been to Boston."

The words froze there, midair.

This was my ending, this was my agony, and she smiled, knowingly.

"Boston?" Jack asked, looking back and forth at us, knowing there was some undercurrent between us he wasn't picking up on.

"You're not the only one who can hire a PI." She looked at me then, a keen reckoning in her eyes. "I worked for the Senator, remember? As you know, Avery, I have his files. All of them."

I must have gasped, because she smiled then.

"It took me years to track down the clues, to pay the right people to get the facts, and I finally have. You lied to Jack. He thinks you can do no wrong, but you're responsible for every single terrible thing in his life. You should've never come back here, trying to steal my husband. My son."

"I did not come home to steal Jack or your son. I would never take a son from his mother, and if you'd think about it for a minute, I think you know that."

She started to say something else, and I held up my hand, stopping her. I put my empty glass on the counter and then did the thing I had hoped and prayed I'd never have to do. I turned to Jack, and said, "I'm sorry. I didn't want to tell you this way."

He looked as puzzled and concerned as I'd ever seen him.

"If I'm honest with you," I choked out, "I didn't want to tell you at all. You had every right to know, but I would have run away again before telling you. Before hurting you like this."

I swayed on my feet, but I wouldn't let Jack touch me, or help me this time. I put a hand on the counter for balance, and then pulled up my shirt so that they both could see the scar, the large vertical cut from my breast-bone to below my navel. Fat, ugly, and somewhat faded now, but still ragged and pinkish. The air went out of the room, an implosion that detonated my heart as Jack's shock broke over him.

CHAPTER TWENTY-EIGHT

Jack's hands trembled as he looked first at the scar, then at me, and back to the scar. How I wish I had died on that operating table. Anything would have been better than seeing Jack's loss, as fresh as if it had just happened.

Well, I guess for him, it had.

"If you think," Marguerite hissed, "that I'm going to let a woman like you, a crazy con artist, a liar, have anything to do with what's mine?"

"Hush, Mags," Jack said, grief swamping him.

She ignored him, plowing on. "She hid your child from you. She knew she was pregnant before she ran. She ran and kept you from knowing, didn't even tell you when she needed medical help. You're a trauma medic, Jack, and she knew that and didn't let you help save your own son. What kind of monster is she? That's the question you should be asking yourself."

I closed my eyes. I couldn't argue with her assessment of me.

"Mags, you need to leave," Jack said, in a broken voice I'd never heard before.

Marguerite bristled, but she also looked puzzled now.

"Jack. I know you've been under a lot of stress, and I know that's clouded your judgment, but now that you can see what she really is—what a liar she is—"

"Get out," he said it so sharply, so quietly, loss images bled around me as Marguerite gasped.

"You can't be serious. Your son *died* because she didn't get help in time. And she knew. She knew—"

I shook my head at Jack, my own horror clouding my eyes.

"I didn't. I swear, Jack, I wouldn't have—"

"Oh, right," Marguerite said, turning to me, "like anyone can believe anything you say. Your parents are con men—yes, the Senator was digging for information on them, too, but he'd already pegged you for a liar, and what I found proves you're a murderer, too—"

"That's it," Jack demanded, his voice snapping the command, the emotional bullets whizzing all around us. "Get out. I am completely serious, Mags; if you don't leave right now, I'll carry you out. I want nothing to do with you ever again."

"But Jack, don't you hear what I'm saying? She destroyed your father. Destroyed your family. Lied to you and hid your child from you—she destroyed your child, and you're just going to forgive her? What kind of father would let her get away with that?"

Tears and mascara ran down her cheeks, and she stepped a few inches closer to Jack. "You're not thinking clearly, Jack. You feel sorry for her, but look what she's done. See who she is. I will not have her around my kid. She's crazy—certifiable."

"The only one certifiable in this room, Mags, is a woman who would abandon her son so she could conduct a witch hunt on a woman who has done her no harm."

With that, Marguerite threw the copies of the hospital records at him and spun away; as they drifted into piles, soft as lullabies, deadly as poison, she yanked open the door to find Gail on the porch, about to knock. Brody saw his mom and ran to her screaming, "Moooommmm!"

"Hey, Baby," Marguerite said, knifing me with looks over his head. "I'm back. I had to take a real important trip, and someone was supposed to let you know."

Brody looked at his dad, swallowing her lies, his gaze hardening.

"I'm sorry for all the confusion. I think your dad got some of my trip days mixed up."

She looked down at the boy, beaming through her tears. "I'm so glad to see you!"

Gail stood stunned on the porch, and then she saw Jack's face—still in shock and grief. "We saw the note at your house," she explained, awkwardly.

224

"It said Marguerite was back and over here. Brody read it—and there was no stopping him."

Jack nodded, "Thank you, Gail. I'm glad you brought him."

I turned away from the happy familial scene and poured myself another glass of juice. I had never been so thirsty in my life. I could not remember the last time so many losses had crashed about my head; I felt off and woozy, wretched and heartsick, and pain lanced through me. Snow drifted from my ceiling, my breath frosted, and I grew so cold. I shivered, aching, watching Jack stand there in anguish, unable to process the import of what Marguerite was saying to Brody or the dagger sheathed in the words of the note she had left for Gail.

"I think I should go," Gail said from the doorway, and Jack nodded.

Brody unleashed his hug on his mom and ran through the snow over to me, beaming, tears running down his face. "You found her! I knew you would. You found my mom!"

I could barely nod, but I somehow managed it, my throat so tight, I could hardly speak. "Sort of. I think she found herself."

I can still see her bloody eyes. Why can I still see them? I didn't dare look up from Brody to Marguerite's satisfied expression.

"I know you're real glad to have your mom home. She's missed you, I'm sure." The words felt garbled even as I said them, and I had to resist the urge to brush my hand through his coal dark hair, resist huffing the snow off his nose. I don't think he heard much of what I said. He'd already danced back over to his mom, leaving me numb. Empty.

Marguerite grasped his chubby little hand and said, "You know what? I think it's time we had a treat. What would you like?"

"Can I, Dad?" Brody asked, automatically, and I saw how much it meant to Jack that he'd done so without worry or fear.

I closed my eyes and tried to shake the image of a sprawled Marguerite, face up, blood gushing over those glassy eyes. Why was I still seeing this?

"Sure, Brody," Jack choked out, and Brody whooped and raced out the door.

Marguerite smiled. "See you in court, Jack."

CHAPTER TWENTY-NINE

We stood for eons there looking at that closed door, I think, both in so much pain we didn't know where to start. Snow piled up in drifts in my living room and kitchen, coating the easel, the paints, the little dining table in the corner. A million years later, Jack shoved his hands in his pockets. His voice was strangled as he fought the words. "An emergency C-section?"

I nodded, and my voice cracked. "I'm sorry."

"Dear God, Avery, you don't owe me an apology. I owe you." He broke then, his shoulders shaking with sobs. "How far along?"

His voice was only marginally audible, but his losses swamped me, killing me.

"Twenty-two-and-a-half weeks."

As a trauma medic, Jack would know that wasn't old enough for his son to have had much of a chance in the world on his own.

"He lived seven hours, forty-one minutes. They couldn't save him." I shook, telling him that. I shook so hard, my teeth rattled.

"Did Nate know?" he asked, the words so low I almost didn't hear them.

"He didn't know. Still doesn't."

Jack leaned against the wall, covering his face with his hands as he inhaled a few ragged breaths. I braced against the counter, my legs threatening to fold—knowing he had so many questions to ask, knowing my answers would only cause him more pain.

"What happened?" Jack's eyes were glassy with tears when he looked up at me, his hands in tight fists.

I couldn't meet his gaze. How do you tell the father of your son that your body killed the beautiful child you had made together? That you knew it was a danger, and yet you didn't ask for help, at least not in time. *How do you explain that?* There is no excuse for it. There is no forgiveness for such carelessness. There is no mercy. There is only hell, and I hadn't wanted him to have to live there, in that dark, dark place where I now lived. Yet here we were, and our shared agony detonated every image of loss that had ever come between us.

"Avery," he said, his voice barely audible. "I need to know."

I took a deep breath, squeezing my eyes shut against the images, and fought for the sanity it would take to tell him.

"It was a seizure. My first big one since I was a little kid. The flood of losses had escalated; I couldn't control them—I don't know why. Maybe the pregnancy? The hormones? My brain chemistry. No way to know."

Every word scraped me raw.

I ignored the snow, falling harder now. Somehow ignored the odd sight of a sleek gray coat of fur disappearing beneath my little table. I was in my kitchen. I knew that. I could feel the chipped texture of the broken Formica counter underneath my hand, see the worn honey tones of the wood floor where the snow piled, smell the familiar scent of man, and sweat, and hay, and turpentine from my paints, over by the easel. My feet were so cold, so cold. My heart hurt like something had rent it in two, and I knew there was never going to be a way to put it back together.

I slid to the floor then, everything in me giving up. There was nothing left. Nothing but hurt.

I dragged out the words, one by one, hard as rocks. "I . . . I tried to get prenatal care, but the doctors had lost patients, lost children, and the pain was exponential when I was trapped in an exam room, so I thought I could read up, study everything. Get a mid-wife, find a quiet place. It was so stupid, not to ask for help from you or Latham."

"It's not your fault. I chased you away," his voice broke, and he put his face in his hands. "God, Avery, I told you I didn't want to have kids with you."

"I couldn't blame you for that, Jack."

"You should."

"No. What I do . . . it's painful to me, to everyone around me. It's not predictable, and I don't know if our son . . ."

I couldn't breathe the words; they were so hard for me. Jack moved toward me, and I stopped him with a shake of my head. The room spun faster, snow fell harder and harder, and I knew only that I wanted to die.

"I will never know if he'd have had some ability or not. Maybe it would have been something different, but it also might have been one even more painful than mine, more painful for him. I couldn't blame you—"

"No," he said, fiercely. "I would have been honored, Av. We would have found a way to help him. To help you. And I should have been the person you could count on the most. I was such a damn idiot that night."

We stared at each other; the heartbreak we had caused had grown into a living, breathing, broken thing between us. I can't explain the slap of shock I felt in that moment: *He didn't hate me.* He was trying to understand, and he didn't hate me. I'd been so certain, so absolutely certain he would despise me.

He had come after me that night so long ago, just a few hours after he'd called me a freak. It had taken only a few minutes to realize his mistake, and a few hours before the police would release him to try to find me. The man he was now would love his son. Maybe the young man he'd been back then would have, too. It was somehow worse to know that.

There are some pains that ride around in your coat pocket—you're aware they're there. They're heavy and beat against you as you walk, but you'll eventually take off the coat and forget you ever carried around something so sharp and misshapen. Other pains, though, brand your soul, changing everything about who you are, how you identify yourself, how you think, how you breathe, how you live. Sometimes, the only reason you go on living is because you feel compelled to bear witness to the loss, to say to the world: "This person lived. He was real, and I loved him."

Jack's losses and my own drummed against me, relentless, a thousand hammers each insistent on leveling a blow. I wanted to reach for him, to comfort him, and I couldn't. I was the cause of so many of them. My sympathy would be a mockery, right now. Some things you don't inflict on other people, especially people grieving their lost child.

"What was his name?"

I told him, and his shoulders shook with quiet, racking sobs. "I hope that was okay. He was baptized before he died."

He nodded, still not able to look at me. Oh, how I wanted to die. To just disappear. Snow blanketed the room, and I shivered again.

I stand as witness. Jackson Francis Thibodaux, Jr., was my child, my heart, my breath. He lived. He should not have had to pay the price of my own selfish stupidity. I owe him a debt; one I still didn't know how to pay. I'd have given anything to have him back. Anything at all.

In my bedroom is a small suitcase I take wherever I go; battered and older than dirt, it is army green and covered in Scooby Doo stickers nearly faded to white and a few foil stars that somehow managed to still have a bit of shine left to them. I had brought it from home when I left Saint Michael's that night. Back then the case had carried only a few clothes. Some make-up, I think. A couple of stuffed animals I'd carted around since I was a kid, though I had no real memory of where they came from; still somehow, I loved them. The clothes were long gone, as was most everything else. Now, it held only my heart. A little box of ashes, with a baby's name. The brass lock, cool to the touch, was tarnished to a near black. I had made out a note to Latham that if something were to ever happen to me, to make sure Jack got it all.

What do you do when the best of who you are is somewhere in the past? Sometimes, you run from it. It doesn't help, though, if you take it everywhere you go.

"Can you tell me the rest?" Jack asked, pulling me back to him, and I realized he might have asked once already.

"It was Boston. I had gotten an apartment. A big happy family lived below. They . . ." Every word hurt. Every breath. I wrapped my arms around myself, shaking yet trying not to show it. My vision blurred at the edges, tremors sweeping through me. "They came home that night devastated. Two dead, a car wreck." I shook. "Their losses were so raw . . . there were stairs. I don't remember falling."

I put my forehead against the kitchen cabinet, leaning into it, an avalanche of emotion tumbling through me. There was not enough air in this room. "They took me to the ER. Losses. Losses everywhere."

"Which made your seizure worse," Jack said, his words bleak as sin.

And I nodded.

"They thought you had preeclampsia," Jack finished for me.

And I nodded again. He slid down then until he was sitting on my floor, his elbows on his knees, his face cradled in his hands.

Everything we might have been spilled off Jack: A family. Parents. Our child growing up, playing on Jack's ranch. Riding a horse. Throwing a ball. A backwards glance over his shoulder, just like his father's, grinning at me as he pedaled his first bike, arguing with me over homework. *Everything everything everything* we'd lost.

We'd lost together.

We'd lost forever.

And we'd lost each other in the bargain.

"It was April seventh," I whispered. "He would be nine now."

CHAPTER THIRTY

I was sitting on the sofa, another glass of OJ in my hands, Jack kneeling in front of me, but how I had gotten there was a blur. The snow was now piled in giant drifts, some as tall as the countertop, and it felt as if we were sitting in a blizzard with Jack's hair blowing in the wind, only we were in my living room. I saw movement out of the corner of my eye and caught a glimpse of a shaggy tail as a big dog ducked behind the kitchen island. I wanted to ask Jack about that, but he was talking, as if I was supposed to be following along. I took a sip of orange juice, grateful the sharp tang helped me push some of the losses aside, helped me focus a little.

"The night you came to the house," Jack was saying, "the night my dad died. You came to tell me you were pregnant. It all makes sense now. You'd been so strange on the phone. The media hell surrounding the Senator's corruption charge had taken over, and it was brutal."

He'd paced his front porch that night, horror and loss and rage throbbing with every step he took, and then he had turned on me, eyes wild with hurt. "Why'd you tell them about the file?"

How could I tell him that I was only trying to show the Senator that he wasn't so high and mighty? That he had to answer to someone for what he'd done to Jack, to others. I didn't even know what was in the damn file, just that the Senator was afraid of it being found. But the Senator didn't want to only end me and Jack, he wanted me to end the pregnancy—a pregnancy Jack didn't even know about yet, and that the Senator had bribed my doctor to discover. The bastard. I fought back the only way I knew how. How was I supposed to tell Jack that, with his father lifeless on the other side of the house?

"My dad is dead in there, Avery, and you as good as put the damn gun to his head!"

"It was a bad night," I said to him now, as we watched each other, both in too much pain, both remembering too much. I turned to look out my window, and where the porch and front yard should have been was a wooded clearing. My heart raced. "I knew I shouldn't have told the reporter about the file—the corruption stuff would have put your dad behind bars, and it would have hurt you. I shouldn't have done that, but I was so hurt, so angry. He wanted me gone, and I lashed out. It's my fault he killed himself."

"It absolutely is not your fault."

Then, as if he'd had a realization: "Wait. What? A corruption file?"

I could see his confused expression beneath the snowflakes caught in his lashes. "The file," I said again, fighting against the swirling snow and the floaty sensations swamping me. "Stuff he'd done. Stolen, I think? I dunno."

I reached up despite knowing better and brushed away a teetering clump of snow that had accumulated on Jack's shoulder.

"I'd been in there to see him earlier that evening," Jack said, like he was discovering something for the first time, "and he told me you'd threatened to give the reporter the file of photos of me he kept."

I could still hear the echo of Jack's voice all those years ago: "You're a liar. A con artist. They were right about you. Get the hell out of my life! You're a freak show." And for a moment, there, he loomed above me, his hand raised, a knife in his hands, and I fled. I was four miles away, in the deep quiet of the woods, before I knew I had left.

I was standing in my own home now, wobbly, but standing on my own, and then Jack was next to me, gently drawing me into his arms.

"Photos?" I asked, and then the images hit me. The photos the Senator had taken of Jack as a boy, naked. Bruised. All his abuses and losses documented. I nearly fell, but he caught me. "Oh God, Jack, I didn't know. I could always just see . . ."

He looked horrified and then resigned, as I explained. "I could always see the losses. The beatings. And I hated the Senator because of them. I didn't realize I was also seeing actual photos."

"You always knew?" He said it with a reluctant acceptance. I nodded. "Yet all those years as a kid, as a young man, you still saw me as *whole*."

"You were always whole to me Jack. You didn't choose what he put you through, but you had the strength to survive it, to keep from turning into what he was. You went out and pushed yourself to be a good man. To save lives."

I reached up, running my fingers through his short hair, brushing the snow away as I did, and my heart lurched as he rested his cheek in my palm. "I don't know if I could have done that. I do know I wished more than once that I could kill him."

"I almost did a few times," Jack said, "until I got big enough to threaten to go to the press. He kept those photos hidden—I'd tried to find them. He said they were his insurance that I'd do as I was told. I think he thought I'd be too humiliated to risk them ever being seen by anyone else. He had a bullshit story already worked out about how he'd found the photos, caught me with a boyfriend. I went into the military, instead of politics like he'd wanted, and dared him to release them. We rarely spoke in all the years after the abuse stopped, but that night, we argued viciously. He claimed you'd gone to the press, and that I'd put you up to it." He pulled me tighter. "Av? Please don't run this time. I know I scared you—"

"You didn't have a knife in your hands that night, did you?" I whispered, and in his shock, he leaned back so he could look me in the eyes.

"Good God, no. What?" Then he squinted at me. "Are you okay? You're pale, and you're shivering; your eyes are dilated too."

"Exhaustion. And it's so cold. I must've left the A/C on too low."

I could feel the blizzard whipping against my back as he led me back to the sofa and handed me the orange juice again.

I knew why I was afraid of Jack, knew from my dad's prediction that I would die at Jack's hands, but I had no idea why I had a memory that I *knew* wasn't true, a memory so firm, it felt like part of my DNA. If I went over that night carefully, step-by-step, almost frame-by-frame, I knew he had never had a knife.

This was important. There was something here I should understand, some mystery danced at the edges of that image, mocking me. It felt like

233

standing in the foyer of a very dark house, seeing a tiny light on all the way across a desolate, cave-like space, and not knowing where the furniture was or how to flip on the other light switches and knowing, knowing beyond a doubt that there were monsters there. I was lost, and something whispered across my senses, taunting me. The cold wind squalled into the kitchen, and the slow drift of snowflakes churned into a near-blizzard. I shivered as the dog prints accumulated around us now, and I could have sworn I saw a wolf out in the hallway. For a moment, just a moment, Calliope was tied to a chair in the center of the room, snow piled all around her. It was but wasn't Calliope, though whoever she was she looked so similar. So familiar.

And blink my kitchen was back, buried beneath snow, little mountains of white piling all around, urgency hitting me in waves, a voice whispering *run, little girl. Run or die . . .*

It was all too much. I couldn't help Calliope. I couldn't help Jack. I was failing so many people.

"I would never threaten you with a knife, Av. I don't know how you could not know that."

"Me, either," I answered, my voice bleak.

Jack looked back at me; his head tilted, like he was trying to figure something out. The dog snuffling through the snow drifts pulled my attention away; he was almost playful, making his way over to the sofa. I could see now he was more wolf than dog, maybe some sort of hybrid. He took a seat next to Jack, his silver eyes echoing Jack's, and I knew that he was, indeed, a wolf. I'd been in denial, but I also knew the wolf wasn't going to hurt me. I just couldn't figure out how I knew that, or why the wolf was there. I drank some more juice, hoping he'd go away, only to have him growl at the glass.

"Quit growling," I said to him.

"I didn't mean it that way," Jack answered, and I tried to shake off the confusion.

"Not you, the wolf," I said, and Jack's eyebrows went up.

He looked around, as if to double-check. "Av? Are you having a vision? Are you seeing images?"

I looked at the wolf-dog and shrugged. "Yeah, let's go with that." Everything around me felt fuzzy, lighthearted in a way that it shouldn't have. "What did you ask?"

"Why didn't you tell me? As bad as all this is, you had to know you could have told me."

I closed my eyes and tried hard to focus, so I could give him as much of the truth as possible. "I have asked myself that every single day. At first, I didn't know how to tell you. I didn't want you to come to us out of guilt and feel trapped by a girl with abilities you loathed."

I took another gulp of OJ for courage, and the wolf growled. I resisted the urge to shush him and leaned forward, resting my elbows on my knees, the once full glass of juice now nearly empty. I handed it to Jack, and he got up to get me another refill.

"After your dad's funeral, you were overseas, in danger, and you needed to focus on that, on staying alive. Then later . . ."

He handed me back the juice, and I swigged it down, feeling powerful, feeling free, light. I could see a teenaged girl spinning in the snow where the front wall of the house ought to be. There was such a joy in her delight, her red snow boots kicking up fans of white dust as she spun, and I made myself not look at her. If I didn't look her direction, she'd go away. Right? I frowned, trying to pull back my train of thought.

"As . . . as . . . the months progressed . . ."

"Av, you don't—"

"I do. When I . . . felt him kick and move, I realized I couldn't make that choice for you, that it wasn't right or fair."

"What stopped you?"

"I thought I had a little more time to come home and let you know." Oh, and by the way my father said I'd die at your hands, so I was afraid it would be when you saw me, with your unborn baby. I didn't want him to die because I couldn't live without you.

We were both crying now, and the snow had blanketed the room. I was never going to be warm again.

"You were that afraid of me."

I didn't answer. I couldn't lie to him and say no, and I couldn't tell him the truth as to why. Had Dad's prediction put the thought of Jack holding a knife in my head? Was it some sort of hypnosis? I'd seen him use hypnosis in some of his cons. Could that have been it? But if it were, why'd it feel so real?

"What I want to know, Av, is why? What made you so afraid? It can't just be that one argument, that I was an asshole and it scared you. Angry, livid, disgusted—all of those make sense. But afraid? I need to understand. I can't tell you how sorry I am that I let you down that night, and I would do anything in my power to change it all for you. For him."

"You should tell him," the girl in the red boots said, and I wanted to clamp my eyes shut. I drained the glass. She wasn't real. She wasn't there.

"Tell him, and then we can have a tea party," the girl sang out, happy, and I couldn't help myself. I looked over at her and gasped. She looked so much like an older version of Calliope, my heart raced. As she spun and laughed, roses grew up out of the floor, climbing the other three walls in the room like a trellis, the deep red petals dusted in snow.

She had the voice of the Old Woman. Was this the Old Woman, only not old anymore? I didn't know how I knew that, or why it made sense. She stood in the front yard just a few feet away; her arms were stretched out and her face lifted to the sky as the snow swirled around us, her braids falling away from her face, her skin glowing as if a light shone from within. She stuck out her tongue, tasting the flakes as she spun in place, the scent of piney woods filling the room. With every revolution, she was younger and younger and younger, laughing, her joy in the snow a beautiful thing to behold. Another turn and she was ten, and another turn and she was seven, and another turn and she was four. She stopped then, smiling at me; so beautiful, so beautiful my heart ached.

"Would you like a cup of tea?" she asked, grinning at me.

I shook my head, and I could tell that made her sad, this girl with the ageless voice. I felt as if I was floating. I couldn't see anything else . . . just the girl, with the sad smile and the red snow boots.

"I don't know you," I whispered, but as I said it I knew I was wrong. She was the girl in the first painting, the one that had sold big to someone I'd never met, the one that launched my career. She was the Snow Angel.

"You should tell him," she said again, "what Dad predicted," and she spun.

"I don't know you," I told her, more forcefully now, my eyesight darkening, shutting out the world, and I could feel Jack's hands as he rubbed my own, trying to warm them.

"Stay with me, Av," he said, from far, far away.

Then the little girl spun again and stopped, suddenly, looking at someone I couldn't see, the rictus of a scream freezing her features, soundlessly. I could see her left arm was now missing, bleeding profusely, and as I watched, something invisible sliced across her throat. Blood arced into the snow.

I closed my eyes and cried and said, "I don't know you, I don't know you *no no no no no no no . . .*"

CHAPTER THIRTY-ONE

"Roses," I said, in awe at how they grew and climbed, even in the snow, then died. A little girl was lying in the snow maybe twenty feet away, and I needed to run. *Run run run, little girl, run.*

"Too much snow," I said, my fingers turning blue with frost. Don't like the snow. *Cold cold cold.* Feet hurt, so cold. I jumped off the sofa, spinning, spreading my arms out, and catching the snowflakes as I spun.

Jack picked up my empty glass, a funny look on his face; he touched his finger to the white residue at the bottom. I think he tasted it. Silly man, there wasn't any left. Everything felt fine, now. It was going to be okay; I would just float away.

"Shit!" He grabbed his phone.

"You can't order juice take out, silly!" I floated by. I grinned. I didn't want to grin; yet I couldn't seem to stop. There was a little girl trapped some-where . . . I could see her. Calliope tied to a chair next to the girl lying in the snow. Damn, I was grinning again. I knew somehow I shouldn't be grinning . . . Horror tumbled below the gurgle of laughter. And the world spun . . .

"Avery! Avery! Talk to me!" A snapshot as I fought to open my eyes: Jack yelling, catching me as I fell, laying me on the floor. Why'd he do that?

Didn't he know I could float? *Floaty floaty*, high up into the sky. Hands were on me—feeling my pulse. I remembered those hands.

"Don't leave me, Av. Please, God, don't leave me."

I felt the force of his determination, his absolutely furious insistence that I stay, and it was so wonderful and sweet that I wanted to answer him but I didn't remember what I was supposed to say. I'd lost him *so so so* long ago, there was no way to have him again, and I was so tired. *So so* tired, I just wanted to sleep.

"Breathe, dammit!" Jack yelled.

I wanted to tell him it was okay, I just needed to sleep a little bit longer, and the light behind my eyes dimmed until all there was left was the dark.

Words, echoed, *soft soft*, farther and farther away. Jack's voice, Jack's beautiful voice . . . *words words words*, and then silence.

Blissful quiet.

When I opened my eyes next, it didn't even feel strange to find myself floating above, looking down on my body prone on the floor, Jack's cell phone near my head. I hovered somewhere near the skylight, while Jack frantically took my pulse, breathed into my mouth. Odd, I swear I could feel the pressure of the air going in and out, in and out, even up here near the ceiling.

Then there was shouting, and Hank bolted in, stopped abruptly, stunned. Jack shot him an order, and Hank ran out, then back in again with a medic bag; all the while Jack never stopped breathing into me.

They both seemed awfully upset. Silly guys. Could they not see I was floating right above them and feeling just *fiiiiiiine* as the color leeched out of the room, and the world went gray. Gray's fine. Gray's nice and soft. Gray's easy. *So sleepy.*

I felt someone take my hand, and I closed my eyes.

Blissful, comfortable, peaceful nothingness.

I wriggled my toes in the cold sand, squishing them into the sand's grit. *That's new.*

CHAPTER THIRTY-TWO

The beach stretched into nothingness on either side of me, shrouded in mist, and it felt enclosed somehow in memory, like an old-fashioned snow globe. The tide slid in along the shoreline to my right, lapping silently, kissing the white sand and rolling away. It was the only movement anywhere—everything but the tide was still as a bone and plucked as bare: just me standing on the beach. No wind, no water spray, no squawks of seagulls. No smell of sand or surf or the coconut suntan lotion traditionally slathered on pasty white skin.

"You're dying, you know," a voice said behind me, and dread crawled over my skin.

I recognized her before I turned to confirm: Old Woman. Missing her arm, bleeding from the stump, the blood running into the sand and spilling into the Gulf. I looked away from her—anything for relief from that bloody stump—and took in the scene's almost monochromatic shades of grays and whites.

"I'd heard you go to a lighter place," I mused, trying not to be terrified, "but I sort of expected it to be, I dunno, *shinier*, somehow."

Old Woman chuckled. "This is the place you made for us."

"Me?" I glanced around again, disappointed at the lack of color and vibrancy, save for the red of her own blood, no vivid detail, except for the Old Woman. My version of hell, I suppose.

"Do you recognize this place?" she asked.

I squinted, and then noticed for the first time farther up the shore: An old hotel. A few other old, ramshackle buildings emerged from the mist, and then a pier or two; it was as if the painter had sketched them in as an afterthought, so faded were they, like looking at an old postcard from the seventies. I spun the other direction, and there was a young girl, about five, building sand castles with a red bucket.

"It's Biloxi?" I said, confusion warping the words into a question.

Why would I hang onto such a bad memory, the place where my ability had first surfaced, the place where I had *seen* that lost red stiletto, the one the woman nearly killed me over? I moved closer to the little girl—and recognized myself, a younger me. I thought I had been six when we were in Biloxi, but I looked younger than that. I . . . she . . . piled sand into the red bucket with an intensity that I still remembered. I watched her scowl as one of the towers on her castle insisted on leaning, and I remembered the next step—how she . . . I . . . packed it down and decided it didn't need to be a tower. It could be an igloo.

I realized the child-me was now speaking to someone. I couldn't hear what she said, and I couldn't seem to walk any closer. I struggled to take a step, straining to hear whoever was there. Panic bubbled deep in my chest. *Run* boiled out of me, hot and sticky and deadly real. I spun around, wondering why the panic. Far down the beach, the woman—the one with the red stiletto—was headed my direction. She carried something shiny in her hand that I couldn't quite make out, and I glanced back at the younger me, still engrossed in a conversation with an imaginary friend.

"I don't want to see this," I whispered, but even so, I tried to push toward the girl. "Who's she talking to?" I asked the Old Woman when it was clear I couldn't reach the child-me.

"Who do you think she's talking to?"

"I don't—" and then, suddenly, there was a younger girl helping the child-me. She was about four years old, and she was trying her best to follow my lead, to do what I did, and she gazed up at the child-me with such adoration, the emotion I felt gut-punched: love. *I loved her.* I fell to my knees in the icy cold sand. I shuddered, freezing, and suddenly, as dreams are wont to do, the child-me was now wearing a threadbare coat. And mittens.

And so was the younger girl. Bright red snow boots. *Just like the girl in my painting.* Bile burned the back of my throat. That woman in the distance

240

kept walking toward us, closer, closer, and my heart pounded so hard, I felt like someone was beating on my chest with her fists.

The Old Woman, who was now closer to my own age, had knelt as well, and she reached out and held my hand with her one good one. Heartbreak in her eyes. The two young girls packed down the castle, the sand gleaming white in the afternoon sun, white, white . . . snow white.

I reached for the sand and scooped up snow instead. The Gulf shoreline slowly changed into rocks. A tree line far away on my left emerged from the mist. We were in a clearing of sorts, with a threadbare motel slumped in the not-too-far distance; the child-me and the smaller girl were oblivious to the change in location, both too busy giggling as we built an actual tower out of snow.

"We did it! We did it!" the younger girl exclaimed, and the children hugged.

We hugged.

Who was she? How were we here? Where was *here*?

"This isn't Biloxi, is it?" I asked the Old Woman, now younger than me, though her eyes still appeared ancient, holding grief the depth of the ocean.

"No, this isn't Biloxi," she echoed, her braids swinging with the shake of her head.

I stood and turned, and fear soured my gut as I saw the woman still walking toward us wasn't a woman at all. It was a man. Tall, scrawny in a red shirt. Someone I knew. Knew he was *bad bad bad bad.*

That's when I grasped what I'd been ignoring: The child-me had no scars. She—I wore no cast.

Run. Runrunrunrun.

"I'm not remembering Biloxi," I told the woman, who was a teenager now, and she shook her head, agreeing. "Biloxi never existed, did it?"

"No," she said. "Biloxi never existed."

"There was no woman in red," I whispered, and I looked again at the red snow boots the youngest girl had on, shock and disbelief warring. "No red stiletto?"

"I'm sorry," she said, her voice echoing softly off the distant rocks. "This is the truth, now."

I trembled, fear tearing through me as the man in the red shirt walked closer. "We're in Nova Scotia. That's where I'm from, isn't it?" *Everything I knew . . . everything I had so long believed . . . was a lie.*

She nodded, ten years old, now. Her eyes, so sad as she squeezed my hand one last time. And then, in a blink, she was gone.

The four-year-old looked over at me and said in the Old Woman's voice, "You must remember. It's time."

Something inside me screamed: I don't want to. Please, God, I don't want to remember any of this.

The girls had flopped down next to their castle and now were making snow angels, laughing, oblivious to the man walking toward them.

When they sat up, the four-year-old turned to the child-me and said, "Would you like a cup of tea?"

The child-me laughed. "Yes, please!"

I dropped onto my knees, my heart hurting so badly, I didn't think I could survive it.

Her name was Téa Rose.

"One lump or two?" she asked, grinning.

"Two," the child-me answered, laughing as my little sister kissed me on each cheek.

She was my little sister.

I had a little sister.

Neither child saw the monster heading for them, the skinny man holding the big knife.

He was my father's cousin, though we had always been told to call him "Uncle," and he made me shiver whenever he was around. He helped our parents with the cons. The grifts and thefts. He had a sly, lascivious stare; his gaze always rested on me just a little too long. I usually hid behind Latham if I had to be in the same room with him, and I always pulled Téa out of sight with me, not able to explain why.

Blalock Swan.

He walked through the snow toward the oblivious two girls as they returned to building their snow castle, and I screamed and screamed and screamed at them to run, but my words could not cut through the muffled winter and the silence of the snow. I tried to rise, to run to them, to block his trajectory, but something pinned me in place, something held me fast, and, oh, God, he reached them and grabbed . . .

Me.

The five-year-old me.

242

CHAPTER THIRTY-THREE

Fear and adrenaline spiked as the child-me tried to yank away from him, and Téa started crying. I wanted to yell for Latham, but we'd drifted too far from the cheap motel room where we were staying. My body tried to recoil from the too tight grip of his calloused hand to no avail. He raked a gleaming appraisal over me, and I whimpered. I knew. I knew this was very bad, and I couldn't even push a scream past the stark fear.

"You're the price," he said, his spittle hitting my face, his breath smelling like spoiled lemons. "Your dad screwed me out of the last deal he's gonna screw me out of. Your mom told me it was you all along—you're the one what can see the lost things." He shook me like a rag doll. "Where are the rubies?"

But I couldn't see rubies when I looked at him. I only saw horrible, oily, evil images. Lust for girls, little girls my age. I didn't understand it then, or know what it meant, couldn't have told you what the word *lust* meant—but I could see what he wanted to do to me and not doing it was a loss. A loss he couldn't live with. A loss he wouldn't abide. Animal instinct told me I was seeing things he shouldn't want—things so evil, they shouldn't be able to exist. But they did, and he liked them all.

Needed them.

He shook me again, so hard I bit my tongue, and blood filled my mouth. His eyes lit up, and he licked his lips, and then licked the blood out of my mouth while I tried to squirm away.

"Where?" His now bloody lips were close, too close as he breathed his lemony breath into my face as Téa kicked at him like a small puppy that doesn't have a clue she too is vulnerable.

"You didn't lose them," was all I could say, my teeth clacking together as he shook me again, and since the rubies weren't his to lose to begin with, there was no way I could see where they were.

He leered down at me, his teeth crooked, his skin chapped from the cold, and his hand twisted hard, snapping my wrist, and I screamed in pain.

"You're their secret weapon. You're mine now."

He started to drag me off, only to have Téa set off on him again, kicking and screaming; he unleashed one last kick and the knife, a machete—I could now see the sun glinting off the blade as it lopped off her arm, and I screamed again. My little sister and I gazed at each other, shock tying our souls together, and then she looked at her bloody arm lying in the snow, and her brown eyes grew so big. That ancient gaze of hers met mine, and before she could even inhale to scream, he slashed again and cut her throat.

I don't know where the wolf came from. I just know he barreled out of the woods, shaggy and scary, and the man dropped my arm and stepped back as the wolf sprang.

I ran blindly before the man could grab me again, ignoring the sounds of battle behind me.

Run. Runrunrun—hide.

Branches slammed against my face, the pain in my wrist so severe I wanted to cry, but I knew if I cried he'd hear me. He'd find me.

Run. *Runrunrunrun.*

Everything went gray, and the next thing I knew, I was standing in Latham's living room, his old Victorian in Saint Michael's.

Latham took one look at me and tried to rush me, to catch me.

But he went straight through.

CHAPTER THIRTY-FOUR

Latham hit his knees, his hands clasping the sides of his head as if it were about to explode. "Oh my God, no! No, Avery, no, not you, Squirt, no!"

I tried to reach for him, and my hand passed through him.

Téa stood next to me, then, and took my hand.

"It's okay," she told Latham. "She remembers now."

"My fault," he said, anguish and self-recrimination killing him, choking me, breaking me. "All my fault. I'm so sorry. I was supposed to be watching you. I was watching TV. Fucking TV. God, Squirt, I'm so sorry." And he broke down into sobs as Aurelia March stepped up and took my other hand.

"He doesn't know who did this," four-year-old Téa said. "He never knew, and we can't seem to tell him so he can understand. I think it's killing him."

Then, one by one, every girl that Blalock had killed appeared, surrounding us, filling the room. There was Jancey and Penelope and Kim and all the other little girls. Latham was dying because he was carrying them all with him; he was feeling their pain every moment of every day, and he felt it as his own. He felt he had failed them, too. I wanted so much to reach for him, to comfort him, but the room grew dim.

"You've died," four-year-old Téa explained matter-of-factly, tugging on my hand to get my attention. "And you're running out of time to go back."

I felt a sharp sting in my thigh and someone—was it Jack?—breathing for me. I recognized the scent of him. I could almost hear his voice between breaths, begging me to live, to stay with him. Aurelia tugged at my other hand.

"You have to go back," she said. "You have to stop the bad man."

Latham passed out, the pain of thinking he had lost me too much to bear. He collapsed on the floor.

A blanket of grief covered me . . .

Téa yanked my hand. "Hurry!"

CHAPTER THIRTY-FIVE

I dropped back into my body like a cannonball into the deep end of the pool—I hit hard, and it stung as I fought for air, battling to overcome the sensation of drowning. I pummeled the concrete wall holding me, hitting Jack as I involuntarily jerked with another spasm. He clutched me to his chest. We still laid on the floor, his legs wrapped around mine, one arm a vise around my shoulder, the other hand cradling my head against his heart.

"It's okay. You're okay; it's just the shot."

I broke through the surface of the feeling, and though the spasms ebbed, I still shook. Hard.

"It's okay," Jack kept saying.

I didn't believe him. It was never going to be okay again. Terror spiked, and once again I couldn't breathe. All I could see was that memory of Téa, real time, see the slice of the machete, as if it was happening over and over again in front of me.

Oh God, run run RUN.

I heard the inarticulate guttural growls of a wounded animal, and it wasn't until Jack kissed me, tears running down his cheeks, that I realized: *The sound was coming from me.*

Everything I'd seen of the child-me spun and crashed through the room, angry wasps of memory. I held onto Jack, grounding myself in his losses, using them to block my own, trying to keep a handle on the *now* versus the *then*, while images of Calliope, Aurelia, Jancey, all of the girls, circled above. Jack looked into my eyes, in that trauma medic sort of way.

"Help me get her into the truck," he ordered someone I couldn't see, someone lost in the snowdrifts piled around us. "The Narcan worked; must've been some form of opiate, but it's going to wear off."

Strong hands raised me up. Terror whistled, bearing down on me. My arms jerked, twitched, and when I closed my eyes, I saw . . . Latham, the guilt on my brother's face as he'd gone down on his knees, tears streaming, begging forgiveness.

Had that been real? Had I been in his home with Téa beside me? Surely no. That was a dream, right?

I realized we were crowding into the back of Jack's truck now, the snow falling in the cab turning red then white then red with the flashing of the emergency lights; his sirens blared as we sped across the rut-filled lane leading from my house. Hank was driving—Hank the Abominable Snowman, of course Hank was there. He'd brought more snow with him, snow swirling the cab of the truck creating a magical wonderland. Except where Jack sat.

Jack remained sunshine and warmth, and I snuggled closer. He cradled my face in one hand as the other held me in his lap, and I sunk into the safety of his palm.

"I'm watching your pupils," he explained. And then he *saw* me, *saw* that I could see the terror, the grief on his face, and he put his forehead to mine. "How did you not notice the orange juice tasted off?"

"I was already seeing things—thought my brain was misfiring. I'm sorry."

"Dear God, Avery, I lost you there for a moment. No pulse. Nothing. I didn't think I could get you back."

"I . . . I died?"

"You quit breathing, and I did mouth-to-mouth, but your heart stopped for what felt like hours, and I was about to start CPR when you snapped back. Thank God." He wrapped his arms around me and whispered, "I don't think I could have survived losing you. It would've ended me."

I had died. It was real. Standing in Latham's house had to have been real as well. I tried to tell Jack: "No! No! Jack! Latham—I saw him . . . he's dying. Gotta get there." I shoved and tried to break free, but Jack held me tight.

"911?" Hank asked.

"Too slow," Jack said, "use the radio there. Call out Sam—he's closest and—"

The rushing noise in my head devoured his words and turned Jack's voice into a hum as he gave instructions to someone—Hank's voice answered, giving Jack some sort of update. Something about a delivery guy found dead—the ArtShoppe guy—but my delivery had arrived . . .

"Nate!" I gasped. "If Nate hadn't shown up that day when he did . . ."

Jack paled. "That was him," I whispered. "That was the LPK."

My head felt loopy with pain and adrenaline, rushing, rushing. Time shrank and expanded and Jack was talking to me.

". . . at Latham's door . . . no answer . . ."

"Tell Sam, living room," I said through clenched teeth, the floaty, flying rush stealing in, taking over, no matter how much I fought against it.

What if it was now too late for my brother? What if I had failed Latham? I clutched Jack closer. *I had died. I had died at Jack's hands.* It was all so crazy, so impossible, so . . . freeing.

Euphoria rode in on a wave, lifting me, and I bobbed in an ocean of happiness. *I died at Jack's hands, and didn't stay dead. Woot! Who saw that coming? Not me!* I laughed, and a puzzled Jack frowned.

"Too fast," he muttered, throwing a worried glance Hank's direction. "Way too fast." He rummaged in a bag at his feet as the silly grin on my face widened. *Floaty floaty floaty.*

"Av, whatever was in that juice, it's strong. The Narcan's wearing off."

I giggled. I didn't care—about anything. I drunkenly tried to flap my arms, flying along with the truck. Nothing I had seen when I died could be real anyway, right? Because, hey, *dead.*

"Hey, Dad!" I said singsongy, "I died and didn't stay dead. *Neeener neeener neener!*"

"Dad?" Jack asked, grabbing my hands to keep me from reaching for the door lock. Hated being cooped up. Wanted to fly. "What's your dad got to do with this?"

"Oh, right! I couldn't tell you." I leaned in, light-headed and dizzy but also *so so so* happy, "You were s'posed to kill me." I giggled. "Isn't that hysterical?"

His grip tightened.

"Ow," I said.

"Sorry," he said, loosening his hold. He spoke gently now, calmly. Too calmly, spacing the words out like armed soldiers. "What do you mean, I was supposed to kill you?"

"*Ah ah ah!*" I wagged my finger at him. "Not s'posed to tell." His annoyed expression was so cute. I grinned, sniggering until I snorted. "Gets very very bad if I tell."

"Who said?"

"Dad." I don't know why he couldn't understand this. Clear as day. "Said I can't tell you. Telling makes it worse. Telling always makes it worse. Told me not to see you. Never supposed to see you again." I imitated my Dad's best actorly voice, "Bad choices—like he's one to talk. All those cons. All those grifts. Avery. Got to go to work now. Huh. Why'd he call me Avery?"

Avery. *Avery Marie.* Had Dad picked that name? Or Leila? How many names have I had?

What is my name?

"Let's see if focusing on something else helps," Jack said over my head, and then, "Avery, what did you mean your dad said I was going to kill you?"

I had the feeling he and Hank had been asking me questions for a while given the perturbed looks on their faces. They should see themselves! So grouchy. I whooshed a wave of snow at Jack, and laughed when he looked so upset.

"Hey, frowny face, it's okay, it's already over. I died!" I laughed again. "That's what Dad does—he sees when you're gonna die. *Eeeeevvvverrryyy*-body he meets, bang, knows how they die. To the millisecond!" I tried to snap my fingers, missed, and cracked up laughing. "*Stilllll heeeeerrreeee*," I sang, waving my hand in front of them as they talked about me like I was invisible.

I leaned into Jack. Any minute now, I was going to float away. "Dad shouldda told me I'd still be here. He shouldda told me. So much bad stuff. So many years. Couldda stopped it." I tried to focus on Jack. "So much bad stuff, Jack." And whoosh, the roller-coaster ride flipped, and the whole inside of the truck bowed and breathed in and out as I hung onto him. "Whoa."

"Avery." Jack pulled me around to look at him.

"Not Avery!" The scenery whizzed past, until the colors blurred and whirled. It was such a rush. "Dunno my real name. Didn't I tell ya? Dad makes 'em up, wherever we go."

"You told me. How long ago did your dad say I'd kill you?"

"Years and years ago." I struggled through the fluffy cotton feeling. "He saw it. Knows when people croak, slips in, steals stuff." I looked at Jack.

"Bad Daddy. Said I'd die by your hands." I looked down at the hands in question. "Your beautiful hands. Strong hands. Did I tell you how much I love your hands?"

Those same wonderful hands slid up my arms to cup my face. Jack seemed to be studying my eyes again. I blinked at him and sighed. How I had missed those hands.

"Dammit," he said, as I floated away on a cloud.

"Shit, hang on, Av!" someone yelled from far, far, far away.

I felt the shocking bite of the needle as it jammed into my thigh, and the bright fire of the drug as it snapped my insides awake, screaming terror burned through me. Adrenaline rushed to my brain, like a million jolts of caffeine. Suddenly, I was caged in Jack's arms again but there. Still alive.

"Dammit!" I hurt and yet I couldn't make myself calm down. My arms and legs twitched, and when I looked out the window—Hank was flying as the world raced by. A blur of cars pulled over to let us by on the two-lane highway. It was all a whirl of lights and dark smudges of trees against what was now a night sky.

"It's okay, Av," Jack said once more as I turned to him. "We'll be at the hospital in about ten minutes."

"No—not the hospital!"

"Have to, Baby. This shit is too strong. You died. I'll be with you every step of the way. Let's just focus on something else. Can you tell me why you never told this to me? About your dad's prediction?"

"Makes it worse, Dad said." Another spasm hit. "He swears it makes it worse." My words stuttered out of fear and rage. "Said he tried to change things once. Got very bad, bigger bad even than what he had seen. Said he shouldn't have told me, but had to keep me from dating you. I didn't listen. Then that night."

I couldn't stop the tears and Jack pulled me closer. He knew which night. He had to have known how his anger must've looked to me. "I got so scared, Jack. I couldn't think. Just that we had a baby. Had to save him." Everything in me broke then. Because I knew. I knew I'd killed our child by running away. "Oh, God, Jack. I thought he was right. I thought he meant I'd die—and if I went back to you pregnant, our son would die, too."

251

I curled into his chest, shivering, tears soaking his shirt. I'd done every-thing wrong. *I'd killed our son.* I had believed my dad meant well when he'd told me, but if he could see *this* death, he could see the final one, and he'd have known I would survive this. He'd known all along that Jack didn't kill me—not in any final sort of way. I had never doubted the prediction. Or questioned how or whether Dad spun it. I knew he hadn't given me a *when*, but he'd still made it sound so definite: *I would be murdered at Jack's hands.*

Dad let me kill my baby. I wanted to die.

How could a father do such a thing to his own child? How could Jack not loathe me?

Jack rocked me, ssshhhing me as he ran his fingers through my hair, soothing.

I'd killed our child. I could never fix that.

Jack hugged me hard, whispering, "You were just as much a victim, Avery, as our son. Just as much." He pulled my hand to his lips, kissed my knuckles. "Right now, though, we need to get you taken care of, you and Latham."

Latham. Panic returned. How had I forgotten?

"Latham's on his way to the hospital, too," Jack answered.

I hadn't even realized I'd spoken out loud. What else had I said? The drug was doing a number on me. I struggled to focus on those still at risk.

"Any news on where Calliope is?" I asked, trembling.

"Not yet." Hank caught my gaze in the rearview mirror for a second, but it was long enough for me to see he, too, was running on fumes. "Did you see something?"

I buried my face in Jack's shirt. How could I explain to him that I had left behind my little sister? How could I tell him that I'd left her so far be-hind that I'd refused to remember her? Refused to hold her, to protect her? The name tore from me, black and bleak, and Jack held me as I shuddered through them.

"Blalock Swan?" Hank asked, on his phone again, relaying everything. "Give me a description."

I did, and Hank frowned. "That doesn't sound like the phony ArtShoppe delivery guy."

"I think it was a disguise. Think he'd used others. I think he was the guy in Chicago, the one who kept hovering around me at my art show." At Jack's puzzled look, I said, "There was this guy who kept asking what inspired me.

He creeped me out. And then someone tried to grab me off the street. That's when the FBI put me in protective custody." I looked at Hank.

I leaned closer to Jack, to safety. "That same night was my first big sale, *The Snow Angel*. I think the Snow Angel was actually my little sister. I think I've been trying to remember all these years what happened to her and wouldn't let myself."

"But if you were that close to him," Hank asked in his logical way, "why didn't you sense him? Or see any images?"

"Because Av wasn't a loss. Not for him," Jack said, better than I could have. "She was something he'd found." Jack's arms trembled as he gripped me tight.

Hank told someone on the other end of the phone to run a search for a Blalock Swan, if that was even his real name. He had been incarcerated, but even my father had passed background checks when Hank had run one on me. He was a step ahead of me on that, though, asking for my father's background file to be reopened and to look at any known aliases of Blalock Swan, cross-referencing them with all known associates to see if my father was in the system under another name. It might help us narrow down information on Blalock that we could use. If we got it in time.

Hank and Jack shared a veiled glance in the rearview mirror, and before I could see what they weren't saying, what they were worrying about, Hank said, "I think from what you said that you were the first. I think he wanted you and killed your little sister in a fit of rage when she tried to stop him. He didn't get to have you, and he's been recreating that ever since. He's punishing each and every one of them for being Téa instead of you."

Jack frowned at him, shaking his head in warning, but Hank plowed on.

"This time—you came here first. I'm almost certain he followed you to Saint Michael's. All of the time lines suggest you came across him in Memphis. We know Evelyn Miers was taken before you got there, and then he was in Chicago next."

Could I have stopped him?

"No, Av," Jack was saying, his voice hoarse, his face damp with tears. "Listen to Hank. He said you came a long time after. A long time."

Hank caught my eye in the mirror. "He'd already moved on when you got there. But my gut is telling me you sensed something, something you didn't understand, and you ended up in the next city—Chicago—where he had settled. I think you were sensing those losses, and I think you were following him without realizing it. And if you were the first, he's not going to leave, or be finished, until he gets you."

"Calliope! She had a little sister!" I sprang out of Jack's embrace, on fire from the pain.

"They all have little sisters, Kid," Hank said. "We didn't ping on that pattern until about the fourth girl, but it didn't help us any. He's been slowly escalating."

I knew what he meant—there had been no rapes in the beginning, but over the last year . . .

"We didn't know if the little sister was a fluke or not," Hank continued, "until we found more of the girls."

"You didn't tell me."

"Couldn't. We kept what details we shared with you to a minimum— didn't want to influence what you saw." He glanced at me. "Or remembered. The press missed it—mostly because some of the girls weren't found until you came on board, and then they were so focused on you, which helped the case. Gave us some room in which to operate."

"Oh, God. All those girls. Hurt, tortured. Because of *me*."

"No," Jack and Hank said simultaneously, vehemently.

"You do not take that on, Av. *He's* the monster. Not you. You didn't know; you didn't have any control over this. It is not your fault because it was not your choice. It's his and his alone." He looked at Hank and the ache in his voice told me he was hurting for me when Jack asked, "Do you think he's the one who got into her house? The one who drugged Avery?"

More snow filled the interior of Jack's truck.

I closed my eyes, trying to hang onto the present.

"Doesn't work for me," Hank said. "Guy like this, he's going to want to get his hands on you. He wants to finish the circle, to teach you that lesson personally."

"So someone else also wants me dead?" I had the weirdest flash of Marguerite holding a pitcher of orange juice, but surely that was just me projecting. That'd be crazy.

I couldn't focus on that—I had to focus on Calliope.

Roses sprang from the floorboard of the truck, as the snow fell harder.

I shivered and realized Téa was sitting next to me, four years old again, wearing such a sad, angelic expression, my heart cracked.

"You have to hurry," she said. "Latham needs you."

CHAPTER THIRTY-SIX

Hank dropped us off near the ER entrance and went to park the truck. Heat radiated off the asphalt parking lot, yet nothing—not the still-high temperature, not the thick, sauna-like humidity, not the presence of Jack—slowed the snow from accumulating at our feet, nor the icicles from forming over his head as we stepped under the entrance awning.

I stopped Jack from shutting the door to allow the pack of shaggy wolf-dogs inside. A part of me knew they weren't real. Nobody but me seemed to notice them as they prowled the ER waiting area, weaving between legs and chairs. I was pretty sure no one else saw the snow either, while I had to work to resist scooping a handful up and packing it into a snowball.

Jack kept his arm wrapped around me, and I used his images to muffle the painful losses spiraling off the patients and staff. He guided me to the reception desk, and when he began talking in medic-speak, the words floated by in little word bubbles that captured only every fifth word or so.

Still in his loose hold, I turned in a slow circle, taking in the pea-green hospital walls and the utilitarian chairs guaranteed to be uncomfortable, probably to discourage as many people as possible from using the ER instead of going to their regular doctor. As if most people had a choice.

The part of me that had worked with Latham for so long noted the choice of materials and furnishings in the place: All utilitarian, made to last. Plain baseboards. Practical linoleum. Sturdy chairs. Fire extinguishers.

Vending machines. All the normal stuff. I, of course, wasn't just seeing the normal stuff. We'd traveled miles past normal long ago, past just seeing snow and roses. Now, trees grew out of the floors, hiding the walls, sprouting into a full forest as I turned and turned. The wolves hopped over roots, seemed mindful of the rocks, and then scampered onto a jagged plateau of boulders I hadn't noticed on my first turn.

Jack kept talking earnestly to the pretty nurse, but his eyes didn't stray from me, and I noticed they narrowed as if he knew my tether to this world was about to break. I had to force myself not to touch the leaves now hanging above me, crusted as they were in ice and snow. I fisted my hands and shoved them in my pockets.

"This way," Jack said in my ear, and I jumped. We followed the nurse through some doors and down a hall. "You okay?"

Jack's worry—projecting his loss of me—whatever it was that I had been to him, impaled my heart. That girl, that person he'd fallen in love with, was someone else. How could we stand a chance when I didn't even know who I was now? I wanted that life with him. I wanted that life for myself. I'd run for so many years *away*, when I should have been running *to*. I didn't want to lose this chance. How could I have not seen that for so long?

Hope. I wanted hope.

"Um. For a dead girl, I think I'm doing pretty good."

Jack grimaced at my poor attempt at humor. Probably best I didn't mention the snow on his shoulder. Or the wolves. The wolves would probably worry him. As I suspected would the trees. I was already used to the trees, but the objects starting to bud from the limbs were a trifle disconcerting. I tried not to look at them: the cell phones, rings, earrings, wallets, briefcases, photos, keys, my God, the keys—does anyone not lose keys?—files, folders, always one shoe or one sock, tools, laptops, balls, bats, gloves, glasses. Everything and anything you could imagine that someone could lose hung from those branches. Every time someone walked by, objects bloomed in their wake.

Jack took my hand, and the nurse led us down a long hall with pale ivory linoleum tiles that stretched the length of the corridor, only now where the tiles should have been, blades of winter grass grew, bent and browned, a carpet racing ahead of me the deeper we pushed into the building. A step ahead, more trees climbed the pale walls, their limbs woven into a canopy where the ceiling should have been. A light flurry of snow fell, dusting gurneys and defibrillators along with patients, nurses, and doctors as the losses of the latter piled around them or lodged in the trees. I had to force myself to resist pulling Jack away from where his head looked like it might hit the dangling tennis racket (he walked right through it) or the snow skis (he walked through them as well). The more the roots invaded the hall, the more lost items that appeared, and the greater my pain—pinpricks became needles tracking my skin, and I ground my teeth, holding onto the reality of Jack's hand.

I had to fight this off. I had to help find Calliope. I had to help Latham.

The stream worried me a bit. It burbled past X-ray, over moss-covered rocks that congregated in front of the MRI doors; the rocks had a dusting of snow, but the water moved around them too swiftly for ice to form. Three or four wolves wove in and out of the trees and the lost debris, and I kept expecting the doctors and nurses moving around the hallway to trip over them. I stopped when Jack stepped into the rushing water that should have been too deep to wade through; he stopped, puzzled, and then turned to me.

"What's wrong?"

"Stream," I said, looking at where it washed over his feet and then further down curved through another little sitting area. I shook my head and said, "Sorry. Nothing. Just scared."

The stream seemed annoyed at my dismissal, and grew.

The nurse led us to an examination room where moss had begun covering the walls, and roots and boulders crowded the monitors and exam table. The light wasn't nearly bright enough. The wolves growled, as the room got darker and darker, closing in. I hated the room.

"Do you have a flashlight?"

"A what?" Jack looked shocked.

I looked away from the boulder jutting out of the poster explaining high blood pressure and caught the fear Jack was stoically trying to hide.

"Um. Nothing." I tapped my head. "Still a little weird up here."

The nurse was kind enough to ignore my ramblings, and wrote down whatever Jack told her. I dragged my gaze away from the VW Bug that now capped a tree growing beside her, and tried not to worry about how long the car could stay there before falling. The nurse took my vitals and attached a monitor cup to my finger that made it glow, and left again—the tree and the VW thankfully disappearing with her.

"When can we see Latham?" I asked Jack, hoping he hadn't noticed my shifting focus.

257

"I'm not sure. You're not freaking out." The walls bent into a small dome, obliterating the light, and the wolf sitting next to me leaned against me, comforting. "With the Narcan, I expected you to be more paranoid, much more jittery. That means a lot of opiates remain in your system."

We could hear people in the next room—a construction worker, I would guess, from the bulldozer protruding from the wall. A bulldozer? Really?

Jack turned my head so that I was looking up into his eyes again. Behind him, the window of a car hovered, a child's bloody handprint against the glass; I couldn't see the car.

"Hey," Jack said, snapping his fingers in front of my eyes. "Are you spacing out, or about to seize?"

"Um. Spacing." I hoped. I didn't have the normal tingling in my hands or the auras that often preceded a seizure, but then again, I had never been this drugged before one, either. Who knew?

Somewhere in this hospital, I reminded myself was my brother. If I was honest, I was scared down to my bones to see him. Part of me was panicking and urging me to run and find him, but the rest of me held back, refusing to get with the program.

At the whiff of roses, I stiffened, and as they broke through the snow—impossible, but still—they climbed the walls until they'd formed an arbor, blooming, the scent so strong, I could taste it.

Téa stood in the doorway and motioned to me, pointing to her left. "That way," she said. "He thinks you're dead. He won't believe me."

"Jack," I whispered, "Téa says Latham thinks I'm dead. I think I'm supposed to let him know I'm okay. I think he needs to know that to get better."

"They're not going to let you leave this exam room or allow us in his, Av," Jack explained, diplomatically avoiding the fact that I was apparently talking to my dead sister.

The boulders seemed bigger now, and the walls were turning into granite with veins of minerals spidering across the ceiling.

"He needs me," I insisted.

Jack sighed. Glanced at the monitor covered with roses, and nodded at what he saw. "I'll see what I can find out." He tipped my chin so I'd focus on him. "Stay right here. Okay? I'll make a couple of phone calls."

A second wolf jumped beside me, whimpering and licking my face. I flinched, trying to ignore him, and Jack threw back his shoulders. He'd fight this, if he knew where to throw a punch. "Don't move. Okay?"

I nodded, ignoring Téa, who stood just inside the door now, tapping her foot on a rock. She watched Jack go and peeked out the door behind him. After a couple of beats, she gave the universal all's clear signal of kids everywhere. I followed my little sister's ghost down a long corridor of moss and rocks and tree roots, a cavern so cold, my breath misted, as the wolves growled and circled us.

Téa stopped at the door of a trauma room, and we could hear a doctor inside, hear a nurse reporting all sorts of medical mumbo jumbo about swelling of the brain and shunts and procedures, and I pushed through the door and saw my brother, ghastly pale, lying on the bed, his head shaved. The shock of that sight slapped me, a vicious strike, and I couldn't form words at first—I just gaped at him like a guppy gasping for air.

"Who exactly are you?" the doctor asked, as the nurse moved to me.

"I'm his sister," I said, trying not to be too obvious that I was holding onto Téa's hand behind my back. "I'm his family. He needs me. He needs to know I'm okay."

"Lily?" Latham asked, and I glanced down at Téa, confused.

"That's your name," she whispered. "Lily Victoria."

Somewhere inside my head, part of me was as shocked as hell. The rest of me said, "Hey," like learning I had a completely different name was no big deal. "I'm here."

"Let him touch you," Téa said, and she motioned me forward. "He's gonna think you're still a ghost."

I stumbled a bit, trying to look like I'd meant to do so, as the doctor and nurse eyed me like I was a possible psych-ward escapee.

"You can have a minute," the doctor said. "We've done a CAT scan, and we have to get a shunt into him. I was just trying to explain the procedure and the reasoning, but I'm not sure how much he understood. The shunt will relieve the swelling in the brain, and then we'll do an MRI to see what's going on. One minute. We'll be right outside."

I nodded, and stepped up to Latham, whose face was swollen, devoid of all his charm, grin, and personality.

"Hey," I said again. "I'm here."

"Dead," he mumbled. "Jack killed you."

"No." I grabbed his hand, and leaned down to whisper in his ear. I squeezed his fingers, hard. "No, Latham, I'm okay. Jack saved me—not the other way around. Dad got it wrong. All wrong. I'm here. I'm alive. Can you

259

hear me?" He didn't answer, so I did what I used to do when we were kids and he'd ignore me. I pinched the living crap out of his arm.

"Ow!" he mumbled, wobbly, one eye opening to look for the culprit. "Meanie." But he grinned as he said it, a little anyway.

I squeezed his hand, hard.

"They're going to do something to relieve the pressure in your brain," I told him, hearing the doctor outside. "You understand?"

He nodded, a weak dip of his chin.

"Then they're gonna run some tests. You fight, Latham. You hear me? You fight. I still need you, big brother."

"Bossy," he muttered, but he squeezed my hand three times. *I love you.*

"Miss," the nurse said, moving in behind me, touching me on the arm; so many losses bloomed off her, I recoiled. "I'm sorry, but we need to get him to OR. We'll find you as soon as we're done, and give you a report."

I squeezed Latham's hand four times back. *I love you, too.* And let the nurse pull me away.

They wheeled him out in his bed, and I followed them into the hallway, and as I saw him disappear around the corner, I doubled over in pain. I could hear Jack shouting for me around the corner, and suddenly, he was there, holding me as I sobbed.

They were taking my brother to the OR to put a shunt in his brain.

There was screaming in my head, the words lodging in my throat, and I couldn't tell Jack what had happened.

"Av," he said, pulling me up, forcing me to look at him. "Brody's missing."

CHAPTER THIRTY-SEVEN

I gasped as I looked into his misery. *Marguerite standing at my counter, an orange juice pitcher in hand.* I blinked, snapping out of that image to the one of a car window, a little boy's bloody handprint on the glass.

" . . . and he said—"

"Wait," I interrupted Jack. "Loopy here—who said what?"

Jack backtracked. "Nate called. You with me?" I nodded. "JoJo Bean saw Marguerite's car abandoned out on Highway 30—and saw a little boy's bloody handprint on the window."

"Oh, my God." I dug my fingers into Jack's arms, trying to find a solid grip on reality. The hallway around us overflowed with lost items, hanging from tree limbs above our heads, popping out of the ground, sitting on the shoulders of orderlies or nurses as they passed us. The roar of the stream was strangely hypnotic, if loud, and the smell of the piney woods overwhelmed the normal hospital scents of antiseptic and rubbing alcohol.

"Brody. In Marguerite's car. I had seen the handprint earlier. Just the handprint. Didn't know it was his. Or her car."

"There's a little blood in the backseat—Nate said like someone slapped him. Not enough to think he . . ." His voice broke. "Can you see him?"

"Orange juice," I said, closing my eyes. "Marguerite. Holding the orange juice."

"Wait—you *see* that?"

261

"Loss. Me. Your loss of me. Shows me her. Cause of your loss."

"Brody? Where'd she take him? Why would she get out of her car?"

I shook my head. I couldn't see anything like that, anything about the car. But I could see her bloody eyes, and I gagged.

He bent to look directly into my eyes, and swore. "You're still reeling, aren't you? You're still feeling the effect of the drugs."

He wrapped me into a tight hug.

"Bloody eyes," I said, finally, through clenched teeth. "Dunno why. Where. When."

"I have to go find him," Jack said, his heart rending in two, hating to leave me.

"Brody," I said, fighting to form the words past Jack's fear of loss. "Go!"

"Kid!" Hank called from the end of the hallway, and I watched as he jogged around boulders, through the stream, and past trees, and so many objects they piled up on each other.

Jack kissed me hard, fast, and limped away, catching the keys from Hank as they passed each other.

"You're staying here?" I asked Hank.

"I'm working with everyone by phone. If Blalock tries to come for you again, he'll have to get through me."

I didn't hear anything else he said after that. I could see Jack running down the long hallway, and in between us, Calliope tied to a chair, sitting in the middle of the stream, Brody tied to a chair next to her. Neither of them looked awake, but they were breathing.

Calliope opened her eyes and looked at me.

Only it wasn't Calliope anymore. *It was me.*

"You know where we are," the child-me said, nodding to the wooden stand next to her, the purplish cloth draped over it.

"Jack," I yelled, pushing as much authority and volume into my voice as I could dig up. "Wait!"

He was torn, and I couldn't blame him.

Around us everyone paused, breath held, as I wended my way toward the girl—Calliope again—in the chair, I crossed the stream, weaving around tree roots and briefcases, toys and enough other odds and ends to fill someone's house, aware that Jack was jogging back to me, trusting me. Trusting me with his son's life. Even as crazy as I must've looked to everyone, including him, he believed in me. As I eased nearer to Calliope and Brody, the

262

stream splashed onto the wooden floor beneath the kids' chairs. Near her, the wooden stand. *It's a pulpit!* The purplish cloth draped over it was one of Father Tomas's stoles, his favorite.

Jack stopped as I held out my hand to prevent him from walking into the scene.

On the pulpit I saw a hand-lettered sign, the words written in precise, block script, and I stepped closer so I could read it.

COME ALONE OR THEY DIE.

I looked up at Jack; my own terror was mirrored in his eyes. After being so wrong about Marguerite, I needed to be careful.

"I don't know if what I'm seeing is real or not."

"I trust you," he said. "What do you see?"

CHAPTER THIRTY-EIGHT

"Avery?" Jack was standing in front of me, his big, warm hands framing my face, looking into my eyes, and grounding me. We stood now in his barn—a cavernous, immaculate structure that seemed like it ought to house NASA equipment instead of horses and hay.

I didn't think we'd been at Jack's long; I was still fighting through the remnants of all the hospital losses while trying to hang on to the details of our plan. The drive from the hospital was a blur of Jack terrified that he was sacrificing my life for his son's; Jack worried I'd have another seizure. Or worse. But I absolutely was not going to stay behind at the hospital where it was even more likely I'd seize and not be able to help. There were two kids' lives on the line.

The choices we had swirled around me, all potential losses. Nate and Hank conferred a few feet away, over a map. Hank was just off the phone with Baton Rouge SWAT; the team had a gunman holed up in a warehouse on the north side of the city, more than an hour away if the gunman could even be subdued and brought in, so we'd be on our own for a while.

Various other first-responders—local agents, sheriffs, police, firefighters—were gearing up and heading this way, planning to meet out of sight of the church. They did not know the terrain nor the church like Jack. I think Hank had weighed the protocol of not allowing a father to be involved against Jack's military experience for about five seconds, taken one look at

Jack and known there was no way to stop him from being involved short of shooting him, and just decided to make the best of it.

"Avery?" Jack asked again, and I blinked.

"I'm okay," I lied, and his expression said he recognized the lie and turned grimmer. "I can do this, Jack."

Truth be told, I was freezing; snow flurries fell inside the barn, and I was worried the wolves would startle the horses.

Wait, the wolves aren't real.

"You still seeing things?"

"Well . . ."

"Avery."

"Maybe a few. It's better though."

It was actually about the same, but why worry him.

One of Jack's stable hands led Pan and Jack's big black gelding, Gambler, over. I'd almost asked how Pan came to be there, then remembered I'd asked that of them several times already. I still wasn't sure of the reason.

I resisted rubbing my hands together to warm them since in reality it was summer and sweltering outside. I also knew if I pulled out my work gloves from Pan's saddlebag, Jack would know I was still cold and be distracted. He didn't need that. What we faced was terrifying enough.

"You remember the plan?" Jack asked as Nate finished up a call with some of his deputies.

"Pay attention to where I step. Look for trip wires, signs of fresh disturbance on the ground, IEDs. Go to the front of the church, stay where y'all can see me, try to get him to come outside, or at least keep him busy talking."

It was the first time I'd been able to remember all of the steps. Jack looked only slightly relieved.

"He wants you in there," Hank reminded me as he joined us, leading another horse of Jack's. "He'll have a clear path to the door. He likes playing with his victims—he's not going to end it quickly with you."

"He's not going to end it with her, period," Jack said, "because we're going to get in, get the kids, and get out while she distracts him outside. She's not stepping in that church."

"Jack," I said, and reached for his hand. "It's okay. Hank doesn't sugarcoat the truth. I know I can trust that. He's like the good version of a dad."

Hank busied himself with something in his saddlebag.

"You listen to me, Avery Marie," Jack said, getting in my face. "You don't sacrifice yourself. You hear me? You do not go in that church. I can get the kids out. I've dealt with similar situations behind enemy lines. I've dealt with IEDs. I cannot deal with losing you again. Understood?"

I nodded.

"Promise me. You won't go inside."

"I promise," I lied, knowing I would do whatever it took to get those kids out. Whatever it took. Calliope and Brody were going to grow up, unlike Aurelia March. No matter what I had to do to make that happen.

Jack nodded, not entirely believing me, and that was all I could hope for. He needed to focus. We mounted the horses and rode out, following Jack on a path that only he could see on the dark swampy floor of the forest; Jack was silent, running through projected failure scenarios (all losses, all blooming around me), while Nate and Hank made last minute calls finalizing what every converging officer and agent needed to do upon arrival. They'd decided on this approach, hoping the odds were better that Blalock couldn't booby trap the entire woods. After everyone was in place, I would go around to the front of the church.

"He still has several hours left with Calliope if he sticks to pattern," Hank added, turning slightly in his saddle to address me.

Welcome back the trees whispered in the dark.

Run, little girl, run. We'll hide you.

"He's going to feel compelled to finish that," Hank continued, and I knew I'd missed something in the middle. "He will want you to watch, to validate his choices. Don't give him that. Delay him. Ask him questions—he wants to talk to you. This is a guy with a God complex—he thinks he's too smart and you're too scared of him to disobey and bring anyone with you. He probably has an escape planned, and another city already lined up. I suspect he believes you're going to be his new partner, that you'll help him and enjoy doing so. His ego won't let him think anything else."

Hank didn't say what else he was thinking, that it could just as easily go the other way—that Blalock would be angry with me for not being that five-year-old anymore. That I would disgust him, and he would kill me immediately out of frustration or rage and then move on to kill Calliope . . . and then Brody. All of those potential losses carpeted the woods around us, and I had to hang onto the saddle to keep from leaning over and retching; watching yourself maimed and killed in various scenarios as someone else's projected loss was surreal and disturbing. Knowing it could easily come true

266

was the sickening part. I wasn't what Blalock wanted anymore. I had not a doubt in this world that this was going to piss him off even more.

"Remember," Nate said from behind me, "We do have help on the way. We just have to buy enough time to get them here. You don't go in. You just keep him talking."

"Got it."

Jack and I rode in single file. Nate had split off earlier so he could come at the church from the woods opposite us, and Hank had circled over to a big live oak that grew thirty yards beyond the front of the church. That tree had low, thick limbs he could climb—the better to get a good sightline on the front door; he had a sniper rifle from Nate's official stash. If I could lure Blalock out the door far enough, Hank could take the shot.

I shivered. So, so cold. Jack watched me and worried.

Between the drugs, and the terror, and the worry over Latham (Sam had called and said he was still in surgery), I was numb. Losses kept manifesting, piling up around me, and they looked so solid, it was becoming almost impossible to distinguish between the real from the imaginary.

Or maybe I was just losing it. Were the drugs screwing with the real losses or the imaginary ones? Was I *actually* seeing Brody and Calliope in the church? I'd already been wrong once about Marguerite. What if I was wrong again? Another wave of losses washed over me: Brody's own images jumbled with Calliope's.

Then I realized what I was seeing.

"Jack!" I reined in Pan as the images inside the church solidified around me, overlaying the forest I should have been seeing. "Brody is seeing explosives by the backdoor of the church, but also under his chair and Calliope's. He's worried that you'll die—that he'll lose you, too—that's why I'm seeing them, I think."

"Son of a—."

Jack called Hank and then conferenced in Nate to relay the problem. We were about thirty yards from the edge of the woods, the trees still so thick we were cloaked in darkness. Blalock wouldn't see us coming, unless he had thermal imaging binocs. Even so, the woods said *you are safe here. Hide, little girl. Hide.*

In the clearing in front of the church, a dark van sat in the drive. "Stolen plates," Jack whispered, news from Hank, on the phone. Blalock's getaway van—pointed out, ready to go.

Somewhere far away, Jack, Hank, and Nate quietly discussed the options, given the new twist of the explosives so close to the children.

"Jack, Brody's image . . . Blalock has some sort of device strapped to his arm. It's hands-free. He's not holding it—or a trigger. There are buttons."

"How many?"

I stared at the image, trying to count, but it was dark in the church, and Brody couldn't see Blalock all that well. "Four, I think. Maybe six."

"Son of a bitch," Jack swore, and then quietly conferred with Nate and Hank again.

Run, little girl. Hide. Hide. Dread ate at my soul.

"What do we do?"

Jack reached over and linked his hand in mine.

"Stick to the plan. Try to draw him out as close to the front steps of the church as you can."

I could see Jack's losses sluicing off him: him not saving his son, losing me. No one watching him would know that, just looking at him. He looked tough, stoic, competent. I could see why men who'd been downed behind enemy lines were always so glad to see him.

"He's got to disengage that bomb to open that door," Jack explained calmly, trying to bolster my confidence, unaware that I could see how tortured he felt, "so he'll do that, even if it's just to try to make you go inside. You stall him, and I'll get in."

Sure, I could do that, though the snow flurries that had turned to a hard blizzard said otherwise. I tried to ignore the wolves circling Pan and growling at the church.

Jack kissed me, and then turned his horse into the woods. All his losses fanned out in his wake: I was there. And Brody was there. And our son, Jackson. I had to close my eyes and count to a hundred to give him time to get in place.

The church stood in a clearing beneath an inky sky chock full of stars and a fat moon, as if all the heavens wanted a front-row seat. The clearing was more or less an oval, with the woods nearer to the backdoor than to the side, where I now stood. There were no lights. No movement.

There had been a clearing like this in the snow. Dogs, no, wolves circling me . . . keeping me warm. Keeping me moving. I stumbled. Fell nearly naked into the snow. No more voice to weep. No more tears. Pain. So much pain. My wrist. Agony. The leader of the wolves licked me, nudged me, cold nose to my side. Nudging me harder to get up, keep moving. I should be afraid of them, but they'd piled on me at night, like I was a lost puppy, and then when I warmed up, they kept me moving moving moving moving. I saw the church. The lights were on, warm. Welcoming. Singing inside. Ave Maria.

A nun worked outside, gathering wood . . .

Everyone's—the men, the children's, even Swan's—losses swarmed me, and I struggled to push away the new memory-images. Maybe I'd lost my mind. How could I trust anything I saw? Anything I thought I remembered? Had there been a nun?

Your name is Lily Victoria, Téa had said in the hospital.

I hadn't told Jack that. Although Hank had surmised that I might have been Blalock Swan's first victim, I could tell Jack clung to the hope that it wasn't true or that if it was true, that I had gotten away unscathed somehow. That my scars really were from a car wreck and not a mad man.

It's funny, the lies we tell ourselves, to survive.

I dismounted Pan, leaving her reins loose—if she spooked, I didn't want her whinnying, panicking, and me not able to get to her, especially in the case of gunshots. I had no idea if that would scare her or not, and I'd rather she ran home to the corral, safe, than fight the reins and get hurt.

She butted my side as we stood there, and I scratched her forelock as she nuzzled me. I pulled the last apple out of my saddlebag and gave it to her.

"I might not see you again. If I don't, then I want you to know you were an absolute pain-in-the-ass horse." She head-butted me again. "Yeah, well, you kinda grew on me, too."

I brushed the snow off her mane, felt its cold in my hands, and watched my breath crystallize in front of me.

It was time.

The snow piled up in small hills as I walked into the clearing, heading for the church like a parishioner on Sunday morning. Goosebumps rose on my skin, and I wished again that I had a jacket. Somewhere in the recesses of my mind, I could see Jack, sweating, crawling through the tall grass behind the church, a saddlebag full of tools he might need slung over his shoulder. Nate worried about losing him as he crawled toward the church from the other direction. The nighttime temps here were lucky to dip below eighty-five in mid-July, but I felt the cold whip of winter wind, tasted the snow on the air, smelled the piney woods, and I stepped out into a blanket of snow.

Just for a moment, I was back there, back in my childhood. Téa and I were finishing up the snow castle, and I caught her big grin as I pulled off the final bucket to expose the last turret on top.

"We did it!" she exclaimed, hugging me, as we jumped up and down with joy.

"Let's make snow angels!" I said, and we ran a few feet away and threw ourselves on the ground, raking our arms and legs up and down, up and down, up and—

"Girl," Blalock's voice exploded from the church some thirty feet away from where I now stood. "You'd better be alone."

The front door was open, but I couldn't see him in the dark behind it. He was smart enough to know not to turn on the lights and make himself a target.

"I'm alone."

"I'll kill these kids, you lie to me."

"I know."

"You wearing a wire? One of those little cameras?"

"No."

"Take off your clothes. I don't believe you."

CHAPTER THIRTY-NINE

"What?" Did he actually think the authorities didn't know who he was, that he was going to just walk away from this night and start over somewhere . . . with me? Was he that delusional?

"You heard me, Girl. Clothes come off, or I cut one of the kids. Not sure which one, yet. Don't much care about the boy; I just grabbed him so you'd see where to go, so he'll probably go first."

I stamped my feet in the snow, and started peeling off my shirt, my sandals, my jeans. I stopped at the underwear, praying its skimpiness would be enough to satisfy Blalock that I wasn't wearing a wire. It was a small thing, a stupid hill to die on, but I knew Hank could see me, and I was mortified. Hank hadn't given the signal that the rest of the SWAT had arrived, so there was that small break.

"Everything," Blalock said. "I know how small those cameras can be."

"Look," I said, stalling, turning, raising my arms, "there's nowhere else for a wire to be." I was not overly endowed, so it wasn't like I had something stuffed in my cleavage.

Then I heard Calliope scream, and a couple of seconds later, he shouted from deeper in the depths of the church: "Everything, or I take her arm off right now."

I stripped. I regretted not having done it already. *Stupid false modesty. She has to make it out alive . . .*

"Now, come in," he demanded.

The snow hung in sheets as thick as a velvet drape, and my fingers had numbed. My toes burned as frostbite set in. It made no sense. I should be warm . . . I should be warm. I kept telling myself the snow wasn't real, and still, I shook, cradling my right wrist with my left hand; he'd broken my wrist, snapped it, and it was excruciating. I wanted to drop to the ground. I wanted to scream or run.

Instead, I walked forward . . . and it hurt.

I remembered the pain but only the pain.

And I walked forward, forward into the cave.

I'd had to scramble over a boulder when I first entered the door, and then I stood dumbstruck and trembling as the walls of the cave closed in around me. The moonlight had turned watery and weak and was giving way to the night, save for a single torch lit somewhere off to my right. *Am I in the church?* a small voice asked somewhere in the back of my mind. Didn't I just climb over Marguerite and sweet Father Tomas?

But I saw no church—only gray granite cave walls, crisscrossed with roots and veining, the skin of an ancient monster sent to devour me whole. Part of my mind processed that a vestibule door in the chapel was open, but what I saw was a crack in the cave wall that led to a larger cave. Where the pews should have been to my left, I only saw camping gear, a pallet laid out with a sleeping bag on it. Stacks of supplies, like someone planned on staying awhile. Why was I seeing this? Was this his loss?

A slice of moonlight streamed in, somehow *through* the cave walls, glinting off a big knife, and then I saw him as he crossed the room to meet me. I felt myself whimper, an animal too hurt to help itself.

I remember those eyes. He had a nasty leer set in a face so plain I could see how he had escaped detection. He was a chameleon, the man no one notices at the office that absconds with millions, the quiet worker on the floor of the factory that shoots his supervisors and coworkers in a fit of rage, the nice neighbor who keeps someone locked in his basement for ten years. Average. Nondescript. Ordinary. His hair was darker blond than I recalled, and he was older now, maybe forty-five, fifty, but he moved as if he was in pain, with the gait of a much older man.

The delivery guy disguise—the extra padding, buckteeth inserts, wig— were gone. In reality, his hair was falling out, only a few tufts left, as if he'd had chemo. The average person meeting him on the street, if he wore a cap, would never notice him, unless they happened to look into his eyes. It was the eyes that told you he was a killer. His losses jammed in my throat: *Dying! He's dying!* I could feel losses from him now, now that I remembered, now that my senses had stopped shutting down in self-defense.

My head throbbed, and my arm hurt. I fought to stay in control. *I'm in a church. Not a cave. Not a cave.*

He stood in front of me, the knife in one hand, a detonator with several buttons casually taped to the other wrist.

"Got tired of waiting for you, Lily," he said, backhanding me with the knife-hand so fast I hadn't even seen him lash out. "You were mine. I told you that. You were mine."

Blood ran from my mouth, and as he stepped a little closer, the smell of his foul lemony breath made me panic. I wanted to run. *Run!!!!!*

But it wasn't possible. Not yet. There were kids here. Somewhere, there were kids here. I couldn't see them yet; I couldn't seem to hang onto the church long enough to get my bearings.

Can't run. Need to buy Jack time. Keep Swan distracted. Please, God, give Jack time.

"I'll . . . I'll go with you. Anywh-where."

Swan said, "It's too late for that. You remember me now, don't you?"

Oh, God, he intends to die in this place. He's not even going to try to finish with Calliope.

"Yeah," he smiled, "you remember."

I nodded, too afraid to talk. I could see images of Jack at the back of the building, unscrewing a piece of plywood. *Jack had remodeled the church. He knows another way in.* Nate was beside him, helping but all the while worried about losing him, losing the kids, losing me.

"Your daddy slithered you away, after those damned nuns rescued you. Got you out of the country. Named you something else. Couldn't find you no matter how hard I looked."

He stepped a little closer, the heat of him terrifying me. He leaned forward, putting the knife at my belly, the point of it right on my scar. When he licked my cheek, his wet tongue leaving a trail, I fell back into time, into that cave. I was a child again, and he had me undressed down to my underwear, lying on that sleeping bag. He pressed my broken wrist, and he laughed as I screamed. Then he started cutting me, little cuts that burned in the cold—up and down my arms and legs.

I sobbed. God, no. No. No *no no no*. Pushed the memory away. *I will not relive this.*

"Yes," he said, touching me with the knife, and I couldn't tell if it was now or back all those years ago in the cave, "you remember now, don't you, you little bitch."

He slapped me again. That was now. That was pain, and I held onto it, trying to hold onto the here and now.

"I know what you can do. You belonged to me for all the shit I went through, for all the shit your momma and daddy stirred up for me. Your daddy owed me. He owed me big. Your mamma said they'd lend you out, but no, your dad, he was greedy. Had to have it all himself. Got me sent to jail, they did." He breathed in my face. "Got me arrested. Set me up, your dad. Thought he was so fucking smart. Thought I'd be in jail for years. Told him then, I'd be out. Be out to get you, to get even.

"He didn't believe me. Thought he was so damn clever. Using you to get all the stuff I was supposed to have. I was the one who could finesse any lock, any security system. Hack anything." He tapped his head. "That's my talent. But I didn't know how to use it, how to time it so I wouldn't get caught. But your dad, he knew. He knew where the lost things were, when to go get them. He used me. Millions, he stole, using you. Millions I should've had. And you. Told you then, you were mine. Always mine." He cut me then, a long, thin, shallow slice across my big scar, and I choked on a scream.

"Then he tipped off the police again. After I did you and your sister, he got even. Tipped off the police about my next job. Three strikes, and he knew I'd be in for a long, long time." He grabbed me by the throat and slammed my head against the wall. "But he didn't think about compassionate leave. About them letting me out because I'm dying. I'm not a risk to society!" And he laughed, and as he slammed my head against the wall again, my ears rang and I saw a new image.

Jack had made it inside the cave. How? *Supposed to be inside the church.* I could feel the heat of his fury all the way over to where I stood, and I could see what he saw, the loss it was to him, what Blalock was doing to me, what he'd done to Brody, to Calliope. He was underneath the choir loft heading toward a door behind the altar. It was so dark it could've been a tomb.

"Twenty years, Lily. Your dad cost me. Then I saw your painting: *The Snow Angel,* and I knew who you were. You painted that day. Our day."

He leaned up against me, and I could feel how excited he was. He smelled of rot and lemons. My eyes watered, and he licked my cheek again. I clenched my teeth to keep from throwing up.

"That's when I knew you wanted me. Missed me. Hadn't been able to find you. Nobody had your address. Damn Feds hid you. But I've been doing up the girls special, so you'd remember. So you'd know it was me and come find me." He sliced a small cut in my arm; his expression set as if he were caressing me. Madness. Madness in his singsong voice. "You shouldn't have run away, Lily. I put lilies on them, just for you. Did you like them?"

Oh, God. No. *No no no no no.*

He squeezed my throat, and I knew he expected an answer.

"P . . . pretty . . . " was all I could muster, and it killed me to utter the words. *Dear Jesus, they all died because of me.*

"But none as pretty as you. None of them could do a goddamn thing, either. You were special. Mine. Now it's too damn late. I should've had all those millions your dad has. I wouldn't be sick, if it wasn't for him. I wouldn't be dying! I'd have had the best of everything, the best doctors."

He leveled a suspicious look at me: "You still working for him?"

"N . . . no. Hate. Him."

He eased off his grip then, before tightening it again and slamming me against the wall. "Liar! I know he's still on the job. But he's going to lose you, Bitch. He's going to lose his little goose that laid the golden egg. His golden Little Princess, he called you."

Little Princess Killer.

I wanted to die. I wanted to go backward in time and die; if I had, back then, back with Téa, maybe, maybe the rest of the little girls would have lived. Maybe he'd have quit long ago.

It was still a cave where Blalock and I stood, but Jack's fury over his losses, of what was happening to me, burned off the manifestation of the cave there, and I could see him and Nate, quietly crawling toward the kids—crawling and projecting potential losses, and it was all just too much, too much pain. I was having difficulty holding onto sanity. Holding onto *now.*

"You let someone else touch you," Blalock said.

His knife scraped another shallow line across my stomach, and it burned and bled. Memories of all the times he'd cut me filled my head—hundreds of cuts, some deep enough to bleed for hours, some shallow but cut to leave a scar. *You were in a car wreck*, my dad had told me. Yet he'd known better. He'd never changed that story and he never told me. Him or Leila, never a word, never a warning. *You got those in a car wreck. Remember?* And the shiny watch swung over me as I curled in a ball on the sofa, lulling me into a trance.

Blalock bent down and licked across my belly where it bled, always keeping the knife on my thigh, able to plunge it in me any time he wanted. He liked to do that. Light cuts, then a deeper one when I thought he wouldn't. Just to keep me off balance.

He slid the knife down my thigh, and I screamed. *That was now.* I whimpered again when he put it to my breast. Jack worked carefully, trying to shove away his fear so he could focus and save the kids. His images pummeled me. I was not letting Jack lose his son. I was not going to let Calliope die. I was not going to let Blalock win. I needed to let Blalock do whatever he wanted. Keep him busy long enough. Just long enough. Please, God. I could see the detonator taped to his arm.

"You grew up," he said, disgusted.

"You're nothing now, nothing. You shouldn't have let someone else touch you, you little bitch," Blalock said, pinching my breast so hard I yelped. He let go long enough to pull a cell phone from his pocket. "And your dad's gonna listen as I cut you one last time. Call him."

I shook so hard, I couldn't hit the numbers on the phone right.

As I dialed, he sliced again, across my ribs, and tears rolled down my cheeks. *Buy time . . . buy Jack and Nate just a little more time . . .*

I remembered a bit more now. He'd been attacked by a wolf and I had run, but he'd killed the poor animal and quickly come after me. I had lost track of the days I'd been in the cave. He'd gone for supplies. I couldn't have told you my name, or where I was. I was just his. I was supposed to serve him. He was going to be rich. He was training me, he said. Sometimes he made me run from him so he could catch me again. Let me try to get away, told me to *run, little girl, run.* Just to teach me I couldn't get away from him.

I was his, like a gun or a knife. His to use as he saw fit.

"Call your dad. Now!" he spat.

It was so cold in the cave. I was filthy, ragged, covered in dried blood from the cuts. My wrist and hand had swollen; I couldn't use my fingers. He'd let me keep my underwear on. Wonder Woman underwear. Five years old, I was going to be a superhero. I still had them on, as stained as they were, but I could see he was working up to making me take them off, to what he wanted next. He'd worked himself up to the point of convincing himself it was right, that I was his to use as he liked, and I knew, I knew if I was there when he came back, what would happen.

He had tied my ankle to a boulder, with just enough length for me to hobble over to a hole to use the bathroom, a shallow pit he'd dug that stank and nearly suffocated me. I couldn't untie the rope. I'd tried the first day, with the one hand, but I couldn't manage it. So I chewed through it. My mouth was swollen from where he'd hit me, but I chewed through that rope like a rabid animal. I'd have chewed my foot off next, if I'd had to.

I don't remember much after stumbling out of that cave. Only worrying that he could be back any minute. Knowing he could track me. I had learned from the earlier times not to cross the clearing. Stick to the woods. Safe in the woods. Try not to whimper. He'd hear. Wolves. Wolves found me. Fainted in the snow. They piled on, warmed me. Warmed me, like I was a baby wolf. Nudged me to move. Pushed me to keep going.

Blalock ran the knife down my body, one long continuous slice as I tried to dial the phone. This was now, not then. No underwear. No Wonder Woman. Just me. Just plain, scared Lily. He raised his hand, the knife now at my breast, my blood smeared on his chin, and he grinned at me—my blood on his teeth. The phone finally connected and rang, and my dad answered, first ring. Like he'd been expecting it.

"Hello, Bill," Blalock said, using one of my dad's aliases. "How you doin', you old sonofabitch."

"Fine, Blalock. How are you?" No surprise in his voice.

"Oh, I'm just fine," Blalock said, pinching me hard, so hard I whimpered, determined not to scream. I didn't want to distract Jack. He was tamping his losses, reining it all in with a ferocious will for the sake of Brody, for Calliope, for me.

"Got your daughter."

"Avery?"

"That's not her fucking name!" Blalock shouted.

"Lily?" Dad asked, and Blalock nodded to me to answer.

"Here."

"Ah," was all Dad said.

"Remember when you warned me to stay away from her, all those years ago?" Blalock asked. "Said I'd die? I'd die in a church?"

"I do recall," Dad answered, and Blalock cracked up laughing.

"Me—in a church! I thought you were lying, you son of a bitch. And then you stole my life from me. You took her and hid her from me. She made you millions, and she was mine. You owed me. You fucking owed me, Bill."

"I think," my father said carefully, "that's just a difference of opinion, Blalock. You didn't deserve her. You broke her."

Broke . . .

While my dad listened, Blalock pinned me to the wall with his knife, and cut me fast; his tongue darted in my mouth, and he swallowed my screams. God help me, the screaming in my head would not stop. I dropped into my five-year-old body, remembering the lessons he'd taught me. The thin sleeping bag underneath me. The rats scurrying in the corners. Him hovering above me. So much pain. So much pain.

"Gonna have her right here, Bill, where you can hear. Right in front of God and the kids." He laughed, scoring a light figure eight on my breast, following the lines of one he'd made before.

"You don't want her," my dad said, and my head reeled.

"She's not a little girl anymore," Blalock said with disgust. "But she's skinny like one. Little, just like I like 'em." His eyes were wild with disgust at how I'd aged; I could see the images of the child-me spiraling off him. He waffled between seeing the me of the now and the child-me of then. The then seemed to be winning.

I tried to close my eyes, to see what Jack was doing—but I couldn't catch an image. *It's not a loss. He's getting Calliope untied* or so I hoped.

"You don't want to do this, Blalock," my dad said, and I couldn't tell if he believed it or was playing a role in case someone was listening in. "You're mad at me, come after me."

"Those damn nuns helped you," Blalock said to me, crazy lust in his eyes. "Killed 'em later. Just so you know, someone helps you they're dead." He laughed, enjoying the inside joke. "Ain't that right, Bill. You know better than anybody that I mean what I say. Gonna wait 'til I've had her a few times, and then call the FBI. Get good ol' Hank in here. Blow us all up. How 'bout that, Bill? Like knowing how much I'm going to hurt her?"

Snow . . . woods . . . safe . . . followed the wolves . . . followed small tracks in the snow, a woman, a tiny church in a clearing. Woman out back, getting wood. I couldn't talk, couldn't ask her for help. Couldn't keep walking. Saw the warm light from the church.

Someone singing, Ave Mariiiiiaaaaa . . .

Nun. Her head snapped up from what she'd been doing. Me there, in the snow. Losses spilling out of her: A child. Save the child.

"We could go away somewhere," I told Blalock.

Jack and Nate, inside now, though I couldn't see them. Not as many losses spinning off them. *They were saving the children.*

"We could go away. I'm sorry I forgot. I'll help you find things. Sell them. We'll get you some medical help."

Blalock laughed. "Tell her, Bill. Tell her what you foresaw all those years ago."

"He's going to die in that church," my dad said. "I told him years ago, but he didn't listen. And now he'll die."

"And I'll take your daughter with me," Blalock shouted. "That's the part you left out, you asshole. You didn't want me to know I'd find her again. And I know you—you see every damn detail." He stabbed my thigh, and I screamed. "Like that, Bill? I'm going to torture her, and then fuck her, and you can't do a damned thing about it. I'm going to break your little tool here, for good. She should've been mine. And now I'm dying, and it's too late. It's all your fault. If I can't have her, you sure as hell won't get richer off her either. I'm gonna love that you'll live a long time with these images."

Jack frantically worked while Nate untied Brody—that bomb disconnected, but Jack worried about it as Nate picked the boy up and carried Brody to the exit behind the choir loft. Nate's projected losses showed me Jack, still taking apart the IED beneath Calliope's chair. The image blurred as Blalock grabbed me by the throat with the same hand that carried the detonator, the knife between my legs, cutting my other thigh, and he shoved me against the foyer wall. "Tell your daddy, Lily. Tell him what I'm doing to you."

"Cu-cutting me."

The potential loss of Calliope evaporated. *Calliope is free.* I moaned to cover the sound of Nate carrying her to the door, handing her to Hank while Jack eased into the choir loft, moving toward me.

"That's right, Girl," Blalock sneered. "You get off on the pain, don't you?"

I could barely breathe. Dizzy, dizzy. My wrist hurt, and I fought it. *It's not broken. Not this time. Be here. Be here, dammit.* He could not take away who I was. What I'd learned. I. Would. Not. Let. Him.

I am Avery Marie Broussard, you fucking coward.

I will be *here.*

279

And as the last word planted in my mind, the cave ebbed away. I was in the foyer of the church again, inches away from Marguerite's slashed throat, her dead eyes staring up at the crucifix above the door, her blood pooled in the vestibule, her body lying across Father Tomas's. The gentle pastor, face down with the back of his head bashed in.

"Will the bomb go off . . . if I?" I glanced down to his khakis, which made him leer.

"Not 'til I want it to. See, Bill. She wants me. You should've let me have her."

He had to press the buttons for the bomb to go off. There were four on the controller, and I just had to keep him occupied for another minute. I pretended to struggle with the snap of his pants, while he squeezed my throat, still cutting off a lot of air, still cutting light slices in my right breast. I felt faint, and my hands were uncoordinated. He eased up a little.

Jack moved along the front pew to the center of the church, the pulpit behind him as he crossed in the moonlight with murder in his gray wolf eyes. Nate eased back toward the pulpit when something creaked, and Blalock turned.

In that split-second, my whole world changed, as Blalock tapped the button before I could move to intercept, and a light pinged on, green, underneath the table that had been placed in front of the pulpit. Jack had his back to the table. He wouldn't see it, but Nate and I could.

Time stopped. I saw Nate's losses overrun the sanctuary: if Jack died, his love of Jack—knowing Jack would never love him like that, knowing it didn't matter, just having Jack alive was enough. I'd known—I'd known since we were kids—and he'd accepted that I knew. But he'd never stopped loving Jack.

He wouldn't stop now.

I saw Nate moving, slow motion, toward that bomb as if time stood still, and a million thoughts raced through my mind, a million heartbreaks screamed through me, as Blalock reached again for me.

Time snapped forward as I elbowed Blalock, shocking him, giving me the brief second I needed, striking a knife-hand to his throat. I grabbed his arm, spinning so my back was to him, so that he couldn't push another button. He wheezed, fighting to breathe as I desperately looked for an off switch, something to reverse what he had begun. In those seconds, Nate ran for Jack, shouting, trying to wave him away, trying to send him in a different direction, but Jack, always the first to run *to* danger, not away, was running the most direct route to reach me.

Nate leaped. He knew he had no time. I could see he knew. He flew like the best blocker in the NFL, his body arched out, shoving Jack out of the way and between two pews.

But Nate landed and rolled, backward, back toward the bomb.

The explosion turned the world inside out, fire and thunder, chaos and loss; the concussion threw me against one wall of the vestibule, threw Blalock against the opposite wall, as every part of the church rained down, fire from hell.

I couldn't see Jack.

Couldn't feel his losses. His or Nate's.

Couldn't feel my arms, or legs, or hear anything above the deafening roar of fire and someone screaming.

CHAPTER FORTY

Everything hurt, and I could hear the flames, smell the smoke. When I opened my eyes, Blalock stood over me, bleeding, covered in soot and ash, absolute madness dancing in his eyes. He raised the knife for the killing blow. My hand closed on something—the cross that had been hanging above Marguerite, broken.

And as he leaned down, I jabbed upward with that crucifix, stabbing him in the upper thigh so hard that the downward arc of his knife stopped midair, so surprised in that moment that he just stared at it, at the blood running from his femoral artery. He drew back his knife for one last kill before he died.

The thundering growl of something inhuman, something like a wolf, made him pause. Blalock glanced toward the sound, and Jack came through the smoke swirling out of the church, blood pouring from wounds in his arms, shoulders, chest; death in his silver eyes, no mercy. He attacked Blalock, so fast I couldn't even comprehend that Jack had knocked the knife away and snapped Blalock's neck in one deadly motion.

Blalock crumpled to the ground, the startled expression in his eyes registering Jack as the last thing he would ever see.

A piece of me wanted my dad's cousin to suffer, wanted revenge for the atrocities he'd inflicted on so many, including me and mine, and then I looked at the man I loved and knew that he'd already lost so much to this monster, to the path that Blalock had set me on, the loss of my childhood, my ability to trust . . . our child . . . that it was fitting that we ended Blalock together.

Jack pulled the debris off me, and checked me for wounds. The only feeling left inside me was relief that it was over. Some day, I hoped that relief would become peace.

"The kids?"

"Safe."

"Nate?"

Jack shook his head, and I saw the horrific image of what he'd seen as the bomb exploded. Nate! Loss seared me as my heart broke.

"Can you move everything?"

I nodded, not trusting myself to speak. He scooped me up, curled me to him, and carried me out as the SWAT guys entered. Hank was there, throwing a jacket over me, my clothes lost in the rubble of what was left of the church. Headlights illuminated the grassy area as if it was daylight—FBI types hustled us out of the way, over to the ambulances blinking red, blue, red, blue.

Brody screamed, "Dad!" and broke from one of the paramedics and ran to us, hugging Jack as we made it the last few steps to the second ambulance where someone exchanged Hank's jacket for a light sheet and began dressing the cuts and slashes Blalock had left on me. Jack held Brody in one arm and then, once I was bandaged and dressed in a pair of old scrubs, curled his other arm around me. Brody's lost-mom images washed over me: The bad man hiding in the backseat as they were leaving my house. The man putting a knife to her throat—making her drive the car after he slapped Brody. Brody's images of loss didn't show anything about the orange juice, and I thanked God for that. He didn't need to know that his mom had tried to hurt me, or worse. He was going to go through hell as it was.

Over in the other ambulance, the Gavins were huddled with Calliope, who clung to her mom like a newborn. When Rachael looked up, she had tears in her eyes, as she mouthed *thank-you for my baby*.

I nodded and laid my head on Jack's uninjured shoulder while the paramedics pulled long splinters out of the other one.

The losses pouring from Jack for Nate and Marguerite were hard, brutal, blinding. Jack bowed his head, and only I, in all the dozens of people there, knew he wept, his heart broken.

We sat together in the back of that ambulance and watched the church burn. As the flames flitted against the backdrop of the forest, something caught my eye, and I turned, looking out and over the levee the church faced. On the other side of the road, where the levee rose a good twenty yards, a man stood at the crest, backlit by boat lights from the river below. He stood alone, watching the church turn to ashes, and then he looked at me, and all the air went out of my lungs.

Nate.

Whole and unharmed.

"I'm staying," I said to Nate, and Jack, thinking I was speaking to him, squeezed my hand. "I'm never running again."

"Thank God," Jack answered.

But as I spoke, I was watching Nate. My best friend nodded, gave a little salute, and turned and disappeared into the light.

And then the light was gone.

CHAPTER FORTY-ONE

I am not sure how long I had been dozing when the dreams came, soft, quiet, like a low tide easing onto the shore. I stood in a clearing in the woods, and warm, inviting sunlight filtered.

Gone was the snow and cold.

"Would you like a cup of tea?" my sister said behind me, and tears filled my eyes, my throat closed in fear, but when I turned, she was . . . *beautiful*. She was sitting on an old chair, the one I had seen in my nightmares, but it was new again, and lovely. The dress she wore had the same pattern of roses as the fabric scraps in my quilt, and I suddenly realized what Latham had done all those years ago when he'd given it to me: he'd given me what he could of our sister.

"Would you like a cup of tea?" she asked again, smiling this time, and I nodded fervently.

"Yes, please."

"One lump, or two?"

"Two!" I laughed, and she rose to meet me, clasping my hands, kissing each of my cheeks.

When she held me in a long embrace, I knew it was the last time I would get to see her like this. I knew it was a gift for us to have this one last moment together.

"I'm so sorry I didn't remember," I said, and she shushed me.

"You were five, Avery. It's not your fault. None of it was your fault. You survived, and you stopped him. It's time to live your life now. It's time to take back what belongs to you."

"Why did I see you as an Old Woman?"

Téa grinned, impish, like the four-year-old she'd once been.

"Perhaps because I have a very old soul." And then she laughed. "Or maybe your brain was trying to find a workaround from the shock, the self-preservation you'd put in place, nudged along by Dad."

I could hear noises beyond where we stood, and the light was growing dimmer, like the sun was setting—only instead of getting darker, everything was fading, and I knew it was time to say good-bye. God knows I didn't want her to go. I had a million questions for her, a million things to say.

And no time.

"Thank you for helping me," I told her. "I love you. I will always love you."

She hugged me tightly, and whispered, "I know. Live big for me. I'll see your joy, and it will be my own."

And with that, she stepped back, holding my hand as she slowly faded away, until softly, softly, she was gone.

CHAPTER FORTY-TWO

I woke up huddled in an uncomfortable chair in Latham's hospital room. Sam stood guard at the foot of my brother's bed.

"You did good," he said, glancing my way, the way gargoyles are wont to do, and then he looked back at Latham. "They said his brain was still swelling, even as they were trying to get the shunt in place, and then all of a sudden, it stopped. Everything just relaxed."

Jack had taken Brody down to the cafeteria after I had refused to see any more doctors. I understood what I had been through, and the PTSD issues and all of that could wait. I just wanted my brother to wake up.

"They said he smiled," Sam said. "Brain lesions seem to have shrunk. The doctor'll be back later tonight to check on him, but for now, he's resting well."

Sam wasn't, though; he was blaming himself for not being there for Nate.

We stayed like that, the two of us, for some time, mourning our losses—Sam willing Latham, whom he'd always considered a brother, to get well. Me? Finally fully aware of how my leaving all those years ago had broken up a much larger family than I had realized at the time.

I must've eventually dozed off. I only knew when I woke, my dad stood silhouetted against the window. I glanced over at the equipment hooked up to my brother, and sighed in relief. Latham's vitals looked good. Jack had taken Brody home a couple of hours ago, and the sun was pinking up the horizon behind Dad.

He looked over at me, sensing movement, and shoved his hands in his pockets. I stretched and pulled out my earphones, turning off the white noise I'd been listening to on Jack's iPhone—a spare he kept—since my iPod had disappeared somewhere under the burning church. I set it down on the hospital table between us, trying to decide exactly what I wanted to say first.

I'd known he would come. Curiosity, if nothing else, would've lured him to the hospital, but I suspected he was here because he wanted to impress me with his side of the story. "Where's Leila?"

Dad chuckled. "We have a good job brewing in Miami, and I've sent her on ahead."

"So everything . . . Biloxi . . . the woman in red . . . everything was a lie." Seemed as good a place as any to start.

"Most of it," he agreed, amiably. Couldn't fault his acting chops.

"Why?"

He shrugged, looking back outside. "How's a father supposed to tell his broken little girl that she was brutalized? Nearly raped by a monster? A relative no less?"

"I lost my sister. Didn't you and Leila think that maybe, just maybe, I might've needed some therapy to get over that? Some professional help to learn to cope, instead of your hypnosis sessions that rewrote my history, and made me forget her?"

He shrugged. "You remember that now, do you?" His expression said he was sort of proud I'd broken through, finally. "Gotta admit, we did one helluva job, though. You didn't remember her, so you weren't grieving. It was a win-win."

"That was . . ." I couldn't begin to describe it. "Horrific."

He shrugged. "My only regret is we'll never know what talents Téa might have had. I knew the day she was born how she'd die, no real surprise there."

I had to grit my teeth to stop my jaw from dropping, to keep from screaming at him: *His only regret?*

"You should have told me, Dad."

He shook his head, grief conveniently drawn up for appearance's sake.

"Look, you didn't even talk the first few months. You were nonverbal. Barely a step above an animal. They wanted to keep you in the hospital, but it was giving you seizures, so we took you out, took you home. Latham tended to you day and night. He was the only one you would let get near you without biting or clawing. The hypnosis helped you cope. We did the best we could in a bad situation."

The losses I saw spilling from him sickened me: Not the loss of my sister. Not the loss of my innocence. But rather, all the marks they'd had lined up for Leila's readings. Rich marks, who'd lost expensive items. Items my parents would have found and fenced with my help. I kept a neutral expression plastered on my face. I'd learned from the best.

"We didn't know if you'd ever come back," Dad said, mostly to the window, not quite trusting himself to face me for his final performance. "That monster kept you nine days. Nine days, and we didn't know where you were. We'd found Téa, and the cops—the cops thought we'd done it. I told them about my cousin, but they didn't believe me. I couldn't tell them everything of course."

"Like how you were in business together."

He nodded, matter-of-factly. "Would've looked bad, put them on to us, maybe. When you finally started talking, you wouldn't answer to Lily. Or Victoria. They hadn't found Blalock, either, and so we moved. I tipped 'em to the crime that should've kept him in jail forever, and I thought maybe if we moved, changed names, we could keep you safe. We moved five times and changed your name each time, before we finally got to Saint Michael's. You seemed to wake up there. You told us your name was Avery—Avery Marie."

Once again, I saw the little church in the clearing and the nun singing *Ave Maria.*

"I don't know where you got that name from, but you started answering to it, which was fine with us. So we became the Broussards, and you were Avery."

He said it all with just the right balance of remorse, horror, and regret. *An extraordinary performance, really.*

I detected not a single hint in his voice as to how angry he'd been to lose his meal ticket. How he'd been forced to regroup and suffered the inconvenience of starting over. How he had to bring back an old grift, finding people who were going to die, casing their homes, and waiting 'til he knew they'd be on the way to the hospital, or morgue, their families in tatters, so he could go in and clean them out, before anyone even knew to watch out for them.

289

"We didn't put you back to work 'til you were about seven, I think. You enjoyed it. I think it gave you a sense of purpose."

He was waiting for the thank-you.

I nodded instead, and his eyes narrowed on me. I wasn't playing the role he'd imagined.

"You killed the Senator," I said instead.

That surprised him, caught him off guard. He tossed me a nonchalant look, but I could tell my words had ruffled his impeccable control. He toyed with denying it, but as I watched him, I could see the pride leaking out around the edges of his cool composure.

"It's Oscar worthy, all these years, holding it in," I told him, "but I can see it in your losses—yeah, I can see them now, Dad, now that my subconscious doesn't have to protect me anymore. And your losses are leafing through all the possible ways you might have screwed up—lost trace evidence, maybe out there, to expose you." I cocked my head. "I just can't figure out why you did it."

Dad shrugged then, as if we were talking about the weather, or bland food.

"The Senator started digging into your background when you got engaged to Jack. He was determined Jack was going to follow in his political footsteps, and he wanted a pedigreed daughter-in-law, not some ragamuffin con artists' spawn."

"You knew, the first time you met him, that you'd be the one to kill him."

"And had fifteen years to figure out why I'd have wanted to, why it was necessary, and how to cover it up. I kept tabs on what he was doing, paid off interns."

"Marguerite." I made the connection, then.

"She was the last, of course. So ambitious. Bled me dry; she'd made a copy of what the Senator had found, and when she had her own reason to, she dug some more. She was going to destroy us all, unless I kept up the big payments. She got greedy."

"But you knew Blalock would kill her."

He nodded absently, like we were talking about chess moves on a balmy day. "That was a lucky stroke."

I nodded, agreeing. There was more here to do. "Why? The Senator was already dead. Why was it lucky that Blalock killed Marguerite?"

"Oh, that started off as bad luck on my part. The Senator had tripped over the fact that your birth certificate indicated you were born in a hospital that had actually burned down the year before. Stupid mistake. I blame the forger.

"The Senator intended on destroying you publicly—he didn't know about Nova Scotia or the cons, but he had enough, and those press hounds would've found the rest, eventually, and I didn't want you to go through that. I hadn't realized until recently—when Marguerite hired a PI to look into your past—and believe me, I kept tabs on her, since she'd worked for the Senator—that she was getting closer to the same truth. I had to send her to Boston to distract her."

And the penny dropped.

He'd used my child's death as a pawn in his game.

Not just my child. Me. *And all those girls.*

"You knew Blalock was out there looking. You let him kill all those girls."

"I didn't know where he was, or under what name. We have all used several, and he was good with disguises. If I tried to find him or stop him, I knew he'd come back after you."

I think he thought I'd be grateful.

"So that made it okay?"

I stood then, and I think that was the first time my dad began to realize that maybe not all was okay. He looked, worried. "You knew how he would die, Dad. You knew why. You were on the phone with us when he died, so in your vision, you had already seen it. All of it. What he'd done to me. To all those girls. To Calliope. To Nate. How it ended. And you knew why. From the first time you ever met him—what? As a child? At a family gathering? You knew. And yet, you used him, anyway. And you said nothing to warn Latham or me."

"My cousin was magnificently gifted with locks, security, technology. That was his ability. That, and the phenomenal hands of a safecracker, but those run in the family. He was crafty. Incredibly sharp. Well, you saw," he said, as if we were discussing something in a textbook, "how he outfoxed the FBI. We pulled some big heists with him, and he was useful. But when it got close to time, I set him up, got him put in prison for theft. Thought that would keep him away from you. It should have!"

It was the first time I'd ever seen him angry, and he reined it in, just as quickly as it had slipped out. "It should have."

He turned to stare back out at the dawn. "It was the only time I ever tried to change what I saw. Your sister—she was supposed to die at his hands, but in the original version, he hit her and she fell. There wasn't a machete. I didn't know the stuff about you—I can't see that kind of stuff, just death. We didn't even know yet what her talent was, or if she had one. So I tried to change her death—got him arrested, thinking he'd be safely behind bars, away from us. But he got out on a technicality. We didn't know he was free, or I'd have packed you kids up and gone somewhere else. Surely, you know that?"

He shook his head, and he seemed upset that I did not understand.

Then he shrugged it off, facing me. "I may have been a crappy father. And your mother was no prize, but I was determined to protect you."

The stunning lack of conscience in the man appalled me.

I pasted as reasonable a tone as any expert actress could into the next words. "You protected me by letting a killer, a pedophile, work with you? You can't claim to not have known that kind of stuff because you saw how he died, what he was doing, what he was saying to you. So you chose to work with him for the short-term benefits, and I'm supposed to be impressed that you stopped when it was close to the time Téa would be killed, and then you tried to get rid of him? And then, when he got out and was killing other girls, that was okay with you? As long as he didn't get in your way—as long as he didn't kill your golden goose? Not to mention when I finally found some happiness, someone who made me feel normal, you scared me away from him?"

He shrugged. "If that's what it took, yes."

And then he threw me an *of course, you'll understand that* look, like he expected the logic of his choices to clear up any of those silly feelings of betrayal I might have.

"You stole everything from me."

I took a step toward him then, letting him see the depth of my fury. He blanched and had the good common sense to step back.

"You destroyed as much of me as Blalock did," I said. "No, actually, you destroyed more."

He flinched, but I would not feel sorry for him.

"You made me run. I ran, Dad, away from the best thing that ever happened to me, away from love." The cold edge of my voice was a knife as we traded truths over Latham's prone body. "You knew my baby would die.

You knew, and you let it happen. Just like all of those beautiful, little girls. All to save your own ass."

I held up my hand to stop the excuses. "No, I heard you. And there may have been something there, some parental moment that leaked through the narcissism, but spare me. I know your cons. I know how you work the mark. Right now, I'm the mark. You didn't want the Senator to dig into my background because he'd find out you weren't who you said you were. You and Mom. That's what you couldn't have happen. You wanted me to stay away from Jack so that the Senator would lose interest in you."

Cold disgust filled the room when he didn't deny it. Couldn't deny it. He moved away from the window, ambling nonchalantly toward the door.

"Could be." He shrugged. "I'm sure that's some of it."

He stopped in the doorway, and glanced sideways at me. "Could be I know other things and wanted to try to spare you."

"Bullshit. All those girls, Dad, died because of you. You could have stopped Blalock before he even had the chance to get to Téa. Or me. Or, even after me, before he hurt the next one. You knew he would keep going. And you let him, to save yourself—to maintain your lifestyle."

He shrugged again. "Your mother said you wouldn't understand. That's the real reason why she didn't come today. But I thought you might, now that you remembered everything. We were a good team back then. We could make a fortune, you know."

The truth slapped me. He thought now that I was *okay*—now that I knew who I was—I'd be his puppet again. I'd want the old life, the way he wanted it.

I saw Hank appear in the doorway behind my father; he nodded at me, and I handed him Jack's phone. I'd recorded everything, as had the FBI. It hadn't taken but a phone call to get the warrant; I knew when Dad heard everything Blalock had said before dying, he'd want to have his own say. Put his own spin on things. He wouldn't be able to resist checking me out either to see if he could spin it to his advantage, get me back in the game.

Or he'd have killed me. That was the loss I saw spinning off him now. *That he'd let me live.* If a tool's broken, you throw it away. If a con's failing, you walk away. If the others get caught, that's their problem, you keep moving.

"I hope you rot in hell, Dad."

"Get out," Latham said from the bed. His head turned, eyes open and on Dad.

I ran to him, and he looked at me, his eyes clear of pain.

"Get out," he said again to Dad, "and don't ever contact either of us, again. You or Leila."

"You'll have to forgive my daughter," Dad said as Hank pulled him out of the room, "for being confused. She's been through a horrible trauma. She doesn't know what she's saying."

"You don't deserve to call her *daughter*," Hank said, looking at me over his shoulder. "She's the best damned person I know. Shut the hell up. Nobody's buying."

CHAPTER FORTY-THREE

The air was crisp and cool, a rare true spring day in Saint Michael's, when the humidity plays hooky and you want to spin in the sunshine. Normally, a day like that, you smile and laugh with a lightness of being, giddy with joy. But for us—for Jack and me—that day, Jackson's birthday, was a quiet one as we walked hand in hand to the little family cemetery Jack had carved out of the backside of our property.

He'd found a spot where an old live oak grew, one that had seen at least a century, maybe even most of two. It seemed appropriate, somehow, that Jackson's little headstone snuggled up beneath it, under a canopy of branches that reached down to embrace the earth. Jackson's suitcase was buried there as well, with gifts from Brody (his baseball card collection) and from Jack (his Purple Heart).

In the days and months that had followed that night in the church, I'd find Jack there, telling his son about the latest LSU game, or filling him in on what his brother and cousins were up to. Some days, like this one, he was just quiet, folded inside himself. It was those days I thought he went mostly to talk to Nate, who was buried not far away. After all this time, Jack was still reeling from the loss of Nate.

We don't get to choose our losses in life. They etch themselves so deeply into our souls we are forever changed by them in ways our successes can never do. But we have a choice—we can let ourselves atrophy, steeped in the loss, or we can remember all of the joy that came before. Would we give up such love, just to be safe, just to feel less? How is that living?

I glanced over at my husband and knew that he only regretted that he hadn't loved more, hadn't given these two more.

Losses don't define us.

Love does.

I laced my fingers into Jack's, and we stood like that, silent as truth, finding comfort in each other. We hold tight to the now, and the result is that most days . . . well, most days were good.

A clattering of children's voices rose over the low ridge, and I saw a passel of them running wild, like the five Saints had done once upon a time, shouting and laughing, darting in and out of the trees, and I grinned. Brody, who seemed to be healing—slowly, and with counseling—was supposed to be in town with his cousins and a few neighbor kids playing video games. Sometimes, when he knew we were walking out here though, he'd come, too, and visit his mother's grave. He'd seemed to be coping a little better as of late, visiting less often. From the shrieks of laughter and the noise, it sounded like all the kids who'd been cooped up inside had finally remembered to be kids and fled outdoors, jumping fences, tossing a Frisbee. I liked seeing them in the sunshine.

Brody slowed for a moment, not twenty yards away, and my heart fluttered hard against my ribcage.

It couldn't be Brody. The boy was taller, darker, with longer hair. He pulled his hands up to shade his eyes against the low evening sunset, and I saw their steel-gray color, wolf-like, just like Jack's.

He had Jack's eyes. And my dimples.

Jackson.

It couldn't be. I knew that. Chills raced through me as I glanced at Jack, and he stared in the same direction, quiet, lost in thought. He didn't seem to hear anything, not even the noisy kids who whooped and hollered as they wound their way beyond the tree where we stood.

Then I looked back at our oldest son, and his smile widened, a gift of pure happiness in his expression.

"Hey, Mom. Dad. I'll be a little while," he said, his voice floating on the wind. "Don't y'all worry, okay?"

I nodded. "Have fun," I told him. It seemed like the right thing to say. He grinned big again and ran off to join the rest of the kids, and just as they rounded out of sight, I saw a young Téa grab his hand and run with him over the ridge into the twilight.

The other kids shrieked with joy, and that's when I saw Aurelia March. Jancey Taylor. And several of the other lost girls. Laughing. Lit up with the glow of a thousand hugs, a million smiles. And then they were fireflies in the dusk, giggles whistling through the woods.

In the silence, we just stood, and stared. Jack put his arm around me, and I startled and glanced up at him. His gaze was focused on the ridge, where the kids had gone.

"I think," he said, his voice halting a moment, hesitant, as he kept his gaze on the ridge, "I think he's having a good time, wherever it is that he's gone."

I stared at Jack, afraid to ask if he was guessing, trying to make me feel better, or if he'd seen what I had.

"He has your smile," he said, his gaze turning back to the ridge one last time. "I always hoped he would."

I have no words that can explain that moment to you, how Jack could see what I could see.

I'm Avery Marie Thibodaux. I find lost things.

Maybe it is as simple as that.

About the Author

T. M. Causey is the pen name of *USA Today* Bestselling Author Toni McGee Causey of the critically acclaimed Bobbie Faye novels. Also a screenwriter, she began her career writing for magazines, including *Redbook* and *Mademoiselle*. She lives and writes in New Orleans, where she and her husband, Carl, are renovating a building in the French Quarter. You can visit her at www.ToniMcGeeCausey.com.